Louise Fuller was a tomboy who hated pink and always wanted to be the Prince—not the Princess! Now she enjoys creating heroines who aren't pretty push-overs but strong, believable women. Before writing for Mills & Boon she studied literature and philosophy at university, and then worked as a reporter on her local newspaper. She lives in Tunbridge Wells with her impossibly handsome husband, Patrick, and their six children.

Growing up near the beach, **Annie West** spent lots of time observing tall, burnished lifeguards—early research! Now she spends her days fantasising about gorgeous men and their love lives. Annie has been a reader all her life. She also loves travel, long walks, good company and great food. You can contact her at annie@annie-west.com or via PO Box 1041, Warners Bay, NSW 2282, Australia.

DEMANDING HIS SECRET SON

LOUISE FULLER

THE GREEK'S FORBIDDEN INNOCENT

ANNIE WEST

MILLS & BOON

First Published in Great Britain 2019
by Mills & Boon, an imprint of HarperCollins*Publishers*
1 London Bridge Street, London, SE1 9GF

Demanding His Secret Son © 2019 by Louise Fuller

The Greek's Forbidden Innocent © 2019 by Annie West

ISBN: 978-0-263-27328-1

MIX
Paper from
responsible sources
FSC® C007454

This book is produced from independently certified FSC™ paper
to ensure responsible forest management.
For more information visit www.harpercollins.co.uk/green.

Printed and bound in Spain
by CPI, Barcelona

DEMANDING HIS SECRET SON

LOUISE FULLER

For Archie:
for sticking at the hard stuff and making life easier
for everyone around you, especially me.
Louise x

CHAPTER ONE

LEANING FORWARD, TEDDIE TAYLOR spread the three playing cards out swiftly, then quickly flipped them over, covering them with her hand and rearranging them. Her green eyes gave away none of her excitement, nor the jump of her heart as the man sitting opposite her pointed confidently at the middle card.

He groaned as she turned it over, holding his hands up in defeat. 'Incredible,' he murmured.

Rising to his feet, Edward Claiborne held out his hand, a satisfied smile creasing his smooth patrician features.

'I can't tell you how happy I am that you're on board.' His blue eyes fixed on Teddie's face. 'I'm looking forward to having a little magic in my life.'

Teddie smiled. From another, younger, less urbane man, the remark might have sounded a little cheesy. But she knew Claiborne was far too well-bred to do anything as crass and inappropriate as flirt with a woman half his age to whom he had just given a job at his new prestigious private members' club.

'I'm looking forward to it too, Mr Claiborne—no, please—' she stopped him as he reached into the pocket of his jacket '—let me get these.' She gestured towards the coffee. 'You're a client now.'

Watching him walk away to talk to someone in the hotel lounge, she took a deep breath and sat down, resisting the urge to pump the air with her fist in time to the victory chant inside her head. She'd done it! Finally she'd netted a client who saw magic as more than just an amusing diversion at a party.

Across the lounge, Edward Claiborne was shaking hands, smiling smoothly and, leaning back in her armchair, she let elation wash over her. This was what she and Elliot had been chasing, but this new contract was worth more to them than a paycheque. Claiborne was fifth generation New York money and a recommendation from him would give their business the kind of publicity they couldn't buy.

Pulling out her phone, she punched in Elliot's number. He answered immediately, almost as though he'd been waiting for her to call—which, of course, he had.

'That was quick. How did it go?'

He sounded as he always did, speaking with that casual west-coast drawl that people sometimes mistook for slowness or lack of comprehension. But to Teddie, who had known him since she was thirteen, there was a tension to his voice—understandably. A three-nights-a-week job of bringing magic and illusion to the brand-new Castine Club would not only boost their income, it would mean they could employ someone to do the day-to-day admin. And that would mean they wouldn't end up with a repeat of today's last-minute panic when Elliot had realised he'd double-booked himself.

For a moment, she considered making him sweat, but she was too happy and relieved. 'He's in!'

Hearing Elliot's triumphant 'Surf's up, baby!' she laughed.

It was one of the things she loved most about her business partner and best friend—the way he reverted to his Californian roots when he was excited. Her heart swelled. That and the fact that, no matter how unjustified it was, he always had complete faith in her.

'I'm not saying I thought it was guaranteed, but honestly—I don't think I've ever met anyone who loves magic so much.'

'So what clinched it? No, let me guess. The three-card Monte. I'm right, aren't I?'

Teddie could practically picture the familiar wicked grin on Elliot's face.

'Yes! But that doesn't mean I forgive you for throwing me in at the deep end.'

He laughed. 'So how about I take you and George to Pete's Grill at the weekend? To make amends and celebrate?'

'You're on.' She frowned. 'How come you're talking to me, anyway? I thought the whole reason I had to do this was because you had a meeting.'

'I do—I'm waiting to go in. Actually, I'm going to have to go—okay, babe? But I'll drop round later.' He whooped. 'I love this job!'

He hung up, and Teddie grinned. She loved her job too, and Elliot was right: they should celebrate. And George loved Pete's.

Thinking about her son, Teddie felt her heart tighten. She did love her job, but her love for George was fierce and absolute. From the moment she'd held him in her arms after his birth, her heart had been enslaved by his huge dark eyes.

He was perfect, and he was hers. And maybe, if this job went well, in a couple of years they'd be celebrating here.

Leaning back against the smooth leather upholstery of a chair that probably cost more than her car, Teddie glanced around the hotel lounge. Well, maybe not here. The Kildare Hotel was new, and completely beyond her pay grade, oozing a mixture of old-school comfort and avant-garde design that she might have found intimidating if she hadn't been feeling so euphoric.

It was clearly the place to be seen, judging by the mix of hip, moneyed guests, although—she stared critically at the two huge Warhol prints that dwarfed one wall—wasn't it a bit corny to have all these copies of famous paintings hanging everywhere. Why not use originals by local artists?

Glancing over to where Claiborne was still chatting, she felt her pulse skitter forward. Really, she should be over there too, networking. It didn't have to be too obvious. All she had to do was smile as she passed by and her new boss would definitely call her over to introduce her to his companion.

She couldn't see the man's face, but even at a distance his glamour and self-assurance were tangible. Silhouetted against the industrial-sized window, with sunlight fanning around him like a sunburst, he looked almost mythical. The effect was mesmerising, irresistible—and, catching sight of the furtive glances of the other guests, she realised that it wasn't only she who thought so.

She wondered idly if he was aware of the effect he was having or if he was worthy of all the attention. Maybe she should just go and see for herself, she thought, emboldened by her business triumph.

And then, as she began picking up the cards that were still strewn all over the table, she noticed that Claiborne was gesturing in her direction. Automatically her lips started to curve upwards as the man standing beside him turned towards her.

The welcoming smile froze on her face.

She swallowed thickly. Her heart felt hard and heavy—in fact, her whole body seemed to be slowly turning to stone. Her euphoria of just moments earlier felt like a muddied memory.

No—no way! This couldn't be happening. He couldn't be here. Not here, not now.

But he was. Worse, having shaken hands with Claiborne, he was excusing himself and walking—no, *swaggering* towards her, his familiar dark gaze locked with hers. And, despite the alarm shrieking inside her head, she couldn't drag her eyes away from his cold, staggeringly handsome face and lean, muscular body.

For just a split second she watched him make his way across the room, and then her heart began pounding like a jackhammer and she knew that she had to move, to run, to flee. It might not be dignified, but frankly she didn't care. Her ex-husband, Aristotle Leonidas, was the last person on earth she wanted to see, much less talk to. There was too much history between them—not just a failed marriage, but a three-year-old son he knew nothing about.

Snatching at the rest of the cards, she tried to force them into the box. Only, panic made her clumsier than usual and they slipped out of her hands, spilling onto the floor in every direction.

'Allow me.'

If it had been a shock seeing him across the room, seeing him up close was like being struck by lightning. It would have been easier if he'd developed a paunch, but he hadn't changed at all. If anything, he was more devastating than ever, and it was clear that he had risen to such a point of power and wealth that he was immune to such earthly concerns as appearances.

But, to Teddie, his beauty was still hypnotic—the knife-sharp bone structure and obsidian-dark eyes still too perfect to be human.

Feeling her pulse accelerate, Teddie steeled herself to meet his gaze.

It had been four years since he'd broken her heart and turned his back on the gift of her love, but she had never forgotten him nor forgiven him for deleting her—and by default George—from his life like some unsolicited junk email. But evidently she had underestimated the impact of his husky, seductive voice—or why else was her pulse shying sideways like a startled pony?

It was just shock, she reassured herself. After four years she was obviously not expecting to see him.

Pushing aside the memory of that moment when he'd dismissed her like some underperforming junior member of his staff, she frowned. 'I'm fine. Just leave it.'

He ignored her, crouching down and calmly and methodically picking up each and every card.

'Here.' Standing up, he held out the pack, but she stared at him tensely, reluctant to risk even the slightest physical contact between them.

Her body's irrational response to hearing him speak again had made her realise that despite everything he'd done—and not done—there was still a connection between them, a memory of what had once been, how good it had been—

Ignoring both that unsettling thought, and the tug of his gaze, she sat down. She wanted to leave, but she would have to push past him to do so, and sitting seemed like the lesser of two evils. He watched her for a moment, as though gauging the likelihood of her trying to escape, and then she felt her pulse jolt forward as he settled into the chair recently vacated by Claiborne.

'What are you doing here?' she said stiffly.

After they'd split up he'd moved to London—or that was what Elliot had been told when he'd gone to collect her things. The apartment hadn't been part of the divorce settlement, and she'd always assumed she'd sold it. But then, he had no need of money, and it probably had no bad memories for him as he'd hardly ever been there.

His level gaze swept over her face. 'In New York?' He shrugged. 'I'm living here. Again,' he added softly.

She swallowed, stung at the thought of him returning to their home and simply picking up where he'd left off. She wished she could think of something devastating to say back to him. But to do so would only suggest that she cared—which she obviously didn't.

She watched warily as he slid the pack across the table towards her.

Catching sight of her expression, he tutted under his breath, his dark brown eyes narrowing. 'I don't know why you're looking at me like that,' he said coolly. 'It's me who should be worried. Or at least checking my wrist.'

His gaze hovered on her face and she blinked. She'd thought her body's unintended and unwelcome response to his was a by-product of shock, but now, beneath the politeness, further down than the hostility, she could feel it still—a thread of heat that was undiminished by time or reason. It made no sense—she doubted that he'd given her as much as a passing thought in the last four years—but that didn't seem to stop her skin from tingling beneath his gaze.

Watching the fury flare in her fabulous green eyes, Aristo gritted his teeth. She was still as stubborn as ever, but he was grateful she hadn't taken the cards from him. If both his hands had been free he might have been tempted to strangle her.

He hadn't spotted Teddie when he'd first walked into the lounge, partly because her dark brown hair was not falling loosely to her shoulders, as it had done when he'd last seen her, but was folded neatly at the back of her head.

In the main, though, he hadn't spotted her because, frankly, he hadn't ever expected to see his ex-wife again. He felt a tiny stab of pain in his heart like a splinter of ice.

But then, why would he?

Four years ago Theodora Taylor had ensnared him with her green eyes, her long legs and her diffident manner. She had breezed into his life like the Sirocco, interrupting his calm and ordered ascent into the financial stratosphere, and then just as quickly she had gone, an emptied bank account and his lacerated heart the only reminders of their six-month marriage.

He gave her a long, implacable stare. Teddie had taken more than his money. She had stolen the beat from his heart and taken what little trust he'd had for women and trampled it into the ground. It had been the first time he'd let down his guard, even going so far as to honour her with his name, but she had only married him in the hope that his money and connections would act as a stepping stone to a better life.

Of course he hadn't realised the truth until he'd returned from a business trip to find her gone. Hurt and humiliated, he had thrown himself into his job and put the whole disastrous episode behind him.

Until he'd bumped into Edward Claiborne a moment ago. He knew Edward socially, and liked him for his quiet self-assurance and old-school courtesy.

Walking into the hotel lounge, he'd noticed him laughing and chatting with uncharacteristic animation to a female companion. But it had only been when Edward had invited him to the new regular magic slot at his club, and then mentioned that he'd just finished having coffee with the woman who'd be running the shows, that he had turned and seen Teddie.

The muscle in his jaw had flexed, kick-starting a chain reaction through his body so that suddenly his heart had been pounding so hard and fast that he'd felt almost dizzy.

He studied her silently now, safe in the knowledge that his external composure gave no hint of the battle raging inside him. His head was telling him there was only one course of action. That a sensible, sane man would get up and walk away. But sense and sanity had never played that much of a part in his relationship with Theodora Taylor, and clearly nothing had changed—because despite knowing that she was the biggest mistake he had ever made, he stayed sitting.

His lip curled as he glanced down at his wrist. 'No, still there. But maybe I should double-check my wallet. Or perhaps I should give Edward Claiborne a call…make sure he still has his. I know you were only having coffee, but you were always a quick worker. I should know.'

Teddie felt her cheeks grow warm. His face was impenetrable, but the derision in his voice as much as his words was insultingly obvious.

How dare he talk to her like that? As though she was the bad guy when he was the one who had cut her out of his life without so much as a word.

Not that she'd ever been high on his list of priorities. Six months of married life had made it clear that Aristo had no time in his life for a wife. Even when she'd moved out and they'd begun divorce proceedings, he'd carried on working as though nothing had happened. Although no amount of his neglect and indifference could have prepared her for how he'd behaved at the end.

It had been a mistake, sleeping together that last time.

With emotions running high after a meeting to discuss their divorce, they'd ended up in bed and she'd ended up pregnant. Only, by the time she'd realised that her tiredness and nausea weren't just symptoms of stress, the divorce had been finalised, and Aristo had been on the other side of the world, building his European operations.

Although he might just as well have been in outer space.

Remembering her repeated, increasingly desperate and unsuccessful attempts to get in touch, she felt her back stiffen. She'd been frantic to tell him she was pregnant, but his complete radio silence had made it clear—horribly, humiliatingly clear—not only that he didn't want to talk to her, but that he didn't want to listen to *anything* she had to say.

It had been during a call to his London office, when an over-officious PA had cut short her stumbling and not very coherent attempt to speak to him, that she had decided doing the right thing was not going to work.

It certainly hadn't worked for her parents.

Sometimes it was better to face the truth, even if it was painful—and, truthfully, she and Aristo's relationship had had pretty flimsy foundations. Judging by the mess they'd made of their marriage, it certainly wasn't strong enough to cope with an unplanned pregnancy.

But it had been hard.

Aristo's rejection had broken her heart, and the repercussions of their brief and ill-fated marriage had lasted longer than her tears. Even now, she was still so wary of men that she'd barely gone out with anyone since they'd parted ways. Thanks to her father's casual, cursory attitude to parenting, she found it hard to believe that she would ever be anything more than an afterthought to any man. Aristo's casual, cruel rejection had confirmed that deep-seated privately held fear.

Much as she cared for Elliot, it was as a sister. Aristo was still the only man she'd ever loved. He had been her first love—not her first lover, but he had taught her everything about pleasure.

Her green eyes lifted to his. And not just pleasure. Because of him she'd become an authority on heartache and regret too.

So what exactly gave *him* the right to stand there with a sneer on that irritatingly handsome face?

Suddenly she was glad she hadn't turned tail. Fingers curling into fists, she glared at him. 'I think your memory must be playing tricks on you, Aristo. Work was always your thing—not mine. And, not that it's any of your concern, but Edward Claiborne is a very generous man. He was more than happy to pay the bill.'

She knew how she was making it sound, but it wasn't quite a lie. He *had* offered to pay. And besides, if it made Aristo feel even a fraction of her pain, then why not rub it in? He might not have thought her worthy of his attention and commitment, but Edward had been happy to give her his time and his company.

'And that's what matters to you, isn't it, Theodora? Getting your bills paid. Even if it means taking what isn't yours.'

He didn't really care about the money—even before his ruthless onwards-and-upwards rise to global domination, the amount she'd taken had been a negligible amount. Now it would barely make a dent in the Leonidas billions. At the time, though, it had stung—particularly as it had been down to his own stupidity.

For some unknown reason he hadn't closed their shared accounts immediately after the divorce was finalised, and Teddie had wasted no time taking advantage. Not that he should have been surprised. No matter how pampered they were, women were never satisfied with what they had. He'd learned that aged six, when his mother had found a titled, wealthier replacement for his father.

But knowing Teddie had worked her 'magic' on Edward hurt—and, childish though it was, he wanted to hurt her back.

Her eyes narrowed. 'It was mine,' she said hotly. '*It was ours*. That's what marriage is about, Aristo— it's called sharing.'

He stared at her disparagingly. The briefness of their marriage and the ruthless determination of his legal team had ensured that her financial settlement had been minimal, but it was more than she deserved.

'Is that what you tell yourself?'

She felt the hairs stand up on the back of her neck as he shook his head slowly.

'Just because it was still a joint account that didn't mean you had the right to empty it.'

'If it bothered you that much you could have *talked* to me,' she snarled. 'But I was only your wife—why would you want to talk to me?'

'Don't give me that,' he said sharply. 'I talked to you.'

'You talked at me about work. Never about us.'

Never about the fact that they were basically living separate lives—two strangers sharing a bed but never a meal or a joke.

Hearing the emotion in her voice, she stopped abruptly. What was the point of having this conversation? It was four years too late, and their marriage couldn't have mattered that much to him if all he wanted to discuss now was their bank account.

And was it really that surprising? His whole life had been dedicated to making money.

She breathed in unsteadily. 'And, as for the money, I took what I needed to live.'

To look after our son, she thought with a sudden flare of anger. A son who even before his birth had been relegated to second place.

'I'm not going to apologise for that, and if it was a problem then you should have said something at the time, but you made it quite clear that you didn't want to talk to me.'

Aristo stared at her, anger pulsing beneath his skin. At the time he had seen her behaviour as just more evidence of his poor judgement. More proof that the women in his life would inevitably turn their backs on him.

But he was not about to reveal his reasons for staying silent—why should he? He wasn't the one who'd walked out on their marriage. He didn't need to explain himself.

His heart began to thump rhythmically inside his chest, and an old, familiar feeling of bitter, impotent fury formed a knot in his stomach. She was right. He should have dealt

with this years ago—because even though he had succeeded in erasing her from his heart and his home, he had
never quite managed to wipe her betrayal from his memory.

How could he, though? Their relationship had been over
so quickly and had ended with such finality that there had
been no time to confront her properly.

Until now.

Teddie stared at him in appalled silence as, leaning back,
he stretched out his legs. Moments earlier she had wanted
to throw George's existence in his face. Now, though,
she could feel spidery panic scuttling over her skin at the
thought of how close she'd come to revealing the truth.

'So let's talk now,' he said, turning to nod curtly at a
passing waiter, who hurried over with almost comical haste.

She nearly laughed, only it was more sad than funny. He
didn't want to talk now any more than he had four years
ago, but he knew that she wanted to leave so he wanted to
make her stay. Nothing had changed. He hadn't changed.
He just wanted to get his own way.

'An espresso, please, and an Americano.' He gave the
order without so much as looking at her, and the fact that
he could still remember her favourite drink, as much as his
arrogant assumption that she would be joining him, made
her want to scream.

'I'm not staying,' she said coldly. She knew from past
experience that his powers of persuasion were incomparable, but in the past she had loved him to distraction. Here,
in the present, she wasn't going to let him push her into a
corner. 'And I don't want to speak to you,' she said, glancing pointedly past him.

He shrugged, a mocking smile curving his mouth. 'Then
I'll talk and you can listen.'

Cheeks darkening with angry colour, she sat mutinously
as the waiter reappeared and, with a swift, nervous glance
at Aristo, deposited the drinks in front of them.

'Is there anything else, Mr Leonidas?'

Aristo shook his head. 'No, thank you.'

Teddie stared at him, a beat of irritation jumping in her chest. It was always the same, this effect that Aristo had on people. When they'd first met she'd teased him about it: as a magician, *she* was supposed to be the centre of attention. But even when his wealth had been visible but not daunting, he'd had something that set him apart from all the other beautiful rich people—a potent mix of power and beauty and vitality that created an irresistible gravitational pull around him.

She could hardly blame the poor waiter for being like a cat on hot bricks when she had been just as susceptible. It was still maddening, though.

Some of her feelings must be showing on her face, for as he reached to pick up his cup, he paused. 'Is there a problem?'

She raised her eyebrows. 'Other than you, you mean?'

He sighed. 'I meant with your drink. I can send it back.'

'Could you just stop throwing your weight around?' She shook her head in exasperation. 'I know it must be difficult for you to switch off from work, but this isn't one of your hotels.'

Leaning back, he raised the cup to his mouth, his eyes never leaving her face. 'Actually it is,' he said mildly. 'It's the first in a new line we're trying out—traditional elegance and luxury with impeccable sustainability.' He smiled at the look of frozen horror on her face. 'And a constantly rotating collection of contemporary art.'

She felt her breathing jerk as out of the corner of her eye she noticed the tiny lion's head logo on the coaster. Cheeks burning, she glanced furtively over at the Warhols.

Damn it, but of course they were real. Aristo Leonidas would never have anything in his life that wasn't one hundred per cent perfect—it was why he'd found it so devastatingly easy to abandon her.

Her heartbeat stumbled in her chest. No doubt he'd only wanted her to stay here so he could point out this latest addition to his empire.

Cursing herself, and Aristo, and Elliot for being so useless at managing their schedule, she half rose.

'Sit down,' he said softly.

Their eyes clashed. 'I don't want to.'

'Why? Are you scared of what will happen if you do?

Was she scared?

She felt her insides flip over, and she suddenly felt hot and dizzy.

Once she had been in thrall to him. He'd been everything she'd wanted in a lover and in a man. Caught in the dark shimmering intensity of his gaze, she had felt warm and wanted.

And now, as the heat spread outwards, she was forced to accept again that, even hating him as she did, her body was still reacting in the same way, unconstrained by logic or even the most basic sense of self-preservation.

Horrified by this revelation of her continuing vulnerability—or maybe stupidity—she lifted her chin, her eyes narrowing, muscles tensing as though for combat.

'I'm not, no. But *you* should be. Or maybe you like your suits with coffee stains?'

His dark eyes flickered with amusement. 'If you want me to get undressed, you could just ask.'

He was unbelievable and unfair, making such a blatant reference to their sexual past. But, despite her outrage, she felt the kick of desire. Just as she had that night four years ago, when her body had betrayed her.

Her heart thudded. How could she have let it happen? Just hours earlier they'd been thrashing out their divorce.

She'd known he didn't love her, and yet she'd still slept with him.

But she could never fully regret her stupidity for that was the night she'd conceived George.

She glowered at him. 'I don't want you at all,' she lied. 'And I don't want to have some stupid conversation about coffee or art.'

He held up his hands in mock surrender. 'Okay, okay. Look, this is hard for both us, but we share a history. Surely if fate has chosen to throw us together we can put our differences behind us for old times' sake,' he said smoothly. 'Surely you can spare a couple of minutes to catch up.'

Teddie felt her heart start to pound. If only if was just the past they shared. But it wasn't, and hiding that fact from Aristo was proving harder than she'd ever imagined.

But how could she tell him the truth? That he had a three-year-old son called George he'd never met. She caught her breath, trying to imagine how that conversation would start, much less end.

More importantly, though, why would she tell him? Their marriage might have been short-lived, but it had been long enough for her to know that there was no room in her ex-husband's life for anything but his career. And, having been on the receiving end of her father's intermittent attention, she knew exactly what it felt like to be a side dish to the main meal, and she was not about to let her son suffer the same fate.

'I just told you. I don't want to stay.' But, glancing up into his dark eyes, she felt a flare of panic, for they were cold and flat like slate, and they matched the uncompromising expression on his face.

'I wasn't actually giving you an option.'

She felt the colour leave her face. Had he really just said what she thought he had?

'What is that supposed to mean?' Instantly her panic

was forgotten, obliterated in a white-out of fury. 'Just because this is your hotel, Aristo, it doesn't mean you can act like some despot,' she snapped.' If I want to leave, I will, thank you very much, and there's nothing you can do about it.'

Aristo stared at her in silence. Was this why he had sought out her company instead of simply retreating? To force a confrontation so that, unlike in their marriage, he would be the one to dictate when she left? Would that heal the still festering wound of her betrayal? Quiet the suspicion, the knowledge, that he had been used like a plaything to pass the time until something, or more likely *someone*, better came along?

He shrugged dismissively. 'That would depend, I suppose, on how you leave and whether you value your reputation. Being removed by Security in front of a room full of people could be quite damaging.' Leaning back in his seat, he raised an eyebrow. 'I can't imagine what your new boss would think if he heard about it.'

'You wouldn't dare,' she said softly.

His eyes didn't leave her face. 'Try me!'

He could see the conflict in her eyes—frustration and resentment battling with logic and resignation—but he knew the battle was already won. If she was going to leave she would already be on her feet.

With immense satisfaction he watched her sit back stiffly in her seat. This wasn't about revenge, but even so he couldn't help letting a small, triumphant smile curve his mouth.

'So…' He gestured towards the pack of cards. 'You're still a magician, then.'

Teddie stared at the cards. To anyone else his remark would have sounded innocuous, nothing more than a polite show of interest in an ex's current means of employment. But she wasn't anyone. She had been his wife, and she could hear the resentment in his voice for she had heard it before.

It was another reminder of why their marriage had failed. And why she should have confronted the past head-on instead of pretending her marriage had never happened. She might have been strong for her son, but she'd been a coward when it came to facing Aristo.

Only, she'd had good reason not to want to face him. Lots of good reasons, actually.

In the aftermath of their marriage he'd been cold and unapproachable, and later she'd been so sick with her pregnancy, and then, by the time she'd felt well again, George had been born—and that was a whole other conversation.

She was suddenly conscious of Aristo's steady, dark gaze and her heart gave a thump. She had to stop thinking about George or something was going to slip out.

'Yes,' she said curtly. 'I'm still a magician, Aristo. And you're still in hotels.'

Her heart was thumping hard against her chest. Did he really want to sit here with her while they politely pretended to be on speaking terms? Her hands felt suddenly damp and she pressed them against the cooling leather. Clearly he did. But then, he didn't have a secret to keep.

He nodded. 'Mostly, but I've diversified my interests.'

She gritted her teeth. So even less time for anything other than work. For some reason that thought made her feel sad rather than angry and, caught off-guard, she picked up her coffee and took a sip.

Aristo looked at her, his gaze impassive. 'You must have done well. Edward Claiborne doesn't often go out of his comfort zone. So how did you two meet?'

His eyes tangled with hers and he felt a stab of anger, remembering Edward Claiborne's proprietorial manner as he'd turned and gestured across the room towards Teddie.

She shrugged. 'Elliot and I did some magic showcases at a couple of charity balls last year and he was there.'

Aristo stared at her coldly. 'You work with Elliot?'

For some reason her defiant nod made a primitive jealousy rip through him like a box-cutter. In his head—if he'd allowed himself to picture her at all—she had been alone, suffering as he was. Only, now it appeared that not only had she survived, she was prospering with Elliot.

'We set up a business together. He does the admin, front of house and accountancy. I do the magic.'

He felt another spasm of irritation—pain, almost. He knew Teddie had never been romantically or sexually involved with Elliot, but he had supported her, and once that had been *his* job. It was bad enough that his half-brother, Oliver, had displaced him in his mother's affections—now it appeared that Elliot had usurped him in Teddie's.

'From memory, he wasn't much of a businessman,' he said coolly.

For the first time since she'd sat down Teddie smiled and, watching her eyes soften, he had to fight an overwhelming urge to reach out and stroke her cheek, for once her eyes had used to soften for him in that way.

'He's not, but he's my best friend and I trust him,' she said simply. 'And that's what matters.'

It was tempting to lie, to tell him that she'd found love and unimaginable passion in Elliot's arms, but it would only end up making her look sad and desperate.

He raised an eyebrow. 'Surely what matters is profit?'

She'd always known he felt like that, but somehow his remark hurt more than it should, for it was the reason her son would grow up without a father.

Her fingers curled. 'Some things are more important than money, Aristo.'

'Not in business,' he said dismissively.

She glared at him, hating him and his stupid, blinkered

view of life, but hating herself more for still caring what he thought.

'But there's more to life than business. There's feelings and people—friends, family—'

She broke off, the emotion in her voice echoing inside her head. Glancing up, she found him watching her, his gaze darkly impassive, and it was hard not to turn away, for the heartbreakingly familiar masculine beauty of his face seemed so at odds with the distance in his eyes.

'You don't have a family,' he said.

It was one of the few facts she'd shared with him about her life—that she was an orphan. Dazed, Teddie blinked. She was about to retort that she was a mother to his son, when abruptly her brain came back online and she bit back her words. Given how he'd behaved, and was still behaving, she certainly didn't owe him the truth.

But George was his child. Didn't he deserve to know that?

Her heartbeat stalled, and for a moment she couldn't breathe. Her stomach seemed to be turning in on itself. Wishing that she could make herself disappear as effortlessly as she could make watches and wallets vanish, she forced herself to meet his gaze.

'No, I don't,' she lied.

And suddenly she knew that she had to leave right there and then, for to stay would mean more lies, and she couldn't do it—she didn't want to lie about her son.

Neither could she carry on lying to herself.

Up until today she had wanted to believe that she was over Aristo. But as she stared into his dark, distant eyes, the pain of pretending erupted inside of her, and suddenly she needed to make certain this *never* happened again.

She'd made the mistake of letting him back into her life before—made the mistake of following her heart, not her head. And although she didn't regret it—for that would mean regretting having her son—after that one-night stand she'd accepted not only that their marriage was over, but that it was the best possible outcome.

Only by staying out of his orbit would she be safe—not just from him, but from herself.

She lifted her chin. This meeting would be their last.

Ignoring the intensity of his dark gaze, and the full, sensuous mouth that had so often kissed her into a state of helpless bliss, she cleared her throat. 'Fascinating though this is, Aristo, I don't really think there's any point in us carrying on with this conversation,' she said. 'Small talk—any kind of talk, really—wasn't ever your strong point, and we got divorced for a reason—several, actually.'

He held her gaze. 'Are you refusing to talk to me?'

'Yes, I am.'

But she didn't want to explain why. Didn't want to explain the complex and conflicting emotions swirling inside her.

Her heart was banging against her ribs and, breathing in deeply, she steadied herself. Reaching into her bag, she pulled out a pen and a notebook and scrawled something on a page inside it. Tearing the page free, she folded it in half and slid it onto the table.

'I don't expect to hear from you again, but if you have to get in touch this is my lawyer's number. Goodbye, Aristotle.'

And then, before he'd even had a chance to react, let alone respond, she turned and almost ran out of the hotel lounge.

Left alone, Aristo stared at the empty seat, a mass of emotions churning inside him. His heart was beating out of time. Teddie's words had shocked him. But, although she had no doubt intended her curt goodbye to be a slap in the face, to him it felt as though she'd thrown down a gauntlet at his feet.

And in doing so she'd sealed her fate. Four years ago she had waltzed out of their marriage and his life and he'd spent the intervening years suppressing hurt and disappointment. Now, though, he was ready to confront his past—*and* his ex-wife.

But he would do so on his terms, he thought coldly. And, reaching into his jacket, he pulled out his phone.

Three hours later, having fed and bathed George and tidied away his toys, Teddie leaned back against the faded cushions of her sofa and let out a long, slow breath. She felt exhausted. Her apartment—her wonderful apartment—with its bright walls and wooden floors, which was usually a place of sanctuary, looked shabby after the high gloss of the Kildare Hotel. And, although her son was usually a sweet-tempered and easy-going toddler, he must have picked up on her tension. Tonight he'd had a huge tantrum when she'd stopped him playing with his toy speed boat in the bath.

He was sleeping now, and as she'd gazed down at her beautiful son she had felt both pride and panic, for he so resembled his father. A father he would never know.

She felt a rush of guilt and self-pity. This wasn't what she'd wanted for herself or for her son. In her dreams she'd wanted to give him everything she'd never had—two loving parents, financial security—but she'd tried marriage and it had been a disaster.

Even before Aristo's obsession with work had blotted out the rest of his life she had felt like a gatecrasher in her own marriage. But then what had they really known about one another? How could you really know someone after just seven weeks?

Maybe if their marriage had had stronger foundations it might have been possible for them to face their problems together. But they'd had no common ground aside from a raging sexual attraction which had been enough to blind both of them to their fundamental incompatibility. He had been born into wealth. She, on the other hand, had grown up in a children's home with a mother dosed up on prescription drugs and a father in prison.

And sex wasn't enough to sustain a relationship—not without trust and openness and tenderness.

Divorce had been the only option, and, although she might be able to face that fact she still wasn't up to facing Aristo. Thankfully, though, she would never have to see him again.

Her pulse twitched as she remembered telling him to talk to her through her lawyer. She could hardly believe that she'd spoken to him like that. But she'd been so desperate to leave before she said anything incriminating about George, and even more desperate to ensure that he would be out of her life for good.

Stifling a yawn, she picked up her phone and gazed gloomily down at the time on the screen. All she wanted to do was crawl into bed, pull the duvet over her head and forget about the mess she'd made of her life.

Unfortunately Elliot was dropping round to discuss the Claiborne meeting.

For a moment she considered calling him to cancel. But being on her own with a head full of regrets and recriminations was not a great idea.

Anticipating Elliot's partisan comments as she relayed an edited version of the day's events, she felt her mood lighten a fraction and, standing up, she walked into the tiny kitchen that led off from the living room.

She was just pulling a bottle of wine from the rack when she heard the entryphone.

Thank goodness! Elliot was early. Buzzing him up, she picked up a bottle of wine and two glasses.

'Don't be thinking we're going to finish this—' she began as she yanked open the door.

But her words trailed off into silence. It wasn't Elliot standing there, with that familiar affectionate grin on his face. Instead it was Aristo, and he wasn't smiling affectionately. In fact, he wasn't smiling at all.

CHAPTER TWO

'I WOULDN'T DREAM of it,' he said softly.

He held out his hand, his eyes locking with hers, and his sudden, swift smile made her heart lurch forward.

'You forgot these, and I was passing so…'

It was the pack of cards she'd left at his hotel.

She felt her breathing jerk. For a few seconds she couldn't answer—couldn't find the words to express her shock and confusion at finding him on her doorstep. Actually, not *on* her doorstep—he was already leaning against the frame, one foot resting negligently over the threshold so that shutting the door wouldn't just be a challenge, but a virtual impossibility, given the disparity in their respective weights.

'You were passing?'

She felt a shiver run over her skin as his dark gaze made a slow inspection of her, from the damp hair tumbling over her shoulders to her bare toes. Even if she'd been fully clothed she would have felt naked under his intense scrutiny, but she was wearing nothing but a T-shirt that was barely covered by her bathrobe.

There was a pulsing silence and then, tilting his head slightly, he glanced past her into the apartment. 'Aren't you going to invite me in? Or do you always entertain your guests in the corridor?'

'You're not a guest. Guests are invited, and I didn't invite you.' She stared at him suspiciously. 'And I didn't tell you where I lived either, so how did you find me?'

'I looked up "beautiful female magician" in the phone book.' His dark eyes glittered with amusement. 'You were there—right at the top.'

Her skin was suddenly prickling, her stomach flipping over in response to his words. She'd spent so long remembering his flaws that she had forgotten he could make her laugh and it was an untimely reminder of why she'd fallen in love with him.

Only, even as her mouth began to curl upwards she knew she was making a mistake. The last thing she needed right now was to give him any hint of her continuing vulnerability where he was concerned so, tuning out the erratic beat of her heart, she shook her head. 'Aristo—'

'Okay, that was a lie.' He shifted against the doorframe. 'I actually looked up "*angry*, beautiful female magician".'

Heart banging against her ribs, she took a deep breath, a rush of panic swamping her as she tried to gauge his mood. Surely if he'd found out about George he would be the angry one.

'Did you follow me?'

His smile widened. 'Of course. I have a second job as a private detective.'

Resisting the overriding urge to slam the door on his obviously expensive handmade shoes, she held his gaze. 'Very funny. So you had somebody find out where I lived?' She shook her head again. 'That's classy, Aristo.'

'You gave me no choice. You left before we'd finished talking.'

His complete inability to understand what had happened back at the hotel sucked her breath from her lungs.

'No, *I* had finished talking, Aristo,' she said irritably. 'That's why I gave you the number of my lawyer.'

'Ah, yes, your lawyer.' Pausing, he glanced over his

shoulder and frowned, pretending concern. 'Are you sure you want everyone hearing about your private business?'

Teddie stared at him helplessly. She could tell from the glint in his eyes that he was not going to leave without saying whatever it was he wanted to say, and she couldn't physically remove him herself.

Maybe she should call for back-up. But who would she call? Her maintenance charge for the apartment included a caretaker who was nominally responsible for security, but she had no idea how to get in touch with him, and Aristo might make a scene and wake George.

So that left her with the choice of having a conversation in the hallway or in her apartment. Her heart contracted with apprehension. Every instinct she had was screeching at her like a banshee not to let him into her apartment, but what if he met one of her neighbours and they mentioned her son?

Maybe there were other options, but right now she was too tired and strung out to work them out—and besides, she wanted him out of the hallway and her life.

Quickly she did an inventory of the apartment—thankfully she had tidied George's toys away, and the only photos of him were in her bedroom. Her skin felt suddenly hot and tight, but of course there was no way Aristo would be going within a mile of that particular room.

'Fine. You can come in,' she said briskly. 'But you can't stay long.'

Mentally crossing her fingers, she hoped that tonight wouldn't be the one occasion when Elliot was on time. She had, of course, given him an abridged version of her ill-starred marriage, only she had carefully edited out all mention of the tangle of unresolved feelings she still carried around with her.

But Elliot would only have to walk through her front door to know that she was upset, and right now she had

enough going on with Aristo. She certainly didn't want to
have to deal with Elliot as well.

'Ten minutes, Aristo, that's all. And you'll have to be
quiet. I have elderly neighbours,' she lied, 'and I don't want
to disturb them.'

His dark, unwavering gaze fixed on hers and she felt a
sudden rush of panic, for it seemed as though he could not
only sense her lies, but also the reason behind them—as
if the T-shirt she was wearing was printed with the truth.

'I can do quiet, Theodora. Or have you forgotten?'

Her pulse fluttered, cheeks suddenly burning. No, she
hadn't forgotten. They had often been caught out by the
strength of their desire, and on one particularly memorable
occasion in a park they had satisfied their passion beneath
the shade of a tree, hidden from passers-by. Quickly she
pushed the thought away, wishing her brain hadn't chosen
to save that particular memory for posterity, but not even
divorce proceedings had weakened the devastating pull of
desire between them.

Ignoring the quivering tension of her body, she lifted
her chin and smiled at him coolly. 'It must have slipped
my memory.'

Turning, she let the door fall back on his foot, his grunt
of pain giving her a momentary but sharp satisfaction.

Stopping what she considered a safe distance away from
him, she watched as he strolled into her living room, his
assessing gaze travelling over the modest interior and no
doubt contrasting it with the luxury of the apartment they'd
once shared. But who cared what he thought? He was only
here under sufferance, and she needed to make that clear
to him.

'I gave you my lawyer's number for a reason. So why
are you here?' she asked stiffly.

She didn't much care, but now that he was standing in
her living room she realised there was no such thing as *safe*

for her where Aristo was concerned. He was still wearing his suit, but he'd unbuttoned his shirt and lost the tie. Only, instead of making him less intimidating, his more relaxed appearance only seemed to emphasise his natural authority.

Add to that the fact that they were completely alone, it was no surprise that her head was starting to swim.

But it wasn't just the tantalising temptation of his nearness that was making her hold her breath. Earlier she'd been so concerned about inadvertently revealing something about George that she'd been able to ignore her guilt at not doing so. In the unfamiliar surroundings of the Kildare Hotel it had felt almost like someone else's life.

Now, though, it felt real, *personal*, and she could feel herself wavering. Could she really go through with this? Could she really cheat him out of knowing his son? Shouldn't she at least give him the chance? And what about George? He'd already asked her why he didn't have a daddy.

So far he was too young to really focus on the issue, but that would change...

'I didn't speak to her.'

It took her a moment to realise that he was replying to her question about her lawyer.

He was standing with his back to her, studying the books on her shelves, and she stared tensely at him, remembering how he'd loved to lie with that same head on her lap and how she'd loved to run her fingers through the thick, black hair...

She jumped slightly as he turned, her cheeks flushing with colour as his all-seeing dark eyes fixed on hers.

'There was no point,' he said blithely. 'Why pay legal fees when we can talk for free?'

Her skin felt suddenly too tight. There was a long, steady silence as she stared at him incredulously. If she hadn't been so stunned, she might have laughed. 'Are you giving me advice?'

There was another long silence, and then he shrugged. 'Somebody has to. Clearly whoever has been doing so up until now can't have had your best interests at heart.'

He watched her green eyes widen, feeling childishly but intensely gratified that his words had clearly scored a direct hit. And then he caught sight of the two glasses and abruptly his mood changed, for clearly she hadn't been planning on spending the evening alone.

Ever since she'd more or less fled from him, he'd been questioning her motives for doing so. Although he knew their relationship was purely professional, Edward Claiborne and Teddie had looked good together, and it had got to him—for, just like his mother, Teddie was not the kind of women to be alone. Despite her denial, he had no doubt that somewhere in the city there was a nameless, faceless man who had stepped into his shoes.

In fact that was why he'd found himself standing on her doorstep. Even just imagining it made a knot of rage form in his stomach, and that enraged him further—the fact that she still had the power to affect him after all these years.

His shoulders tensed. 'Or perhaps they have their own agenda.'

Teddie felt a rush of anger spread over her skin like a heat rash. '*Nobody* has been giving me advice. I make my own decisions—although I wouldn't expect you to understand that.' Heart thumping, she lifted her gaze to his. 'It was always a difficult concept for you, wasn't it, Aristo? My being an independent woman?'

His eyes flickered, and she could almost see the fuse inside of him catch light.

'If by "independent" you mean self-absorbed and unsupportive, then, yes, I suppose it was.'

She caught her breath. The room felt suddenly cramped and airless, as though it had shrunk in the face of his anger—an anger which fed the outrage that had been simmering inside her since meeting him earlier.

'*You're* calling *me* self-absorbed and unsupportive?' She glared at him, the sheer injustice of his statement blowing her away. She could feel her grip on her temper starting to slip. How dare he turn up here, in her home, and start throwing accusations at her?

But even as she choked on her anger, she wasn't really surprised. Back when she'd loved him, she'd known that he had a single-minded vision of the world—a world in which he was always in the right and always had the last word. Her refusing to talk to him now simply didn't fit with that expectation.

Her motives, her needs, were irrelevant. As far as he was concerned she had merely issued him with a challenge that must instantly be confronted and crushed.

Queasily, she remembered his cold hostility when she'd refused to give up her job. Was that when their marriage had really ended? It was certainly the moment when she'd finally been forced to acknowledge the facts. That marrying Aristo had not been an act of impulse, driven by an undeniable love, but a mistake based on a misguided hope and longing to have a place in his life, and in his heart.

But Aristo didn't have a heart, and he hadn't come to her apartment to return a pack of cards. As usual, he just wanted to have the last word.

Crossing her arms to contain the ache in her chest, she lifted her chin. 'If you believe that, then perhaps I should have given you the number for my doctor, as you're clearly delusional,' she snapped. 'Wanting to carry on doing a job I loved didn't make me self-absorbed, Aristo. It was an act of self-preservation.'

Aristo stared at her, his shoulders rigid with frustration. 'Self-preservation!' he scoffed. 'You were living in a penthouse in Manhattan with a view of Central Park. You were hardly on Skid Row.' He shook his dark head in disbelief. 'That's the trouble with you, Teddie—you're so used to performing you turn every single part of your life into a stunt, even this conversation.'

They were both almost shouting now, their bodies braced against the incoming storm.

Her eyes narrowed. 'You think this is a conversation?' she snapped. 'You didn't come here to converse. I bruised your ego so you wanted—'

'Mommy—Mommy!'

The child's voice came from somewhere behind her, cutting through her angry tirade like a scythe through wheat. Turning instantly, instinctively, Teddie cleared her throat.

'Oh, sweetheart, it's all right.'

Her son, George, blinked up at her. He was wearing his pyjamas and holding his favourite toy boat and she felt a rush of pure, fierce love as she looked down into his huge, anxious dark eyes.

'Mommy shouted...'

He bit his lip and, hearing the wobble in his voice, she reached down and curved her arm unsteadily around his stocky little waist and pulled him closer, pressing his body against hers. 'I'm sorry, darling. Did Mommy wake you?'

Lifting him up, she held him tightly as he nodded his head against her shoulder.

Watching Teddie press her face against the little dark-haired boy's cheek, Aristo felt his stomach turn to ice.

He felt winded by the discovery that she had a child. No, it was more than that: he felt *wounded*, even though he could come up with no rational explanation for why that should be the case.

His pulse was racing like a bolting horse, his thoughts

firing off in every direction. He could hardly take it in, but there could be no mistake. This child was Teddie's son. But why hadn't she told him?

Thinking back to their earlier conversation, he replayed her words and felt an icy fury rise up inside of him. Not only had she said nothing, she'd lied to his face when he'd asked her about her family. Of course he'd been talking about siblings, cousins, aunts—but why hadn't she told him then? Why had she kept her son a secret?

At that moment the little boy lifted his face and suddenly he couldn't breathe. At the periphery of his vision he could see Teddie turning to face him, and then he knew why, for her green eyes were telling him what her mouth—that beautiful, soft, deceiving mouth—had failed to do earlier.

This was his son.

Like a drowning man, he saw his whole life speeding through his head—meeting Teddie at that dinner, her long dark hair swinging forward half-hiding a smile that had stolen his breath away, the echoing emptiness of his apartment, and that moment in the Kildare when she'd hesitated...

He breathed out unsteadily, and abruptly his pulse juddered to a halt.

Only, he wasn't drowning in water, but in lies. Teddie's lies.

The resentment and hostility he'd felt after she'd left him, the shock of bumping into her today—all of it was swept aside in a firestorm of fury so blindingly white and intense that he had to reach out and steady himself against a bookcase.

But the luxury of losing his temper with Teddie would have to wait. Right now it was time to meet his son.

'I'm sorry too,' he said gently, making sure that none

of the emotions roiling inside his head were audible in his voice as he smiled at his son for the first time.

'But you don't need to worry.' Skewering Teddie with his gaze, he took a step closer. 'Mommy and I are going to have a chat, aren't we?'

He turned to Teddie, making sure that the smooth blandness of his voice in no way detracted from the blistering rage in his eyes. Hearing her small, sharp intake of breath, he felt the glacier in his chest start to scrape forward. It had been barely audible, but it was all the confirmation he needed.

Forcing herself to meet his gaze, Teddie nodded mechanically, but inside her head a mantra of panic-stricken thoughts was beating in time to her heartbeat. *He knows. He knows George is his son. What am I going to do?*

Clearing her throat, she smiled. 'Yes, that's right. We're going to have a grown-ups talk. And you, young man, are going to be taken back to bed.'

Although, given that her legs felt as though they were made of blancmange, that might be easier to say than do.

Aristo stared at her coldly. 'But not before you've introduced me, of course.'

Her chin jerked up, but his glittering gaze silenced her words of objection.

'This is my son, George,' she said stiffly.

'Hello, George.' Aristo smiled. 'I'm very honoured to meet you. My name is Aristo Leonidas, and I'm an old friend of your mommy's.'

Gazing into his son's eyes—dark eyes that were almost identical in shape and colour to his own—he felt his stomach tighten painfully. George had his jawline and his high cheekbones; the likeness between them was remarkable, undeniable. At the same age they would have looked like twins.

As George smiled uncertainly back at him he felt almost

blinded with outrage at Teddie's deceit. His son must be three years old. How much had he missed during that time? First tooth. First word. First steps. Holidays and birthdays. And in the future, what other occasions would he have unknowingly not attended—graduation, wedding day…

He gritted his teeth.

Maybe he'd not actually thought about becoming a father, but Teddie had unilaterally taken away his right to be one. How was he ever going to make good the time he'd missed? No, not *missed*, he thought savagely. Teddie had cheated him of three years of his son's life. Worse, not only had she deliberately kept his son a secret from him for all that time, she had clearly been planning to keep him in ignorance of George's existence for ever.

Hell, she'd even lied to him tonight, telling him that he had to be quiet because of her elderly neighbours.

Glancing up, he refocused on his son's face and, seeing the confusion in George's eyes, pushed his anger away. 'I know you're not ready to shake hands yet and that's a good thing, because we need to get to know each other a bit better first. But maybe we could just bump knuckles for now.'

Raising his hand, he curled his fingers into a fist, his heart contracting as his son copied him, and they gently bumped fists.

'Hey, what's that? Is that a boat?' Aristo watched as George uncurled his fingers.

'It's my boat,' he said solemnly.

'I love your boat.' Aristo glanced at it admiringly. 'I have a real boat like that. Maybe you could come for a ride on it with Mommy. Would you like that?'

George nodded, and Teddie felt her chest hollow out with panic.

Watching the sudden intimacy between her ex-husband and their son, she felt something wrench apart inside her, for the two of them were so close—not just physically but in their very likeness. It was both touching and terrifying, almost overwhelmingly so.

Clearing her throat, she smiled stiffly. 'That would be lovely, wouldn't it, George? Right now though, it really is time to go back to bed.'

In his bedroom, she tucked him under his duvet, keeping up a steady stream of chatter until his eyelids fluttered shut.

If only she could just crawl in beside him and close her eyes too. Remembering the look on Aristo's face as he'd worked out that George was his son, she felt her pulse begin beating in her neck like a moth against glass. Despite his outer calm, she knew that he was angry—more angry than she had ever seen him, more angry than she could have imagined possible.

Not that she could blame him, she thought, guilt scraping over her skin like sandpaper. Had their roles been reversed she would have been just as furious. And the fact that part of her had always wanted to tell him the truth didn't feel like much of a defence.

She really should be relieved, though, for it had been getting harder and harder to keep lying.

But now she would have to pay the price for those lies and face his anger. That was bad enough, but more terrifying still was the sudden knife-twist of realisation that Aristo had both a moral *and* a legal right to be in his son's life. It didn't matter about their divorce. George was his son, and if he wanted to press that point home he had the power and the money to do so emphatically—not just here in her apartment but in court.

The thought of facing Aristo in court made her want to throw up.

So face him now, she ordered herself. And, taking a deep breath, she stood up and made her way back to the living room.

He swung round towards her, and her heart began beating so fast she thought it would burst through her ribs. She had thought he was angry before, but clearly each minute that had passed during her absence had increased his fury exponentially, so that now, as he walked towards her, it was the arctic blast of his contempt that held her frozen to the spot.

'I knew you were shallow and unscrupulous,' he said, his eyes gleaming like black ice, 'but at what point exactly did your morals become so skewed that you decided to keep my son a secret from me?'

'That's not fair—'

His black eyes slammed into hers. '*Fair?* You're really quite something, Teddie. I thought you just stole money from me. Turns out you stole my son.'

'I didn't steal him—' she began, but he cut her off.

'Oh, I'm sure you've post-rationalised it. What did you tell yourself? *What he doesn't know won't hurt him?*' he imitated her voice. *'It'll be for the best.'*

'I did do it for the best.' Her voice was shaking, but her eyes were level with his. 'I did what was best *for me*, Aristo, because there was only me.'

He felt his breathing jerk. 'Not true. You had a husband.'

'*Ex*-husband,' she snapped. 'We were divorced by then. Not that it would have made any difference. You were never there.'

His eyes didn't leave hers. 'You really can't help yourself, can you? It's just lie after lie after lie.'

Teddie swallowed. It was true—she had lied repeatedly. But not because she'd wanted to and not about the past. It wasn't fair of Aristo to judge her with hindsight. He might be in shock now, but she'd had just the same shock four years ago when, thanks to him, she'd been homeless and alone.

'I was going to tell you—' She broke off as he laughed, the bitterness reverberating around the small room.

'Of course you were.'

'I didn't mean now—today. I meant in the future.'

'The future?' He repeated the word slowly, as though not quite sure of its meaning. 'What's wrong with the present? What was wrong with this morning?'

'It all happened so quickly.' She looked at him defensively. 'I wasn't expecting to see you.'

Aristo stared at her in disbelief. 'And that's a reason, is it? Reason enough for my son to grow up without a father? Or have you got some surrogate daddy in mind? Is that why you ran out on me this morning?'

The thought stung. He might not have been celibate, but dating—certainly anything serious—had been the last thing on his mind for the past four years. Work—in particular the expansion of his empire, and more recently his upcoming flotation on the stock exchange—had taken up so much of his time and energy. On those occasions when he'd needed a 'plus-one', he been careful to keep her at a distance.

Clearly Teddie had found him far easier to replace.

His eyes narrowed. 'I mean, it's just what you *do*, isn't it, Teddie? That's your real act! Not all this nonsense.' He held up the box of cards. 'You set it all up.' *Set me up*, he thought savagely. 'Then take what you want and move on.'

'If you're talking about our marriage, I had plenty of reasons to leave. And I didn't take anything.'

She felt a sudden sharp pang of guilt as she thought of her son—*their* son—but then she repeated his sneering reference to her work as 'nonsense' inside her head, and pushed her guilt aside.

Glaring at him, she shook her head, whipping her dark hair like a horse swatting flies with its tail. 'And not that it's any of your business but there is no man in my life, and there's certainly no daddy in George's.'

The outrage in her voice sounded real, and he wanted to believe her for his pride's sake, if nothing else. But, aside from the faint flush of colour creeping over her cheeks, she had already told so many different lies in such a short space of time that it was hard to believe anything she said. Clearly lying was second nature to her.

His heart was suddenly speeding and his skin felt cool and clammy with shock—not just at finding out he was a father, but at how ruthlessly Teddie had played him.

'So let me get this clear,' he said slowly. 'At some un-specified point in the future you were planning on telling me about my son?'

Teddie hesitated. If only she could plead the Fifth Amendment but this was one question that required an answer. Actually, it required the truth.

'I don't know. Honestly, most days I'm just trying to deal with the day-to-day of work and being a mom to George.'

And grieving for the man I loved and lost.

Blocking off the memories of those terrible weeks and months after they'd split, she cleared her throat. 'We were already divorced by the time I found out I was pregnant. We weren't talking, and you weren't even in the country.'

His eyes bored into eyes. 'And so you just unilaterally decided to disappear into thin air with my child? He's my *son*—not some prop in your magic show.'

Stung, and shocked by the level of emotion in his voice, she said defensively, 'I know and I'm sorry.'

He swore under his breath. 'Sorry is not enough, Ted-die. I have a child, and I fully intend to get to know him.'

It wasn't an outright threat, more a statement of intent, but she could see that his shock at discovering he was a fa-ther was fading and in its place was that familiar need to take control of the situation.

She felt a ripple of apprehension run down her backbone. Where did that leave her?

Last time she and Aristo had gone head to head she'd been cast out from his kingdom, her unimportance in his life no longer just a private fear but an actuality.

But four years ago she'd been young and in love, unsure of her place in the world. Now, though, she was a successful businesswoman and a hands-on single mother—and, most important of all, she understood what she'd been too naive and too dazzled to see four years ago.

Aristo had no capacity for or interest in emotional ties. She'd learned that first-hand over six agonising months spent watching his obsession with work consume their marriage and exclude her from his life.

She brought her eyes back to his. Yes, she should have told him the truth, but he'd given her no reason to do so—no reason other than biology for her to allow him into George's life.

And now? Maybe if Aristo had been a different kind of man she would have caved, but she knew that no matter how insistent he was now about wanting to get to know their son, it was only a matter of time before he lost interest—like her own father had. But George would not grow up as she had, feeling as though he was at the bottom of his father's agenda.

'*Our* son is not some chess piece you can move about on a board to suit you, Aristo. He's a person with feelings and needs—'

He cut her off. 'Yes, he is, and he needs to see me—his father.'

Folding her arms, Teddie glared at him, anger leaping over her skin in pulses. 'He needs consistency and security—not somebody offering him trips on a speedboat and then disappearing for days.'

He shook his head dismissively. 'I'm standing right here, Teddie.'

'For how long?' she countered. 'A day? A week? I mean, when exactly *is* your next business trip?'

His jaw tightened. 'That is irrelevant.'

'No, it's not. I'm being realistic about your limitations.'

Looking away, she clenched her fists. And her limitations. Her life might be bereft of romance and passion, but it was peaceful. The thought of having Aristo flitting in and out of her and George's life was just too unbearable to contemplate.

'I have rights, Teddie,' he said quietly, and something in his voice pulled her gaze back to his face. 'I'm guessing you can live with ignoring that fact—you've managed it for four years. But George has rights too, and I'm wondering what's going to happen when he realises that he has a father—a father you kept at arm's length. Can you live with that?'

Teddie stared at him, her heart pounding, hating him for finding the weakness in her argument.

'Fine,' she snapped, her hands balling into fists. 'You can see him.' But it was absolutely, definitely *not* going to be in her apartment. 'I suggest we find somewhere neutral.'

'Neutral—that's an interesting euphemism.'

He suddenly sounded amused, and she felt her pulse accelerate as she realised that his anger seemed to have faded and he was now watching her intently in a way that made her breathing come to a sudden, swift stop.

'If you're trying to find a place where you and I will feel "neutral" about one another, then I think you might need a bigger planet. Maybe a different solar system.'

She swallowed. His words were reverberating inside her head, bumping into memories so explicit and uncensored that she had to curl her fingers into her palms to stop her hands shaking.

'I don't know what you're talking about,' she said hoarsely, trying her hardest not to notice the way her stomach was clenching.

She felt heat break out over her skin as he took a step towards her.

'Yes, you do, Teddie. I'm talking about sex. And about how, despite all this, you still want me and I still want you.'

An ache like hunger, only more insistent, shot through her and she stared at him, her green eyes widening in shock at the bluntness of his statement.

He raised an eyebrow. 'What? Are you going to lie about that too?' He shook his head dismissively. 'Then you're a coward as well as a liar.'

'I'm not a coward,' she snapped. 'I just don't happen to agree with your unnecessary and rather crude remark.'

His dark eyes locked onto hers and she knew that this time her lie might as well be written in block capitals across her forehead.

'Yes, you do. You're just scared that you feel this way. Scared that you want me.'

Teddie breathed out shakily. He was close now—close enough for her to see the tiny flecks of grey and gold in the inky pools of his eyes. Close enough that she could smell his clean, masculine scent. So close that she could not just see the curves of muscle beneath his sweater but reach out and touch them—

'You're so arrogant.'

He took another step closer and lifted his hand. Her pulse fluttered as he traced the curve of her jaw with his thumb.

'And you're so beautiful, but neither of those statements changes the facts.'

She could feel his gaze seeking hers and, looking up, she saw that his eyes were shimmering with an emotion she recognised and understood—because she was feeling it too.

'Like it or not, we still burn for one another, and I know you feel it too. There's a connection between us.'

She stared at him, hypnotised not just by the truth of his words but by the slow, steady pulse of heat in her blood. And then, in a split second of clarity, she saw herself, saw his hand capturing her face, saw where it was heading, and was instantly maddened by his audacity and ashamed of her weakness.

Jerking her head away from his hand, she lifted her chin. 'You're wrong, Aristo. It's all in your head. It's not real,' she lied again.

He stared at her, his gaze taking in her flushed cheeks and the pulse beating at the base of her throat. 'Not real?' he softly. 'It looks pretty real from where I'm standing.'

Her whole body throbbing, she breathed out unsteadily. 'That's magic for you, Aristo. It plays tricks with the senses...makes you believe in the impossible. And you and I are impossible.' Fixing her green eyes on her ex-husband's breathtakingly handsome face, she gave him a small, tight smile. 'You being George's father changes nothing between us.'

His expression was unreadable, but as his dark, knowing gaze locked with hers she knew that she wasn't fooling either of them, and his next comment reinforced that fact.

'You're right, it doesn't,' he said into the tense silence. 'So perhaps from now on we can both stop playing games.'

He took a step backwards, his satisfied expression making her heart thump against her chest.

'I'll call you, but if in the meantime you want me desperately...'

Eyes gleaming, he reached into his jacket and held out a small white card. 'That's my number.'

'Well, I won't be calling it,' she snapped. 'As the chances of me wanting you "desperately" are less than zero.'

He smiled. 'Of course they are.'

She wanted to throw his remark back in his face, to claim that he was reading the signals all wrong, but before she had the chance to think of a suitably withering response he turned and strolled out of the room with the same swagger with which he'd entered it.

Heart pounding, she waited until she was sure that he'd left the building before darting across the room to close and bolt the door. Only, like the stable door, it was too late, she thought as she sank down onto her sofa with legs that were still unsteady. She'd not only let him back into her home, but into her life.

CHAPTER THREE

WALKING INTO HIS APARTMENT, Aristo stared blankly across the gleaming modern interior, a stream of disconnected, equally frustrating thoughts jamming his brain. He'd barely registered the hour-long drive home from Teddie's apartment. Instead he'd been preoccupied by that simmering undercurrent of attraction between them.

They'd both been so angry, and yet even beneath the fury he had felt it, strumming and intensifying like the vibrating rails beneath an express train.

Of course he'd known it was there since this morning—from that moment when he'd turned around in the Kildare and his stomach had gone into freefall. It had been like watching flashes of lightning on the horizon: you knew a storm was heading your way.

And he'd wanted the storm to come—and so had Teddie—right up until she'd told him that it was all in his head.

Not that he'd believed her. It had been just one more lie in a day of lies.

He breathed out slowly, trying to shift the memory of her final stinging remark to him.

'You and I are impossible. You being George's father changes nothing between us.'

Wrong, he thought irritably. It changed everything.

No matter how much she wanted to deny it, there *was* a connection between them—and it wasn't just based on sex, he thought, his heart tightening as he remembered his son bumping fists with him.

He still couldn't believe that he was a father. A *father*!

The word kept repeating inside his head like a scratched record.

Suddenly he needed a drink!

In the cavernous stainless steel and polished concrete kitchen, he poured himself a glass of red wine and made his way to the rooftop terrace that led off the living area.

Collapsing into a chair, he gazed moodily out at the New York skyline. Even from so high up he could feel the city's energy rising up like a wave, but for once he didn't respond to its power. He was too busy trying to piece together the life that Teddie had shattered when she'd walked into his hotel.

And if that hadn't been enough of a shock, she'd then lobbed a grenade into his perfectly ordered world in the shape of a three-year-old son.

Welcome to fatherhood, Teddie-Taylor style.

Thanks to her, he'd gone from nought to being the father of a miniature version of himself in a matter of seconds, with Teddie presenting George to him like the proverbial rabbit being pulled from a hat.

He ran his hand slowly over his face, as though it might smooth the disarray of his thoughts. It felt surreal to be contemplating even the concept of being a father, let alone the reality. He'd never really imagined having a child—not out of any deep-rooted opposition to being a father, but because work and the expansion of his business empire required all his energy and focus.

He frowned. But maybe there were other reasons too? Could his father's decision to opt out of his responsibilities have made him question his own programming for parenthood? Possibly, he decided after a moment's thought. Apostolos Leonidas had been an intermittent and largely reluctant presence in his life, and maybe he had just assumed that he'd be the same.

And up until now he'd more or less given his father a free pass—having been made to look a fool, his father had understandably wanted nothing to do with his adulterous wife, and that had meant having nothing to do with his son either.

But even when Aristo had been blinded with shock and anger earlier he'd felt no resentment towards George, no sense of panic or dismay. Gazing down into his son's dark eyes, he had felt his heart tighten in recognition—and love.

His shoulders stiffened. The same love that Teddie clearly felt for George?

Resentment still simmered inside him, but he couldn't stop himself from reluctantly admiring his ex-wife. Whatever else she might be, Teddie was a good mother. George clearly adored her, and she loved their son—not with his own mother's chilly, grudging variety of love, nor the nod of recognition that had passed for love in his father's head. Just love—pure, simple and unselfish.

Imagining how it must feel to be the focus of that kind of affection and tenderness, he felt something tauten inside him—not just a sense of responsibility, but of resolve. He was George's father, and it was his job to make sure his son had the love and security that he himself had been denied as a child.

His parents' divorce and subsequent remarriages had left him rootless and unsure of his place in the world, and he knew instinctively that George needed both his parents. But if that was to happen then this time Teddie wouldn't be running anywhere—ever. Only, judging by how quickly she had bolted from his life last time, he needed to make that clear sooner rather than later.

'Well, if you ask me, it could have been a lot worse.'

Elliot raised his elbows swiftly off the breakfast bar as

Teddie swept past him with a wet cloth, cleaning the evidence of George's cereal from the surface and wishing she could wipe Aristo from her life just as effortlessly.

Elliot hadn't appeared the night before but had arrived at breakfast, bringing doughnuts and his usual reassuring patter, and she'd been both grateful and relieved to see him.

It wasn't that he could do anything to change what had happened, but he made her feel calmer, more rational. Less like the woman she'd been last night.

Her fingers tightened around the cloth and she closed her eyes.

That, in short, was the problem. Maybe it was because he was so uncompromisingly masculine physically, but Aristo made her feel like a woman—fierce and wild and hungry to touch and be touched. They'd felt so right together; he'd felt so right against her. And, even though she despised herself for being so shallow, she couldn't pretend that anything had changed. When he was near her she was still so aware of his body, his breathing, the heat of his skin…

Her insides felt suddenly hot and tight and, breathing out a little, she opened her eyes. She'd done everything she could to excise the memory of what it felt like to be held in Aristo's arms, only for him to turn up on her doorstep and make a mockery of all her efforts. It wasn't fair—but that didn't mean she was going to roll over and let him turn her and George's lives upside down.

'It could?' Turning, she stared at Elliot disbelief. 'How, Elliot? How could it be worse?'

He shrugged, his expression innocent. 'He could have kissed you.'

Remembering how close she'd come to letting that happen, she scowled at him, a blush of colour heating her cheeks. 'He didn't.'

'Or you could have kissed him— Hey, it was a joke.'

Grinning, he caught the cloth that Teddie threw at him. 'Where's your sense of humour?'

Collapsing onto the stool beside him, she shook her head. 'It packed its bags and left shortly after Aristotle Leonidas arrived.'

She felt a sudden rush of panic, remembering that standoff between them—the prickling of her skin and the intensity of his gaze, his dark eyes scanning her face, all-seeing, hungry, unwavering... Her stomach tightened, her hands curling into fists. She might not have given in last night, but this thing, this 'connection' between them wasn't going to just disappear.

But she could.

The thought popped into her head unbidden, fully formed, because of course that was still her gut instinct. Before Aristo, years of her life had been spent living out of suitcases, staying in hotels and motels, always ready to leave, to flee like a getaway driver after a heist. Running away had been her quick fix, her go-to solution for dealing with any problem in her life, any time things got hard.

It was a hangover from a childhood spent dodging unpaid bills and bailiffs and a legacy from her father—not that she'd ever thought of him as that. Wyatt Taylor had never stayed around long enough for the name 'Dad' to stick. Just long enough to teach her a couple of magic tricks and to make her miss him when he left.

Her heart began to pound.

Only, how could she run with a child? George's life was here, in New York. He went to nursery here, he had friends, a routine. He was the reason she'd stopped running.

As though sensing her panic, Elliot reached over and pushed a stray strand of hair away from her face.

'Come on, Teddie, I know he was a pig to you, and maybe it wasn't ideal, him turning up here out of the blue, but...' He hesitated, his expression becoming uncharacteristically serious. 'But whatever you're telling yourself, you're wrong. You can't run this time, babe.'

As she glanced up guiltily he gave her a lopsided smile.

'I've known you since I was twelve years old. I don't need supernatural powers to read your mind. This isn't something you can run away from, and deep down I don't think you really want to.'

She lifted her chin, narrowing her green eyes. 'And yet strangely, on a superficial level, I feel completely certain that I absolutely do.'

Elliot poked one of her clenched hands with his finger. 'No, you don't. I was there, remember? I know how often you tried to call him. I know how many messages you left, how upset you were.' His jaw tensed. 'I'm no fan of Aristotle Leonidas, but—' he frowned '—he's still George's father and he's got a right to see his son. Right now it's a shock, but once you get used to the idea it'll be okay, I promise. I mean, loads of couples share custody of their children.'

Teddie gave him a small, tight smile.

Thinking about a future in which she would have to see Aristo on a regular basis, speak to him and have him turning up on her doorstep, was not her definition of okay. But maybe over time her feelings for him would diminish, like radioactivity—only didn't that take, like, decades? Not that it mattered how she felt, or where she was. She could run but, as Elliot said, she couldn't hide from the truth any more. Aristo was George's father and she was just going to have to suck it up.

Pushing back his stool, Elliot stood up. 'I gotta go, but I'll call you later.' Sliding his arms into his jacket, he kissed her forehead. 'And don't worry. Leopards don't change their spots, baby, and from everything you've ever told me about your ex he's not the kind to stick around long enough for this to become a problem.'

Watching Elliot let himself out of the apartment, she

knew he was trying to reassure her. And she should feel reassured—it was, after all, what she wanted, wasn't it? For Aristo to disappear from her life for good? Only, for some strange reason, that thought didn't seem quite comforting as she'd imagined it would.

While George took his afternoon nap Teddie tidied the apartment, moving automatically to pick up the tiny toy cars and miniature dinosaurs that were scattered everywhere. Eventually she stopped beside her bed and, kneeling down, pulled out a cardboard box.

Feeling a lump start to build in her throat, she hesitated, and then sat on the floor. Lifting off the lid, she gazed down at the contents.

Was that it? Had her marriage really amounted to nothing more than a shoebox shoved under a bed?

Pushing aside the letters and documents, she reached to the bottom of the box and pulled out a small blue box.

Her hand twitched and then slowly, heart thumping erratically, she opened it and stared down at the plain gold band. For a moment she couldn't move, but as her breathing steadied she picked up her wedding ring and slid it onto her finger.

She still wasn't sure why she had kept it. But the answer to that was not as simple as the question implied.

At first, in the weeks after she'd moved out of Aristo's apartment—and it had always felt like *his* apartment—she'd kept wearing it because even though it had become clear to her by then that her husband was a different person from the impulsive lover she'd promised to love and honour and cherish, she hadn't been ready to give up on her marriage.

And then later it had been the one thing he'd given to her that he hadn't and could never take away—of course that had been before she found out about George.

Her throat tightened. She could still picture the exact moment that she'd finally decided to stop wearing it.

It had been on the taxi ride home from that night she'd spent in Aristo's arms, hoping and believing that they'd been given a second chance.

He'd followed her out of their meeting with the lawyers earlier and they'd argued, both of them simmering with fury, and then they'd looked into each other's eyes and desire had been stronger than their anger combined. Unreasonable, but undeniable.

But then what did desire ever have to do with reason?

They'd rented a hotel room like newlyweds, kissing and pulling at each other's clothes in the lift, hardly noticing the other guests' shocked or amused expressions as they'd run to their room.

But even before the sheets tangled around their warm, damp bodies had grown cold she'd realised her mistake.

That night hadn't been some eleventh-hour reprieve for their marriage. Aristo hadn't acknowledged his part in their marital problems, or been willing to listen to her point of view. Instead he'd just wanted to get his own way and, having failed to convince her with words he'd switched tactics. Like the hopeless, lovestruck fool she had been then, she'd let herself be persuaded by the softness of his mouth and the hard length of his body.

But, waking in the strange bed, she'd realised her mistake instantly.

She breathed out unsteadily, remembering how his face had grown hard and expressionless, the post-coital tenderness in his eyes fading as he'd told that he'd pay for the room, but that would be the last dollar she'd see of his money.

It hadn't been. Three weeks later she'd emptied one of the bank accounts they'd shared—the one with the least amount of money in it—partly to prove him wrong, but mostly so his unborn child would have something from its father.

Sliding the ring off her finger, she put it back in the box and got slowly to her feet. Elliot was right. She needed to face reality, and it would be easier to do so if she was in control of what was happening rather than sitting and stewing, waiting for Aristo to call.

Walking back into the living room, she picked up the card he'd given her the night before and punched out his number on her mobile before she had the chance to change her mind.

'Hello, Teddie.'

She hadn't expected him to pick up quite so quickly, or to know it was her, but that wasn't why she slid down onto the sofa. It was just that hearing his voice down the phone again felt strangely intimate, and for a split second she was reminded of how they'd used to talk when they'd first met. Conversations in the early hours of the morning after she'd finished performing and she was lying in bed in some hotel on the other side of the country.

It hadn't mattered what time she'd called—he'd always answered and they'd talked sometimes for hours. She felt her skin prickle. And not just talk… Sometimes he'd made up stories to help her fall asleep.

Curling her fingers around the phone, she gripped it more tightly. Remembering Aristo doing that for her was like waking to find a handcuff around her wrist, linking her to him in a way she hadn't imagined.

Steadying her breathing, she pushed the memory to the back of her mind. 'We need to talk,' she said bluntly. 'About George.'

'So talk.'

'No, not on the phone. We need to meet.'

There was a short pause, and her chest tightened as she

imagined him leaning back in his chair, a small triumphant smile curving his mouth.

'I can come to your apartment.'

'No.' Hearing the panic in her voice, she frowned. But there was no way he was coming to the apartment again, not after what nearly happened last time. 'I'll come to your office.'

She glanced at the time. She could drop George off at Elliot's and then go on into Manhattan.

'Shall we say about five?'

'I look forward to it,' he said softly.

At exactly five o'clock she was staring up at a tall, gleaming tower as all around her crowds of tourists chatted and laughed—no doubt on their way to see the Empire State Building or some other world-famous landmark.

If only she was a tourist too, enjoying a well-earned holiday, instead of having to face her clever, calculating ex-husband. But the sooner she faced Aristo the sooner she could return home, and so, heart pounding, she slipped through the revolving doors into the cool smoked glass interior of the Leonidas Holdings' headquarters.

Five minutes later she was riding up in an elevator, only just managing to force her mouth into a stiff smile as the doors opened.

'Ms Taylor.' Smiling politely, a young male assistant stepped forward. 'If you'd like to come with me, Mr Leonidas' office is this way.'

But not Mr Leonidas, Teddie discovered as the assistant showed her into the empty office. She wondered if Aristo had absented himself on purpose. Probably, she decided. No doubt he was trying to psyche her out by making her wait, by giving her a glimpse of his personal fiefdom.

She glanced slowly around the room, her narrowed gaze taking in the dazzling panoramic views of New York, the

Bauhaus furniture and the huge abstract painting that hung behind his desk.

'Sorry to keep you waiting.'

She turned, her body tensing automatically as Aristo strolled into the room, his dark eyes sweeping assessingly over her black cigarette trousers, burgundy silk shirt and towering stiletto heels.

He stopped in front of her and she felt her stomach flip over. He'd taken off his jacket, and the sleeves of his cornflower-blue shirt were rolled up, the collar loosened. Her eyes darted involuntarily between the triangle of golden skin at the base of his neck and the fine dark hair on his forearms.

Her breath pedalled inside her chest. He looked both invincible and stupidly sexy, and any hope she'd had that she might have miraculously developed an immunity to him in the intervening hours since she'd seen him evaporated like early-morning mist. Even just being in the same space as him was sending her body haywire, her chest constricting and a prickling heat spreading like a forest fire over her skin.

If Aristo was feeling as uncomfortable as she was, he wasn't showing it. But then in the six months of their marriage she'd never really known what he was thinking—she might be a mistress of illusion on stage, but he was a master at disguising his feelings. Her lips tightened. Although that, of course, presupposed that he had any.

'It's fine,' she said stiffly. 'I know you're a busy man.'

His gaze hovered over her face and she cursed herself silently, for she knew what he was thinking.

Aristo's obsession with work had quickly become an issue for her. The long hours he'd spent at the office and his single-minded focus on building his business had slowly but inevitably excluded her from his life. Not that either of them had done much to stop it eroding their marriage.

For Aristo it had only ever been *her* problem, and she had found it impossible to tell him the truth. That she wanted the man who had craved her, who had been so hungry to share her life that he hadn't been willing to wait.

She swallowed, pushing back against the sudden swell of misery spreading through her. It was her own fault. She should have known what to expect when he'd cut their honeymoon short to fly halfway across the world to buy a resort. But of course when he'd pulled her into his arms and told her it was a one-off she'd believed him. She'd wanted to believe him, and to believe that she hadn't just made the biggest mistake of her life.

Only, her brief doomed marriage was not what she wanted to talk about now. They'd moved way past the point where there was even a 'them' to discuss. As far as she was concerned, the less she had to do with him the better, and after this meeting hopefully there would be no reason for her to see him except briefly and occasionally.

Watching the conflicting emotions flitting across his ex-wife's face, Aristo felt a ripple of frustration. She had always been so unsupportive of his career, when all he'd been trying to do was build a life for her, for them.

Glancing round his office, he steadied his breathing. Surely now she could understand what he'd been trying to do? But, either way, he wasn't going to let it get in the way of what really mattered.

He shrugged. 'Very busy,' he said softly. 'But let's not get distracted. I'm sure you didn't come here to talk about my work.'

She gave him a small, tight smile. 'We need to make arrangements. Something stable and uncomplicated. Because what's most important to me is that George feels happy and safe.'

He nodded. 'And I want that too.' Gesturing towards a cluster of easy chairs and a sofa grouped in front of the windows, he smiled slowly. 'So, why don't we sit down and talk about how we can make that happen?'

Teddie gazed at him warily. So far it was all going better than she'd expected. Her heartbeat scuttled forward. Only, it wasn't fair of him to smile like that. It would be so much easier for her to keep a clear head if he was cold and dismissive. When he smiled that extraordinary smile it was difficult to think straight. Difficult to think about anything other than that beautiful mouth.

Feeling his dark gaze, she ignored both his hand and the sudden rapid pounding of her heart and nodded, then walked as casually as she could manage across the room.

She purposely avoided the sofa and sat down in one of the chairs, but regretted her decision almost immediately as, dropping down into the chair closest to hers, he stretched out his long, muscular legs and began to speak.

'Look, Teddie, before we start I have something I need to say to you.'

'So say it.' She had been aiming to sound casual, offhand. Instead, though, her voice sounded stiff and unnatural.

His eyes fixed on hers. 'I know this can't be easy, having me back in your life and in George's life. But I'm going to try to make it as painless and unproblematic as possible for both of us. All I want is to be a good father.'

She held his gaze. It was on the tip of her tongue to tell him that he *wasn't* back in her life. But to be fair he was trying to meet her halfway, and it seemed churlish to nitpick over his choice of words.

Glancing away to the skyline, she shrugged. 'I hope so. That's why I'm here.'

It was true, and she wanted to believe Aristo, to take his words at face-value—only after everything he'd said and done in the past it was just so hard to trust him. But if this was going to work, for her son's sake, she was going to have to put the past behind her and concentrate on the present.

She took a quick, steadying breath and said quickly, 'I know it probably doesn't seem like it to you, but I really do want George to get to know you.'

The air seemed to still, like a held breath, and, looking up, she found Aristo watching her so steadily and intently that for a moment she forgot where she was. Suddenly the huge office seemed as though it had shrunk, and his body seemed way too close to hers.

Before she could stop herself she shifted in her seat, drawing her legs in tighter and then regretting it immediately as his eyes dropped to her throat, taking in the jerkiness of her pulse.

'So what do you suggest?'

It was a straightforward enough question, and his expression was blandly innocent, but something in his eyes made her body tense, her muscles popping and suddenly primed for flight as she quickly went through the options she'd rehearsed on her journey to his office.

'I thought perhaps we could meet in a park,' she said hopefully. 'George loves swings, and we have a nice park just down the street.'

She felt her pulse begin to hopscotch forward as slowly he shook his head.

'I was thinking of something more than just a trip to the swings. How about you bring George to the apartment for a weekend? That way we'll have more time, and plenty of space, and of course there's the pool.' He raised his dark gaze to hers. 'You *have* taught him to swim?'

She glared at him. 'Yes, of course I have. But—'

'Excellent, so we're agreed.' His smile widened but she started to shake her head.

'No, Aristo. We are not agreed.' She gritted her teeth. How had she ever thought this would be easy?

'Then I'll come to yours,' he said coolly.

Her back stiffened. He absolutely definitely wasn't coming to her apartment, and nor did she want to go to back to the apartment that had once been her home, with all its many reminders of their shared past.

So tell him what you do want then, she told herself.

'I don't think that's a good idea.' She spoke quickly, trying to inject a businesslike tone into her voice.

'No? But you do want to *arrange* something, right?'

He lounged back, his arm resting easily against the side of the chair, and suddenly she wanted to reach out and touch the golden skin, run her fingertips over the smooth curve of muscle pressing against the fabric of his shirt.

'Yes—yes, of course I do.' She dragged her eyes away, up to the compelling dark eyes and dangerous curves of his face.

He nodded. 'Something stable and uncomplicated, I think you said.'

'Yes, that's what I want, but…' She gazed at him uncertainly, wondering exactly where the conversation was going.

'Then the solution is staring us in the face.'

He went on as if she hadn't spoken, his voice curling over her skin, soothing and unsettling at the same time.

'What do you mean?' she said hoarsely.

He smiled. 'Isn't it obvious? We need to get married.'

The air was punched out of lungs. She stared at him in a daze, the beat of her heart suddenly deafeningly loud inside her head. She was mute with shock—not only at the audacity, the arrogance of his words, but at the heat building inside her.

How could she feel like that? Their marriage had been a disaster, and yet she could feel a part of herself responding with an eagerness that shocked her.

Ignoring the quivering sensation in her stomach, she forced herself to meet his gaze. 'That's not funny, Aristo.'

'It's not meant to be.' He looked at her, his gaze impassive. 'If I'm to be a permanent fixture in George's life then I need to be a permanent fixture in yours. Marriage is the simplest solution. We marry and George gets two parents and a stable, uncomplicated home life.'

She stared at him in disbelief. 'Is that what you think our marriage was like? Stable and uncomplicated?' She wanted to laugh, except that it wasn't even remotely amusing, just horribly familiar—for wasn't this exactly why they'd got divorced? Because Aristo had made assumptions without so much as considering her point of view or her feelings.

'I am not marrying you—*remarrying* you,' she corrected herself.

Tipping back his head, he stared down into her eyes. 'Why not? It's not something you haven't done before.'

She gaped at him. 'And it didn't work.' She enunciated each word with painstaking emphasis.

His dark gaze roamed so slowly over her face that she felt it like a caress.

'As I recall it worked very well.'

Her breath was trapped in her throat. 'I'm not talking about that,' she said quickly. 'I'm talking about everything else about our marriage. None of that worked.'

'Didn't work *last time*.' He dismissed her remark with a careless lift of his shoulders. 'But engaging with past mistakes is crucial to an improved performance, and this time we'll be operating from a position of experience, not ignorance.'

She felt her heart beat faster. He sounded as if he was presenting a business plan, not discussing getting married. But then, even before their marriage had ended work had already consumed his life to the exclusion of everything else—including her.

'This isn't some management strategy,' she said witheringly. 'This is my life, Aristo.'

His eyes didn't so much as flicker but she felt a sudden rise in tension.

'No, Teddie. This is our son's life. A son who doesn't know who I am. A son I've already let down. No child should feel like that.'

He stopped abruptly, his jaw tightening, and Teddie felt some of her anger deflate. There was something in his response that made her flinch inside, as though the words had been dragged out of him.

Aristo caught his breath. Remembering his own childhood, the constant nagging sense of not belonging, he felt suddenly sick. Whatever else happened, his son was going to feel wanted by *both* his parents.

'You haven't let him down.'

Teddie's voice jolted him back into real time and he gritted his teeth. She might have been his wife, but he'd never discussed his childhood with her. But the past was history. What mattered was George.

'I wasn't there—' He broke off and stared away, his face taut and set. 'All I want to do is make it up to him. And that is going to take more than a couple of trips to the swings.'

'You're right. I'm sorry.'

Teddie stared at his profile, her heartbeat rocking back and forth like a boat on a choppy sea. She could sense pain beneath his stilted words and she felt ashamed. Up until that moment she hadn't truly considered his feelings beyond shock and anger, and that had been unfair of her— for how would she be feeling right now if the situation was reversed?

'Maybe we should go away somewhere. That way you and George can spend time getting to know each other and we can start being open and honest with each other, because that's the only way we're going to make this work.'

Her words echoed inside her head, and for a moment she couldn't believe that they had actually come out of her mouth. But it was too late to take them back—and anyway, with a mixture of shock and relief she realised that she didn't actually want to. She needed to know now if Aristo was capable of being the father he claimed he wanted to be. Not in a few months, when it would destroy George if he left, just as she had been destroyed whenever her own father had disappeared from her life.

'Do you mean that?' His eyes were on hers, almost black, steady and unblinking.

'You want to get married again?' She phrased it as a question deliberately. 'Well, let's see if we can manage to spend a week together without wanting to kill each other.'

His eyes on her face were dark and intent. 'Or to tear each other's clothes off.'

Her pulse jolted forward, her body rippling into life as a wave of heat skimmed over her skin. For a moment she couldn't speak. Her brain seemed to have seized up and she stared at him in silence, stalling until finally she could lift her chin and meet his gaze.

'It would mean you taking time off work.' She tried and failed to keep the challenging note out of her voice.

There was a fraction of a pause. 'How does next week sound?' he said softly.

Her head snapped up. 'Next week?' The words made her feel giddy, but she could hardly back down now. 'That sounds fine. But won't it be a problem, going somewhere at such short notice?'

His eyes didn't leave hers. 'It won't be a problem at all. You see, I have an island—near Greece—and a plane to take us there.'

His mouth curled at the corners, his smile knocking the air out of her lungs.

'All you have to do is pack.'

CHAPTER FOUR

'Look, Mommy, look!'

Glancing up from the magazine lying open on her lap, Teddie smiled across the cabin to where George was waving a toy car at her.

'I can see, darling. Oh, wow!'

She made a suitably impressed face as he made the car fly up and then crash land on the headrest of his chair.

Over the top of her son's dark head her eyes met Aristo's, and quickly she looked away, not quite ready to share the moment with him.

She was still coming to terms with the fact that she was sitting on a private jet that was flying above the Atlantic Ocean. Obviously it had been her idea that they take a holiday. But, aside from her foreshortened honeymoon in St Bart's, she'd only ever been on day trips away. Now she was on her way to Greece! And not to the mainland but a private island—Aristo's island.

Out of the corner of her eye she could just see his smooth dark head, his black hair and light gold skin gleaming in the sunlit cabin. He was dressed casually, in jeans and some kind of fine-knit grey sweater, but he still exuded the same compelling air of authority and self-assurance.

She felt her heart beat faster. Everything was moving so fast. A part of her was glad about that, for if she'd had longer to think she would probably have been paralysed with indecision. And yet something about the speed with which everything had been set in motion made her feel uneasy.

Tucking a strand of dark hair behind her ear, she gazed meditatively out of the window at the horizon.

No doubt some of that feeling was down to being suddenly confronted by the true scale of Aristo's wealth. Four years ago his empire had been in its infancy—now, though, evidence of the Leonidas billions was visible everywhere, from his chauffeur-driven limousine to the powerfully built men in identical dark suits who had accompanied him onto the plane and were now seated at the other end of the cabin, studiously examining their phone screens.

She glanced over to where George and Aristo were playing with a sturdy wooden garage. It had been a gift from Aristo, supposedly to help occupy George during the long flight to Greece, but she had sensed that, more importantly for Aristo, it was an opportunity to connect with his son.

Her throat tightened. He could give George anything he wanted and, although she knew her son was happy and contented with his life, he was just as susceptible to the excitement of new toys or a promised trip on a speedboat as any other child. What would happen as he grew up? What if George chose to live with his glamorous, prosperous father?

One day he would have to choose because, whatever Aristo might think, she had no intention of marrying him again—ever.

Beneath the magazine, her hands balled into fists. *Don't go there*, she told herself, letting her long dark hair fall in front of her face. But it was too late. Like a dog proudly retrieving a stick for its owner, her brain had revealed the real reason why the haste and impulsiveness of this holiday had got under her skin.

She and Aristo had first got together after a particularly demanding week for her, and a charity dinner that she'd thought would never end. Aristo had been a guest at one of the tables.

Aged twenty-two, she'd had boyfriends, but never fallen in love, and she certainly hadn't been intending to fall in love that night. Even now she still wasn't quite sure how it had happened. Just that there had been something about the tilt of his head and the intensity of his gaze that had jolted her.

She'd picked him out to be her 'assistant', correctly identifying the card he'd chosen and then pickpocketing his watch.

Of course he'd had to come to the bar to retrieve it, and then he'd stayed, and when the bar staff had started to clear up around them she had leaned forward and kissed him.

He'd kissed her back, and she'd taken his hand and led him upstairs to her room. They'd only just made it.

That first time had been fast, abandoned and fully clothed. The second time too. When finally they'd managed to undress, and were lying naked and spent in one another's arms, she had already been half in love with him.

To her surprise, they'd carried on seeing one another—meeting in hotels across America whenever his frequent trips abroad and her show schedule had permitted them to do so. And then, less than two months after they'd met, he'd surprised her in Las Vegas and said the words that had changed the course of her life.

'You can't keep on living out of a suitcase and I can't wait any longer—for you to be my wife.'

Given the example set by her parents, marriage had been the last thing on her mind, and yet she hadn't hesitated.

Her chest tightened. And look how that had turned out.

Two hours later George had finally succumbed to the excitement of the day, and lay sleeping across two seats, his car clutched tightly in his hand. Gently, she reached over and smoothed his dark hair away from his forehead, her heart contracting painfully.

He was so beautiful, so perfect, even given a mother's bias, and she loved him completely and with an intensity that made her feel both superhuman and yet horribly defenceless.

More importantly, he would be out for the count for at least an hour, so now was her chance to send Elliot the text she had promised him and have a little freshen up at the same time. In the small but luxurious bathroom, she splashed some water onto her face, retied her thick, dark hair and then, walking back to the jet's bedroom, she tapped out a short but reassuring message to Elliot and sent it before she could change her mind.

Whatever she wrote, she knew he was still going to worry, but all he needed to know right now was that she had everything under control. But as she sat down on the chair beside the bed, she felt a sliver of panic slip down her spine, and the cheery bravado of her text seemed suddenly a little premature, for standing in the doorway, two cups of coffee in his hands, was Aristo.

Her body tensed, her heart thudding against her ribs like a wrecking ball as he held them up by way of explanation.

'I thought you might like a coffee as we had such an early start.' His dark eyes rested on her face. 'You always used to hate getting up early.' There was a short, suspended silence.

Teddie felt her insides tighten and a prickling heat began to spread over her suddenly over-sensitised skin as she remembered exactly what it had felt like to wake in Aristo's arms.

Tuning out the memory of his hard golden body on hers, she lifted her chin. 'Now I have a three-year-old son,' she said coolly. Her breath fluttered in her chest as he put one of the cups on the cabinet beside her bed.

'How long does he normally sleep?'

'An hour and a half—maybe two today. He was so excited last night he couldn't settle.'

His mouth curved upwards into a slow, sweet smile that made it impossible for her to look away.

'I would have been just the same at his age. Will it mess up his routine?'

She shrugged. 'A little. He didn't eat much breakfast, so he's probably going to be really hungry.'

'We can have lunch when he wakes up.'

She felt a cool shiver shoot down her spine as Aristo dropped down into the bed opposite her. Clearing her throat, she nodded. 'That's a good idea.'

He hesitated. 'I don't know what he likes—I thought pasta, maybe, or pizza.'

He sounded conciliatory, disarmingly unsure, and she felt some of her tension ebb. Maybe this was going to work—and she wanted it to, for George's sake at least.

Nodding, she gave him a stiff smile. 'Pasta or pizza will be fine. Although he's actually not fussy at all.'

She hesitated. Aristo had never been good at small talk or casual conversation—the silence between one of her questions and his answer had once stretched to twenty-three long drawn-out seconds—and the only times he'd ever unbent and seemed relaxed enough to chat had been during those long-distance phone calls late at night. But now, glancing up at his dark eyes, she saw that he was watching her without any hint of impatience.

'If he sees me eat something then he seems to think it's all right for him to eat too.'

'Smart boy,' Aristo said softly, and his eyes gleamed. 'Must take after his mother.'

It was the corniest of compliments, the sort of remark that didn't really warrant a response, but despite that she felt her cheeks grow warm beneath his dark, unblinking gaze.

'So,' he said softly into the taut silence, 'George seems to be getting used to me.'

'He likes you.' She raised an eyebrow. 'But I'm sure that will change when he gets to know you better.'

He stared at her steadily. 'We can make this work, Teddie.'

'I'm sure we can,' she said evenly. 'It would be pretty difficult not to. I mean, it's a holiday on a Greek island.'

She picked up her coffee, wishing that the cup was large enough for her to climb inside and hide from his dark, level gaze.

'I wasn't talking about the holiday.'

His expression was gently mocking, and she felt her heart start to beat faster. She'd known, of course, that he wasn't talking about the holiday, but she'd been hoping to keep away from that particular subject. But if he wanted to talk about it, then, fine.

She breathed out slowly. 'I know that you want this week to be some kind of first step towards me changing my mind about marrying you, but that's not why I'm here,' she said firmly. 'I'm happy for you to be in George's life but, honestly, something truly incredible—unimaginable, in fact— would have to happen for me to want to be your wife again. So could we drop this, please?'

He didn't respond, but she could sense a shift in his mood, sense something slipping away.

'What alternative is there?'

The bluntness of his question caught her off-guard. 'I don't know. The usual options, I suppose. Shared custody. Holidays and weekends— What?'

He was shaking his head and she felt a flare of anger.

'We don't work as a couple. You know that.' She stared at him, a beat of frustration pulsing in her chest. 'So stop pretending that marriage is an option.'

His eyes hardened. 'Only if you stop being so stubborn and try see it from my perspective for once.'

She glared at him. 'We should never have got married in the first place, so why would I ever want to do it again? In fact—' she took a breath, and straightened her shoulders '—why would *you* ever want to do it again? No, please, Aristo—just explain to me why you'd want to do something that made you so unhappy and angry.'

Aristo stared back at her in silence, his heart pressing against his ribs, caught off-guard by this unexpected and startling assessment of their relationship. 'I wasn't angry,' he said finally. 'I was confused because you were so dissatisfied.'

He watched her shake her head.

'Angry...dissatisfied...what does it matter anyway? We were both unhappy, so why would we do it again?'

His chest tightened and he felt a rush of anger and frustration with her for pushing—and with himself for thinking she would understand.

Before he could stop himself—before he even fully understood what he was about to do—he said, 'Because I know what it feels like when your father turns into a stranger.'

Listening to his words bounce around the quiet cabin, he felt his back tense and a hum of panic start to sing inside his head. What was he thinking? He'd never discussed his past with anyone. *Ever.* So why choose this of all moments to start spilling his guts about his childhood?

There was a tiny, sharp silence, like a splinter of ice, and through his dark lashes he could sense her confusion.

'I thought you inherited the business from your father?' she said slowly.

'I did.' His voice sounded sharp, too sharp, but he didn't care. He just stared past her, his back aching.

'So, when did he—?' She stopped, frowned, and then

tried again. 'How is he a stranger? Did something happen? Did you argue?'

Looking up, he found her watching him, and for a second he felt light-headed, almost as though he was floating. He was shocked to see not just confusion in her wide green eyes, but genuine concern too.

He hesitated. Now the words were out, he wasn't sure what to say next, or what Teddie was expecting to hear. The truth, probably. But the truth was way more complex and revealing than he could bring himself to admit, and to Teddie most of all.

'No, we didn't argue,' he said finally, with a firmness that he hoped would dissuade further discussion. 'Just forget about it.'

Teddie stared at him uncertainly, her mind doing cartwheels. She felt as if she had stepped through a wardrobe into a strange new country. This was not the Aristo she knew.

But then what did she really know about her aloof, uncompromising ex-husband? Their relationship hadn't been based on mutual interests or friends. The first few weeks of their affair had been carried out long-distance, and those long phone calls that she'd so come to enjoy had been about the present—his latest deal, her hotel room—and how much they missed one another, how much they missed making love.

They had never once been about their pasts or their families. She hadn't asked and he hadn't volunteered—and in a way hadn't she been grateful? In fact, she might even have encouraged it. She'd certainly discouraged speculation about her background and awkward conversations about her own parents. Maybe a part of her had even found it romantic that he'd wanted it to be just about the two of them.

Now, though, it seemed his reticence had been based not

on romance, or the speed of their relationship, but something more fundamental.

Watching Aristo rub the corners of his eyes, Teddie felt a sudden ache of misery, for it was exactly the same gesture that George made when he was tired or upset. And suddenly she knew why he was so insistent that they remarry.

'Did they get divorced?'

The question sounded ludicrously, simplistically trite, but she didn't know how else to begin—how else to get past that shuttered expression on his face. All she knew was that it had taken six months of a failed marriage and four years of separation to get to this moment, and she wasn't about to back off now. Even if that meant nudging at the boundaries of what he clearly considered off-limits.

Finally, he nodded. 'When I was six.'

His face was carefully blank, but she could hear the strain in his voice. Once again she had that sense of words being forcibly pulled out of him, and she knew that he'd never told this story before.

'That's young,' she said quietly.

He stayed silent for so long that she thought perhaps he hadn't heard her speak, and then, breathing out slowly, he nodded. 'My mother got remarried to this English lord, so they sold the house in Greece and I moved to England with my mother, to live with her and my stepfather, Peter.'

Her mind rewound through her rudimentary knowledge of Aristo's life. How had she not known about this? She'd been married to this man, loved him and had her heart shattered by him, and yet she knew so little. But she was starting to understand now why he was being so insistent about them remarrying. The adults in his life had made decisions based on their needs, not their son's, and in his eyes it must seem as if she had done the same with George.

'And what about your father?'

His shoulders stiffened, as though bracing against some hidden pain. 'He moved to America.'

She stared at him in silence, wanting to pull him close and hold him closer, to do anything that might ease the bruise in his voice and the taut set to his mouth. Except she was too afraid to move, afraid to do anything that might make him stop speaking.

'How did you get to see him?' she asked softly.

His shoulders shifted almost imperceptibly again. 'With difficulty. After we moved I was sent to boarding school, so there was only really the holidays, but by then my mother had a new baby—my half-brother, Oliver—and my father had remarried so everyone had got other stuff going on.'

Everyone but me.

She heard the unspoken end to his sentence, could picture the lonely, confused six-year-old Aristo, who would have looked a lot like their own son.

A muscle flickered in his jaw. 'After a couple of years it sort of petered out to one visit a year, and then it just stopped. He used to call occasionally—he still does.' He looked away, out of the window. 'But we don't really have anything to say to one another.'

He hesitated.

'I dream about him sometimes. And the crazy thing is that in my dreams he wants to talk to me.' His mouth twisted. 'Probably the longest conversation I actually had with him was when he signed the business over to me.'

He fell silent and, her heart thudding, she tried to think of something positive to say. 'But he did give you the business. Maybe that was his way of trying to show how much he cared.'

'I hope not.' Aristo turned to meet her eyes, his mouth twisting—part grimace, not quite a smile. 'Given that he was on the verge of filing for bankruptcy. The company was a wreck and he was up to his neck in debt—he hadn't even been paying the staff properly.'

'And *you* turned it around,' she said quickly. 'He could have just walked away, but I think he had faith in you. He knew you'd do the right thing.'

Her chin jerked upwards, and he watched her eyes narrow, the luminous green like twin lightning flashes.

'You've worked so hard and built something incredible. I know he must be proud of you.'

Teddie stared at him, her heart thudding so hard that it hurt. At the time of their marriage she'd hated his business, resented all the hours he'd spent working late into the night. But this wasn't about her or her feelings, it was about Aristo—about a little boy who had grown up needing to prove himself worthy of his inheritance.

She felt a little sick.

Was it any surprise that he was so intently focused on his career? Or that success mattered so much to him. He clearly wanted to prove himself, and felt responsible for saving his father's business—that would have had a huge impact on his character.

She felt his gaze, and looking up found her eyes locked with his.

'I don't expect you to understand how I'm feeling,' he said eventually. 'All I want to do is be the best father I can possibly be. Does that make sense?'

She bit her lip.

'The best father I can possibly be.'

His words replayed inside her head, alongside a memory of herself on the night that George had been born. Alone in her hospital room, holding her tiny new son, seeing his dark trusting eyes fixed on her face, she'd made a promise to him. A promise to be the best mother she could possibly be.

'I do understand.'

She was surprised by how calm and even her voice

sounded. More surprised still that she was admitting that fact to Aristo. But how could she not tell him the truth when he had just shared what was clearly such a painfully raw memory of his own?

'I felt exactly the same way when I was pregnant. And it's what I wake up feeling most mornings.'

Hearing the edge in her voice, Aristo felt something unspool inside his chest. She looked uncertain. Teddie—who could stand in front of an audience and pluck the right card out of a deck without so much as blinking. He hated knowing that she had felt like that, that she still did.

When he was sure his voice was under control he said carefully, 'Why do you feel like that?'

It seemed irrational: to him, Teddie seemed such a loving, devoted mother.

She shrugged. 'My mom struggled. And my dad was…'

She hesitated and he waited, watching her decide whether to continue, praying that she would.

Finally, she cleared her throat. 'My dad was always away on business.' The euphemism slipped off her tongue effortlessly, before she was even aware that she was using it. 'And my mom couldn't really cope on her own. She started drinking, and then she had an accident. She fell down a staircase and smashed two of her vertebrae. She was in a lot of pain and they put her on medication. She got addicted to it, and that's when she really went downhill.'

Even to her—someone who was familiar with the whole squalid mess that had been her childhood—it sounded appalling. Not just tragic, but pitiful.

Breathing out unsteadily, she gave him a tiny twist of a smile. 'After that she really couldn't cope at all—not with her job, or the apartment, or me…with anything, really.'

He frowned, trying to follow the thread of her logic, aching to go over and put his arms around her and hold her close. 'And you thought you would be like her?' he asked, careful to phrase it as a question, not a statement of fact.

She pulled a face. 'Not just her—it runs in the family. My mum was brought up by foster parents because *her* mother couldn't cope with her.' Her lips tightened.

'But you do cope,' he said gently and, reaching out, he took her hand and squeezed it. 'With everything. You run your own business. You have a lovely apartment and you're a wonderful mother.'

Abruptly she pulled her hand away. 'You don't have to say those things,' she said crossly, trying her hardest to ignore the way her pulse was darting crazily beneath her skin like a startled fish. 'You can't flatter me into marrying you, Aristo.'

Dark eyes gleaming, he leaned forward and pulled her reluctantly onto the bed beside him.

'Apparently not. And I know I don't have to say those things,' he added, his thumbs moving in slow, gentle strokes over her skin. 'I said them because I should have said them before and I didn't. I'm saying them because they're true.'

Releasing her, he reached up, his palms sliding through her hair, his fingers caressing then tightening, capturing her, his touch both firm and tender.

'So could I please just be allowed to say them? To you? Here? Now?'

Teddie blinked and, lifting her hand, touched his face, unable to resist stroking the smooth curving contour of his chin and cheekbone. She felt her fingertips tingling as they trailed over the graze of stubble already darkening his jawline.

Somewhere in the deepest part of her mind a drum had started to throb. She wanted to pull away from him—only not nearly as much as she wanted to feel his skin against hers, to lean into his solid shoulder.

'I suppose so.'

His thumb was stroking her cheek now. It was tracing the line of her lips and she could feel her brain slowing in time to her pulse.

'Aristo...' she said softly. The nearness of his drowsy, dark gaze nearly overwhelmed her.

'Yes, Teddie?'

'I don't think we should be doing this.'

The corners of his mouth—his beautiful mouth that was so temptingly close to hers—curved up into a tiny smile. 'We're not doing this because we should,' he said softly. 'We're doing this because we want to do it.'

Her stomach flipped over and she stilled, too scared to move, for she knew what would happen if she did. She knew exactly how her body would melt into his and just how intensely, blissfully good it would be.

But if she gave in and followed that beating drum of desire where would it lead? She might consider herself to be sexually carefree and independent, and maybe with any other man she could be that woman. But not with Aristo. Sharing her body with him would be fierce and intimate and all-consuming. She knew she would *feel* something— and that would make her vulnerable, and she couldn't be vulnerable around this man. Or at least not any more vulnerable than she already was.

And, whatever Aristo might argue to the contrary, when he talked about wanting to marry her again she knew deep down that what he was really thinking about was sex. Only, no matter how sublime it was, there was more to a relationship than sex—as their previous marriage had already painfully proved. She wouldn't—she couldn't—go there again.

Yes, she wanted to touch him, and she wanted him to hold her, and she was fighting herself, torn between wanting to believe that they could try again and knowing it was an impossibility. Maybe in another life, if the timing had been different...

But Aristo was already her first love, her ex-husband and the father of her child. Did she really need to add another layer of complication to what was already a complex and conflicted relationship? And besides, she should be looking forward, not back, and that meant keeping the past where it belonged.

'I know,' she said quietly. 'But this isn't about what you and I *want* any more. It's about being honest and open.'

His eyes moved over her face. 'So tell me, honestly, that you don't want me.'

He was so close she could see herself reflected in the dark pools of his eyes, and it took every atom of will in her body to resist the tractor beam of his gaze and her own longing.

'I can't. But I also know that I can't have everything I want. Maybe I thought I could once, but not any more.'

As the words left her mouth she knew that they were just that—words—and that if he chose to challenge her or, worse, if he leaned forward and kissed her, she would be lost.

She stared at him, mute, transfixed, mind and body wavering between desire and panic.

But he didn't lean forward.

Instead, his dark eyes calm, his expression unfathomable, he gently ran a finger down the side of her face and then, standing up, walked slowly across the cabin. As the door closed she breathed out unsteadily, searching inwardly for the relief she'd expected to feel.

But it wasn't there. Instead she had never felt lonelier, or more confused.

CHAPTER FIVE

STEPPING OUT OF the shower, Aristo reached for a towel and rubbed it briefly over his lean, muscular body. He smoothed his damp hair against his skull and, still naked, stepped into his dressing room. Stopping in front of the shelves, he let his dark eyes scan their colour-coded contents momentarily, before picking out a pair of dark blue swim shorts and a lighter blue T-shirt.

He sighed. If only the rest of his life could be as organised and straightforward.

Sliding his watch over his knuckles, he glanced down at the time and frowned. It was early—far too early for anyone else on the island to be awake. But although it was the first day of his holiday his body still insisted on acting as though it was just another day at the office.

Actually, not *all* of his body, he thought grimly.

Twelve hours on a plane with Teddie had left him aching with a sexual frustration that made not just sleep but relaxing almost impossible.

He grimaced. Only, in comparison to what was going on inside his head, the discomfort in his groin seemed completely inconsequential.

His heart began to beat unsteadily.

Had he really told Teddie all that stuff about his father? He could hardly believe it.

He'd spent most of his adolescence and adult life suppressing that hurt and disappointment, building barriers between himself and the world, and especially between himself and his wife. Ordinarily he found it easy to deter personal questions. But yesterday Teddie had refused to take no for an answer. Instead she had waited, and listened, and coaxed the truth out of him.

Not the whole truth, of course—he would never be ready to share that with anyone—just the reason why he was so determined to remarry her.

It had been hard enough to reveal even that much, for it had been the first time he'd ever really tried to untangle the mess of emotions he felt for his father. The first time he'd spoken out loud about Apostolos's indifference and almost total absence from his life.

It had been a rare loss of self-control—one that he still couldn't fully explain. But Teddie had been, and was still, the only person who could get under his skin and make him see fifty shades of red. She alone had overridden all his carefully placed defences, and it wasn't the first time it had happened. Despite her being the wrong woman in the wrong place at the wrong time, he'd not only led her to his bedroom but up the aisle.

His mind took him back to the moment when he'd first become aware of the existence of Teddie Taylor at the opening of his first major project—the Rocky Creek Ranch. It had been a vision nearly two years in the making: a luxury resort offering all-American activities on a three-thousand-acre mountain playground.

He'd wanted his mother, Helena, to be there, but inevitably—and despite his reminding her frequently about the date—there had been a clash. His half-brother, Oliver, had been playing in some polo match, so his mother had missed what had been up until then the most important moment in his career.

He'd almost not gone to the opening. But as usual business had overridden emotion and he'd bitten down on his disappointment and joined the specially selected guests to watch the evening's cabaret.

He wasn't entirely sure when Teddie had stopped being just the entertainment. He'd barely registered the other acts and, although he'd thought her beautiful, she was not his usual type. Only, at some point, as she had effortlessly shuffled and cut the cards in front of her captive audience, he'd been unable to look away—and, despite believing himself indifferent to magic, he'd found himself falling under her spell.

Catching a glimpse of green eyes the colour of unripe olives, he'd willed her to look at him, and just as though he'd waved a magic wand she picked him out from the crowd. Even now he could still remember the jolt of electricity as their hands had touched, but at the end of the performance she'd turned away to mingle with the other guests.

Only, of course that hadn't really been the end of her performance.

She'd been waiting for him in the bar.

With the watch she'd removed from his wrist.

Seven weeks later they had been married, and six months after that they'd been divorced.

Angry and hurt, he'd cast her as the villain, believing that she'd seen him as a warm-up act—a means to gain access to the kind of society where there would be rich pickings for a beautiful, smart and sexy woman like Teddie Taylor.

Now, with hindsight, he could see that it had been easy to persuade himself that those were the cold, hard facts, for there had been a deeper anger there. An anger with himself. Anger because he'd allowed himself to be drawn to a woman like her after all he'd been through and seen.

He frowned. Four years ago it had all seemed so simple. He'd thought he understood Teddie completely.

Now, though, it was clear that he'd never really understood her at all. Worse, his previous assessment of her seemed to bear no relation to the woman who had been so worried about him on the plane. Or to the woman who had financially supported herself and their child on her own.

A light breeze ruffled the white muslin curtains and he turned towards the window, his eyes lingering on the calm blue sea that stretched out to the horizon in every direction. Had the single-mindedness that had always been his greatest strength actually been a weakness? Had he put two and two together and made minus four?

Frowning again, he stepped towards the window, pondering how that could be the case.

Although he'd condemned her as shallow and grasping when they'd split up, he couldn't ignore the facts, and the truth was that Teddie had neither challenged the modest settlement she'd received at the time of their divorce—a settlement which had obviously not included raising George—or pursued him for more money.

In fact she had successfully supported both herself and their son *without him*, and reluctantly, he found himself contemplating the astonishing possibility that he might actually have misjudged Teddie. That maybe he'd cut and pasted his parents' mismatched and unhappy relationship onto his own marriage, making the facts fit the theory.

But what *were* the facts about his ex-wife? What did he really know about Teddie?

He breathed out slowly and started walking towards the door. Judging by that conversation on the plane, not as much as he'd thought he did. Or as much as he should.

Teddie had been his wife. He might not remember his vows word for word—there had been too much adrenaline in his blood, and a sense of standing on the edge of a cliff—but surely her husband should have been the person who knew her best.

Thinking about her baffling remarks on the plane, he felt his shoulders tense.

Yesterday she'd as good as admitted that she wanted him—why, then, had she held back? And what had she meant by telling him that she couldn't have everything she wanted?

He felt his heartbeat slow.

In principle, this holiday was supposed to be all about getting to know his son, but clearly he needed to get to know his ex-wife as well. In fact it wasn't just a need—he *wanted* to get to know Teddie, to get close to her.

His legs stopped moving, and something exploded inside his chest like a firecracker as he realised that he wasn't just talking about her body. No, what really fascinated him about his beautiful, infuriating, mysterious ex-wife was her mind.

His heartbeat doubled, a flare of excitement catching him off-guard.

Last time they hadn't got to know each other as people. It hadn't been that kind of relationship, or even any relationship really—just desire, raw and intoxicating as moonshine.

Marriage had been the furthest thought from his mind. Even now he didn't understand why he'd done it. Watching his father be taken for a fool should have been warning enough to steer clear of matrimony, but Teddie had slipped past his defences.

And now she was the mother of his child, and the logical and necessary consequence of that fact was that they should remarry, for it was his job to take care of his child and the mother of his child.

Only, this time it would be different—more like a business deal. There would be no messy emotions or expectations. He would set the boundaries, and there would be no overstepping them, and then he would have it all—a global business empire, a beautiful wife and a son.

All he needed to do now was convince Teddie to give him a second chance.

He blew out a breath. Judging by her continued resistance to even the possibility of renewing their relationship, that was going to be something of a challenge—particularly as he didn't know where or how to start.

But so what if he didn't have all the answers? What he did know for certain was that as of now he was going to do whatever it took to find out what made Teddie Taylor tick.

And, feeling calmer than he had in days, he started walking towards the door again.

'Wait a minute, George.' Turning her son gently to face her, Teddie rubbed sunscreen into the soft skin of his arms, marvelling as she did every morning that she'd had anything to do with producing this beautiful little human.

His small face was turned up towards hers, the dark eyes watching her trustingly, and she felt her heart contract not only with love but at the knowledge that she had never felt as her son did. He had been raised to feel secure in a world where he was loved and protected. Whereas she had known nothing but a life spent in flux, with parents who had been absent either in body or mind.

She thought about herself at the same age. Of her mother, drifting through the house in a haze of painkillers, barely registering her small daughter. And then she thought of herself a few years later, at school, when her constant fear had been that her mother's fixed smile and narcotised stare would be obvious to others.

It had felt like a dead weight inside her chest, a burden without respite—for of course her father had been away, his wife and daughter no match for whatever get-rich-quick scheme he had been chasing.

'Mommy, are we going in the pool now?'

'We are.' She smiled down at her son's excited face. He

had been talking about nothing else since he'd woken up. 'Just let me find your hat.'

He frowned. 'I don't want to wear it.'

'I know,' she said calmly. 'But it's hot outside and you need to protect your head. I'm going to be wearing *my* hat.' She pointed to the oversized straw hat she'd seen and then impulse-bought in a shop on her way home from work.

George stared up at her. 'Does Aristo have a hat too?'

Her smile stiffened. 'I don't know. He might do.'

Looking down into her son's dark eyes—eyes that so resembled his father's—Teddie felt her stomach flip over, as it did every single time George mentioned Aristo's name.

But it was a small price to pay for being permitted into paradise, she thought, closing the tube of sunscreen as she glanced at the view from her window. The island was beautiful. Although just an hour by motorboat from the mainland, it felt otherworldly, mythical.

It was a wisp of land with bleached sandy beaches and coves, and luminous turquoise water so clear you could see every ripple on the seabed. The villa itself looked like something you might read about in one of those glossy lifestyle magazines, dazzling white beneath the fierce sunlight. There were views everywhere of the sky and sea, and occasional glimpses of the elliptically-shaped pool—blue on blue on blue. And if all that wasn't enough, there was a garden filled with fruit trees and the drowsy hum of bees.

It was untouched and timeless, and in another life she could have imagined switching off and losing herself in its raw, unpolished beauty and sage-scented air.

But, despite the sun-drenched peace of her surroundings, and her own composed appearance, she felt anything but calm.

She'd woken early from a dream—something familiar but imprecise—and it had taken her a wild moment to remember where she was. Lying back against the pressed white linen pillowcase, she had steadied her breathing. Her restless mind, though, had proved harder to soothe.

Ever since she'd walked out of Aristo's office she'd been trying to come to terms with everything that had happened and how she was feeling about it.

Or, more specifically, how she was feeling about the man who had just barged back into her life—for, as much as she'd have liked to pretend otherwise, it wasn't this heavenly island that was dominating her thoughts but her ex-husband.

Perhaps, though, that was progress of a sort. For at least now she could admit, even if only to herself, that Aristo had always been in the background of her life.

Of course she'd wanted to forget him. She'd tried hard to make it appear as though he'd never existed. And outwardly she'd succeeded. She had a job and friends and an apartment, and they were all separate from her life with Aristo. But she could see now that her unresolved feelings for him had continued to influence the way she lived. Why else had she kept every other man except Elliot at a distance? Even the sweet single dads she met at nursery.

Her fingers tightened around the sunscreen.

Not that it would have made any difference if she'd welcomed them with open arms. What man was ever going to be able to match Aristotle Leonidas? He had shaped her life and he was an impossible act to follow on so many levels—not just in terms of his wealth or even his astonishing beauty. There was an elusive quality to him that fascinated her. He was like a mirage that shimmered in the distance, hazy and tantalising, always just out of reach, slipping between her fingers like smoke.

Her heart began to beat faster.

Except yesterday, when out of nowhere he'd suddenly unbent, opening up to her about his childhood in a way that she would never have imagined possible. It had been a brief glimpse into what had made him the man he was, but also a fairly damning reflection on their marriage— for how could she have known so little about the man who had been her lover and her husband?

It wasn't all her fault, though, she thought defensively. Aristo had been as reluctant to discuss his past as she had, and a part of her couldn't help but wonder if it wouldn't have been a lot easier if they'd had that conversation four years ago,

Instead, though, he had stonewalled her, and she'd run away.

And if she hadn't been marooned on an island on the other side of the world that was what she should be doing now—beating a dignified but hasty retreat from his unsettling, dangerously tempting presence.

Picking up George's hat, she shivered at the memory of how close she'd come to giving in to that temptation. She was just so vulnerable where Aristo was concerned... Only, it went deeper than that. Her need to exonerate and turn a blind eye was rooted in a childhood spent craving and competing for her father's attention.

It had been the pattern of her early life: Wyatt's intermittent absences followed by his inevitable reappearance. No matter how unhappy and angry she'd been, every time he'd come back she'd let herself believe his promises, allowed herself to care. And every time he had left she had felt more worthless than the time before.

And that was why she wasn't going to fall into the same pattern with Aristo.

No matter how sexy or charming he was, one shared confidence couldn't change the facts. It was too little, too late. They didn't trust each other, and that was why their marriage had failed—why she couldn't give in to the sexual pull between them now.

Making love with Aristo again would undoubtedly be unforgettable, but she knew from experience that the people she cared about found it exceptionally easy to forget *her*.

That episode in the plane had hinted at what would happen if she gave in, how quickly everything would start to unravel…

She breathed out slowly. Was that true, or was she overreacting? After all, what was really so wrong about two people who had once shared a unique and powerful chemistry getting together again? Plenty of people did it: Elliot for one.

Only, this was different. There was George to consider, so there would be no way out…nowhere to run.

Her mouth was suddenly dry and she felt a rushing panic, like a stone dropping into the darkness. And besides, this wasn't some game of spin the bottle—and Aristo wasn't some old flame she could casually reignite.

He was a forest fire.

One touch was all it had taken to awaken her body from hibernation. One more touch and she would be lost. And next time she felt like giving in to the heat of his body and the strength of his shoulders she needed to remember that.

Outside on the terrace, George instantly tugged his hand free and scampered towards Aristo. She followed him reluctantly, suddenly conscious of the fact that both she and Aristo were semi-naked, and wishing that she'd packed a one-piece as well as her bikinis.

George was gazing up at his father. 'I want you to take me swimming.'

Aristo laughed. 'So let's go swimming.' He hesitated. 'Is that all right?' Glancing over, he stared at her questioningly, and she almost burst out laughing, for his expression so closely mirrored their small son's.

Nodding, she turned towards George. 'Yes, but you have to do what Aristo tells you.'

She felt it on her skin before she saw it: the slow upturn of his mouth, the teasing glitter in his dark eyes.

'Does that go for you too?' he asked softly.

Her heartbeat faltered. Somewhere beyond her suddenly blurred vision she heard the faint splash of waves as a pulse of excitement began beating beneath her skin. For a sharp, dizzying second they stared at each other, and then, glancing pointedly back at George, she smiled.

'I'm going to read my book, darling. I'll be just over here, okay?'

Ignoring the amusement in Aristo's eyes, she quickly sat down on one of the loungers that had been arranged temptingly around the pool. Unwrapping her sarong, she stretched out her legs and glanced over to where Aristo had been sitting. Instantly her mood shifted. A mass of documents were spread out over the table and beside them, open in the sunshine, was his laptop.

Seriously? Had he really brought work with him?

Her eyes narrowed. But when had Aristo ever put work anywhere but first on his agenda? She thought back to the long, empty evenings she'd spent alone in their beautiful cavernous apartment, feeling that same sense of failure and fear that she was not enough to deserve anyone's unswerving attention.

Fleetingly she considered saying something—but it was only the first day of their holiday, so maybe she should give him the benefit of the doubt. After all, he had walked away from his office at a moment's notice, and that would have meant unpicking a full diary of meetings and appointments.

Out of the corner of her eye she caught a glimpse of hard, primed muscle, and instantly a heat that had nothing to do with the Mediterranean sun spread slowly over her skin.

Picking up her book, she opened it at random, irritated

that, even when faced with evidence of his continuing obsession with work, her body still seemed stubbornly and irrationally determined to ignore the bad in favour of the good.

There was a loud splash, and automatically her eyes darted over to where the 'good' was unapologetically on display. In the shallow end of the pool Aristo was raising George out of the water on his shoulders, droplets of water trickling down the muscles of his arms and chest, and in the dazzling golden light he looked shockingly beautiful.

She gritted her teeth. Why couldn't he own a ski lodge? Some snowbound chalet where quilted jackets and chunky jumpers were practically mandatory? she thought, her heart thumping as Aristo stood up and began to walk out of the water, the wet fabric of his shorts clinging to the blatantly masculine outline of his body.

Fully clothed and in a crowded hotel he had been hard to ignore, but half naked on a private island he was almost impossible to resist.

As though reading her mind, Aristo chose that particular moment to look over at her, and she felt a cool tingle run down her spine as his dark eyes drifted over her face, homing in on her mouth in a way that emptied the breath from her lungs.

She wanted to look away, but forced herself to meet his eyes—and then immediately wished she hadn't as his piercing gaze dropped to the pulse beating agitatedly at the base of her throat, then lower still to the curve of her breasts beneath the peach-coloured bikini.

'Look at me, Mommy! Look!' George waved his hands excitedly.

'Don't worry, George,' Aristo said softly, his dark eyes gleaming. 'Mommy's looking.'

Her skin was prickling as, still carrying their giggling son, he walked slowly towards her. Depositing George onto his feet, he dropped down lightly onto the lounger beside her, his cool, damp body sending a jolt over her skin like sheet lightning.

'Here.' Grabbing a towel, she unceremoniously pushed it into his hands. 'Why don't you dry off?'

'I thought you might like to take a dip with me.'

His voice was cool and controlled, but the taunting expression in his eyes made her breath catch in her throat.

'Or are you scared of getting out of your depth?'

Their gazes locked and she wondered how it was possible that one little sentence could make her feel her so naked and exposed.

She tried to think of something smart to say, but she was struggling to control her voice. 'No, of course I'm not scared.' She glared at him.

His eyes hadn't left her face. 'Did you hear that, George?' He glanced slyly over at his son. 'Mommy's going to come swimming with us.'

'I didn't say that—' But as George began jumping up and down, she gave up. She held up her hands. 'Okay, okay— I'll go swimming. But later.'

Her face grew warm as she felt his dark eyes slowly inspect her, his narrowed gaze rolling over each of her ribs like a car over speed bumps.

'That colour really suits you,' he said softly.

Leaning forward, he tipped her book upwards to glance at the cover and she felt his thigh press against hers. Her mouth suddenly dry, she stared across at him.

'Thank you.' She felt her lips move, heard her voice, but none of it felt real. Nothing felt real, in fact, except the hard length of his leg.

'Mommy? Please may I have a juice?'

Turning towards her son, she nodded. 'Of course, darling.'

'I'll take him.' Aristo stood up, and she clenched her

muscles against the sudden, almost brutal feeling of loss as she watched her son trotting happily beside her ex-husband towards the villa.

Later, she joined them in the pool, and then she dozed in the sunshine while Aristo taught George to do a kneeling dive.

It felt strange, watching the two of them. In fact she felt the tiniest bit jealous of her son's fascination with Aristo, for up until now it had always been just the two of them. Mainly, though, she was stunned but happy at how quickly and effortlessly they had bonded, and at the fact that Aristo seemed as enchanted by George as she was.

A knot began to form in her stomach. It had caught her off-guard, Aristo being so gentle and patient with his son. Growing up, that had been all she'd ever wanted from her own father—to be more than the fleeting focus of his wandering attention. And the blossoming relationship between Aristo and George was not merely a reminder of what she'd missed out on growing up, it also confirmed what she'd already subconsciously accepted—that there was no going back. They were going to have to tell George the truth.

Gazing down at the open but unread page of her book, Teddie felt a flicker of panic. Not about her son's likely reaction to the news, but about what would happen when they left the island and returned to normal life.

Aristo might appear to be fully focused on George right now, but this was the honeymoon period, and she knew how swiftly and devastatingly things could change. Back in New York, her son would no longer be the only item on Aristo's agenda. He was going to have to compete for his father's time against the allure and challenge of work.

The tension in her chest wound tighter and tighter and she gripped the edges of the book, remembering how glorious it had been to feel the warmth of his gaze. And how cold it had felt when she'd been pushed into the shadows.

But it was too late to worry about that now. George wasn't going to stay as a three-year-old for ever, and sooner or later he was going to want to know who his father was. And—as she'd already discovered—there was never a right time to tell the truth.

'I thought we might eat together later tonight. Just the two of us.'

Aristo's voice cut into her thoughts and her chin jerked up. They were lazing by the pool beneath a gleaming white canvas canopy. His gaze was steady, his voice measured.

'We need to talk,' he said quietly. 'And, much as I love having our son around, it'll be easier to do that when he's not there.'

She knew her face had stilled. Her heart had stilled too, at the thought of spending an evening alone with him. But, ignoring the panicky drumming of her heart, she nodded. 'I agree.'

And then, before her face could betray her, she lowered the brim of her hat and leaned back against the sun lounger.

Three hours later, the heat of the day was starting to drop and a faint breeze was riffling the glassy surface of the pool.

Glancing down at her cup of coffee, Teddie felt her spine tense. The meal would soon be over, but she still hadn't managed to say even one word of what was whirling inside her head.

Looking up, she felt her heart drop forward like a rollercoaster. Aristo was watching her, his gaze so calm and knowing that she felt as if she'd been caught with her hand in his jacket. Except he wasn't wearing a jacket.

Just a washed-out black Henley and a pair of cream linen trousers.

'You're quiet,' he said softly.

'Am I?' She felt her cheeks flush, hearing the nervousness in her voice.

'Yes, unnervingly so.' His eyes looked directly into hers and she suddenly wished that it was whisky, not coffee that she was drinking.

She frowned. 'I'm just thinking…'

'Whoa! I wasn't getting at you. I don't want to fight.'

He held up his napkin and waved it in a gesture of surrender, but she barely noticed; she was too busy following the lazy curve of his smile.

Her own smile was instant, instinctive, unstoppable. 'I'm not looking for a fight either…' She hesitated. 'I was just thinking about us, and George, and…'

He sat watching her, waiting, and she looked away, fearful of what she would see in his eyes.

'And… Well, I think we should tell him tomorrow that you're his father.'

There was a stretch of silence.

Aristo studied her face.

Caught between the flickering nightlights and the darkness she looked tense, wary, apprehensive and he could sense the effort her words had taken.

Of course, logically, now he and George had met, it was inevitable that they should tell him the truth, and it was what he wanted—or at least a part of what he wanted. But, as much as he wanted to acknowledge his son as his own, these last few days had taught him that the decision needed to come from Teddie.

And now it had.

He exhaled slowly, relief vying with satisfaction. It wasn't quite the hand of friendship, but it was a start.

His eyes wandered idly over the simple yellow dress she was wearing, lingering on the upward curve of her breasts. And anyway, he wanted Teddie to be a whole lot more than just a friend.

'Are you sure?' He spoke carefully. 'We can wait. *I* can wait.'

He was rapidly becoming an expert in waiting. Shifting against the ache in his groin, he gritted his teeth and glanced away to the white line of slow-moving surf down on the beach.

Teddie felt her heart jump against her ribs. Incredibly, Aristo was giving her a choice, but to her surprise she realised that now was the right time.

'I'm sure.'

And once they did then there really would be no going back.

She felt a spasm of panic, needle-sharp, like a blade beneath her ribs. Was she doing the right thing? Or had she just doomed her son to the same fate that she'd endured? A childhood marked with uncertainty and self-doubt, with a father who would cloak his absences beneath the virtuous task of supporting his family.

'He needs to know.' Hearing the words out loud, she felt tears coming. Quickly she bolstered her panic. 'But I need to know that you understand what this means.'

He frowned. 'If I didn't I wouldn't be here.'

Pushing back her chair, she stood up unsteadily. 'So this is all about you, is it?'

'That's not what I'm saying.'

He was standing now too.

'That's what it sounded like.'

She heard him inhale and her anger shifted to guilt. It wasn't fair to twist his words when she wasn't being honest about her own feelings.

'I just mean that being a father is a lifetime commitment.'

His face hardened. 'I'd like to say that's not something I'm going to forget but, given my own childhood, I can't.

All I can say is that I am going to be there for George—for you.'

Teddie fought the beating of her heart. He was saying all the right things and she wanted to believe him—only believing him set off in her a whole new spiral of half-thought-out fears and uncertainties.

'Good.' She was trying hard to let nothing show in her eyes but he was staring at her impatiently.

'Is it? Because it doesn't sound like it to me.'

He moved swiftly round the table, stopping in front of her. The paleness of her face made her eyes seem incredibly green, and he ran his hand over his face, needing action to counteract the ache in his chest, unsure of his footing in this uncharted territory.

'Teddie...' He softened his voice.

She lifted one hand to her throat and raised the other in front of her, as though warding him off. It was a gesture of such conflicting vulnerability and defiance that he was suddenly struggling to breathe.

'I'm not just saying what I think you want to hear.'

'I know.' She gave him a small, sad smile. 'And I want you to be there for George. It's just it's only ever been me and him. I know you're his father, but I've never had to share him before and it feels like a big deal.'

Aristo stared down at her. The fact that Teddie loved her son so fiercely made something wrench apart inside his chest and, taking a step forward, he pulled her gently towards him.

'I'm not going to take him away from you, Teddie,' he said softly. 'I couldn't even if I wanted to. You're his mother. But I want to be the best father I can be. The best *man* I can be.'

He felt some of the tension ease out of her spine and shoulders, and then, leaning forward unsteadily, she rested her head against his chest.

Listening to the solid beat of his heart, Teddie felt her body start to soften, adrenalin dissolving in her blood, his clean masculine scent filling her chest.

The air around them was suddenly heavy and charged. She felt weightless, lost in the moment and in him, so that without thinking she curled her arms around his body, her fingers following the contours of the muscles of his back. And then she was pushing up his T-shirt and touching smooth, warm skin.

His hand was sliding rhythmically through her hair, tipping her head back, and his mouth was brushing over her cheeks and lips like the softest feathers, teasing her so that she could hear her own breathing inside her head, like the waves rushing inside a seashell.

She took a breath, her hands splaying out, wanting more of his skin, his heat, his smooth, hard muscle. Her heart was pounding, the longing inside of her combusting as she felt the fingers of his other hand travel lightly over her bare back. And then her stomach clenched as he parted her lips and kissed her open-mouthed, his tongue so warm and soft and teasing that she felt the lick of heat slide through her like a flame.

Her head was swimming.

She wanted more—more of his mouth, his touch, his skin—so much more of him. Reaching up, she clasped his face, kissing him back, pulling him closer, lifting her hips and oscillating against him, trying, needing to relieve the ache radiating from her pelvis.

Heat was spilling over her skin and, arching upwards, she felt his breath stumble, and then he was sliding a hand through her hair, holding her captive as he kissed her more deeply, his warm breath filling her mouth so that she was melting from the inside out.

Her fingers were scrabbling against his skin… She moaned…

There was a second of agonising pulsing stillness, and then slowly she felt him pull away.

His eyes were dark with passion. For a moment he didn't speak, and she knew as he breathed out roughly that he was looking for the right words, looking for *any* words because he was as stunned as she.

'Sorry. I didn't mean to do that.'

She stared up at him, an ache like thirst spreading outwards. 'Me neither.'

'So I suppose we should just forget it ever happened.'

He made it sound like a statement, but she knew it was a question from the dark and unblinking intensity of his gaze. Suddenly she could barely breathe.

Should they? Would it really be so very bad to press her foot down on the accelerator pedal and run the red light just once?

She could feel something inside her shifting and softening, and the urge to reach out was so intense and pure that she almost cried out. But her need for him couldn't be trusted on so many levels—not least the fact that no man had come close to filling the emptiness that she'd been ignoring for four years.

'I think that would be for the best,' she said quickly, lifting her gaze, her green eyes meeting his. 'Just be a father to him.'

His steady, knowing gaze made her heartbeat falter and she glanced away, up to a near perfect moon, glowing pearlescent in the darkening sky.

'Thank you for a lovely evening, but I should probably go and check on George.'

And, taking a fast, hard breath, she sidestepped past him and walked on shaking legs towards the villa.

In the darkness of her son's room she leaned against the wall, seeking solace in its cool surface.

She shouldn't have agreed with him.

She should have told him that he was wrong.

Then remembering his open laptop, she tensed. They might have called a ceasefire, but she still didn't trust him.

And it wasn't just Aristo she didn't trust. She didn't trust herself either.

Four years ago she'd let her libido overrule not just her common sense but every instinct she'd had, and it had been a disaster. Nothing had changed except this time she knew the score.

Aristo might be the only man who had made her body sing, but she knew now that if she allowed herself to be intimate with him then she ran the risk of getting hurt—and she'd worked so hard to un-love him.

So that left friendship. Not the sort of easy affection and solidarity that she shared with Elliot, but the polite formality of former lovers now sidestepping around each other's lives and new partners.

Her heart lurched as visions of Aristo with a new wife flooded her head and she felt suddenly sick. It had been hard enough getting over him last time. Far worse though was the thought of having to witness him sharing his life with someone else.

CHAPTER SIX

IT WAS THE most perfect peach Teddie had ever seen. Perfectly plump, sunset-coloured, it was half concealed by a cluster of pale green leaves, like a shy swimmer hiding behind a towel on the beach.

She'd spotted it yesterday evening, when she and George had joined the housekeeper, Melina, as she'd wandered around the garden, choosing ingredients for the evening meal. In the end they had collected fat, dark-skinned figs to go with the salty feta and thyme-scented honey that had followed a dessert of delicious homemade strawberry ice-cream—George's favourite.

She let out a quiver of breath, remembering her son's re-action as she'd told him that Aristo was his father. Watching his face shift from confusion to shy understanding, she'd felt her heart twist—as it was twisting now at the memory, although not with regret. And she knew George had no regrets either, for he was happily 'helping' Melina crack eggs for the *strapatsada* they were having for breakfast.

Standing on tiptoe, she stretched out her arm, her fingers almost touching the peach's skin. If only she was just a little bit taller...

She breathed in sharply as a hand stole past her and gently pulled the peach free.

'Hey!' Turning, she stared up at Aristo in outrage. 'That's mine.'

He looked her straight in the eye and kept on looking. 'Not according to the evidence.'

Her fingers twitched. She was tempted to make a grab for it, but already his proximity was sending her senses haywire and she didn't want to risk reaching out to touch the *wrong* soft, golden flesh...

She swallowed. Her desire for him chewed at her constantly, and already her insides felt so soft and warm it was as if she was melting.

Watching the play of emotions cross her face, Aristo felt his body tense. He could sense the conflict in her and it was driving him crazy. For once they'd had only to be alone and they would be reaching for one another—his hand circling her waist, her fingers sliding over his shoulders...

His blood seemed to slow and thicken and his limbs felt suddenly light as he stared at her profile, at the dark arch of her eyebrow above the straight line of her nose and the full curving mouth. There was a sprinkle of freckles across her cheeks and he wanted to reach out and touch each and every one.

Instead, though, he glanced down at the peach, turning it over in his hand, his thumb tracing the cleft in the downy flesh. 'What will you give me for it?' he asked softly, his mouth curving upwards.

Teddie swallowed. This was Aristo at his most dangerous. That combination of tantalising smile and teasing dark, dark eyes. And, even though she knew she shouldn't, she held his gaze and said lightly, 'How about I *don't* push you into that lavender bush if you hand it over?'

Laughing, he held out the peach. 'And I was going to offer to share it with you.'

His fingers brushed against hers as she took the peach and she felt a tremor down her spine like a charge of electricity. 'So let's share it,' she said casually. 'There's a knife in that basket.'

'Are you sure it won't spoil your appetite?'

A suspended silence seemed to saturate the air around them and, staring past him, she said quickly, 'The basket's on the bench.'

She watched as carefully he halved the peach, then pitted and sliced it, his profile a pure gold line against the intense blue sky. The creamy golden flesh was still warm from the sun and heavy with juice, and as she bit into it the intense sweetness ricocheted around her mouth.

'Wow! They don't taste like that in New York.'

Folding the knife, he dropped it back into the basket. 'No, they don't. But then everything tastes better here.'

She frowned at the edge that had entered his voice. 'You make that sound like a *bad* thing.'

A light breeze stirred between them and the air felt suddenly over-warm, the sunlight suddenly over-bright.

He shrugged. 'It's not a bad thing—just a consequence of living in a fantasy. When you go back to civilisation, reality doesn't quite match up.'

Her heart was pounding against her chest. He was referring to the peach, but he might easily have been talking about their marriage—for wasn't that what had happened? They had married on impulse, without really knowing anything about one another—certainly not enough to make till-death-do-us-part vows. And even before the honeymoon had been over it had become clear to both of them that what they'd shared in all those hotel rooms across America was too fragile to survive real life.

And yet here they both were in this idyllic sun-drenched garden sharing a peach.

She felt a flutter of hope. Okay, this wasn't real life, but they weren't newly weds either and Aristo wanted to make this work. They both did. And that was the difference between now and then. Four years ago they hadn't wanted the same things, but that had been before George.

Remembering how at breakfast Aristo had answered their son's questions about his motorboat patiently, giving him his full attention, she released a pent-up breath.

'I think you're looking at it the wrong way,' she said slowly. 'I mean, peaches in New York might not taste like the peaches here—but what about the cheesecake? You can't tell me that they have cheesecake here like they do at Eileen's.'

He frowned. 'I wouldn't know. I've never eaten there. Actually, I've never had cheesecake.'

'Really?' Teddie stared at him in disbelief. 'Well, that's not right. As soon as we get back to New York we're going out to have to fix that.'

Aristo laughed. 'We are?'

He seemed pleased.

'They do all kinds of flavours. When I was pregnant I had these terrible cravings for baked cheesecake and it just kind of carried on. Now it's a regular thing. Last Saturday in the month. You could come too.'

'It's a date,' he said softly.

Her heart was suddenly beating too fast. 'I didn't mean just the two of us,' she said quickly.

Was that how it had sounded? Or was he just accepting her invitation?

Aristo held her gaze, but the anticipation that had been flickering through his veins had abruptly dissolved. His shoulders tensed. After the moment of intimacy the swift rejection was unsettling, but it was the confirmation he needed that he couldn't be casual with her in the way he'd been with other women in his life.

She had been his wife, and he was determined that she would be again. Only, he wasn't going to get emotionally played.

He turned and looked at her, his expression unreadable.

'Of course not. Are you supposed to be picking something for Melina?'

Reaching down, he picked up the basket and she nodded, grateful for a shift in conversation.

'Yes, I was—lemons and thyme.'

For a moment she thought he was going to offer to help her. Instead, though, he held the basket out to her. 'Then I'll leave you to it.'

And before she had a chance to respond he had turned and was walking back towards the villa.

'Hurry up, Mommy.'

For the second time in so many minutes Teddie felt George's hand tug at the edge of her shorts.

'I'm trying, sweetie. Just let me check this one last pocket.'

Fumbling in the side of her suitcase, she smiled distractedly down at her son, who was sitting on the floor of her dressing room.

Her hat was great when she was sitting on the sun lounger, but it was difficult to wear in the pool and she was trying to find the hairbands that she'd packed—or at least thought she'd packed—so that she could put her hair up to protect her head.

'Mommy, come *on*!'

'Darling, the pool will still be there—' she said soothingly,

But, shaking his head, George interrupted her. 'I don't want to go to the pool. I want to see the pirate boat.'

Pirate boat! What pirate boat?

Giving up on her search, she pushed the case back into the wardrobe and turned to where George was sitting on the floor beside a selection of toy vehicles, his upturned eyes watching her anxiously.

'What are you talking about, darling?' Gently, she pushed a curl away from his forehead.

'The pirate boat.' He bit his lip, clearly baffled by his mother's confusion. 'Aristo—I mean, *Daddy*…'

He paused, and her heart turned over as he looked up at her. The word was not yet automatic to him.

'They left it behind and Daddy said he'd take us to see it.'

Teddie frowned. She had some vague memory of Aristo talking about pirates when they were eating breakfast that morning, but she'd been only half paying attention, she thought guiltily. Most of her head had still been spinning from that almost-kiss they'd shared last night.

'Okay—well, we can do that. I was just going to tie my hair back.' Leaning forward, she gave him an impish grin. 'But I've had a much better idea!'

Ten minutes later she was walking through the villa with George scampering by her side. Both of them were wearing blue and white striped T-shirts and Teddie had drawn a moustache and stubble on their faces.

'Shall we scare him?' George whispered, accelerating into a little run.

He seemed giddy with excitement at the prospect, and Teddie nodded. But as they crept out onto the terrace the giggle she'd been holding back subsided as she saw that the pool was empty.

'Where is he?' George's hand tightened around hers and instinctively she gave it a squeeze.

'He's probably getting changed.' She gave him a reassuring smile.

Ten minutes later, though, they were still waiting by the pool.

'Do you think he's forgotten?' George whispered.

He was starting to look anxious, and she couldn't stop a flicker of uncertainty rippling down her spine.

She shook her head. 'No, of course not,' she said firmly. 'Why don't we give it another five minutes and then we'll go and look for him? I'm sure he'll be here any moment.'

But Aristo didn't arrive. Finally, Teddie took George's hand, and they walked back into the villa just as Melina came rushing towards them.

'I was coming to find you! I completely forgot Mr Aristo said that he was going to be in his office. He has a very important work call.'

Nodding, Teddie pinned a smile on her face, but inside she could feel a rising swell of angry disappointment as she asked Melina to take George to the kitchen. Disappointment and relief—for hadn't she been expecting this to happen?

She bit down on her misery. An important work call! No, scratch that, a *very* important work call, she thought bitterly. Her throat tightened. Had she really thought that things could be different? Or that Aristo could change? She should have realised how this holiday was going to pan out that first morning, when she'd spotted his laptop crouching like some alien in the blazing Mediterranean sunshine. But, idiot that she was, she'd assumed it was a one-off.

Aristo's office wasn't hard to find, and his voice was clearly audible as she walked stiffly up to the open door.

'No, we need total transparency. I *want* total transparency—exactly.'

He was standing by his desk, his phone tucked against his ear, the tension in his body at odds with the casual informality of his clothing. She stepped into the room, her heartbeat ringing in her ears as he looked up from his laptop, his frown of concentration fading.

'I'm going to have to call you back, Nick,' he said quietly. Hanging up, he stared at Teddie impassively. 'So you got my message?'

'Loud and clear,' she snapped. Stalking into the room, she stopped in front of the desk. 'I was a bit stunned at first, but I suppose it wasn't that much of a surprise. You put work first during the whole of our marriage, so why should a holiday to get to know your son be any different?'

His face creased into a frown. 'I don't know what you're talking about. It's *one* call—'

Her response to his words was instant, visceral, making her heartbeat accelerate, emotion clog her throat. It was everything she'd dreaded—only it had happened so much more quickly than even she had thought possible. Literally within hours of him claiming that he wanted to be there for her and George.

But how many times had her father made just such a claim?

'I'm talking about *this*,' she interrupted him. 'About you, sneaking off to close some deal—'

She broke off abruptly. The misery inside her chest was like a block of ice and she was starting to feel sick.

Aristo felt the pulse of anger start to beat beneath his skin. Ever since they'd told George that he was his father Teddie had been acting strangely, oscillating between a suspended tangible hunger and a maddening aloofness, but this—her anger, her baseless accusation—was so unexpected, so unfair.

And she was dressed as a pirate—although clearly she had forgotten that fact.

Just at that moment his phone started to ring and, glancing up at the ceiling, she rolled her eyes in a way that made him want to find a plank and make her walk it.

'I'm not going to answer that,' he said coolly. 'And I wasn't *sneaking* anywhere. Something important came up and I needed to deal with it. I told Melina to give you a message, and she did.'

Why was this so hard for her to understand? He'd taken a week off work, but that didn't mean his business was on hold. And who did she think he was doing all this for—and why? Women might talk about needing love and being loved, but what that translated into was a relentless desire for money and status—as his mother had proved.

His phone was still ringing and her green eyes narrowed like a cat's. 'We're not some junior members of your staff you can just fob off.'

'I wasn't fobbing you off.'

She stared at him incredulously. 'George is *three years old*, Aristo. He was so excited.' Her voice quivered and she paused, then straightened her shoulders determinedly. 'You didn't even give him a second thought, did you? But the thing about three-year-olds is that if you say you're going to do something then you have to do it. You can't lie to him.'

His phone had finally stopped ringing, but his chest felt suddenly so tight that he couldn't breathe.

'That's rich—coming from you.'

He watched the colour drain from her face, but he told himself that she deserved it.

'You lied to him from the day he was born. And you lied to me too.' He shook his head dismissively. 'All those years, and not once did you consider telling me the truth.'

'That's not true.' Her face blazing with anger, Teddie took a step forward. 'I did try and tell you.'

'Don't give me that.' The coldness in his eyes made her stomach churn. 'You could have contacted me in any number of ways.'

'I did,' she said flatly, the flame of her anger dying as quickly as it had ignited, smothered by the memory of the phone calls she'd made to his various offices around the globe, and the polite but cool indifference of the Leonidas staff.

'I tried them all. By the time I realised I was pregnant, you'd left America, so I tried calling you, but you blocked me on your phone, so then I called your offices and left messages with your staff asking you to call me back but you never did. And I wrote to you, every year on George's birthday but I never got a reply.'

There was a long silence.

Aristo could feel his heart pounding, the shock of her words pricking his skin like bee stings. She was telling the truth. He could hear it in the matter-of-fact tone of her voice. And yes, he *had* blocked her number, told his staff not to bother him with any kind of communications from Teddie… And they had done what they'd been told. But he'd been angry and hurt—and also scared that if he even so much as heard her voice he would do something stupid, like listen to his heart…

He'd just wanted to put it all behind him—to forget her and his marriage—

'So you gave up?' His pride might have contributed to him not finding out about his son, but the bulk of the responsibility was still hers.

Watching her eyes widen with anger and astonishment, seeing the sudden shine of tears, he felt harsh, cruel—only before he could say anything she took a step towards him.

'Yes, I gave up! Because I was on my own and I was sick and I was scared.' She breathed out unsteadily. 'But even if I hadn't given up, and you had got my messages, you wouldn't have called me anyway. No doubt something *very important* at work would have come up and you'd have had to deal with that instead.'

He stared at her in silence, his face set and tense, his dark eyes narrowing like arrowheads. 'Not this again.' He shook his head. 'Unlike you, Teddie, I'm not a magician. I can't just pull a hotel out of a hat and take a bow. I work on global projects that employ tens of thousands of people. I have responsibilities, commitments.'

His face looked cold and businesslike. It was the face he'd used on her when he'd been late home from work, or cancelled dinner, or spent all weekend on the phone. Behind him, through the window, the flat, shifting blues of the Mediterranean seemed an oddly serene backdrop to their heated argument.

'*Responsibilities…commitments…*' Her voice echoed his words incredulously. 'Yes, you do, Aristo. Four years ago you had a wife—me—and now you have a son—George.'

'I was working to build up the business for you, so you didn't have to worry about money!'

Surely she could understand his motives for working so hard? Had they stayed together she would have been the first to complain, for women were never satisfied with just enough—they always wanted more.

'Well, I didn't marry you for your money.'

He heard the catch in her voice and his chest tightened as he watched her lip tremble.

'And you're already fantastically wealthy. So why are you still working as though your life depends on it?'

There was a short, strained silence, and then, as his phone started to ring again, she took a deep breath.

'You should probably answer that,' she said quietly. 'We clearly have nothing left to say.'

And, turning, she walked swiftly out of the room.

Twenty minutes later, having got directions from Melina, she and George reached the right cove. The pirate boat was at the back of the beach on the dunes, its wooden hull bleached like the bones of some marine animal. It was more of a rowing boat than an actual pirate ship with masts, but it was still recognisably a boat and, on seeing it, George began towing her down the dunes.

'Look, Mommy, *look*!'

'I can see it, darling,' she said quickly.

He'd been unusually quiet during the walk, and she was grateful to hear a hint of his former excitement back in his voice.

After walking out of Aristo's office she had collected him from the kitchen, explaining in an over-bright voice that, 'Daddy is very sorry that he can't come right now, but he wants us to go without him.'

Watching her son's face fall, she had wanted to storm back into Aristo's office, snatch his phone and hurl it out of the window along with his laptop. She knew exactly how George was feeling, and the fact that *she* had somehow let it happen, by letting her selfish, workaholic ex-husband into his life, felt like a dagger between her ribs.

'Do you want to have a look inside?' she whispered.

He nodded and, leaning down, she picked him up. They inspected the ship carefully, but aside from a few small startled crabs they found nothing.

George sighed and, glancing down at him, she saw that his eyes were shining with tears. With an intensity that hurt, she wished she had planned ahead and hidden something for him to find.

'Daddy would know where the treasure is,' he said sadly.

She breathed out silently. *But Daddy isn't here. He's holed up his office, expanding his empire.*

'He might—but we haven't really looked properly. And most treasure is buried, isn't it?' she said reasonably.

'Yes, it is,' said a familiar male voice as a shadow fell across her. 'And no self-respecting pirate would ever leave his treasure lying about on his ship.'

'Daddy!'

George launched himself at his father.

Looking up at Aristo, Teddie felt her heartbeat accelerate. He was wearing a white shirt unbuttoned at the neck, and a pair of rolled-up dark trousers. He'd borrowed what looked like a scarf and tied it bandana-style around his head. The stubble, however, was his own.

He looked incredibly sexy—but she wasn't about to let his looks or her libido wipe the slate clean, and nor was she about to expose George to any further disappointment.

'I think we should be getting back now,' she said stiffly. 'We can look for treasure another time.'

Their eyes met, and she glared at him above George's head.

'Trust me,' he said softly. 'I've got this.'

He headed off along the beach with George scampering beside him. Gritting her teeth, she watched them crouch down near a rocky outcrop, then stand up again. And now they were heading back towards her.

'Mommy, *look*!'

George was jumping up and down, and even at a distance she could see that his eyes were wide with excitement.

'I'm coming,' she called.

She half-walked, half-ran across the sand, to where he was pointing excitedly at a large white stone clearly marked with an *X*. Her heart seemed to slide sideways and she glanced up at Aristo in confusion.

The sun was behind his head, casting a shadow across his face, but she could feel his eyes, sense their intensity, and suddenly she understood what he'd done.

'We must have walked right past it,' she said, when she was completely sure her voice was composed.

Aristo lifted the stone, and then he and George scooped out sand with their hands until finally their fingers found the edges of a wooden box. To Teddie's eyes it was obviously far too well-preserved to be a pirate's relic, but she could see that her son had no doubt that it was genuine.

She watched him pull it free, and open it.

'Oh, George,' she whispered. The box was filled with gleaming golden coins. 'You are so lucky.'

He looked up at her, his face trembling with astonishment. 'Can I take it home?'

'Of course.' Reaching out, Aristo cupped his son's chin in his hand. 'This is my island, and you're my son, and everything I have is yours.'

* * *

Back at the villa, they ate early. George was exhausted, and could barely keep his eyes open, so Aristo put him to bed and then joined Teddie on the terrace.

There was a short, delicate pause.

'I wanted to say thank you for earlier,' she said quietly. 'It was magical, and so thoughtful of you.'

'All I can say is that real pirates had it easy.' He groaned. 'Honestly, cleaning those coins nearly killed me. It took so *long*.'

She laughed. 'Aristo Leonidas wearing his fingers to the bone! I really wish I'd seen that.'

His eyes on hers were suddenly serious. 'Well, I'm glad you didn't. It was my turn to make magic happen for you.' His mouth twisted. 'I'm sorry about the phone call.'

'I'm sorry too.' She squeezed his hand. 'I shouldn't have jumped to conclusions.'

'You didn't. I took the call and I shouldn't have done,' he said simply.

Turning his gaze towards the blue sheet of water below, Aristo frowned. Crossing the dunes earlier, his breath had seemed to choke him, and with every step he'd grown more convinced that he'd blown it.

Now, though, beneath a pink sunset, with Teddie sitting opposite him wearing that same simple sundress, his reaction seemed ludicrously out of proportion.

Or it would have done but for the unasked question that was reverberating inside his head and had been since she'd stormed out of his office.

'Did you mean it?' he said abruptly. 'Did you mean what you said earlier—about not marrying me for my money?'

He could see the confusion in her eyes. 'Yes, of course. I would have married you if you'd been penniless.'

'So why did you keep working, then?' Another question—this one older, but just as pressing. 'In New York?'

She frowned. 'I needed to—I need to have that control.'

The words left her mouth unprompted, unedited, and she stared at him, embarrassed and angry, because up until that moment that fact had been private, not something she could even really admit to herself.

Sensing his curiosity, she hesitated, but his dark gaze was calm and unfazed and she felt her heartbeat steady itself.

'My mum was terrible with money. She was so out of it sometimes she'd forget to pay the rent. And she was always upping her medication, so it would run out, and then we'd have to buy other people's prescriptions. Otherwise she'd steal them.' She swallowed. 'I know my life isn't like that any more, but...'

Gazing down, she saw that her hands were clenched in her lap, and with an effort she forced her fingers apart.

'I can't seem to stop that feeling of dread.'

'I didn't know that was how you felt,' he said slowly.

She shrugged. 'Having a regular income, however small, just makes me feel calmer.' Finishing her sentence, she glanced towards the door. 'We should probably go back in.'

For a moment Aristo didn't respond, and then he nodded slowly and they stood up and walked back through the silent house.

'You asked me why I work. And you're right—it's not the money, or even how work makes me feel...'

He had stopped at the top of the stairs and was staring back down, as though considering his next step, his next sentence. Finally he turned to face her.

'I do like being in control...having a focus—but it's more than that. It's about creating something that matters beyond just making me rich.' His gaze fixed on her face. 'I want my brand, my name—George's name now—to be indelible.'

And he was prepared to work relentlessly to reach his

goal, Teddie thought miserably. Even when he was just talking about it, she could see the fire in his eyes, the relentlessness and determination to succeed, and her stomach clenched. How could she or George compete with that?

As though reading her thoughts, he shook his head. 'I know what you're thinking. And you're right. Work was too important to me—more than it should have been. But only because I let it be. I can change. I'm already changing.'

He took a step forward and his fingers brushed against hers lightly, then he caught her hand in his.

'We both are. Look at us talking.'

His hand tightened around hers and he sounded so vehement that she found herself smiling.

It was true. Last time he had stonewalled her, and she had run away rather than face their problems, but here they were discussing things. Only...

'Aristo, I'm glad we're talking, but...' She hesitated. 'I'm not sure that's enough for us to find a way back to how we used to be.'

'Good.' He pulled her against him so that suddenly their eyes were level. 'Because I don't want what we had before. What we had before needed improving. This time you and George are going to be my top priority.'

Her heart was beating too fast; she couldn't keep up with him. Or with the rush of longing that was racing through her blood. 'Did *everything* about us need improving?'

His dark gaze rested on her face. 'No, I can think of one thing at least that was utterly incomparable,' he said softly. 'But if you don't believe me then maybe I could remind you.'

His words rippled over her skin like the softest caress. He looked so handsome, so certain. She could feel the smooth tension of his hard body next to hers, and his eyes were darker than the night sky. She knew she should disentangle herself, but instead she reached up and touched his face.

She heard him breathe out softly, and the sound made something inside her chest crack apart like ice breaking. She wanted him so badly that she felt she might catch fire. So why was she fighting it? Fighting herself? What point was she really proving to Aristo, or herself, by denying the attraction between them?

They already had a bond through George. Nothing could be more permanent and binding than a child, and she had managed to come to terms with that by setting boundaries.

So stop making everything way more complicated than it needs to be, she told herself. *Than you want it to be*.

His hand was firm against her waist, his eyes steady on her face, and she could feel his longing, sense the power beneath his skin. But she knew that he was holding himself back, waiting for permission.

She ran her finger along the line of his jaw and tilted his head down so that their mouths were almost touching. 'I don't need reminding,' she whispered.

His mouth brushed against hers, barely touching, teasing her, and his hand slid up to cup her breast, his fingertips grazing her nipple. Feeling the swell of blood beneath her skin, she breathed in sharply, leaning into him, and then, taking his other hand, she led him slowly towards his bedroom.

They were just over the threshold when he pulled back, then stopped, his eyes narrowed, his face taut with concentration.

'Is this what you want, Teddie?' he said hoarsely. 'Me... this?'

She stared at him in silence, her body throbbing. Maybe it was just the island working its magic on her, subtly, irresistibly, but it—*he*—was what she wanted.

'Yes.'

In one swift movement he pushed the door shut and, leaning forward, kissed her fiercely, his hand sliding up beneath her hair to cup her head, his kisses spilling like warm liquid over her mouth and throat and breast.

The touch of his warm mouth was making everything tingle and tighten, so that she could hardly bear it. She moaned softly and then her body started to shake and she began pulling at his clothes, her hands clumsy with desire.

Sucking in a breath, he lifted his mouth and, stepping back, peeled off his shirt, reached for his shorts.

'No, wait, let me,' she said hoarsely.

His eyes narrowed in protest, but as she reached out and ran her fingertips over the muscles of his stomach he stayed still. Gently, she caressed his smooth skin, following the path of dark hair down to his waistband, then lower still. As she traced the thickness of his erection, feeling it twitch and swell and harden beneath his shorts, she heard him groan and felt his hand lock in her hair.

Slowly, carefully, she undid the cord around his waist and pulled him free. Heart thudding, she stared at him in silence, her mouth dry, her breath quickening.

'My turn now,' he said softly.

His fingers were light but firm. Unbuttoning her dress, he let it slip to the floor and breathed in sharply. She was wearing no bra, just a pair of the palest peach panties, and her body was flecked with sand. He stared at her, spellbound, and then, taking her hand, he led her into the bathroom and pulled her into the shower.

As his hands spread over her ribs, Teddie closed her eyes. Warm water was trickling over her skin and her belly was tight and hot and aching. She curled her hands into his wet hair, reaching out for his hard, muscular body, trying to shake some of the dizziness in her head. She wanted him so much, wanted the ache inside her to be satisfied, and helplessly she arched up against him, pressing, pulling, pleading with her fingers...

But as he lowered his mouth and sucked fiercely on her nipples she gasped, stepping unsteadily back against the wall of the shower.

Aristo stilled, the soft sound bringing him to his senses. Closing his mind against the heavy, insistent beat of hunger in his groin, he lifted his head. 'Are you protected?'

She stared at him dazedly, then shook her head.

Groaning, he backed out of the shower, his heart pounding. When he returned she had stripped off her panties and his body stiffened in instant response. Gritting his teeth, he rolled the condom on and then kissed her again, parting her lips, plundering her mouth with his tongue. His hands were roaming over her belly and between her thighs and, feeling her move against his fingers, he was suddenly struggling to breathe.

Teddie moaned softly. Her body was aching now and, reaching out, her hand found his erection. Hardly breathing, she slid her fingers over the rigid, pulsing length, pulling him closer, opening her legs. She heard him breathe in raggedly and then he was lifting her up, bracing himself against the wall. Shifting against him, panting, she guided him inch by inch into her trembling body to where a ball of heat was starting to implode.

Flattening himself against her, Aristo began to thrust, out of sync at first, then in time to the pulse beating in his head. His mouth found hers and he felt her respond, deepening the kiss. His heartbeat was accelerating and, closing his eyes, he felt his body start to cut loose from its moorings. Teddie arched upwards, her hands gripping his shoulders, nails cutting into the muscle. He felt her tense, heard her cry out, and then his body shuddered and he erupted into her.

CHAPTER SEVEN

IT WAS EARLY when Teddie woke up. She wasn't sure what time it was, but as she opened her eyes she could tell from the pale wash of light spreading through the room that dawn was not far away.

She blinked. They must have forgotten to close the shutters—but then they'd had no thought for anything except each other. Her face grew hot as she remembered how Aristo had stripped her naked, his hands smooth against her skin, smooth and hard and urgent.

How she had needed his touch, craved the frenzy of release that he alone had given her. And she had wanted to touch him too, splaying her fingers over his body, pressing her thumbs into the muscles of his shoulders and down his back, her hands shaking with eagerness.

Glancing over at Aristo, she felt her breath still in her throat. He was deeply asleep, his long dark lashes grazing his cheekbones, one arm loosely curling over the pillow. She loved how smooth his skin was—and his smell: salt and sunlight and some kind of citrus. She lay for a moment, trying to hear his heartbeat in the silence, feeling the gravitational pull of his body.

And she would have carried on lying there, except that her mouth felt dry, and there was a sharp ache beneath her ribs, like thirst only more intense. Pushing back the sheet carefully, so as not to wake him, she slid out of bed.

Tiptoeing into the bathroom, she turned on the tap and,

grabbing her hair to one side, held her mouth open beneath
the running water. It tasted good and she swallowed greed-
ily, and then, standing up, she caught a glimpse of her reflection in the mirror.

She stilled. She had been fighting herself for days now,
and giving in to her desire had felt like such a big step,
with such serious, far-reaching consequences, that she had
expected to see a sign. But then when it had finally happened she had never felt more certain of anything—except
when she'd found out she was pregnant and had decided
to keep the baby.

Some things were just meant to be, and leading him into
his bedroom had given her a peace that came from being
part of something greater and beyond her control.

And now? How did she feel *now*?

She searched anxiously inside herself for feelings of
regret—but how could she regret what had happened last
night? He'd felt so right against her, their bodies seam-
less against one another, and even now the memory of
his touch made her head swim. It had been wonderful,
incredible… The corners of her mouth turned up and she
realised she was grinning stupidly at herself in the mirror. *Magical!*

And it wasn't just the sex. She'd been there before, tumbling into bed with Aristo after that meeting with their lawyers, but then it had felt so different—off-key, every word a
misstep, their bodies desperately seeking a way to resolve
what they hadn't even tried to address.

Only, now they'd talked—really talked—and there had
been no desperation, just a sense of irrefutable rightness.

So, no, she didn't regret any of it—but nor, she realised,
had the ache in her chest subsided. It wasn't water she
wanted.

Back in the bedroom, she slipped under the sheets and
felt him shift beside her. Gazing down, she saw that his

eyes were open, and then his hand was sliding over her stomach and her body rippled into life and she reached for him urgently.

An ivory-coloured light greeted Aristo when he blinked his eyes open several hours later. For a few moments he lay on his back, watching the white muslin curtain flutter weakly in the barely there breeze, and then slowly he stretched out his arms above his head.

For days now, ever since he'd walked into the Kildare lounge and spotted Teddie, his body had been on edge, vibrating with the muscle memory of what it had been like to hold his ex-wife in his arms, to feel her body arching beneath his and hear her soft gasp of climax.

Last night had transformed memory into reality, and now, lying among the warm mussed-up bedding, breathing in the scent of her skin, his body was already craving her again.

Unsurprisingly.

Right from the moment she'd reached for him he'd been enslaved. And not just by her beauty or the way her body had melted into his. She'd taken the heaviness from his heart, made the blood run more lightly in his veins, and he'd never met anyone like her before or since.

Despite the undeniable attraction between them, Teddie had been keeping him at arm's length. Until last night, when she had led him to his bedroom and he had felt like an exile returning to the promised land.

He breathed out once, then got up swiftly and walked into the bathroom. Stepping under the shower, he closed his eyes, tipping his head back under the warm water, and instantly he felt his body harden, his brain dazzled by the memory of Teddie naked, sliding down his body, cupping him in her mouth—

His eyes snapped open and he punched off the water. It

still didn't feel real: to be able to touch her again, to have her consent to kiss and caress her freely, to stretch out her body beneath his.

But it had happened.

And the relief was unimaginable—as intoxicating and potent as wine. And even more potent was the knowledge that she had felt the same way too. Even if she hadn't stated her desire out loud, he'd have felt the urgency in her, felt a need as explicit and unequivocal as his own, and the tautness of her nipples and the slick heat between her thighs had been answer enough.

And holding her whilst she slept… He had liked it that she had curled against him, had enjoyed almost against his will the possessive feeling it had provoked, even though it was the kind of primitive he-man response he would normally despise.

But it was daunting, knowing how easy it would be to lose himself in Teddie. Look at how he was feeling now. Already he could feel the previously insurmountable barriers around his heart starting to crack apart, like pack ice feeling a spring sun.

Only, that wasn't going to happen.

Not this time.

Yes, he wanted Teddie back in his bed full-time. But now, knowing now what he did about her childhood, he knew what was required to make her stay there—she needed stability and certainty, something vast and unshakable, and with his business about to go public he was in a position to give her and George what they deserved.

Because last night hadn't been just about sex.

A muscle flickered in his jaw. It had been about momentum and, just like in business, once you had momentum that was the time to push on to the next step.

In Teddie's case that meant convincing her to marry him.

Outside, he heard George's voice and Teddie's reply. Instantly his skin was prickling, his heart bumping against his ribs as he walked out of his bedroom, down the stairs and into the brilliant sunshine.

Teddie was leaning forward, laying the table, her dark hair swinging loosely across her shoulders, and in her pale pink sleeveless blouse and sawn-off denim shorts she looked like a very sexy castaway. Beside her, George was eating a bowl of yoghurt.

'Daddy—Daddy, we're having...we're having...' Looking up from his breakfast, George hesitated, a small frown of concentration creasing his forehead. 'What are we having, Mommy?'

Glancing over to where Aristo was standing behind her son, Teddie felt her heart start to beat unevenly.

Waking for the second time, she had found it agonisingly hard to leave the lambent warmth of Aristo's body. But she'd had no choice. Like most young children, George woke early and, although he'd been sleeping in longer since they'd arrived on the island, she hadn't wanted to risk him waking up and discovering her bed empty.

Her pulse fluttered forward like a startled deer.

Or, worse, waking up and finding her in Aristo's room.

Daylight hadn't changed her mind. But although she was willing—eager, in fact—to share his bed, she had no illusions. Sublime sex hadn't been enough to save their marriage four years ago, and it was not enough to rebuild their relationship now.

That didn't mean that she regretted what had happened. On the contrary, she knew it would happen again and she wanted it to—because she wanted him: the one, the only man whose touch left her begging for release.

Especially here, on this beautiful island paradise. Here they were far away from the demands of real life, and it was easy to live in the moment and not think further. And when it ended, as it undoubtedly would, when they returned to New York, she would move on with her life.

So why expose George to this sudden temporary change to her sleeping arrangements? He was three years old. Plus, he'd only just found out that Aristo was his father and, although he'd taken it very well, she understood enough about children—and her son in particular—to know that it was a huge, *permanent* tectonic change to his life.

Besides, he had no understanding of sex, let alone the complex dynamics of his parents' relationship, so how could she hope to explain that she and his father hadn't loved each other enough to make their marriage work, but the sexual charge between them was too powerful to resist?

The thought of trying to do so made her brain feel as though it was being pressed in a vice.

She cleared her throat. '*Pites*—I think that's what Melina said they're called.' She forced herself to look at Aristo.

He nodded. 'You mean the little pies?' Reaching down, he ruffled George's hair. 'They used to be my favourite when I was your age. They're delicious.'

George twisted round to look at Teddie. 'I want to have them *now*, Mommy.'

He tugged at her hand and she let him pull her from her chair. 'Well, I don't know if they're ready...'

'Can I go and ask Melina? Can I?'

Her arm tightened around her son but, resisting the urge to draw him against her leg like a shield, she nodded. 'Don't run—and don't forget to say please,' she called after him.

There was a small sea breeze shimmying across the terrace and she tucked a stray strand of hair behind her ear. She knew she should say something, only she couldn't think of a single word.

As Aristo took a step closer she felt a rush of panic. What if he tried to kiss her and George saw?

Edging behind the table, she gave him what she hoped was a casual smile. 'Did your mother make them?'

'Make what?'

He stared at her in a way that made her muscles tense. Not quite hostile, but wary. Her smile stiffened, her heartbeat suddenly swift-moving, erratic.

'The pies?' she prompted. 'You said they were your favourite when you were George's age. I thought your mother...' Her voice faded. His expression hadn't altered outwardly, but there was a slight tension in his manner that hadn't been there before.

Aristo shrugged. 'My mother's more of a hostess than a cook.'

He studied her face calmly. Last night she had not only acknowledged and accepted the irresistible sexual pull between them, but she had also shared her past with him, and he'd been hoping that if he could get her to drop her defences again then maybe, finally, she might consider sharing the future with him.

Only, judging by Teddie's cool demeanour this morning, she was still not ready to trust him completely. For a moment he considered giving her some space, but he had a responsibility to make this work, to make her see why it had to work.

'What are your plans for later?' he asked abruptly.

She glanced up at him, her eyes wide and clear. 'Nothing. The pool, probably—why?'

'Because I thought you and I might spend the afternoon together.' His dark gaze roamed her face. 'Just the two of us. There's something I want you to see...'

'You're sure that Melina is okay about this?'

Turning towards Teddie, Aristo picked up the hand that

was clenched between her knees and squeezed it. It had taken some persuasion to convince her to leave their son back at the villa. Now that she was here, though, he was determined to let nothing interfere with his plans.

'I'm one hundred per cent sure,' he said firmly. 'You *are* allowed to have child-free time. Besides, Melina adores George, and he loves spending time with her—and if there's any problem we can be back in ten minutes. That's why we're taking the boat.'

Grinning, he gestured towards the front of the speedboat, where Dinos sat with one hand resting lightly on the wheel.

'And Dinos gets to go fishing without Melina getting on his case, so everyone's happy.'

Teddie shook her head, smiling back. 'I've never really understood fishing—it seems so boring.'

'It's not boring—it's shopping, but with a rod.'

His eyes gleamed and she punched him lightly on the arm. 'Clearly you've never been shopping.'

'Clearly you've never been fishing,' he countered.

Her eyes widened. 'And *you* have, I suppose?'

She felt a rush of heat as his gaze swept over her.

'Only once.'

He lowered his head, brushing his mouth against her cheek, his warm breath sending a flutter of sensation across her skin so that she felt a bite of hunger low down.

'But I was careless and I let her get away,' he whispered.

His head dipped and he kissed her mouth softly, his hands tangling in her hair, pulling her closer as the boat's engine slowed and then stopped.

Lifting his mouth, he glanced past her. 'We're here.' Turning towards her, he held out his hand. 'Come on—let's go see the rest of my island!'

It was more rugged at this end, Teddie decided as Aristo led her away from the beach and an extremely happy Dinos.

Instead of being sandy, the beach was pebbled and the sea was a deep nautical blue.

The light was soft through the olive trees, but as the path climbed upwards she soon started to feel breathless.

'Sorry!' Slowing his pace, he glanced down at her, his expression contrite.

Frowning, she stared at the olive grove. 'It didn't seem like a hill from down there.'

He grinned. 'It's not far now.'

She could hardly believe it was the first time she had left the villa since arriving. But it was hard to keep track of time on the island, and the days had blurred in a haze of eating, swimming and sleeping.

Although neither of them had slept much last night.

The thought popped into her head and this time the heat on her face had nothing to do with the sun.

'This is it.'

Aristo had stopped beside her and, turning with relief to where he was looking, she felt her heartbeat skip backwards as she stared down at the ruins of some kind of monument.

She breathed out softly.

'It's actually why I bought the island.'

He spoke quietly but she could hear the emotion in his voice.

'It's incredible.'

She shook her head, hardly able to take in what she was seeing. Juxtaposed against an impossibly turquoise sky, the pale stone columns looked fantastical, so that she half expected a centaur to step out from behind one.

'Can we get any closer?'

Nodding, he drew her against him, his hand sliding up her back as his mouth covered hers.

Heat flooded her and she could feel herself melting, her body softening against the hard breadth of his chest.

Breathing out unsteadily, he lifted his mouth, and stared down at her, his dark eyes gleaming. 'Is that close enough?'

Heart thudding, she gave him what she hoped was a casual smile and lightened her voice. 'I was talking about the ruins.'

'Come on, then.'

He caught her hand in his and they followed the sage-scented track down the hillside, past clumps of almost violently pink cistus.

Up close, the ruins were breathtaking. Standing in the shadow of the columns, it was impossible for her not to be impressed by their size—and the fact that they were still standing. But it wasn't just about size or age, she thought, gazing at them in silence. It was about the human cost of building it. How had they got the stone there? And how long had it taken for them to carve it with such precision?

His hand closed around hers and, turning to him, she smiled. 'Is it a temple?'

He nodded. 'To Ananke,' he said softly. 'Goddess of destiny and necessity. She's very important because she directed the fate of gods and mortals.'

He was kissing her as he spoke, feather-light but feverish kisses against her mouth and throat. She was losing concentration, losing herself in the feel of his lips on her skin.

Drawing back slightly, she frowned. 'I've never heard of her.'

'Shh!' He held up his finger to his lips, but he was smiling. 'I need to keep in her good books until after I've floated the business.'

Teddie glanced at him uncertainly. Why was he bringing up work now—here? It seemed almost sacrilegious, not to say out of place, but the hazy sunshine was touching his dark eyes with gold and she felt dizzy with a longing that was almost like vertigo.

'I thought it was hard work and a go-getting attitude that built your empire,' she said teasingly.

His mouth curled upwards and he took a step closer, so that suddenly she was breathless with his nearness.

To hide the tangle of desire and excitement twisting inside her, she slipped free of his grip, stepping sideways and behind a pillar, darting out of reach as he followed her.

'You're not telling me you really believe in all that stuff about destiny?' she said, as he caught her wrist and spun her against him. Her pulse butterflied forward as she felt his muscles tighten.

'I used to not,' he said slowly.

She swallowed. There was a tension in the air, a stillness and a silence, as if a storm was about to break, and she had to count the beats of her heart to steady herself.

'So what changed your mind?'

He lifted his head, and their gazes locked. 'You did. When you decided to meet Edward Claiborne in my hotel.'

She looked startled—and confused, Aristo thought as her green eyes widened.

'I don't understand.'

'That's okay. I didn't either. Not until we got here.'

He stared past her at the ruined temple, his pulse oscillating inside his head, wanting, needing to find the words that would make her change her mind—

'That first evening, when you and George went to bed, I was so tense I couldn't sleep. So I went out for a walk and I ended up here.' He frowned, remembering how he'd felt suddenly calm and resolute as he'd wandered between the columns. 'I couldn't stop thinking about everything that's happened. You being at the Kildare. Me going to your apartment. All of it so nearly didn't happen—and yet it did.'

Her hand tightened in his. 'I wasn't even supposed to be there. Elliot was. But he'd double-booked himself so I had to go instead,' she said quietly.

'That's exactly what I'm talking about. Don't you see, Teddie? You and me meeting again—it's fate. Every single thing that's happened could have gone a thousand different ways, but each time fate's pushed us closer. We're meant to be together…we belong to each other.'

Teddie blinked. She wanted to believe him, and he made it sound so compelling, so plausible, so certain. It was why she'd fallen in love with him.

Remembering those long late-night phone calls, she felt her pulse jump in her throat. But then Aristo had always been able been a good storyteller. Only, she already knew how their story would end.

Something of her thoughts must have shown on her face. Dropping her hand, he took a step closer and captured both her arms, tightening his hands around her shoulders.

'Are you happy?'

She looked up at him in confusion. 'What do you mean?'

'Are you happy? Here? With me?'

His words sent her stomach plunging, but even as she considered lying, she was nodding slowly. 'Yes, but—'

'But what?'

She frowned. 'But it's not that simple.'

'It could be,' he said fiercely. 'And I want it to be. I just need you to give our relationship a second chance. To give *me* a second chance so I can be the husband you deserve and the father George needs. I want you to marry me.'

She couldn't speak. She was too scared that she would agree to what he was asking—just as she'd done four years ago.

Her heart gave a thump.

She was scared too, of what would happen if she said yes. Their marriage might have lasted six months on paper, but even before their honeymoon had ended she had taken second place to his work. And now his empire was even bigger, his workload more demanding. How was he going to find the time for a wife *and* a child?

Wyatt had certainly never managed it, and she and her mother had just learned how to live with his absences. But she didn't want that for George. To know what he was missing but be powerless to change it.

Only, what would happen if they split up? How would George react? Having only just bonded with his father, he might choose to stay with Aristo. Would she lose her son as well this time?

The thought made her legs start to shake.

'George needs me.'

'Of course he does.' He sounded genuinely shocked. 'I would never take him away from you. You've done an incredible job, caring for him on your own for three years, but I don't want you do have to do it on your own any more. I want to be there for you—for both of you.'

'I can't marry you.' She pressed her hands against his chest until she felt him release his grip, and then he took a step backwards, giving her space. 'I'm sorry, Aristo, but I can't—I know it feels like things can work out between us, because I feel it too. But this isn't real life, and once we leave the island it won't be the same—you know that.'

Her throat felt as if it was lined with sandpaper.

'You and I—' she looked up at him, her eyes blurry with tears '—we are impossible.'

'Any more impossible than Elliot choosing to meet Claiborne at *my* hotel? Or you stepping in for him at the last moment?' His dark gaze was burning into her face. 'The impossible happens all the time, Teddie.'

She shook her head. 'You hurt me.'

The tremble in her voice seemed to belong to a completely different person. She hadn't meant to say it so bluntly, let alone out loud and to Aristo, and the shock of her admission silenced her.

'We hurt each other,' Aristo said after a pause. 'But we're not those people any more, so let's forget them and what happened then. Marry me and we can start again.'

Teddie stared at him in silence. It would be so easy to say yes. So much between them was good, and she knew how happy it would make George, and how miserable he was going to be if they returned home without Aristo. But how much worse would it be if his father was a full-time presence in his life?

She gave a small shake of her head. 'That's not going to happen, Aristo.'

Her voice was calm. Everything was so beautiful—the sunlight, the temple, the shimmering blue sea stretching away to the horizon, their new mood of intimacy and of course Aristo himself—and she didn't want to make it ugly with a stupid, pointless argument.

Nothing moved in his face. He held her gaze. 'We could make it happen.'

'But we don't need to.' She tried again to lighten the atmosphere between them. 'You asked me if I'm happy, and I am. We both are. So why add unnecessary complications?'

She could almost see him examining her words, deliberating and weighing up his response. Her heartbeat accelerated. His expression was one she recognised, for she'd seen it often, when he had been on the phone or at his laptop at their home, and it hurt that he was treating his ex-wife and child like some glitch at work.

Aristo frowned. He could sense her retreating from him—could feel their mood of easy intimacy starting to shift into something more strained—and even though he'd been the one to introduce the topic of marriage he felt irrationally angry with her.

'For someone claiming to want honesty and openness you're being a little disingenuous. Surely marriage would simplify matters between us. It will certainly simplify matters for George.'

Teddie stared at him in silence for a moment. 'How? By moving him away from the only home he's ever had to live in some uptown mausoleum? I told you before—he has friends, a routine, a life.'

'And now he has a father. Or am I less important than some random three-year-old he sits next to at lunch?' He shook his head dismissively. 'Kids change friends all the time at that age, Teddie.'

'I know that,' she said sharply. 'And, no, I don't think you're less important—just deluded. Listen to yourself! We bumped into one another in a hotel less than a week ago and now you want us to remarry. I mean, who does that, Aristo?'

He kept his gaze hard and expressionless. 'We did. Four years ago. Okay, it was seven weeks, not one.'

'And look how that turned out!' She stared at him in disbelief. 'It was hardly a marriage made in heaven.'

Aristo steadied himself against the pillar. The script he'd prepared inside his head was unravelling—and faster than he could have imagined. *Focus*, he told himself. *Remember why you brought her here.*

'This time will be different. In six weeks I'm floating my business on the stock exchange. Leonidas Holdings will soon be a household name. I can give you and George everything you need, everything you've ever wanted.' Some of the tension left his muscles and he exhaled slowly. 'You could both come to the ceremony. They might even let George ring the bell.'

Teddie felt as though her legs were going to give way. She felt dizzy, misery and fury tangling with her breath. She'd thought they were talking about getting married, and yet somehow they'd ended up talking about his business.

Even now, when he was proposing, she was somehow relegated to second place.

'So that's what this is about? Some photo op for the Leonidas empire.'

'No, of course not.'

'Why "of course not"?' she said shakily. 'Everything you do is ultimately about business.'

Uncoupling her eyes from his, she took a step backwards, her shoulders tensing, her slim arms held up in front of her chest like a boxer. Only, somehow the gesture made her look more vulnerable.

'We should never have married. Whatever happened in your bed last night doesn't change that, and it certainly doesn't mean we should marry again.'

'Teddie, please...'

'Can't you see? I don't have a choice.' She could feel the tears, and knew she couldn't stop them. 'There's no point in talking about this any more. I'm going to go back to the boat now.'

As she darted past him she heard him swear softly in Greek, but it was too late—she was already halfway up the path, and running.

CHAPTER EIGHT

SLAMMING HER BOOK SHUT, Teddie tossed it to the end of her bed.

It was a romantic novel, with a heroine she really liked and a hero she currently hated. She'd been trying to read for the last half-hour, but she couldn't seem to concentrate on the words. Other more vivid, more significant words kept ping-ponging from one side of her head to the other.

She could practically hear Aristo's voice, feel the intense, frustrated focus of his dark gaze, smell the scent he wore on her own skin—even though she'd showered, his phantom presence was still flooding her senses. Her heart was suddenly beating too fast.

The walk back to the boat had seemed never-ending. She had half expected him to follow her, if only to have the last word. Then she'd been scared that he'd wait and make his own way back, leaving her to somehow explain his absence to Dinos.

But she needn't have worried on either count. He had turned up perhaps five minutes after her and seamlessly picked up where he'd left off earlier in the day, engaging Dinos in conversation about his day's catch.

Back at the villa, their son's innocent chatter had been a welcome distraction, but the whole time she'd been dreading the moment when they would be alone again.

Only, again she needn't have worried, for Aristo had politely excused himself after kissing George goodnight.

And she should have been pleased—grateful, even—that he had finally got the message. Instead, though, she had felt oddly disappointed and, lying here now, she still couldn't shift the sense of loss that had been threatening to overwhelm her since she'd turned and walked away from him at the temple.

Rolling on to her side, Teddie leaned over and switched off the light, reaching inside herself for a switch that might just as easily switch off her troubled thoughts.

But her brain stayed stubbornly alert.

Perhaps she should close the shutters.

Normally she only shut the muslin curtains, liking the way the pale pink early-morning light filtered softly through them at daybreak. But tonight the room felt both too large and yet claustrophobic, and she knew closing the shutters would only add to the darkness already inside her head.

Besides the temperature had risen vertiginously during the afternoon, and she wasn't prepared to shut out the occasional whisper of cool sea air.

It hardly seemed possible that only this morning she had made peace with herself, accepting that the sexual longing she felt for Aristo was not shameful in any way, nor something she would come to regret. That it just *was* and there was no point in questioning it or fighting it.

But, although she was willing to give in to the temptation of a sexual relationship with Aristo, marriage was something she was going to continue resisting. She'd spent too long dealing with the chaos and devastation caused by the men in her life to let it happen again to her or her son.

Gazing at the moonlight through the curtains, she felt her heart contract. Maybe a fling wasn't what she would chosen if she could have had exactly what she wanted. But, as she'd already told him, she couldn't have that, and right now it was enough. All she wanted to do was live each minute as fully as possible until the inevitable moment of their separation when they returned to New York.

And it could have worked—only, typically of Aristo, he'd had to push for more—

Her stomach muscles tensed, frustration slicing through her. Nothing was ever good enough for him. He had a beautiful home in one of the most vibrant, exciting cities in the world, another in Athens, this mythically beautiful island and who knew how many other properties scattered across the globe? He owned a string of hotels and resorts and could probably retire now. But she knew he would never stop, that there would always be something driving him onwards, chasing him to the next goal.

Right now it was getting Teddie to marry him. And if she agreed to that then it would be something else.

Why couldn't he have left things as they were? Why couldn't he have just enjoyed the absence of complication in this new version of their old relationship? What was so wrong with allowing things to remain simple for just a few more days?

She didn't understand why he couldn't be satisfied, and she was tired of not understanding. Suddenly and intensely she wanted to talk to him.

Swinging out of bed, she snatched up a thin robe, pushing her arms into the sleeves as she walked determinedly across her bedroom. But when she reached the door she stopped, the rush of frustration and fury that had propelled her out of bed fading as quickly as it had arisen.

Did she really want to have this conversation now?

No. *Only, how could she not?*

Maybe he wasn't her husband any more, but she was going to have to deal with Aristo on a regular basis—and how would that ever work if she allowed the issue of re-marrying to sit unquestioned, unanswered between them?

Knowing Aristo as she did, he wasn't going to give up without a fight. So why not take the fight to him?

Heart thumping, she opened the door and walked purposefully out into the softly lit hallway. But before she had gone even a couple of paces her feet faltered and she came to an abrupt standstill, her pulse beating violently against her throat as though it was trying to leap to freedom.

Aristo was sitting on the floor, his long legs stretched out in front of him and blocking her way. As she stared down at him in stunned silence his dark gaze lifted to her face, and instantly she felt her shoulders stiffen and her heart begin to beat even faster.

'What are you doing?' she said hoarsely.

Holding her breath, she watched as he got to his feet in one smooth movement.

He shrugged. 'I couldn't sleep. So I got up to do some work, only I just couldn't seem to concentrate.' He looked up at her, his mouth curving crookedly. 'This may come as a surprise to you, but apparently everything isn't ultimately about business after all.'

She recognised her own words, but they sounded different when spoken by him. Less like an accusation, more self-deprecating. But even if that was true, she knew he was probably just trying a new tactic.

'So…what? You thought you'd stretch your legs instead?' she said, glancing pointedly at his long limbs, her green eyes wide and challenging. 'What do you want, Aristo?'

His gaze didn't shift. 'I want to talk to you. I was going to knock on your door.'

'But you didn't.'

'Your light was off. I thought you must be asleep.'

She hesitated, then shook her head. 'I couldn't sleep either. Actually, I wanted to talk too. I was coming to find you.'

Aristo felt his chest tighten.

Watching Teddie practically sprint away from the temple, he'd had to summon up every atom of willpower to stop himself from chasing after her and *demanding* that she agree to what was clearly the only possible course of action open to them. Despite his frustration at the relentless circular dynamics of their relationship, and her stubborn, illogical opposition, he'd held back.

He'd felt too angry. Not the cold, disbelieving anger he'd felt four years ago, when he'd returned to their apartment to find her gone, or even the gnawing, twisting fury at learning he was father to a three-year-old he'd never met.

No, his anger had been hot and tangled with fear—an explicable fear, not new but still nameless—and that had angered him further because he couldn't control what he didn't understand. He'd known that he needed time to cool off, so he'd forced himself to stand and watch her disappear, to wait until his heart beat more steadily. And then back at the villa, he'd made himself turn in before her.

Of course he hadn't been able to sleep. His room still resonated with her presence from the night before. But even if it hadn't, he would have been incapable of thinking about anything but her.

And it wasn't just about the sex.

In a lot of ways that would have been easier, more straightforward. He gritted his teeth. But then nothing about Teddie was straightforward. She was an impossible to solve magic trick—thrilling and compelling and mystifying.

Look at her now. She might say she wanted to talk, but the expression on her face was an almost perfect hybrid of defiance and doubt, and he could sense that she was holding her body ready. Maybe ready to fight but, knowing Teddie, more likely ready to flee.

He felt the muscles of his face contract. He didn't want to fight with her any more, and he certainly didn't want to make her run.

Only, they couldn't just stand here in the darkness for ever.

'I don't want to force this...' He spoke carefully, willing her to hear his words as an invitation, not a trap. 'So I'm going to go downstairs and sit by the pool. If you want to join me that's great, and if not then I'll see you in the morning.'

Outside, the air was slightly cooler and he breathed in deeply, trying to calm the thundering of his heart. Had he said enough to reassure her that they could survive this conversation?

He wasn't sure, and as the silence stretched out into the night he was on the verge of turning and walking back into the villa. Then he saw her walking stiffly out onto the deck.

She stopped in front of him, close enough that he could see her eyes were the same colour as the wild pines that grew in the centre of the island, but not so close that she couldn't bolt back into the darkness.

'I don't want to argue,' he said after a moment.

She held his gaze. 'And you're saying I do?'

He held up his hands. 'No—that's not what I meant. Look, Teddie, I'm not looking for a fight. I'm just trying to fix this.'

'Fix what?' She glanced up at him, and then away into the darkness. 'Me? Us? Because I don't need fixing, thank you very much, and there is no us.'

'So what was last night about?'

'Last night was about sex, Aristo.'

'Not sex—passion,' he said softly.

'Whatever! It's just chemistry, pheromones.' She made her voice sound casual, even though her fingernails were digging into the palms of her hand. 'That's all.'

'*That's all?*' he repeated incredulously. 'You think last night was run of the mill?'

'No, of course not.' Her cheeks flushed. 'I'm not saying what we have isn't special. I know it is—that's why we've got this arrangement. So can't we just enjoy it? Do we have to keep talking about marriage?'

A muscle flickered in his jawline. 'Yes, we do. This "arrangement" works here, but it's not practical long-term.'

'Practical?' She took a deep breath. 'I thought we were talking about passion, not putting up some bookshelves.'

He gazed at her steadily, but she saw something flare in his dark eyes.

'So how do you see it working, then, Teddie? Is it going to be sex in the afternoons, when George is at school? Are we going to have to get up early and move beds every time one of us sleeps over?' His lip curled. 'But I'm guessing you don't even have a spare bed, so what will happen? Are you expecting me to sleep on the sofa?'

Her hands clenched into fists. 'That's the point. I'm not expecting anything. And you shouldn't expect anything from me—particularly marriage.'

She might as well not have spoken. Even as she watched him searching through that handsome head of his for some new line of attack he was already speaking.

'You told me you wanted us to be honest with one another.'

Heart pounding, she stared at him in mute frustration. 'So be honest! What you really want from me is sex, but you *need* me to be your wife because you want a wife.'

'Not just *a* wife. I want *you*.'

She shook her head. 'You don't want me—not really.'

'I know you don't believe that.'

'You don't know anything about me,' she snapped. She was starting to feel cornered, hemmed in by his refusal to see anything except from his own point of view. 'And what's more you don't want to know.'

Watching his jaw tighten, she knew that he was biting down on his temper.

'That's not true.'

'Yes, it is. You have this idea of what a wife should be, and I'm not it, Aristo.' She took a breath, trying to stay calm. 'Please don't bother trying to pretend I'm wrong. There's no point. I know I'm not enough. I've known that since I was five years old—'

She broke off, startled not just by the stunned look on Aristo's face but by the words she'd spoken out loud, for up until now her the subject of her father had always been a conversational no-go area.

'What are you talking about?' he said slowly.

She shook her head, not trusting herself to speak, frightened by what she might say next. 'It's nothing,' she said finally. 'Just a sad little story you don't want to hear.'

His heart in his mouth, fearful of losing her but more fearful of chasing her away, he watched her walk into the darkness, counting slowly to ten inside his head before following her.

She was sitting by the pool, head lowered, feet dangling into the water.

'I do want to hear it. I want to hear everything.'

The beams from the underwater lights lit up her fine features as though she was standing on a stage, about to perform a monologue—which she was, in a way, he thought, watching her slim shoulders rise and fall in time with her breathing.

There was a tight little pause, and then she said quietly, 'The first time my dad left I didn't miss him. I was too young—just a baby. He came back when I was about George's age, maybe a bit older.'

She lifted her face and his breathing stilled at the expression on her face. She looked just as he imagined she would have done as a little girl, just like George had looked when he'd told him that he was his father—solemn and shy, eyes wide with wonder.

'What happened?' He made himself ask the question but he already knew the answer. He could see it in the pulse beating savagely in her throat.

'He stayed long enough that I minded when he left, which was when I was about five. And then again when I was eight, then nine.'

She looked up at him briefly and he nodded, for he had no idea what to say.

'He was always chasing some get-rich-quick scheme, making promises he couldn't keep, borrowing money he couldn't pay back, gambling the money he did have on the horses. And sometimes he'd get out a pack of cards and teach me a trick. He was good—he probably could have made a career out of magic—but he liked taking risks and that's what he did when I was fourteen. He pretended to be a lawyer and got caught trying to con some widow out of her life savings.'

She looked away, and Aristo could tell that she was fighting to stay calm.

'I think he'd been lucky up until then. He was so handsome and charming he could usually get away with most things. But maybe his luck had run out or his charm couldn't hide all his lies any more. Anyway, he got sent to prison for eight years.'

Her eyes met his and she gave him a small, bleak smile that felt like a blade slicing into his skin.

This time he couldn't stay silent. 'I'm so sorry... I can't imagine what that must have been like for you.'

Nor had he ever tried. Of course he hadn't known the full story, but he had been too wrapped up in his own fears and doubts to consider it.

He'd sensed a wariness in her but, looking back, he knew that each time she'd hesitated he had simply ignored the signs and used his charm to convince her—just like he'd done in Vegas.

'Do you know what's the really sad part? Him being in prison was okay. It was actually better than how it was when he normally disappeared. You see, it was the first time I actually knew where he was. And he was pleased to see me, and that had hardly ever happened before. Usually he was distracted by some stupid scam.'

And then she'd met *him*, Aristo thought, swallowing, feeling shame burning his throat. A man who had brought her to a tall tower in a strange city, showered her with gifts and promises he hadn't known how to keep, then neglected her—not for some stupid scam, but for the infinitely more important and pressing business of building an empire.

No wonder she found it so difficult to trust. Her father had laid the foundations and he had unthinkingly reinforced her reasons to feel that way.

'I don't know how you survive something like that,' he said quietly. Except Teddie hadn't just survived. She'd faced insurmountable obstacles and triumphed.

She shrugged. 'It got worse before it got better. My mum lost it—big-time. I kept having to stay home to take care of her so my school got involved, and then I had to go and live with foster parents. Only, we weren't a good fit and I kept running away, so basically I ended up in care.'

Teddie swallowed. She couldn't look at him, not wanting to see the diffidence or, worse, the pity in his eyes.

'It wasn't all bad, though. That's where I met Elliot,' she said defiantly.

'Teddie...'

She tried to block the softness in his voice, but then she felt his hand on hers.

'Don't be nice to me.'

She pushed him away. If he touched her she would be lost, but he was taking her hand again, wrapping his fingers around hers, and she was leaning into him, closing her eyes against the tears.

'I don't want your pity.'

'Pity? I don't pity you.'

He lifted her chin and, looking into his fierce, narrowed gaze, she knew that he was telling the truth.

'I'm in awe of you.'

She bit her lip, stunned by his words. Four years ago she'd thought that hearing the truth would give him a bulletproof reason to walk away, and yet he was here, holding her close, his heartbeat beating in time to hers.

'I should have told you the truth before. But I thought you'd get bored with me before then.'

He shook his head, clearly baffled. 'Bored! Yeah, you're right—I can understand why you thought that might happen.' When she didn't respond, he frowned. 'Seriously?' he said softly. 'Don't you *know* how smitten I was?'

Her heart gave a thump; her eyes slid away from his. 'It was all so quick…and I guess you weren't really my type.'

His eyes looked directly into hers. 'You had a type?'

'Yes—no. I just meant the other men I dated weren't like you.'

Her cheeks felt hot. How could she explain his beauty, his aloofness, the compelling polished charm of a man born to achieve?

'They were scruffy guys I met in bars. You didn't even look at the bill before you paid it.'

The faint flush of colour on her cheeks as much as her words did something to soothe her remark about him not being her type, but he was still trying to understand why she thought he would have got bored with her.

There was a drawn-out silence. Teddie could feel the curiosity behind his gaze, but it was hard to shape her thoughts, much less articulate them out loud.

'It wasn't about you really—it was me. Even before we

got married I felt like an imposter. And then when I moved into the apartment I panicked. It felt like when I was child, with my dad. I just couldn't seem to hold you—you were so focused on work.'

'*Too* focused.'

He breathed out unsteadily, knowing now how difficult it would have been for her to admit how vulnerable she was—how difficult it must still be.

'You're an incredible person, Teddie, and your father was a fool not to see that. You deserved better than him.'

He brushed his lips against her forehead, the gentleness of his touch making her melt inside.

'You deserved better than me.'

Reaching up, she rested the back of her hand against the rough stubble of his cheek and his arm tightened around her.

'I never meant to hurt you,' he said. 'I just wanted it to be different with you.'

'Different from what?' she asked.

He frowned. It was the first time he'd ever spoken those words out loud. The first time he'd really acknowledged his half-realised thoughts to himself.

'From what I imagined, I suppose.'

She glanced down into the pool and then back up to his face, her expression suddenly intent. 'What *did* you imagine?'

He hesitated, his pulse accelerating, but then he remembered her quiet courage in revealing her own painful memories and suddenly it was easier to speak. 'My parents' marriage.'

Her green eyes were clear and gentle. 'I thought you said it was civilised?'

His mouth twisted. 'The divorce was civilised—mainly because they had nothing to do with it. But the marriage was positively toxic. Even as a child I knew my mother was deeply unsatisfied with my father, their friends, her home…'

He paused, and she felt the muscles in his arm tremble. 'And me,' he said.

Teddie swallowed. She felt as though she was sitting on quicksand. Aristo sounded so certain, but that couldn't be true. No mother would feel that way. But she knew that if she was upset George always worried that he'd done something wrong…

'She might have been unhappy, but I'm sure that didn't have anything to do with you. You're her son.'

He flexed his shoulders, as though trying to shift some weight, and then, turning, he gave her a small, tight smile. 'She has two sons, but she prefers the other one. The one who doesn't remind her of her mediocre first husband.'

Her hand fluttered against his face and she started to protest again, but he grabbed her fingers, stilling them.

'When I was five she moved out and took an apartment in the city. She left me behind. She said she needed space, but she'd already met Peter by then.'

Catching sight of Teddie's stunned expression, Aristo felt his throat tighten. But he had told her he was going to be honest, and that meant telling even the most painful truths.

'It's fine. I'm fine with it.' He stared down at the water and frowned. 'Well, maybe I'm not. I don't know any more.'

Teddie stared at him uncertainly. Her own mother had been hopeless, but she had never doubted her love—just her competence.

'But she must be so proud of you—of everything you've achieved. You've worked so hard.'

His profile was taut. He was still like a statue. 'Yes, I work. Unlike my half-brother, Oliver, who has a title and an estate. Not that it's *his* fault,' he added. 'It's just that her feelings were more obvious after he was born.'

His voice was matter-of-fact, but she could hear the hurt and her chest squeezed against the ache of misery lodged beneath her heart.

'But you like him?' she said quickly, trying to find something positive.

He shrugged. 'I don't really know him. He's seven years younger than me, and I was sent to boarding school when he was born. I guess I was jealous of him, of how much love my mother gave him. I've spent most of my life trying to earn that love.'

Her fingers gripped his so hard that it hurt, and he smiled stiffly.

'She left my father because she thought he wasn't good enough, and I guess I thought all women were like her— always wanting more, wanting the best possible version of life.'

'I never wanted that,' she said quietly.

The crickets were growing quieter now as the evening air cooled.

'I know. I know that *now*,' he corrected himself. 'But back then I suppose I was always waiting for you to leave me. When I came back from that trip after we argued about you giving up work, and you'd gone to see Elliot, I over-reacted. I convinced myself that you were lying. That you didn't just want space.'

He could still remember how it had felt—that feeling of the connection between them starting to fade, like a radio station or mobile phone signal going out of range so that there would be periods when they seemed to skip whole segments of time and conversation. He'd been terrified, but it hadn't been only the sudden shifting insubstantiality of their relationship that had scared him, but the feeling that he was powerless to stop it.

'I did just want space.' She looked at him anxiously. 'I wasn't leaving you.'

'I *know*.' He pressed her hands between his. 'I'm to blame here. I was so convinced that you'd do what my mother did, and so desperate not to become my father, only I ended up creating the perfect conditions to make both those things happen.'

'Not on your own, you didn't!'

He almost smiled. 'Now who's being nice?'

She struggled free of his grip, clasping his arms tightly, stricken not just by the quiet, controlled pain in his voice but by what they had both pushed away four years ago.

'I was lonely and unhappy but I didn't address those problems—I didn't confront you. I ran away just like when I was a teenager.'

'I'd have run away from me too.' His face creased. 'I know I wasn't a good husband, and that I worked too hard, but it was difficult for me to give it up because work's been so important to me for so long. I didn't understand what it was doing to you—to us—but I've changed. I understand now, and you're what's important to me, Teddie—you and George.'

She wanted to believe him, and it would be so much easier to do so now, for she could see how her panicky behaviour must have appeared to him.

Last time the spectre of her parents' marriage—and his parents'—had always been there in the background. They'd both been too quick to judge the other. When the cracks had appeared he had overreacted and she had run away.

Her eyes were blurred with tears as she felt barriers she had built long before they'd even met starting to crumble.

Maybe they could make it work. Maybe the past was reversible. And if they both chose to behave differently then maybe the outcome would be different too.

Aristo reached out and drew her closer and she splayed her fingers across his chest, feeling his heartbeat slamming against the palm of her hand.

'Please give me a second chance, Teddie. That's all I'm asking. I just want to put the past behind us and start again.'

His gaze was unwavering, and the intensity and certainty in his eyes made her heart race.

'I want that too,' she said hoarsely. 'But there's so much at stake if we get it wrong again.'

She thought about her son, and the simple life they'd shared for three years.

'I know,' he said softly. 'But that's why we won't get it wrong.'

If he could just get her to say yes…

She hesitated, her green eyes flickering over his face. He felt a first faint glimmer of hope, and had to hold himself back from pulling her into his arms and kissing her until she agreed.

'This time it will be good between us,' he said softly. 'I promise.'

Her head was spinning. It was what she wanted—what she'd always wanted. *He* was all she'd ever wanted, and she'd never stopped wanting him because she had never stopped loving him.

From the moment she'd chosen him to walk up onto that stage, his intense dark eyes and even darker suit teasing her with a promise of both passion and purpose, the world had been *his* world and her heart had belonged to him.

Her pulse fluttered. Around her there was a stillness, as though the momentousness of her realisation had stopped the crickets, and even the motion of the sea.

She searched his face. Could it be possible that Aristo felt the same way?

Looking up into his rigid, beautiful face, she knew that right now she wasn't ready to know the answer to that question, or even to ask it. She still hadn't replied to his marriage proposal—and, really, why was she waiting? She knew what she wanted, for deep down it was what she'd never stopped wanting.

'Yes, I'll marry you,' she said slowly, and then he was sliding his fingers through her hair, pulling her closer, kissing her deeply.

And there was only Aristo, his lips, his hands, and a completeness like no other.

CHAPTER NINE

SHIFTING AGAINST THE MATTRESS, Teddie blinked, opening her eyes straight into Aristo's steady gaze. It was the last morning of their holiday. Tomorrow they would be back in New York, and they would spend their first night as a family in what she thought of as the real world.

It was three days since she had agreed to become his wife—again—but even now just thinking about it made her breath swell in her throat.

She loved him so much—more, even, than she had before. Four years ago she had been captivated by his perfection. Now, though, it was his flaws that had enslaved her heart, the fact that he could feel insecure and trust her enough to admit it.

'What time is it?'

She stretched her arms slightly, her eyes fluttering down the line of fine dark hair on the smooth golden skin of his chest to where it disappeared beneath the crumpled white sheet. His hand slid over her stomach and she felt something shift and spiral down in her pelvis.

'What time do you want it to be?'

His finger was tracing the shape of her belly button, and suddenly she was struggling to speak.

'Early,' she whispered.

'Then you're in luck.' He gave her waist a gentle tug, pulling her closer so that she could feel the warmth radiating from his body.

Leaning forward, he kissed her softly, brushing his lips against her mouth, then down her throat and back to her mouth, and she pulled him closer, her fingers splaying over his shoulder as he stretched out over her.

He pushed inside her, gently at first, easing himself in inch by inch, then with more urgency. He breathed in sharply, his face taut with concentration, and she knew that he was having to hold himself back. She shivered, enjoying the power she had over him.

As though sensing her thoughts, he swore softly under his breath and then rolled over, taking her with him so that she was lying on top of him. Reaching up, he covered her breasts with his hands, playing with the nipples, feeling them harden, his dark eyes silently asking for and receiving her unspoken consent as he grasped her arms and pinned them against her body.

And then his mouth closed around her nipple, nipping and sucking at it fiercely, moving to the other breast until he felt her arching against him. He heard her gasp and, lifting his mouth, gazed up at her flushed cheeks, his dark eyes narrowed and glittering.

'You're so beautiful,' he murmured. 'I want to watch you.'

Teddie rocked against him. She could feel the impossibly hard press of his erection, could feel him growing thick, then thicker still, and she rocked faster, guiding his movement, wanting the merciless ache inside her to be satisfied.

Groaning, he let go of her arms, pulling her closer for more depth, driving into her until she began lunging forward, her whole body shaking as he tensed against her, his muscles clenching in one last breathless shudder.

Afterwards, they lay sprawled against one another, bodies damp and warm, fitting together with a symmetry that seemed to her as miraculous as any magic trick. The morning light was growing sharper, and soon they would have to get up, but for now it felt as though the beating of their hearts and the soft shadows at the edge of the room were holding back time.

Lifting her fingers, he flattened her hand against his. '"And palm to palm is holy palmers' kiss",' he said softly.

Tilting her head back, she looked up at him, her green eyes widening. 'Are you quoting Shakespeare?'

She felt her face grow hot and tight. Despite privately acknowledging her feelings for Aristo, something still restrained her from telling him that she loved him. Of course, she'd rationalised her behaviour, arguing to herself and to her conscience—in other words, Elliot—that the baseline of her love needed no public announcement or reciprocation.

Only occasionally did she wonder if it had more to do with a fear of how he would react.

Either way, it was getting harder to stay quiet—particularly if he added an ability to quote romantic lines to his armoury of charms.

He raised an eyebrow. 'Don't look so surprised. I don't just sit hunched over my laptop drooling over my bank balance. I have seen the occasional play.'

His fingers were lazily caressing her hip, and her breath caught as his lips brushed her collarbone. She leaned closer. He was so wonderfully sleek and warm, and the ceaseless rhythm of his fingertips was making it difficult for her to concentrate.

'So you like *Romeo and Juliet*?'

'Of course.'

His eyes gleamed, and she could hear the smile in his voice even before his mouth tugged upwards.

'Although I always thought there was scope for a sequel, where the paramedics arrive with an antidote.'

She held his gaze. 'You think they deserved a second chance at happiness?'

'Doesn't everyone?' He stared down at her intently, and she felt her pulse accelerate.

'That's not fair,' she said lightly. 'You can't quote Shakespeare and then look at me like that.'

Glancing down at her naked body, he groaned, and she felt him harden against the soft curve of her buttocks, felt her skin tighten in instant uncontrollable response.

'You're in no position to talk about fairness.'

Shifting forward, she slid her hand over his stomach. 'Who said anything about talking?'

Later, body aching, muscles warm and relaxed, she lay curled on her side, listening to the splash of water as Aristo showered. Outside, nothing was moving, and the faded crescent of last night's moon hung in the washed-out sky, a pale, fragmented twin for the blush-coloured sun that was starting its morning ascent.

She felt incredibly calm—and happy. There was hope now, where before there had been only doubt and fear and two damaged people circling one another. She knew Aristo now—not just as a lover but as a man. She knew where he came from, the journey he'd made to reach her, and he knew her journey too.

And from now on it would be *their* journey.

Her stomach flipped over as he walked back into the bedroom, a towel wrapped around his sleek, honed torso. His body looked as though it had been spray-painted bronze, and she lay breathless with heat and longing as he stood in front of the open doors, sunlight falling on his bare shoulders.

'Don't look at me like that,' he said without turning.

She blinked, her fingers clenching guiltily against the sheets. 'Like what?'

He walked towards her, and the single-minded focus in his dark eyes made a sharp, tugging current shoot through her.

He didn't answer, just dropped onto the bed beside her and leaned over, sliding his hands over her waist, pulling her body closer, kissing her, opening her mouth and, just like that, she was melting on the inside all over again.

Groaning, he lifted his mouth and rested his forehead against hers. 'You're not making this very easy for me...' he said softly. He shook his head. 'I can't believe we have to leave for New York this evening.'

Curling her fingers underneath the edge of his towel, she pulled him gently onto the bed beside her. 'Is that a problem?'

He sighed. 'I just want to stay here with you for ever.'

She rubbed her face against his cheek, then shifted against the pillows to meet his gaze. 'I want that too, but...'

'But what?' Reaching out, he ran his fingers through her hair, wrapping it around his hand, drawing her head back, letting his eyes roam hungrily over the length of her throat. 'We could easily stay a couple more days—a week, even.'

She stared at him, her head spinning. Did he even realise the full magnitude of his words? It wasn't just that he was offering to stay on the island but that he was prepared to neglect his business to do so.

Her heart was thumping. She'd been trying to ignore it, but their imminent return to reality had been ticking away in the back of her mind like a timed explosion, waiting to go off.

For the last few days she had been sublimely happy. They'd hardly spent a moment apart, and Aristo had never been more attentive, but part of her hadn't been able to help but wonder if that would change when the plane touched down in New York. If his promise of change would disappear along with the sand in their shoes.

Now, though, she realised that—incredibly—he had meant what he'd said, for he had just given her the proof she'd been subconsciously seeking that she didn't need to measure her happiness in days or weeks any more.

'We could…'

Sitting back, he studied her face assessingly. 'You're turning me down?'

Green eyes flaring, she nudged him with her foot. 'I don't want to wear you out. I mean, you're not as young as you used to be—'

She broke off, yelping as he grabbed her foot and jerked her towards him, his dark eyes gleaming with amusement.

'Is that right?'

His fingers began sliding up her legs, over her ankles, moving lazily over her skin, and she breathed out unsteadily, feeling her body tighten in response.

'Of course I want to stay…'

She hesitated. Her job had always been such a contentious issue between them, but she couldn't run away this time. More importantly, she didn't want to.

'But I've got opening night at the Castine on Saturday. I have to be there.'

She wondered how he would respond to her putting *her* job first, but his eyes were impossible to read.

There was a short silence, and then, leaning forward, he kissed her gently. 'Then we'll be there.'

For a moment she didn't register his choice of words, and then suddenly she realised what he'd said.

Taking a breath, she said tentatively, 'I didn't know you were planning on coming.'

His gaze was steady and unblinking. 'I wouldn't miss it for anything.'

And, tugging her body towards him, he lowered his mouth and deepened the kiss.

* * *

The next two days fell into a pattern. They woke early, then made love until the morning light grew bright enough to wake their son. They had their meals on the terrace, swapping between the pool and the beach as the sun rose. Then, after George had gone to sleep, they retreated to Aristo's bedroom where they stripped one another naked, making love until they fell asleep.

It was the hottest day today, and they had gone to the beach in search of a breeze.

Stretching out her legs, Teddie gazed up at the cloudless sky. 'I forgot to tell you—Elliot texted me.'

Aristo frowned. 'Is there a problem?'

He watched as she glanced across to where George was jumping over the tiny waves that were undulating across the pale sand. Her uncomplicated connection with their son was still a source of wonder and joy to him. As was the new easiness between them.

She shook her head. 'No, it's good news. Apparently Edward's invited a whole bunch of his celebrity friends to come to the opening night. There's a tennis player, some actors, and that singer who sang at the Super Bowl—I can't remember her name.'

Picking up her hand, Aristo kissed it. 'It doesn't matter. They're going to love you.'

Teddie smiled automatically. *But not as much as I love you.*

Her heart beat faster as he leaned forward and brushed a few grains of sand from her arm, apparently unmoved by her words.

Unsurprisingly, as they'd been inside her head.

She glanced up at him, and then quickly away. Why was she being so spineless about this? It was the perfect opportunity to tell him the truth, but the words stayed stubbornly in her throat as he laced his fingers with hers.

'Of course they probably won't all turn up.' She smiled.

'They will. And I'll be there too,' he whispered, nuzzling her neck, his warm breath making her pulse jump.

'Thank you for doing this.' She gave his hand a quick squeeze. 'You'll probably find it insanely dull as you already know all my tricks.'

His eyes gleamed. 'Not *all* of them,' he softly. 'If last night was anything to go by.'

He had never felt so relaxed. No—not just relaxed, he thought reflectively. He felt liberated. Not only had he won Teddie back, he hadn't thought about work for days. Of course he was checking his email, once in the morning and once again in the evening, but the project he'd been working towards for years no longer seemed quite as important as the woman sitting beside him and their son.

How could anything compete with getting to know George and sharing his bed with Teddie?

He glanced down at their hands, at the way her fingers were entwined with his. And it wasn't just about sex. He wanted to hear her laugh, to *make* her laugh. He wanted to watch her fix her hair into that complicated bun thing that seemed to defy gravity. To hear her mischievous voice as she pretended to be the lonely giraffe in George's favourite bedtime story.

Four years ago he'd always had a sense that she was holding herself back, and he'd mistakenly assumed it was because she wasn't committed to him. Now, though, she had admitted the truth about her past. He had gained her trust. And that knowledge was an aphrodisiac more potent than any sexual act.

He looked up as, pulling her hand free, she nipped his arm with her fingers.

'You're about to be taken off the guest list,' she said threateningly, but she was laughing.

He grinned. 'Wouldn't matter. It's your big night. Whatever happens, I'm going to be there in the front row—that's a promise.'

She leaned against him. 'I can't believe it's happening.'

She couldn't. Nor that Aristo was going to be there. It was a touching sign of his commitment both to her *and* her career. And yet another reason to reveal the depth of her feelings.

But right now she needed to concentrate on her upcoming show. She never got stage fright on the night, but in the days running up to a performance her nerves always got the better of her. And she hadn't so much as picked up a deck of cards for nearly two weeks.

Thankfully she'd brought a couple of packs with her, and now, leaving George and Aristo building an elaborate fortress out of sand on the beach, she returned to the villa and worked her way through her repertoire of tricks, some of which had taken five years to perfect.

As usual, she lost track of time, and it was only when she heard the sound of Dinos's motorboat, returning from its morning trip to the market, that she realised how long she'd been practising.

Packing away her cards, she ran quickly through the villa, down to the beach.

'Sorry,' she said breathlessly. 'I didn't realise how late it was.'

'Look what we built, Mommy!'

Grabbing Teddie by the hand, George hauled her over to where Aristo stood grinning beside a huge sandcastle.

'Wow! That's amazing! I think that is the best sandcastle I've ever seen.'

Eyes dancing, she stood on tiptoe and kissed Aristo softly on the mouth.

'And the biggest!'

Drawing her closer, he laughed.

'Daddy, can you take a picture?'

'Yes, of course he can, darling.' Teddie glanced down at her son. 'Do you want to be in it?'

Pulling out his phone, Aristo took a step backwards.

'Okay—hold your spade up, George.'

Aristo held his arm above his eyes to shield them from the sun, and was just starting to crouch down when his phone vibrated.

'Hang on a minute…' Glancing down at the screen, he frowned. 'I'm going to have to take this.'

Teddie watched in confusion as he held the phone up to his ear.

'What?' he said tersely. 'Well, can you explain to me why that's even happening?'

Without even looking back, he began walking away.

'Mommy?' George was standing beside her, staring uncertainly after his father. 'Where's Daddy going?'

'He's just got to talk to somebody. He'll be back in a couple of minutes,' she said quickly.

But five minutes later Aristo was still talking.

As Teddie tried to distract their son she could see Aristo out of the corner of her eye, pacing in circles, still talking, his shoulders braced.

It was obvious the call was work-related and, judging by the palpable frustration in his voice, there was some kind of problem—but was it really that urgent?

After another five minutes she took a reluctant George back up to the villa, having promised that Daddy would definitely not forget to take a photo of his sandcastle.

Standing in the living room, she gazed down at the beach, feeling her frustration starting to rise. But Aristo was the CEO of a huge global company, and she couldn't really begrudge him one phone call, no matter how long-winded. She was just lucky to have Elliot at home, fielding any potential work problems for her.

She glanced down to where Aristo was still pacing across the sand. It was obviously not a happy conversation, but a cup of his favourite *sketos* coffee would help restore his mood.

She was just about to head off to the kitchen when she saw him heading up the steps from the beach, moving fast, the phone still pressed his ears.

'I agree. I can't see a way round it. Okay. Thanks, Mike. We'll speak on the flight.'

Striding past her into the room, he tossed his phone onto one of the sofas. His jaw was tense, the skin of his face stretched taut across his cheekbones and, her heart hammering against her ribs, she stood in silence, feeling invisible, extraneous, frozen out.

'Is everything okay?'

He turned and stared at her blankly, almost as if he didn't know who she was, and then, frowning, he shook his head. 'No, it's not.' His eyes narrowed and he ran his hand over his jawline. 'But it's my own fault. This is what happens when I go off-grid.'

'What's happened?'

The air around him seemed to vibrate with tension.

'There's a problem in Dubai. For some incomprehensible reason they've been using single-use bottles out there and I need them replaced.'

Was that all? She felt a rush of relief. 'It's obviously just a mistake. Surely all you have to do is get someone to replace them?'

He stared at her impatiently.

'This isn't just about replacing bottles, Teddie. Leonidas hotels and resorts are supposed to be eco-friendly. If this gets out it's going to look like I'm greenwashing my business, and I can't have publicity like that—particularly when I'm about to float the company.'

Glancing down at his swim-shorts, he grimaced.

'I need to change,' he muttered and, turning, he began walking purposefully towards the stairs.

Change? She followed him, feeling slightly off balance. 'Are we going somewhere?'

He stopped, one foot on the first step, and to her agitated mind, he looked ominously like a sprinter waiting for the starter gun to be fired.

'Not we.' Turning, he locked his eyes with hers.

'I don't—'

'You don't need to go anywhere.'

Finishing her sentence, he smiled politely and she had a rush of *déjà-vu*—a familiar unsettling sensation of being demoted to 'any other business'.

'Look, this shouldn't take more than a couple of days,' he said calmly. 'Melina and Dinos will take care of you while I'm away.'

She felt a head-rush, his words pulling the blood away from her heart.

'What? You're going to Dubai?' Her legs felt flimsy suddenly, and she reached out to grip the bannister. *'Now?* Can't you send someone else?'

He stared past her, his features hard and closed. He could see the confusion in her eyes, and the disappointment in her clenched fists, and it hurt knowing that he was the cause, but he couldn't risk handing this over to someone else.

'Of course not. I need to be on the ground. I'll need to talk to the staff, and if anything's leaked out then I'll need to talk to the media. Otherwise it'll look as though I don't care about the promises I make.'

'Promises?'

Her grip against the bannister tightened. There was an ache inside her chest, cold and dark and heavy, spreading like an ink stain. 'What about the promises you made to *me*?' she heard herself saying.

His eyes didn't so much as flicker. 'Teddie, this is important. Otherwise—'

She cut him off. 'You said I was important to you,' she said flatly. 'You promised me that this time it was going to be good between us. You promised that you'd be at the opening of the Castine. In the front row.'

He frowned. 'And I will be—'

'How?' She interrupted him again. 'The opening show is on Saturday. Did you forget? Or maybe you just don't care.'

He said nothing and the chill seemed to spread to her limbs.

Aristo stared at her in silence. Her accusations stung—primarily because he couldn't deny them. He hadn't forgotten about her show, but he'd downgraded its importance—obviously, how could he not have done? There were always going to be other shows, but if he didn't go to Dubai then he would be jeopardising everything.

'Of course I care. That's why I'm going to Dubai.' His face felt so rigid with tension that it hurt to speak. 'Look, I don't want to leave you—'

'So don't!' Her eyes were fierce, the green blazing like the Aurora Borealis. 'Stay here with us—that's what you said you wanted.'

He stared at her, their conversation washing over him like the waves outside, pulling him in and drawing him away all at the same time.

He didn't want to leave her, but they couldn't stay here for ever, and this happening now was a reminder of what was at stake back in the real world—what he risked losing. Teddie might have told him that she didn't care about money and status, and he believed her, but now that she'd agreed to marry him he was determined that this time it would be perfect.

And if things got out of hand in Dubai then that wouldn't happen.

Glancing over, he saw that her eyes were too bright, but he let his anger block the misery twisting in his throat. He hadn't planned any of this, and he had no choice but to fix it in person. So why was she making it so hard? Just for once couldn't she just give him her unconditional support?

Reaching out, he took both her hands and, gripping them tightly, pulled her closer. 'Of course I care. Look, it's just one show. And I wouldn't be going to Dubai if there was any other option. But I can't risk the damage it will do to my reputation.'

Nor the knock-on consequences that damage would have when he came to issue a share price—because that was his goal. Then he would be able to join the business elite and leave his rivals in the dust.

That was his priority, in his role as husband and father.

Teddie swallowed past the lump in her throat.

She didn't recognise the man standing in front of her. Had he really just spent hours building a sandcastle with their son? Looking down at his hands, she felt her heart contract. She could feel his pulse beating frantically, urgently through his fingertips, and suddenly she understood.

This wasn't about some mess in Dubai, or his business reputation, this was about a childhood spent trying to win the love of his mother. And now he was trying to do the same with her and George. To earn their love.

That was why work mattered so much to him and why he wanted his name to be indelible.

But what would happen if he found out he was already loved? Unconditionally. Now and for ever. Maybe she could quiet the urgency inside him.

'I don't want you to go,' she said softly. Looking up into his eyes, she smiled unsteadily. 'And you don't need to go.

If you don't ever float your business, whatever that means, it won't change how I feel about you, or how George feels about you.'

She cleared her throat.

'I love you, Aristo.'

Silence.

His dark eyes rested on her face and then, lifting her hands to his mouth, he kissed first one and then the other gently.

'I can't do this now.'

His voice was quiet, careful, almost as though he was scared of breaking something.

She stared at him, her heartbeat slowing. She'd never told anyone she loved them before—not even Aristo. Other phrases of love, maybe, but not those three specific words. But she knew that the correct response wasn't, *'I can't do this now.'*

'Is that all you're going to say?' she said shakily. 'I just told you I love you…'

'I can't, Teddie.' He let go of her hands.

Her chest was too tight, and then she felt her veins flood with shock and misery as she realised that what he'd been scared of breaking was *her*.

She opened her mouth to speak, but no words came out. She'd thought she knew what heartbreak felt like but she'd been wrong.

'I'm sorry,' he said stiffly. 'I really need to change. We can talk properly when—'

Her body felt numb, and it took an effort to shake her head. 'There's nothing to talk about.'

What was there to say? That she had stupidly fallen in love with a man who saw marriage as a means of tying up loose ends? She wasn't even going to try and deny the sexual chemistry between them, but everyone knew that passion burnt itself out. And if she hadn't been the mother of the heir to the Leonidas empire their relationship would no doubt have ended when they'd finally satisfied their hunger for one another.

He frowned. 'We'll talk when I get back. If you don't want to stay here, then go to the apartment. I'll make arrangements.'

'There's no need.' She was striving for calm. This wasn't going to turn into some slanging match. At least then this trip would be a happy memory for George. 'We won't be moving into the apartment. I'm not going to marry you, Aristo.'

His eyes narrowed. She could feel his disbelief, his frustration.

'Because I'm flying to Dubai? Don't you think you're overreacting a little?'

Time seemed to wind back four years, and suddenly it was as though they were back in the bedroom of that tall tower in New York, when he'd told he was going on yet another business trip.

She shook her head. 'No, I don't. This isn't about you flying to Dubai, it's about us being honest—or did you forget that too?'

He didn't respond, but his jaw tightened. 'I have been honest. I didn't plan this mess, and I can't just delegate it to someone else.'

He looked so serious, and so very beautiful, and she loved him so much, but it wasn't enough to make her turn a blind eye like her mother had done. She knew Aristo was telling the truth—only they were small, inconsequential truths. She needed security in her and George's life, the emotional not the financial kind, and there was nothing to be gained by avoiding the bigger, uglier truths.

She took a deep breath. 'Just tell me the truth. Would you honestly have asked me to marry you if I hadn't had George?'

He glanced away, and in that small gesture she knew that it was over.

Her face didn't change. 'You should change, and then we need to tell George you're leaving.'

Silently, she willed him to look at her, but after a moment he turned and began walking upstairs.

CHAPTER TEN

TAKING A DEEP BREATH, Teddie closed the door to her wardrobe and gazed at her reflection in the mirror.

It was the first time she had been able to look at herself since getting back from Greece. Up until now she'd been too hollowed out with misery and despair to face the red-eyed proof of her failure, but tonight she had no choice.

Tonight was the opening night of the Castine, and she was going to be up on stage in front of the fifty personally invited guests of Edward Claiborne. Getting to this moment had been brutal, and the pain had been like nothing she'd ever experienced. But tonight was her night—hers and Elliot's—and she wasn't going to let herself or him down.

Turning slowly, she glanced over her shoulder. The jumpsuit was black...fitted. The top was guipure lace, long-sleeved, buttoning up the front to a high collar. The trousers were plain except for the long fringe that was really only visible when she moved.

Spinning round on her towering heels, she stared at herself critically, pressing her hand flat against her stomach in an effort to calm the jumping jacks twitching inside her.

She looked serious but that was okay. Perhaps a little intimidating. But that was okay too. An audience should have a healthy respect for magic, not see it as some kind of sideshow at a kids' party.

And it was a beautiful jumpsuit. Too expensive, of

course, but she would be earning real money now, and for the past few days she had been uncharacteristically reckless in her spending. She'd given Elliot a new evening suit, as a thank-you for looking after the business, and she'd been lavishing George with presents too.

Her throat tightened. Not to say thank-you to him, but sorry. Sorry for giving his stupid, selfish father a second chance.

As soon as she'd seen Aristo in the lounge at the Kildare she should have walked straight past him and into a lawyer's office. Instead she'd not only let him back into her bed, but into her heart, had even agreed to marry him.

Her mouth trembled. She could forgive herself for falling into his arms. Given the sexual pull between them, it had been inevitable. But she had no excuse for falling in love with him again.

Breathing out unsteadily, she closed the wardrobe door.

She'd always been so concerned about not turning into her mother, but maybe she was actually more like her father, for she had let herself be seduced by daydreams instead of seeing the reality. And, just like Wyatt, she'd stupidly believed she could beat the house.

Gazing at her reflection, she let her hand drop.

One small mercy was that, thanks to some last vestige of self-preservation or common sense, she hadn't told George that she and Aristo were getting married. But she'd still had to explain to their overtired and confused son why they weren't going to Daddy's apartment.

She blinked back tears as she remembered their journey back from Greece.

When Aristo had left the island George had been moderately upset. But he'd assumed that they would be staying there until his father returned. It had only been when Teddie had told him that they were going back to New York without Aristo that he'd got hysterical.

She hadn't wanted to lie, and the truth was that she didn't know when—*if*—George would see his father again, but she had told him how much Aristo loved him, how much *she* loved him, and just saying the words had made her feel more confident. Whatever happened, she would be there for her son.

Her stomach clenched and she felt suddenly sick. She wished that she hadn't actually thought of Aristo by name. Ever since she'd got back home she'd been trying not to do so, even in her head. It just seemed to make her feel so much worse, and right now she didn't want to feel anything.

George had been inconsolable, refusing to leave Melina and then crying himself to sleep on the plane. Then and only then had she allowed her own tears to fall.

Thankfully, Elliot had been waiting outside her apartment. Opening the door of the taxi, he'd pulled her into a bear hug with one arm, scooped George into the other. He'd taken charge of everything—paying the driver, carrying in the suitcases and then ordering pizza.

He hadn't cross-examined her, but then he hadn't had to ask anything. He knew her well enough to see the pain behind her careful smile as she'd cut the pizza into triangles.

George had calmed down, but she was still worried about him. He hadn't slept in his own bed since they'd got back, and he seemed quieter than usual. Thankfully he loved his babysitter, Judith—a retired pre-school teacher and grandmother of twelve—so at least she wouldn't have to worry about leaving him tonight.

She heard the doorbell ring and instantly froze, her heart hammering against her ribs. But of course it was only Elliot's voice drifting through the apartment.

'Teddie?'

She took a breath. 'I'll be right there,' she called, knowing that she was wasting her time. He would see right through the over-bright note in her voice.

She felt suddenly guilty and stupid for wishing that it was Aristo waiting patiently in the living room for her to emerge instead of her friend—her good, loyal friend.

Guilty because Elliot deserved better, and stupid because right now she had no reason to believe that she would ever see Aristo again, given that he hadn't so much as texted her once.

Her mouth trembled and, feeling the threat of tears, she picked up her bag and walked quickly across her bedroom. She'd promised herself that tonight she was not going to cry any more tears for Aristotle Leonidas until the show was over.

And that was what was going to happen, for—unlike her ex—she actually kept her promises.

'You okay, babe?'

Edward Claiborne had sent a limo to collect them and, glancing across its luxurious interior, Teddie saw that Elliot's face was soft with worry.

She nodded. 'I will be.' She gave him a small crooked smile. 'And this evening will help, you know—being up there. I'll forget everything but the cards.'

Maybe she might even forget her shattered heart.

'I know.' He grinned. 'And I know I'm your buddy, and that makes me not really a guy, but I gotta say you look smoking hot tonight, Teds!'

She managed a real smile then. 'You look good too, Els.'

The limo was slowing, and she could see the doorman stepping forward to greet the car. Her pulse started to accelerate. They had arrived.

Elliot held her gaze. 'You ready?' he said quietly, holding out his hand.

Nodding, she reached out to take it as the door swung open.

The Castine was the perfect setting for a magic show.

There was no sign outside the door, and it was situated in a side street far away from the hustle of the city. On the first floor there was a bar and dining room, and on the second a jewel-coloured lounge that, despite its size, offered both intimacy and drama.

She could hear the buzz of people talking and the clink of glasses beneath the beating of her heart, and as she stepped under the spotlight she knew that all eyes were on her.

They just weren't his eyes.

And, despite knowing it was pointless, she still couldn't stop herself from quickly scanning the front row, unable to quell one last tiny hope that he would be there.

Of course he wasn't.

But they were an easy crowd to please—and not just because of the waiters discreetly circulating the room with bottles of *prestige cuvée* champagne. Clearly, like their host, they appreciated magic, and as their applause filled her head she was finally able to admit what she had been fighting so hard to deny. She missed Aristo. Missed him so much that words were simply not adequate to describe the sense of loss, the loneliness, the aching bruise of his absence.

She already knew that she would never again share that dizzying chemistry with a man. But, together with their son, it was something nobody could ever take away from her—it would always be there inside her. And now, looking out into the blur of faces, she felt a tingling heat run down her spine, for she could almost feel him there in the audience, a shadow memory of that first time they'd met.

Two hours later it was over.

'Teddie, that was marvellous.' Edward Claiborne was the first to offer his congratulations. 'I honestly think she's a genius, don't you, Elliot?' He massaged his forehead. 'I've watched a lot of very talented magicians in my time, but with you I find it impossible to separate technique from performance. When you're doing a trick, I know something's happening but I just don't see it.'

'Well, he's happy,' Elliot said softly as they watched him shaking hands with an Oscar-winning actress. 'And he has some great connections.' He grinned. 'Hollywood, here we come!'

She punched him lightly on the arm. 'Hollywood is in California. You hate California, remember? That's why you moved to New York. Besides, it's hardly convenient for George's nursery.'

She made her way slowly back to the dressing room. In some ways the evening had been a triumph, but it had been a bittersweet triumph, for she knew now that no amount of applause and admiration would ever make her feel as complete as lying in Aristo's arms.

But there was no point in thinking about that now. *This is supposed to be your night, remember,* she told herself. And, taking a deep, cleansing breath, she walked into her dressing room.

And stopped.

Aristo was sitting on a chair, his head bowed, what looked like a phone clamped between his hands. As she took a faltering step backwards, her fingers gripping the door frame for support, he looked up, his dark eyes fixing on her face.

'Aristo.'

He was wearing a dark suit, and it was a shock seeing him dressed so formally, but of course this was real life now, and that meant work. Her stomach clenched as he stood up, but she forced herself to hold his gaze.

'Hello, Teddie.'

She stared at him in disbelief, trying to ignore the pain ripping through her chest. 'What are you doing here?'

Her arms had lifted to cross automatically in front of her body, and she willed her legs to stay upright.

'I came back for the show,' he said quietly. 'I told you I wouldn't miss it for anything.'

Her heart thumped inside her chest. 'Except you did. It just finished. But it doesn't matter.'

Her voice sounded wrong, too high and breathless, and she knew it didn't match her careless words, but she was past caring what he thought of her.

'You had something more important to do. You had to fix a crisis in Dubai.'

He shook his head. 'There was no crisis in Dubai.' His mouth twisted. 'Only, I'm such an idiot I had to go all the way there to work that out.'

'I thought you had to be there to talk to your staff and the media.'

Staring down into her eyes, he let out a long breath. 'I was wrong. I realised the only person I needed to talk to, the only person I *wanted* to talk to, was you. That's why I flew back to New York.'

He ran his hand across the face, and with a jolt she realised that although he was dressed in a suit, he looked nothing like the suave businessman who had left her on the island. His shirt was creased, and his unshaven face looked paler than usual, and he was actually holding his passport, not his phone.

He must have come straight from the airport and he must be exhausted. The two thoughts collided inside her head.

But, remembering how he'd let go of her hands when she'd told him she loved him, she pushed the thought away.

'Well, I'm sorry you had a wasted trip,' she said stiffly. 'Two wasted trips.'

'Teddie, please—'

'No, Aristo. I don't want to do this.' She shook her

head. Her whole body was shaking now. 'If you want to see George, then talk to my lawyer.'

'I don't want to talk to your lawyer. I want to talk to you.'

He took a step forward, and even if she hadn't heard the strain in his voice she would have seen it around his eyes.

'I made you a promise. I said I'd be here, and I was. I know I wasn't in the front row. I got here too late for that. But I was at the back the whole time.'

She stared at him, blinking, remembering that moment when she'd felt his presence, how she'd thought it was just a phantom memory of the first time they'd met.

'I should never have left you. I knew I was making a mistake, but…' He paused, then frowned. 'But when you told me you loved me I panicked.'

His choice of words felt like a slap to the face. Could he make it any plainer that her feelings were not reciprocated? Her heart was a lead weight in her chest and she felt suddenly brutally tired.

'I don't need to hear this, Aristo,' she said flatly. 'I just want to go home.'

He shook his head. 'Not until you understand.'

Reaching out, he took hold of her arms, but she shook him off.

'I do understand. You don't love me and you only wanted to marry me because of George. I get it, okay? And now I want to go home.'

'Your home is with *me*, Teddie. And not just because of George.'

She started to shake her head, but he took her face between his hands and this time she didn't pull away.

'Look at me,' he said softly.

At first she resisted, but finally she lifted her chin.

'Maybe it was true at first, but not any more. George is our son, but he's not the reason I want to marry you. I want you to be my wife because I love you.'

'If you love someone you don't panic when she tells you she feels the same,' she said stubbornly.

He shook his head, his dark eyes narrowing. 'Not true. I love you, Teddie. And I did panic. As soon as you said those words I couldn't think straight. I just knew that I couldn't let anything mess up my business, the sale of the shares.'

'But I told you I don't care about any of that.'

He nodded. 'I know you don't—but I did. Look, I know it sounds crazy, but I've been chasing perfection all my life—first at school, then with work. And each time I reached my goal I'd set myself a new one.'

He frowned, as though baffled by what he was saying.

'When you told me you loved me I couldn't just say the words back to you. I wanted to *show* you how much I love you, and I thought that meant fixing things in Dubai, that if I couldn't do that then I didn't deserve to win you back. I was so desperate to make that happen, and so scared that it wouldn't. But as soon I got there I realised that I wasn't fixing anything, only breaking *us*, and that's why I came back to New York—'

His voice cracked, and he breathed out unsteadily.

'Because I can't lose you again, Teddie. The business, my career—none of that matters if we're not together. That's all I want...to be with you.' He stopped, his dark eyes on hers. 'If you'll have me. Do you think that's possible?'

Her heart was fluttering against her ribs, but her love for him felt solid and unbreakable. 'I do,' she said softly. Holding her breath, she searched his face, saw hope and love shining in his eyes.

He pulled her closer, wrapping his arms around her, burying his face against her hair. 'I thought I'd broken us.'

She felt his grip tighten.

'I was so scared that I'd ruined it, that I'd lost you.'

'You can't lose me. You're my husband, my heart.' Lifting her face, she smiled weakly. 'But if you'd told me you were coming I'd have saved you a seat.'

He loosened his grip. 'I think I left my phone on the plane.'

She looked up at him. 'What about Dubai?'

'I don't know.' He frowned, then slowly began to smile. 'And what's more I don't care. I really don't.'

'I need to sit down,' she said shakily.

He led her into the dressing room and pulled her onto his lap, his arms curving around her body so tightly that she could feel his heart beating in time to hers.

'You're an incredible magician, Teddie.'

Leaning back into his chest, she felt her face grow warm. 'Thank you. It went really well. But Elliot and I are definitely going to have to find some other acts to keep it fresh. Maybe a hypnotist—people always love watching that.'

'Maybe I could have a go. I've been practising a trick.'

His eyes were warm and steady on her face.

'You have?'

'You can never have too much magic in your life.'

His gaze drifted slowly over her face and she felt her pulse start to accelerate.

'Well, you can certainly audition.'

'Right now?'

'Okay.' She laughed. 'Do you have a stage name?'

He shook his head. 'I don't think I'm going to need one. It's going to be a one-off performance.'

She smiled. 'So what trick are you going to do?'

'It's one I made up myself.'

His face was soft and unguarded and she stared at him, transfixed by the glitter in his dark gaze.

'It's called the reverse disappearing ring.'

'Do you want me to tell you when to start?'

His eyes locked onto hers and she felt her blood lighten as he shook his head.

'No need. I'm done.'

She frowned, and then as he lifted her hand she felt her heart open up as she gazed down at the beautiful emerald ring on her finger.

'It was a bit last-minute in Vegas,' he said hoarsely. 'But I wanted to do it right this time.'

'I love it,' she whispered, her eyes filling with tears. 'And I love you.'

'I love you too.' Dipping his head, he kissed her gently. 'More than I ever believed I could love anyone. So much more. And it's going to be so good between us.'

Reaching up, she stroked his cheek. 'Do you promise?'

'Oh, yeah,' he said slowly.

And she believed him because she could see the certainty and love he was feeling reflected in his eyes as he lowered his mouth to kiss her again.

EPILOGUE

DESPITE THE WEATHER forecast predicting rain, the clouds emptied from the sky just as the limousine turned slowly into Broad Street. Glancing up at the sun, and then back down to the diamond ring on her third finger, Teddie smiled. She knew from personal experience that predicting the future was an extremely unreliable business.

'Do you like it?'

Looking up into Aristo's face, she nodded slowly. The ring was a surprise gift to mark six months of married life—*happily* married life—and it was stunning, but the soft grip of his hand around hers was what was making her heart swell with love.

Any fears she might have had of history repeating itself were long forgotten. Aristo had been true to his word and as eager as she to make sure that the mistakes of the past stayed in the past.

'Of course I do.' Reaching up, she stroked his cheek, her green eyes suddenly teasing.

'Do I get one every six months?'

He laughed, and then his face grew serious. 'I know it's not an official anniversary—it's just that I wanted to give you something…you know, because last time—'

'I know.' Leaning forward, she kissed him, cutting off his words.

Their engagement had lasted a year, and both of them had enjoyed the wait. They'd argued a little, and laughed a lot, and then finally they'd had a small private wedding with friends and colleagues that they'd planned together. Elliot had given Teddie away, and George had been a very solemn page boy, and now six months had passed and they had never felt closer.

'I love you,' she said softly.

Sliding his hand around her waist he pulled her closer. 'I love you too.' His eyes were steady and unblinking. 'And I know it's been a difficult lately, but that's going to end today.'

'It's fine. I understand.'

Today, after months and months of intense preparation, Aristo was finally floating his business on the New York Stock Exchange. He'd been working long hours, and she knew he was trying to reassure her now, but it was something she no longer needed.

The unhappy memories of their first marriage were just memories.

Now, instead of staying late at the office, he'd invite his team back to the apartment so that she and George could be a part of the process, and she wasn't left feeling isolated and lonely. And on the odd occasion when he had been forced to travel he had kept his trips as short as possible, often returning earlier than expected or taking her and George with him.

She squeezed his hand. 'And today's going to be better than fine.' Feeling the limo start to slow, she kissed him fiercely, her eyes burning with love. 'I'm so proud of you, Aristo.'

He shrugged. 'I work with some good people. They're really what's made this possible.'

'You do, and you've worked incredibly hard too.' Her gaze fixed on his face. 'But I wasn't talking about the business,' she said softly. 'I was talking about you.'

Aristo stared down into her clear green eyes, his heart pounding.

The limo had stopped. If he looked out of the window he would be able to see the six Corinthian columns of the New York Stock Exchange. For so long he had dreamed of this moment—the short walk to the legendary neoclassical building that would turn his business into a global brand.

But over the last eighteen months he'd made a far more important journey with the woman sitting beside him. Teddie had transformed his life. She had taught him how to hope, to believe and to love.

Of course he was pleased that the IPO was happening, but the appeal of the big deal had dimmed. His life with Teddie and George was far more satisfying and exciting than any boardroom negotiation, and he savoured every moment spent with his wife and son for he had come so close to losing them.

As soon as they stepped out onto the pavement time seemed to speed up exponentially, so that one moment the second bell of the day was ringing to start trading on the Leonidas stock and the next they were mingling with underwriters and executives from the business.

And now they were back in the limousine, on the way to a party for the staff at Leonidas headquarters.

Teddie breathed out slowly. After the frenzy of the trading floor the car seemed incredibly calm and quiet.

She felt Aristo's gaze on her face and, turning, she smiled up at him. 'Happy?' she said softly.

He nodded. 'It went well.' Leaning forward, he tapped on the glass behind the driver's head. 'Bob, can you take us to the apartment now, please?'

Teddie frowned. 'But what about the party? Don't you want to celebrate?'

He shook his head. 'I spoke to the staff this morning. They know how pleased I am, and this party will be a lot more fun for them without the boss breathing down their necks.'

Biting her lip, she touched her fingertips to his cheek. 'Does that mean I get to have you all to myself?'

Pulling her into his arms, he laughed.

'Yes.' He paused. 'And no. I thought we needed some time as a family, so I've arranged for us to spend a week at the island. We're just going to pick up George on the way.' His eyes dropped to her mouth. 'But once we're there we should have time to celebrate...*privately*.'

The dark heat in his gaze took her breath away. 'I like the sound of that,' she said slowly. 'And we have got a lot to celebrate.'

More than she would ever have imagined, and more than Aristo knew.

Watching her expression shift, Aristo frowned. 'I'm happy it's all over, Teddie, but going public with the business isn't what I want to celebrate.'

His face was so serious, so open, that she could keep the secret to herself no longer.

'I wasn't just talking about the business.'

Leaning closer, she fixed her eyes on his handsome face, wanting to see his reaction. He looked at her uncertainly and, picking up his hand, she pressed it gently against her stomach.

'We're having a baby.'

For a moment he didn't speak—neither of them could: their emotions were too intense, too raw. But it didn't matter. She could see everything he was feeling in his heart, everything she needed to see burning in his eyes as he pulled her closer and kissed her passionately.

* * * * *

THE GREEK'S
FORBIDDEN
INNOCENT

ANNIE WEST

This story is for Helen Sibbritt.
Thank you so much for your enthusiasm,
support and never-failing good cheer!

CHAPTER ONE

'TAKE A DEEP BREATH, Carissa, and tell me slowly.' Mina held her friend's shoulders tight. 'And another.' She nodded encouragingly as Carissa's breathing grew more normal. 'That's better.'

While Carissa focused on her breathing, Mina's gaze searched for the source of her friend's distress. But there was nothing unusual in the entry to the other woman's apartment. No blood. No disarray. No intruder. Just a large pink suitcase.

Yet something was definitely wrong. Carissa, the most easygoing person she knew, had grabbed Mina before she could open the door to her own apartment and yanked her in next door. There was real fear in Carissa's china-blue eyes.

'Come and sit and tell me about it.'

'No!' Carissa shook her head and a cloud of golden curls spilled around her shoulders. 'There's no time. They'll be here soon. *But I don't want to go.* I *can't* go.' Tears filled her eyes as her voice wobbled. 'I want Pierre! But he's not here in Paris. He's abroad.'

That at least made sense. Pierre was Carissa's boyfriend.

'Don't fret. No one's going to make you go anywhere you don't want to.' Mina kept her voice calm, ushering her friend into the small sitting room and gently pushing her into a seat. Carissa's whole body shook and her face was stark white.

Mina had received enough bad news herself to recognise shock. Her mother had died when she was young and just five years ago, when she was seventeen, her father had died unexpectedly from a brain aneurism.

Memories stirred of that terrifying time, held hostage

in a palace coup after her father's funeral. Then her sister Ghizlan's sacrifice, forced to wed the coup leader, Huseyn, so he could become Sheikh. It seemed a lifetime away from Mina's life now in France.

'Tell me what's up so I can help.' Mina pulled a chair close and took Carissa's hands. Her face was, for the first time Mina could recall, bare of make-up and her shirt wasn't buttoned right. For Carissa this was a fashion catastrophe. More like Mina's usual look than her own.

Mina's frown deepened. 'Has someone hurt you?'

Her stomach clenched as she remembered the day of the coup, the drench of icy fear as a soldier manhandled her, stopping her escape with brutal efficiency. She recalled the adrenalin rush galvanising her to fight back. It was the first time anyone had laid a hand on her. The first time she'd become aware of the sheer, physical power men could exert over women. Until then, Mina's royal status had protected her.

Carissa was trusting and gentle, always looking for the best in people. If someone had taken advantage of her—

'No, it's nothing like that.'

Mina's shoulders sagged. Relief rushed through her. In the years they'd studied together at a prestigious Paris art school, and since, she'd never seen Carissa distraught like this.

'So who is coming? Where don't you want to go?'

Carissa's bottom lip quivered and she blinked hard.

'Alexei Katsaros is sending someone. They'll take me to his private island.' A shudder ran through her. 'But I don't want to go. I can't. Even when Dad told me about it, I never thought it would actually *happen*! You have to help me, Mina. Please.'

Mina's worry eased and with it her frantic heartbeat. Not a life-and-death situation, then. She knew who Alexei

Katsaros was. Who didn't? He was a megawealthy IT entrepreneur. Carissa's father was one of his executives.

'Is it an invitation to visit your father? I'm sure Pierre would spare you for a short vacation.'

Carissa shook her head. 'This isn't a vacation. It's an arranged marriage! Dad told me he hoped to organise it but I never thought he'd bring it off. Alexei Katsaros can have his pick of women.'

Mina said nothing. Carissa was extraordinarily pretty and sweet-natured. That, plus her innate desire to please, would appeal to lots of men.

'I can't go through with it, Mina.' Carissa's fingers bit into hers. 'I could never love a man like that, so hard and judgemental. He wants a trophy wife, who'll do what he wants when he wants. My father's told him I'm pretty and biddable and...' Her shoulders shook as the tears became sobs. 'I never thought it would come to this. It seemed impossible, laughable. But I don't have a choice. My father's *counting* on me.'

Mina frowned. Arranged marriages she knew about. If her father had lived he'd have organised one for her.

'I'm sure no one will force you into anything.' Unlike in Jeirut. Her sister had been forced into an unwanted marriage and Mina remembered feeling utterly helpless at being unable to prevent it. It had been a miracle when, against the odds, the pair later fell in love. The match had seemed doomed to end in misery. 'Your father will be there. If you explain—'

'But he's *not* there,' Carissa wailed. 'I don't know where he is. I can't contact him. And I can't say no to Mr Katsaros. Dad warned me there'd been some trouble at work. He didn't say what, but I think his job's on the line. He's hoping this marriage will smooth everything over.' Carissa clung to Mina's hands, her fingers curling into talons. 'But I could never marry such a hard man. He has a new woman every week. Besides, Pierre and I are in love. We're getting married.' A flicker of happiness transformed her teary features.

'You're getting married?' Mina stared. She shouldn't be surprised; the pair were besotted.

Carissa's smile died. 'We were planning to elope next weekend, when he's back from this business trip. Pierre says it will be easier to face his family with a fait accompli.'

Pierre rose in Mina's estimation. He was a lovely guy but he'd never stood up to his stiff-necked family who wanted him to marry someone from old French money.

'But I can't marry him if I'm forced to marry Alexei Katsaros!' Carissa's tears overflowed.

'Did Katsaros *say* he wanted to marry you?'

'As good as. He said my father had told him about me and he was anxious to meet. He believed we'd find a lot in common and that we had a future together.' Carissa bit her lip. 'I tried to fob him off but he didn't hear a word I said. He cut me off and said his staff would be here in an hour to collect me. What will I do?'

Mina frowned. She didn't like the sound of this. He might be rich but that didn't excuse rudeness or give him the right to order Carissa around.

'Tell me again exactly what your father told you.'

But as Carissa spoke, Mina's hope that her friend had overreacted dissolved. There'd recently been a rift between her father and his employer. After years of faithful service it seemed Katsaros might dump him. Mina couldn't approve of Mr Carter's plan to use Carissa to cement his position, but such things happened. Several of Mina's peers in Jeirut had been married to older men they barely knew to strengthen family or business links.

She gritted her teeth, watching Carissa's hands flutter as she related the one-sided conversation with Alexei Katsaros. He hadn't invited Carissa to his island hideaway but simply informed her of the travel arrangements. As if she were freight to be transported, not a woman with a life of her own.

Mina's temper rose like steam from a kettle.

She prized her freedom, appreciating how different her life was in Paris, away from a world where every major decision was made by the male head of her family. Western women accepted freedom as their right, not knowing how precious that was. And here was some billionaire bully, trying to snatch that from Carissa. With the help of her own father!

It wasn't right.

'And there's nothing I can do.' Carissa sniffled.

'Of course there is. They can't force you onto the plane. Or into marriage.'

'I can't not go. What about my father's job?' She hiccupped. 'But if I go, what about Pierre? His family will find a way to stop our wedding.'

Mina wanted to tell Carissa to grow a backbone and stand up for herself. But Carissa wasn't made that way. Besides, she cared for her father, though he'd got her into this mess. Plus it sounded, from other things she'd said, as if Mr Carter hadn't recovered from his wife's recent death. That might explain why he'd slipped up at work. A good employer would make allowances for grief. Mina suspected Alexei Katsaros was a domineering tyrant, considering no one but himself.

Irresistibly, her thoughts dragged back to those fraught days after her father's death. Her future and her sister's had hung in the balance, their fate determined by a man with little sympathy for their hopes and wishes.

Mina remembered the horror of being utterly powerless.

She refused to let Carissa become a chattel to buy her father out of trouble, or satisfy Katsaros's desire for a convenient, biddable wife.

'I've packed a bag. I can't reach my father, so I'll have to go. But it means leaving Pierre.' Carissa wrung her hands and Mina felt something snap inside.

Carissa was sweet but she had as much grit as a marshmallow. Between them, Katsaros and Carter could herd her into a marriage that would make her miserable for the rest of her life. Mina couldn't change her friend into a woman who'd look a thug in the eye and send him packing, or tell her father he couldn't marry her off to a stranger. But she *could* delay things long enough for Carissa and Pierre to marry. A few days, a week at most.

'How long before they collect you?'

Carissa's answer was drowned by a sharp rap on the door. She gasped and grabbed Mina's hands.

The last shred of doubt fled Mina's brain as she read her friend's terror and despair. Carissa was a pushover, but Mina wasn't.

She got to her feet.

'Still no sign of Carter, sir. He hasn't been home.'

Alexei's grip tightened on the phone and he ground his teeth in frustration. But he refrained from chewing out the head of his London office. It wasn't MacIntyre's fault Carter had done a bunk. Alexei should have acted sooner, but initially he hadn't wanted to believe Carter's guilt. The man had been at his side for years, the only person Alexei really trusted.

That was why his betrayal cut so deep. Trust came hard to Alexei. He'd seen his mother betrayed and cast aside, made into a victim and her life shortened, because she trusted too easily.

Alexei bore a lot of the blame. He'd been gullible, falling for his stepfather's charm, believing the man genuinely cared. He'd persuaded his mother to let the guy into their lives. Too late they discovered he'd only cultivated

Alexei to get to his mother and her dead husband's insurance payment.

No one could accuse Alexei of gullibility now.

That was what made it so remarkable that, despite his caution, he'd come to believe in Carter. It wasn't just his way with numbers. His almost uncanny knack for identifying problems and possible solutions. It was his reticence, his scrupulous separation of business and personal life. He'd been the perfect executive.

Until his double-dealing came to light.

Alexei felt that sucker punch of betrayal. Worse this time because he should have known better. He was no innocent kid.

'Keep me informed. Have the investigator check in daily.'

'Yes, sir. Of course, sir.'

Alexei ended the call and scraped a hand through his hair, telling himself he'd grown soft. He should have acted sooner. Now he had to play catch-up.

He swung round to pace, ignoring the turquoise water and white sand beyond the window. He didn't want to be in the Caribbean, no matter how restful his private retreat. He wanted to be wherever Carter was. The man's depredations had been deep. Not enough to destabilise Alexei's business but enough to send a ripple of disquiet through anyone savvy enough to discover Alexei had been duped.

Despite his policy of employing the best, most innovative people in the industry, Alexei Katsaros *was* his company as far as the market was concerned. He'd worked hard to establish one of the world's leading software companies and build a reputation as a canny entrepreneur. His nose for success was only rivalled by his company's groundbreaking IT solutions. News of his fallibility would crack that image and damage his company's position.

Damn Carter. Where was he hiding?

Alexei slammed to a halt as he heard a vehicle through the open window.

At last. The ace up his sleeve.

Alexei breathed deep, easing cramped lungs, assuring himself that now, *finally*, he had the upper hand.

He crossed to the window and watched as the four-wheel drive pulled up. The driver's door opened but before Henri could get out the front passenger door swung open and someone alighted.

Alexei's brow twitched into a frown. That couldn't be her. He waited for the rear door to open but it stayed steadfastly shut. Henri walked ponderously to the rear of the vehicle and pulled out a single suitcase of candy pink.

That was all. One suitcase and one passenger, though not the passenger he expected.

Alexei's frown became a scowl. The call from Paris had assured him that she'd been collected from her apartment and deposited on his jet. Yet surely this wasn't Carter's daughter. He'd expected a fashion tragic with mountains of luggage.

His gaze rested on the svelte figure of a woman who stood, hands on her hips and head back, surveying his home. Far from being addicted to high-end fashion as he'd been led to believe, she wasn't dressed in designer casuals for a tropical island holiday, but for…what? A yoga class? An artist's garret?

Understanding took root. *That* was it.

Carter, when he'd raised the preposterous idea of a match between Alexei and his daughter, had waxed voluble about the girl he'd never mentioned in years of employment. He'd wittered on about her beauty and charm, her sweet disposition and eagerness to please. And her aspirations to be an artist in between shopping. She lived in Paris, playing at an artistic career, no doubt funded by the money Carter had embezzled from Alexei.

Pain radiated from Alexei's jaw down his neck to his tight shoulders.

He yanked his thoughts from Carter's crimes to the man's daughter.

She took her pretensions seriously. Or perhaps the outfit was for his benefit, though surely it wasn't designed to please a man. Flat black shoes, black leggings and an oversized black T-shirt that gaped over one shoulder.

Definitely not Alexei's style. He preferred a woman who dressed like a woman.

Yet even as he dismissed Carissa Carter as not his type, his gaze lingered on the length of shapely legs silhouetted in black. Long legs, the sort of legs he'd enjoy wrapped around his waist during sex.

His gaze flicked higher, skimming her slight figure. He supposed, in the right gear, she'd be a perfect clothes horse, but personally he preferred a woman whose curves were more abundant.

Then the tilt of her head altered and he found himself face-to-face with her.

She was too far away for him to make out her features properly. Just good bone structure and dark hair pulled ruthlessly back into a bun. He had the impression of a wide, mobile mouth, but he wasn't paying attention. His thoughts were on the sudden throb pulsing through his belly.

It couldn't be attraction. Not for the daughter of a criminal. A woman whose lifestyle had probably fed her father's depredations. He had no proof Carissa Carter knew of her father's crimes, but she'd benefited. Maybe she'd been in on the scheme, eager to fund her easy life in Paris. Alexei couldn't trust her. He'd play the part of eager suitor, pretending he was in the market for a wife.

As if he needed a third party to find him a woman!

He stared back at her, expecting her to duck her head and pretend not to see him.

Instead she stood motionless, watching as if *he* were under the microscope. It was a curious feeling. Alexei was used to people inclining their heads in agreement or deference. Except women, who tended to stare.

Carissa's bold regard was something altogether different. It sent heat skittering down his spine, drawing every sense to hyperalert.

Finally, after she'd looked her fill, she turned to Henri. Alexei caught a flash of white teeth as she smiled but it was the coltish grace of her movements that held his attention. There was a fluidity to her supple body that reminded him of a Russian ballet dancer with whom he'd once shared a fiery affair. Alexei recalled not only the dancer's grace but her athleticism and body awareness that had taken sexual pleasure to a new level.

He watched Carissa Carter saunter towards his house. Shoulders back, head up, yet she didn't march. Instead that loose-limbed stroll was a symphony of sensual femininity.

For his benefit?

Of course.

His guest might play at being the bohemian artist, but if she was her father's daughter, she'd have her eye on the main game, getting Alexei's money.

For the first time since he'd learned of Carter's betrayal, Alexei smiled.

He didn't want the woman here, except as bait to draw her father. The fact she'd accepted his summons told him she'd sell herself into marriage with a man she didn't even know. Though she knew the size of his bank balance. That regularly featured in rich lists around the world.

It could be amusing watching her try to seduce him.

CHAPTER TWO

MINA KNEW ABOUT WEALTH. She'd been born royal. But her family riches and privilege were tied to duty, responsibility and service. The palace where she'd grown up had been the nerve centre for her country's administration.

This was pure sybaritic indulgence.

As if it wasn't enough to own a tropical island rimmed with beaches so white they looked like sugar frosting, Alexei Katsaros's home was the last word in luxury. The pool wrapped around the house so every room looked out on water. There was a bar actually in the pool too, so he and his guests wouldn't have to stir from the water to get a drink.

Four-poster daybeds were scattered around the pool, their gauzy hangings romantic and alluring. Her artist's eye appreciated the cushions in turquoise, teal and jade that reflected the vibrant shades of the tropical garden and the sea beyond. Then there were the sculptures in pale stone, which she glimpsed through the greenery. She itched to detour and investigate.

Forcibly she yanked her attention back to the house. The huge entry door stood open. Beside her, Henri waited for her to precede him.

Strange, this momentary hesitation.

All the way from Paris she'd been buoyed by indignation on Carissa's behalf. Now though, Mina knew an uncharacteristic moment of doubt. A wariness at odds with her practice of facing problems head-on.

Her impulsiveness, her father would have said.

Why? Mina wasn't overawed by Katsaros's wealth, or cowed by any threat he could make.

Yet for a moment, as her gaze locked on the big man watching her from inside, something unfamiliar quivered through her. Something starkly unsettling.

An inner voice urged her to flee while she had the chance.

Of course she lifted her chin and stared right back instead.

The bright bowl of azure sky above her seemed to drop lower, the air thickening as she drew a slow, steadying breath. Still, he held her gaze.

Her bloodstream fizzed, making her fingers and the soles of her feet tingle. For a second she wondered if she'd been hit by a bolt of lightning out of the clear sky, till reason told her that was impossible.

Deliberately she turned away, feigning interest in her surroundings. Yet the image imprinted on her retinas wasn't the white mansion with its picture windows, but the powerfully built man whose eyes locked on her. Everything about him, from his wide-set stance to that deep, muscled chest revealed by his open shirt, screamed strength.

Well, Mina was strong too. No bossy tycoon would intimidate her.

Nodding to Henri, she headed for the door.

She was greeted by Henri's wife, Marie, whose smiling eyes and lilting accent made Mina relax in spite of herself.

'Alexei is eager to meet you but perhaps you'd like to freshen up first?'

Mina smiled and shook her head. The flight by private jet had been far from onerous. 'Thank you, but no. I'm eager to meet my host.'

'How…charming.' The deep voice came from beyond Marie. Its cadence drew Mina's skin tight, as if someone dragged a length of rich velvet across it. A shimmer of heat flared low in her body and she had to work to keep her expression bland.

Slowly, so slowly she seemed to feel each muscle and joint move, she turned her head towards the shadows.

Never had Mina been more grateful for her royal upbringing. She'd spent seventeen years learning to look composed and calm, even if she'd never quite mastered regal. At twelve she'd sat on podiums listening to interminable speeches. At fifteen she'd held her own at royal dinners. Her polite interest expression could fool everyone but her sister.

Which meant the man watching her through narrowed eyes had no idea she felt as if someone had sliced the tendons at the backs of her legs.

Mina's knees shook for the merest instant before she stiffened them, but her cool smile remained steady. As for the sizzle in her blood, no one else knew about that.

She waited for him to frown and say she wasn't Carissa Carter. Yet he simply stared down at her from his superior height. Could it really be that he didn't know what Carissa looked like? That flaw in her plan had kept her awake on the flight from Europe. Yet, against the odds, it appeared he didn't. So sure of himself. Arrogant enough to expect everyone to obey his every whim. So unquestioning.

Mina let her mouth curve slightly. 'Mr Katsaros. How lovely to meet you at last.'

'At *last*, Ms Carter? You've been waiting to meet me? Surely your trip was admirably quick?' His hint of indolent surprise and the tilt of one slashing eyebrow gave him an air of smug superiority.

'Oh, it was.' Mina looked down and flicked lint from her sleeve. 'Admirably so. Why, I didn't even have time to check my diary for commitments that might clash before I was whisked away. Or to arrange for someone to keep an eye on my apartment.'

She let her brow pucker in a frown. 'I hope the fruit I bought doesn't spoil while I'm away. And the milk.' She let her smile widen. 'But I understand. I'm sure you're used to wanting something and having it happen immediately. No time to waste on boring niceties like invitations or queries about whether the dates suited me.'

Below his rumpled black hair grooves corrugated that wide brow. Mina raised her hand. 'Not that it matters. I know how terribly valuable your time is. After all, what could I *possibly* have scheduled that could be nearly as important?'

From behind her Mina heard a snuffle from Henri that sounded suspiciously like a stifled laugh. Then he excused himself, murmuring something about putting her luggage away and prudently followed his wife down a corridor.

Which left Mina alone with Alexei Katsaros.

He didn't even seem to notice Marie and Henri leave. All his attention was on Mina.

If she were in the mood to feel fear it would have swamped her now, for the man watched her with the hyperawareness of a hunter. Then there was the sheer size of him, not only tall but well-built, all muscled strength beneath those straight shoulders. She'd caught a glimpse of a well-developed chest and taut abdominals that confirmed this man did far more than sit behind a desk, making money. His thighs beneath the faded jeans were those of a skier or a horseman, honed hard and strong.

Without taking his eyes off her, he slowly finished buttoning his white shirt. Then he tucked it into his faded jeans with a casual insouciance utterly at odds with the speculative gleam in his dark eyes.

Mina's manufactured smile solidified as he took his time shoving the material down, his hand disappearing behind the denim. For reasons she couldn't fathom the sight of him dressing made her pulse quicken. Her palm prickled as if her own hand slid down that flat abdomen.

'I'm sorry, did my arrival wake you?' The snap in her

words betrayed her discomfort but Mina compensated for it by slowly taking stock of his tousled black hair and the dark shadow of beard growth across that solid jaw.

His hands fell to his sides and he stepped out of the shadows. The light hit sharply defined cheekbones, a well-shaped mouth and a stern blade of nose, down which he surveyed her. Mina was reminded of precious icons she'd seen. But whereas those old saints had looked flat and unreal, this man exuded raw energy and the glint in his dark eyes was anything but unworldly. Alexei Katsaros was too… physical for sainthood. With his imposing size and posture he could model for a cavalry officer from a previous century, supercilious and deadly in a bright uniform, with a sabre at his side.

Mina repressed the warm shiver that started at the base of her spine and threatened to crawl, vertebra by vertebra, up her back.

'You know you didn't wake me. We watched each other.' His voice was both rough and dangerously soothing.

Mina couldn't explain it but he made the simple words sound almost indecent. As if they'd been naked at the time, or as if she'd watched him doing something—

'So, you're concerned about your groceries, is that right?' One dark eyebrow rose and it took a second for Mina to follow the change of subject. She was still lost in a hazy daydream of Alexei Katsaros stripping his shirt away and reaching for the button on his jeans. 'I can have one of my staff deal with your apartment, Ms Carter, since I put you to such inconvenience.'

Mina wrenched her thoughts back to the man before her. The man whose satisfied smile told her he knew he'd unsettled her. Whose tone conveyed that she'd managed to needle him with her pointed comments about being dragged away.

'That's very kind, Mr Katsaros.' She blinked up at him,

mimicking Carissa, then thought better of it. She'd never batted her eyelashes in her life and wasn't about to start.

'Something in your eye, Ms Carter?' Not by a whisker did he betray a smile yet Mina knew he laughed at her.

To her surprise, Mina had to stifle a smirk of her own. He was right. She couldn't pull off such feminine wiles. She was better to stick at being herself.

'Sand, probably.' She blinked again. 'My own fault. I insisted on driving with the window down to enjoy the breeze.'

Carissa would have shrieked at the thought of her hair getting messed up, but Alexei Katsaros didn't know that. Mina would have to get by with pretending to be a Mina version of Carissa. Less fluttery and uncertain, less overtly feminine, less willing to be bullied.

'Thank you for the offer to take care of my apartment but I prefer not to have my home taken over by strangers. I'm sure you understand.'

He understood all right. His smugness fled as he registered that she referred to his staff who'd politely yet inexorably ushered her from Carissa's flat.

'My staff disturbed you? You felt threatened in some way?' His voice was sharp.

Had he really thought she'd be happy, herded by armed bodyguards?

Mina remembered Carissa's tears and frantic fear. How would she have coped, confronting those big men with cold eyes and suave suits?

They'd been impeccably solicitous but Mina read in them the same quality she'd seen in her father's royal guards. Beneath the polish were men trained to use force. If she'd refused to go, they'd have bundled her onto that private jet without a qualm.

'Oh, I didn't feel at all threatened by anyone else while I

was with them.' She paused, letting him absorb her words. Would he understand *they'd* been the threat?

His expression didn't alter.

Clearly he had no idea how frightening it was for a woman not used to close personal protection to have stony-faced men wearing shoulder holsters usher her into an anonymous vehicle.

Suddenly weary, Mina suppressed a sigh. What was the point? He wouldn't care even if he understood.

'Your staff were polite and incredibly…efficient. I'm sure no express parcel could have been delivered to your door more quickly.'

She looked away, letting her gaze rove the white marble foyer, taking in the carved Cycladic figurine in a niche on the far wall. Mina's pulse quickened with interest but she couldn't afford to be distracted. Slowly she turned back to her host, whose hands, she noticed, were bunched in fists at his sides.

He stepped forward and Mina's nape prickled. This close she realised those intent eyes were a stunning dark green, opaque and intriguing. She'd never seen the like. Momentarily she was mesmerised. Then she dragged her thoughts back to their conversation.

'I prefer to make my own arrangements, Mr Katsaros. I'm sure you understand.'

Alexei understood all right.

He was being taken to task by a woman who didn't know she was playing with fire. Or did she believe she could set her own rules because he contemplated marriage?

That had to be it. There was no other explanation.

He'd wondered if Carter's daughter was a spoiled princess. As far as he could tell, she'd lived for years off her father's, and by extension his own, largesse, while enjoying a dilettante's life.

Now he had his answer. Carissa Carter was used to getting her own way. Spoiled rotten, he had no doubt. Her father had led her to expect an advantageous match and she seemed sure it would happen.

Yet her words disturbed him. Had she really been frightened of his security staff? Alexei barely noticed them now, just considered them a normal part of life.

He stared down at the woman who continued to surprise him. It wasn't only her plain outfit, or the accent that wasn't quite as he'd heard it over the phone, but then there'd been interference on the line. He'd imagined someone more eager to ingratiate herself. More overtly charming.

Carissa Carter was more complex than he'd imagined.

She was confident yet not in the way of a woman used to trading on male admiration. She carried herself with an intrinsic elegance that, when she looked down that straight nose at him, bordered on condescension. That intrigued. As did the intelligence shining in those sherry-coloured eyes and in the snarky undercurrent of her conversation.

He'd imagined Carter's daughter more eminently dismissible. The man had said her nature was sweet rather than incisive and that she wasn't cut out for business. Alexei had assumed she was pretty but vacuous.

How wrong he'd been.

Nor was she as he'd expected her to look. He saw no resemblance to Carter in her dark hair, luminous eyes or expressive mouth. Her skin was golden, not pale, and she met his gaze with a direct curiosity that, at any other time, he'd appreciate.

It evoked a hungry gnawing in the pit of his belly, a reminder that, despite his preoccupation with her father, Alexei was a vigorous man with healthy appetites.

He drew a slow breath, marshalling his thoughts, and was fascinated to see that, despite her sugared verbal barbs, Carissa Carter wasn't immune to him after all. Her eyes tracked the rise of his chest, her pupils dilating as if mesmerised. Then she blinked and turned away, feigning indifference.

Satisfaction stirred. He'd disliked her jabs about the way he'd got her here, had even felt a stirring of remorse. Seeing that chink in her armour pleased him.

'How remiss of me to keep a guest standing in the foyer.' Alexei smiled and watched a tiny wrinkle appear above the bridge of her nose, as if she concentrated on not reacting. Fascinating.

'Won't you come in?' He stood aside and gestured for her to precede him into the main sitting room.

'Thank you.' She inclined her head in the slightest nod.

Alexei caught a hint of perfume as she passed. Another surprise. He'd expected some expensive designer scent but this was one he'd never encountered. Instead of florals or cloying sweetness, she'd chosen a fragrance that hinted at the exotic Near East. Alexei inhaled cinnamon and spice and a warm, earthy richness that made him think, bizarrely, of veiled temptresses in gauzy silks. He canted towards her.

Fortunately she didn't notice. She entered the sitting room with that leisurely, swaying stroll that spoke of casual confidence. As if she were accustomed to a billionaire's luxury lifestyle. But then, given her father's thievery...

He watched as she caught sight of the ancient sculpture against one wall. The torso of a young man, the musculature and veining of chest and arms superbly executed, the filmy fabric of his tunic the work of a master. She stiffened and drew a sharp breath. A second later she stood before the ruined masterpiece, her hand stretching momentarily towards it before dropping to her side.

'It's magnificent.' There was genuine awe in her words. Alexei recognised it. He felt the same way about the piece.

His mouth twisted. Despite all expectation he found Carissa Carter…refreshing. Perhaps it wouldn't be so tough pretending to be interested in her till her father arrived.

'It was discovered at the bottom of the sea.'

As if his words broke the spell of artistic appreciation, she spun around, that oversized black T-shirt swirling wide. What did she look like beneath it? The rest of her was slim and beautifully formed.

'You have a very nice home, Mr Katsaros.' Her voice appealed too. It was low and musical. Not high and breathy as he recalled it from the phone call. Though he'd probably taken her by surprise with his invitation.

Alexei's mouth tightened. She was right. It had been a demand, not an invitation. Carissa had made him sound brutish and that annoyed him. But the situation demanded a swift resolution. He didn't have time for niceties.

Her eyebrows arched when he didn't respond to her small talk.

'Call me Alexei.'

'Thank you, Alexei.' Her voice slowed on his name and he felt the oddest sensation, as if she'd reached out one slim hand and trailed it down his chest, right to his belly. Abdominal muscles clenched in response. 'Please, call me Carissa.'

'Carissa.' He tested the sibilant on his tongue and saw her eyes darken. The sight sent another ripple of awareness through him. She was definitely attracted. 'You have an interesting accent. Not the same as your father's.'

Intriguingly she stiffened as if he'd hit a weak point. It was the tiniest movement but unmistakeable to a man who'd spent so long studying the vulnerabilities of business opponents.

'My father's accent is English. But we moved around a lot when I was young. I suppose mine's a hybrid.'

Alexei watched the unblinking way she held his gaze and wondered what she hid.

'Yours is interesting too.' She spoke quickly, clearly wanting to divert his attention.

Alexei was interested to find that despite his fixation on locating and punishing her father, his curiosity about Carissa increased by the moment.

He gestured for her to take a seat and sank down onto a leather lounge, crossing his ankles and leaning back.

'Russian mother, Greek father, moved to London as a kid.' He shrugged. 'Like yours, my accent's a hybrid.' More like mongrel, he silently corrected. He'd spent too long living precariously in places where the predominant language was that of the violent gangs who ruled through intimidation.

Silently Carissa nodded and sat opposite him. In contrast to her casual clothes her posture was graceful. With that long, slender neck and perfect poise he was reminded again of a dancer sweeping into a low curtsey. He could picture a tiara on her smooth, dark hair and a sheaf of flowers in her arms.

'Tell me, Carissa, have you heard from your father?'

'He's not here?' Her expression flickered but too fast for him to read it.

'No, but I'm expecting him soon.' As soon as Ralph Carter heard his precious daughter was staying at Alexei's private island he'd hotfoot it here, hoping the marriage he'd suggested would save him from Alexei's wrath. If that didn't work, Alexei had the perfect hostage to lure him from hiding.

'I see.' She chewed the corner of her mouth and then, as if aware of his scrutiny, offered a small smile. 'That will be lovely.' Once more her direct look suggested she hid something. What?

'So you haven't heard from him?'

'No. He seems to have his phone switched off. Do you need to contact him urgently?'

Alexei fought impatience. His desire for retribution against the one person he'd actually *trusted* in decades hadn't eased. Fury curdled his gut. He couldn't believe he'd been foolish enough to let Carter con him.

'Not at all. In the meantime we can get to know each other better.' That prospect grew more enticing by the moment.

She shifted in her seat, her first overt sign of nervousness. Intrigued, Alexei took his time surveying her, his fingers tracing a lazy circle on the soft leather of his chair's arm.

'I want you to be happy here, Carissa. Let me know if there's anything you want.'

'That's very kind of you, Alexei. For that matter, very kind of you to let me holiday here in this glorious place.'

She'd changed her tune. Fifteen minutes ago she'd been complaining about his staff and the speed with which he'd brought her here. What had changed?

Every sense stirred. He scented not fear but caution, as if Carissa suddenly felt out of her depth. Not so sure of herself after all?

She wasn't his target; her father was. Yet that didn't stop a frisson of satisfaction at the suggestion Ms high and mighty Carter had second thoughts about her situation. If she was cast in the same mould as her father, it would do her no harm to learn she couldn't have everything her way. Especially if she'd spent the past few years living off money her father had stolen from Alexei.

'Oh, I don't consider it a kindness, given our special situation.'

She stilled. It looked as if she didn't even breathe. 'Our special situation?'

'Of course.' This time Alexei's smile was genuine. 'Since we're marrying.'

CHAPTER THREE

MINA'S MOUTH DRIED as she watched a slow smile transform Alexei's face. It wasn't a polite expression of friendship or amusement. It was a wide grin that she could only describe as dangerous.

More than that. *Hungry.* As if he wanted to sink those strong white teeth into her flesh.

She shivered as heat licked through her. Disgust, of course. She wasn't some dish served up to satisfy his appetite.

Yet, on the thought, Mina realised her response wasn't so simple. A shiver drew her breasts tight till her nipples beaded. Astonished, she realised she was torn between annoyance and excitement.

As if she *wanted* to satisfy Alexei Katsaros's animal appetites. And hers, as well.

The realisation had her fingers clawing the arms of her chair as she fought the urge to reel back. As much at her own confusing reaction as at his overtly *masculine* perusal. He surveyed her like a man who'd just bought a woman.

She despised him. Yet despite her outrage, Mina felt a thrill of anticipation.

By the time she'd conquered her shock, there was no sign of that feral hunger in his expression. Had she imagined it?

Mina wasn't an expert on sex but she'd had her share of admirers. Men whom she found it easy to resist. For some reason they were fine as friends, but when they wanted more, Mina didn't. Yet she knew what sexual interest looked like.

She couldn't see it in his face now.

'We've only just met.' Her tone was cool.

One dark eyebrow rose. 'It was your father's suggestion that we'd make a good match. He told me you'd agreed. Are you saying that's not the case?'

Mina swallowed, ignoring the sandpaper abrasion of her throat, and wondered how best to play for time. All the way here she'd told herself Carissa had been mistaken and that Alexei Katsaros couldn't want *marriage*. He didn't need to marry a stranger. He was rich, successful and good-looking.

Also impatient, determined and self-obsessed, if his idea of finding a wife was ordering her to his island and giving her no choice!

What had she landed herself in? Surely he hadn't brought her here for a wedding!

Shock jagged through her, stealing her breath. If so, then this masquerade would be over before it began. Mina forced herself to take a deep breath and think.

'He did mention a possible marriage, but...'

'But?'

'We don't know each other! I can't agree to marry someone I don't know.'

He said nothing, just crossed his arms, the movement drawing Mina's attention to the depth of his broad chest and the muscled power of his biceps. He was a man whose physical size and fitness could daunt a woman who wasn't strong enough to stand up for herself.

'So you're here to what? Get to know me?'

'Is that so unreasonable?' Mina jumped on the idea like a lifeline. 'We're talking about a lifetime commitment.'

The hint of a smile flickered at the corner of Alexei's mouth. 'That's a refreshingly...old-fashioned view.'

Mina let her eyebrows climb. 'Marriage is a serious commitment. Why enter into one if you don't plan to make it work?' She wasn't sure why she didn't simply shrug off his comment. But marriage, like the right to make her own decisions, was something she felt strongly about. Her mother had married her country's Sheikh not for love but because her family decreed it. It hadn't been a happy match.

'I see your point.' Alexei nodded.

'So you understand I need time to determine if a marriage would work. Surely you want that too.'

'To assess if we're *compatible*?' Alexei didn't move, nor did his expression alter, yet the quality of that stare flicked a warning switch. Adrenalin surged in Mina's blood. Heat consumed her as if he'd surveyed every inch of her body with that searing scrutiny, instead of merely holding her gaze.

How did he do that?

More important, why did she react so?

Mina wasn't oblivious to men but she'd never been swept off her feet, or into bed, by one. Her history made her cautious about ceding control to any man. Before his death, her father had mapped out her life, giving her no choice, even about the clothes she wore and the subjects she studied. Since leaving Jeirut for Paris she'd devoted herself singlemindedly to art, determined to carve a career in the field she loved. The guys who tried to sidetrack her into a relationship had never caused a ripple in her world.

Now it wasn't a ripple she felt but an earth tremor.

Mina wouldn't let that daunt her.

She lifted one hand negligently. 'Before we worry about *compatible* perhaps we should start with finding out if we'd survive the marriage without killing each other.'

Alexei gave a crack of laughter. 'Good point, Carissa.' The light dancing in his eyes made him look completely different. Like someone she wanted to know.

Mina stiffened.

The first time she'd seen Alexei Katsaros, something happened that had never happened before. Her certainty had wavered and with it her confidence. Mina couldn't abide the idea of being tentative around him, like some gullible, awed girl. It was easier to confront him. She suspected if he exerted himself to be nice it would be too easy to feel the force of his charm.

Now, abruptly, as she met his smiling look, the events of the last twelve hours took their toll.

Exhaustion slammed into Mina. Despite her determination not to back down before this man, she felt herself slump. Adrenalin had kept her going. Now that dissipated, leaving her overtired limbs shaky and her head swimming.

She had to get out of here before she made a mistake. Mina was too weary to guard her tongue and thinking straight became harder by the second. This man with the piercing green eyes would trip her up, especially since she wasn't practised at lying.

If he discovered the truth, all this would have been for nothing. Carissa needed time to get away with Pierre and cover her tracks.

'I'm sorry, you'll have to excuse me.' Mina lifted her hand to cover a yawn, only to discover the fake yawn was real. 'I'm suddenly very tired.'

'You didn't sleep on the flight?' He looked surprised.

Mina shook her head. She'd been ushered onto the private jet late in the evening for the overnight flight to the Caribbean. But despite the comfortable bed, she'd had too much going on in her head to sleep.

'It's been a very long day.' She glanced at her watch, trying to calculate the time difference but to her surprise, her mind was too foggy. Tiredness and stress took their toll. 'I've been awake more than twenty-four hours.' And yesterday had been a long day, even before Carissa had dragged her into this mess. Or, to be fair, since she'd thrust herself into it to protect her friend.

Time to regroup before she said something she shouldn't.

Mina pinned on a smile, the multipurpose one she reserved for royal meet and greets. She hadn't used it in years and it felt rusty. 'I'm sorry, Alexei, but I'll have to leave you for now.' She rose, surprised at the effort it took to stand tall. Her knees were unsteady, and for a second she swayed.

'Could you point me towards my room, please?'

He loomed before her, the beginnings of a frown creasing his forehead. 'You look pale.'

'I'm fine,' she lied. How many hours had it been since she'd eaten? She hadn't been in the mood for food on the plane, refuelling on coffee and lots of it, but now the caffeine had worn off and she felt as powerful as a dandelion in a strong wind. 'If you could show me the way?'

When Alexei didn't immediately answer, Mina swung round towards the entry, remembering Henri heading down a corridor from there.

As she turned, another wave of tiredness hit and her movements lost their usual precise control. Her foot caught the edge of the plush carpet.

She didn't trip or stagger, just paused, swaying as she caught her balance.

'I'll take you.' The deep voice came from beside her ear as, to her astonishment, Alexei bent and curled his arms around her back and legs. An instant later she was in the air. Or, more precisely, in his arms, pressed against a hot body that seemed to be all solid muscle.

Mina's breath stalled, then released on a shaky sigh at how extraordinary this felt. No one had ever held her like this. She registered conflicting feelings: shock, pleasure and an unexpected desire to burrow closer. As if Alexei were someone she trusted. Or desired.

'There's no need.' The words were crisp, at odds with the strange wobbly feeling in her middle. It was impossible to sit straighter and assert control when she lay in his arms, unable to get any purchase.

Alexei ignored her words, marching out of the room.

With each step Mina felt her body move against his in a swaying rhythm that was surprisingly appealing. In other circumstances…

In other circumstances this wouldn't happen, ever.

'Thank you for your consideration,' she said between barely open lips. 'But I prefer to walk.'

That made him pause. He angled his head to look down at her and Mina was bombarded with impressions. The hard perfection of his squared-off jaw. From this intriguing angle, it was a study in obstinate power. The soaring, proud cheekbones that spoke of ancient Slavic heritage. The flare of arrogant nostrils and the fly-away effect of his winged eyebrows. The steady pump of his heart against her ribs and the power of those iron-hard arms encircling her.

Something shivered to life in the pit of Mina's belly. Something that grew as she inhaled a tempting cedar-and-citrus aftershave that melded with the hot, salt scent of male skin. Her nostrils twitched appreciatively and the shiver amplified.

Astounded, Mina watched his eyes darken, the pupils dilating.

The world eclipsed to the dark mystery of that shadowy stare, heating her in all sorts of places.

When he spoke the sound vibrated from his chest into her body. She'd never experienced anything as intimate as his voice reverberating through her while his eyes devoured her.

'Relax. I'm not going to hurt you.'

Despite the certainty he wouldn't drop her, Mina couldn't ignore the inner voice screaming at her to get away. Being this close to Alexei Katsaros was perilous, whatever his stated intention.

'I prefer to walk. If you'll kindly put me down.' Tiredness vanished, replaced with quivering watchfulness.

'And have you trip and hurt yourself?' He shook his

head, his rumpled locks swinging free. 'I wouldn't forgive myself.'

His tone was admirably sincere yet Mina read the tiny creases at the corners of his mouth and knew he was enjoying himself. Could he feel her heart hammer? She hated being vulnerable to him.

Before she could read any more, he looked away and began walking down the hall, carrying her easily, as if he carted unwilling women around every day.

Maybe he did.

'Contrary to what you might have heard, Mr Katsaros, women are capable of thinking for themselves. We don't appreciate he-men making our decisions for us. I—'

'Is that what you think I am?' Annoyingly his pace didn't falter. 'What exactly does that mean?' His jaw jutted as he ruminated. 'Someone very masculine? Someone who sees an exhausted guest and looks after her so she doesn't hurt herself?'

Mina counted to ten. If she thought it would do any good, she'd struggle against his hold. But, though fit, she was no match for all that hard-packed muscle, especially given his superior size. He was well over six feet. If Alexei Katsaros didn't want to release her she couldn't make him. The knowledge infuriated her and she began stringing together curses in her own language that she couldn't say lest he wonder how she knew Arabic.

She forced her gaze away from that annoyingly superior chin, focusing on the play of light and shadow on the ceiling as they passed down the hall.

'After all,' he continued, 'as you pointed out so eloquently, it was my fault your trip was so…precipitate. If I'd been more conscious of your comfort I'd have organised for you to travel during the day, or ensured the bed on the plane was more comfortable. I'll have it replaced.'

'There's no need for that. The bed was quite comfortable.' Even to her ears her voice sounded thin. She held on to her temper by a tiny margin. All her life she'd been taught not to reveal anger. This time she dared not lose control because he'd see it as a victory.

'Then it's a wonder you didn't sleep. Perhaps—' she caught movement in her peripheral vision and turned to see him send a teasing look her way '—you couldn't sleep because you were excited about visiting me.'

Excited! About as excited as if she visited a zoo to see a rattlesnake. Mina sucked in a rough breath, then stilled as the movement made her more aware of Alexei's big hand on her ribs, close to her breast.

'Perhaps I didn't sleep because I was busy contacting people to reschedule things for the period I'll be away. Since I had no opportunity earlier.' She slanted him a frosty stare only to find that smile lurking around his mouth.

'Ah, yes, no doubt your agenda is full of priority appointments.' His expression didn't change but his tone revealed how unlikely he thought it.

Mina didn't bother to disabuse him. She might not run a multinational corporation, but nor was she idle. As well as the exhibition she was preparing for, she volunteered with disabled kids and at a nearby nursing home, doing art therapy. Plus, there was some admin work at a women's shelter, the latest design commission for the perfumery in Jeirut and another from a French company that had seen her perfume bottle designs and wanted something similar.

'Mr Katsaros.' Her patience was perilously close to failing. One more jibe and she'd forget her resolve. 'I really must—

'Alexei, remember?' His voice rumbled through her like an intimate caress. It was the final straw.

'Put. Me. Down.' Her voice rose from request to imperious command. 'Now!'

Mina caught a flash of white teeth, a glimpse of glinting eyes and suddenly the world fell away as she dropped from his arms.

'As you wish, Princess.' He spoke as she landed with a puff of expelled air on her back. She was on a bed, looking up into dark, laughing eyes. But Mina was too tired and stressed to be amused. She didn't appreciate being the butt of his jibes or his arrogant certainty that her life was of negligible importance.

Mina jackknifed to a sitting position, swiping a cushion off the bed with one hand and throwing it in the same, fluid movement. She had the satisfaction of seeing it hit him square on his superior chin.

'Be thankful that wasn't anything heavier. My aim is as good as any man's.' She heaved a breath that, to her horror, felt far too shaky. 'Now, if you'd have the decency to leave, I'd like to catch up on some much-needed sleep.'

Damn. Damn. Damn.

Alexei stalked away from the guest wing to the master suite.

What had got into him? Half an hour with Carissa Carter and he'd veered between anger, attraction, approval and amusement. And far too much of all of them. He always controlled his emotions; he wasn't undercut by them.

He hadn't expected to be impressed by Carter's precious princess. He'd been ready to write her off as a pampered bimbo who viewed the world through the prism of her greed for an easy life. Instead he'd discovered someone witty, incisive, challenging and sexy. Ridiculously sexy, given her defiantly unfeminine clothes.

On Carissa Carter even a baggy T-shirt and leggings made his hormones surge. And that mouth. She was sharp-tongued in a superior way that made him want to take her mouth and discover what sweetness lay beneath its cutting edge.

There was definitely sweetness. He'd been surprised, when he held her, at the fretful way her pulse raced. He'd been mesmerised by her contrary reactions as she pretended not to respond. Her breathing had quickened, her pupils dilated, and he'd read confusion beneath her scorn and defiance. Even her awe as she admired the sculpture in the sitting room had charmed him.

He'd lit from within at the feel of her, supple, streamlined and, he discovered, curved in the right places.

What would happen if he followed her down onto that bed? He couldn't remember the dark frenzy of desire ever being so immediate or urgent.

The very fact he'd thought about it was a concern. Did he really want an affair with Carter's daughter?

Logic demanded an unequivocal *no*. Instinct screamed *yes*.

Which was an excellent reason to pull back. Apart from the fact he didn't take advantage of vulnerable women.

Alexei rubbed a hand across his jaw as he entered his suite and crossed to the window to stand staring across the infinity pool to the sea beyond.

Guilt trickled down his spine. Bad enough that there'd been a kernel of truth in Carissa's accusation about how he'd got her here. It had solidified into a jagged shard of ice when he'd heard the hint of a wobble in her voice as she stared up at him from her bed. She'd been flushed and furious and he'd revelled in his power to rile her, till he'd heard the tiny crack in her façade of superiority. Suddenly it hadn't seemed amusing.

It hit him that he'd behaved like a kid pulling a girl's pigtails, desperate to get her attention any way he could.

Him, desperate?

Hardly. Certainly not for the likes of Carissa Carter.

Except she wasn't as he'd expected.

He scraped his hand across his chin, feeling the stubble

he hadn't bothered to shave. He shouldn't allow himself to be diverted by her. She was incidental to his plans.

But, pending Carter's arrival, there wasn't much he could do to bring those plans to fruition. Steps had been taken to contain the damage, and while Alexei checked in daily, working via computer and phone, his team was working hard.

Which gave him leisure to ponder his would-be bride.

Alexei's brow scrunched. Funny. He'd assumed Carissa would be eager to marry. Her father had come up with the idea, no doubt desperate to cement personal ties that would save him when his embezzlement came to light. The fact a woman in her mid-twenties was willing to go along with such a plan pointed to her being venal, marrying for money and position.

Too many women had tried to tie him down. Not for love, but as their ticket to wealth and privilege. Alexei didn't fool himself into believing they were attracted by his character or sense of humour. Some were drawn by his looks but money was the deciding factor.

Yet Carissa hadn't given an unequivocal yes.

Why? Did she believe if he had to work for what he wanted, he'd appreciate her more? Because men enjoyed the chase?

He huffed a breath. Maybe she had something there. If she'd walked in the door and promptly agreed with everything his interest wouldn't have been piqued.

Except by that delectable body, which he'd discovered was curvier than he'd first thought.

Except for her intelligence and sensitivity.

Alexei shoved his fists in his pockets and rocked back on his feet, annoyed. He'd been so caught up in the need to draw Carter out of hiding, he hadn't bothered researching the man's daughter.

He'd acted rashly, driven by fury that the one person he'd trusted since his mother died had betrayed him.

That was a slashing wound that wouldn't heal till Carter was made to pay. It overset Alexei's equilibrium, evoking unwanted feelings that interfered with his decision-making.

It wasn't so much the money, but the personal affront of betrayal. The cold slap of horror that he'd let himself be gulled into believing the man, *liking* him.

Carter had made a fool of him, conning him into giving his trust. Not just because of the man's work qualities.

But because Carter reminded him of his father.

Like Alexei's father, Carter appeared taciturn to outsiders, but his features broke into smiles when he mentioned his family. Uncannily, Carter also had a mannerism, a tilt of the head, that echoed Alexei's precious memories of the father who'd died when Alexei was six.

Then there was his utter devotion to his spouse. There'd been no mistaking the man's devastation when his wife was diagnosed with a terminal illness. His stoic determination to do all he could for her had touched a chord with Alexei. Plus there was that unexpected weakness for silly puns and his scrupulous honesty, both hallmarks of his dad.

Alexei shook his head. Scrupulous honesty!

For years Alexei's motto had been trust no one. He and his mother had suffered because they'd been taken in by a conman. After his stepfather there'd been others, loan sharks, employers, landlords, vultures who'd preyed on his vulnerable mother, turning her life into a misery till finally loss and disappointment crushed her.

Alexei scraped a hand across his jaw, dragging himself back to the present. To the woman in one of the guest suites.

He'd acted instinctively, securing her to give him an edge. He should have ordered a dossier on her so he knew something about her before acting.

All he remembered from Carter's conversations was

that she lived in Paris, where she'd attended an exclusive art school. She loved fashion and shopping and wasn't cut out for a commercial career. Alexei had gained the impression of a pampered airhead pretending to be an artist. A blonde airhead, he remembered from the photo Carter had waved before him and which he hadn't bothered to take in.

So Carissa Carter had dyed her hair. That was one extra fact about her.

Alexei considered ordering a full report on her. But why bother?

She was here. Whatever Alexei wanted to know, he'd find out for himself. He'd enjoy the process.

CHAPTER FOUR

MINA STARED AT the bathroom's enormous, full-length mirror and suppressed a groan. She looked like a stranger.

Carissa had said pink calmed her and made her feel centred. It was proof of how stressed she'd been that she'd packed only for her favourite colour. Almost everything in the case was pink. Candy pink, flesh pink, cerise, rose madder and more.

Mina's mouth curled in an unwilling laugh as she surveyed herself. She wore a candy-pink skirt with matching strappy sandals and a pale pink top with a silver logo that incorporated a highly stylised Eiffel Tower and an open book. Carissa had designed it for an indie book festival in Paris, one of her first commissions.

Had Carissa really planned to wear these clothes to visit Alexei Katsaros? If so she'd clearly had the Caribbean's casual, sunny reputation in mind, rather than any desire to dress up.

Or was her friend savvier than Mina gave her credit for? Maybe this wardrobe was her secret weapon, to prove she wasn't cut out to be a billionaire's wife.

That stifled Mina's humour.

Carissa needed her help and Mina wasn't quite as sure now about her ability to deal with her host.

Especially in a skirt that rode high on her thighs and a top that was more fitted than anything she usually wore. Mina wasn't ashamed of her body, but she covered more of it than her friend did. Plus Carissa was shorter and smaller in the bust, so the top was a snug fit. As for the miniskirt...

Mina shrugged. She had more to worry about than how much bare leg she displayed. Her only clothes were what she'd worn on the plane and the ones Carissa had packed. Besides, she was on a tropical island. Alexei Katsaros would be used to guests wearing shorts or swimsuits. Or, given his reputation and the knowing gleam in those remarkable eyes, nothing at all.

How many beautiful women had he seduced here?

Mina blinked as she caught the direction of her thoughts. *That* wasn't her concern. Deftly she caught up her long hair, winding it round and up into a tight knot at the back of her head. She jabbed in a securing pin and turned away.

If Alexei dismissed her because of her clothes, or because she wasn't the biddable woman he'd imagined, all the better. Clearly he hadn't expected her to voice her opinions or have more than a couple of brain cells to rub together.

It would be better if he concentrated on running his multibillion-dollar empire than on her. It hadn't even occurred to him that getting to know the woman he planned to marry was a good idea.

Remarkable!

Unbelievable!

What sort of man thought like that?

One who didn't expect to be questioned.

Who expected everyone to bend to his wishes.

Mina put away the hairdryer she'd used and entered the palatial bedroom where she'd slept like the dead for hours.

Her gaze rested on the bed she'd remade after her nap. Inevitably the image that filled her mind was of looking up from there into that fabulously sculpted face, into eyes alight with mockery, and knowing that physically she was at his mercy. It had infuriated Mina, for she'd had no choice but to put up with his macho posturing and derision.

That still smarted. She drew taller, pushing her shoulders back, as she relived the scene and wished she still had the small jewelled dagger she'd worn as a ceremonial courtesy in Jeirut. It had been decorative but deadly, and Mina had insisted on knowing how to wield it. Would he have taken her more seriously if he'd known she was fully capable of looking after herself, no matter what the situation?

The idea conjured suitably satisfying images, but her smile faded as she faced the real source of her concern.

Her reaction to Alexei Katsaros.

It wasn't only fury she'd felt. He'd been *interesting*.

Lips twisting, Mina shook her head. He'd been fascinating. That combination of bold assurance and blatant sexuality would catch any woman's attention. Especially since physically his form was...pleasing. But add to that occasional glimpses of humour and penetrating understanding that punctured her initial estimate of a smug bully, and you had a man who left her unsettled.

Mina tried to tell herself the disorientation of tiredness had made her react to him. But innate honesty wouldn't let her pretend.

She had to face the truth.

She disliked Alexei Katsaros and his high-handed ways. He was exactly the sort of man to make her hackles rise. Yet he made her blood heat.

She was attracted to him.

The situation she'd rushed into for Carissa's sake became fraught with unseen snares, like the notorious patches of quicksand in the desert of her homeland.

She hadn't reckoned on anything like this when she'd blithely decided to help her friend. Dimly, she heard her father's voice in her head, the memory of his disapproval as he complained of her impulsive ways. She'd tried to make him proud, do her duty no matter how dull or out of tune with her own interests. But she'd been a source of frustration for him.

Face it, Mina. Nothing you did could satisfy your father. He didn't want a daughter who craved love, but an automaton who could be diplomatic on every occasion, no matter what the provocation.

She'd failed there, hadn't she?

Abruptly she spun on her foot and crossed to the glass doors that gave out onto a crystal pool and, beyond that, the tropical garden.

Mina's eyes were drawn to the profusion of flowers, cadmium yellow, pale ochre and magenta. She felt the old temptation to reach for her sketchpad. To find peace by losing herself in art.

Instead she simply stood a little longer, inhaling the fragrance of salt air and unfamiliar floral perfumes, then set her shoulders and turned away. She couldn't hide forever. It was time to face her host.

She found him on a deep, shaded veranda. Overhead, a fan rotated lazily and the combination of wicker furniture and wide, wooden floorboards hinted at gracious days gone by, though the sprawling villa was modern.

Alexei sat, feet up, on a lounger, typing into a tablet. His hair was ruffled as if he'd combed his fingers through it and his shirt was open again. Mina saw the dark smattering of hair on his sculpted pectorals and jerked her gaze away.

That tiny sizzle deep inside didn't bode well. She'd felt it before, when he carried her in his arms. Now just the sight of him set it off.

Frowning, Mina surveyed the garden, trying to control feelings she couldn't fully identify. On the other side of the pool, a sculpture caught her eye.

'You're awake. Excellent.' Reluctantly Mina turned, fixing a bland expression on her face. She'd known this would be difficult but she'd hoped her earlier response to him had more to do with fatigue than genuine attraction.

Fate was clearly laughing at her naivety.

Alexei set the tablet aside and swung his feet to the floor.

'Please don't get up on my account. You're working. I'll come back later.' She was only too happy to delay being alone with him.

'No, I've finished.' He gestured to the seats grouped around him and she had no choice but to take one.

Instead of a recliner, Mina selected an upright chair, conscious of the way her skirt rode even higher up her legs as she sat. Resisting the urge to tug her hem in a futile attempt to gain an extra few centimetres, she crossed her ankles and tucked her feet under her chair. She didn't look directly at her host but *felt* his gaze. It raked her from head to foot, then lifted again to linger on her legs and higher—

Mina swung her head up abruptly and met his enigmatic dark gaze.

Had she been wrong? She could have sworn he'd been ogling her. Or did her sensitivity about wearing Carissa's clothes make her imagine things? The way her breasts tingled—

'What would you like to drink?' As he spoke Marie rounded the corner of the veranda, as if in response to the summons of a silent bell.

'Something cold would be good.'

'Champagne? A cocktail? Gin and tonic?'

Mina glanced at her watch. Early afternoon. Obviously his usual guests indulged themselves. Mina, on the other hand, needed a clear head. Besides, she was in no mood to kick back and pretend this was a holiday. She felt too agitated around Alexei Katsaros.

'A juice would be lovely, thanks.' She smiled at Marie.

'Of course, ma'am. And I'll bring some food.'

Mina was about to protest that she wasn't hungry, then remembered she hadn't eaten in ages. She'd feel stronger after food. She'd better!

Marie turned to Alexei, a question on her face. In response he shook his head and gestured to a half-full jug of iced water. 'I'm fine.'

So he expected Mina to indulge while he stuck to cold water. Interesting. But then, he'd been working and he hadn't built a hugely successful corporation by drinking the day away. Mina shot a glance at that firm chin and those uncompromising features and guessed Alexei Katsaros was good at discipline and control. Then her gaze collided with his and the impact sent a silent shudder of reaction through her.

She suspected he was also excellent at letting go and indulging. There was a sensuality about that steady gaze that would unnerve her if she let it.

'I'm sorry I slept so long. I didn't—'

His raised hand cut her off. 'You needed the rest. I hope you slept well?' It was a simple question, the sort any host might make. Yet holding Alexei's gaze, feeling heat wash her skin, Mina tensed, conscious of undercurrents.

She took in his relaxed posture, the small smile, yet sensed concealment. One long finger drummed on the arm of his chair and there was an intensity about that stare…

'Thank you, yes. It's a very comfortable bed.'

And just like that, it hit her what this undercurrent was. Sexual attraction. Potent and perilous.

Mina blinked but kept her expression serene, despite the frenzied rush of shock. In her room she'd acknowledged the attraction, but the potency of her reaction unnerved her.

She'd been attracted to guys before. But this was a blast of lightning compared with the weak flicker of a single match. It was the mighty Khamsin wind that scoured the desert and shifted whole ridges of sand, compared with a gentle zephyr that merely rustled the leaves in a courtyard garden.

Mina sank back, forcing down shock, fear and excitement.

It was the excitement that worried her most. She'd always found it hard to resist adventure and challenge.

But not with this man. Not with a man who treated people like pawns on his personal chessboard. She'd be crazy to go there.

'I'm the one who should apologise.' His words snagged her attention. 'I'm sorry if I distressed you earlier, carrying you to your room.'

Mina felt again that powerful pulse of connection and refused to acknowledge it. Was he apologising for carrying her or because he'd recognised how close she'd come to losing command of herself? Please, not the latter!

She inclined her head. 'You were concerned for me. I understand.' It didn't excuse the deliberate way he'd goaded her, but there was no point going over that again. 'I have a favour to ask.'

'Ask away.' He sat forward and Mina sensed he'd been waiting for this.

'Can I borrow a vehicle? There are some things I need to buy.' Like underwear. Mina drew the line at wearing Carissa's lacy thongs.

'I'm afraid that's not possible.'

Mina's eyebrows lifted. Was he really so petty as to deny her transport? 'You don't trust me with your vehicle?' She'd learned to drive on unpaved mountain roads and desert dunes. She'd bet she could handle a four-wheel drive better than him.

'It's more the lack of shops that's the problem.'

'Lack of shops?'

'There aren't any. We get supplies by boat. It's not easy to indulge in retail therapy here.' He spread his hands and Mina caught the ghost of a smile. She recognised the same teasing amusement she'd seen when he'd provoked her. Had Carissa's reputation as a bargain shopaholic preceded her?

Her friend was always searching for second-hand items to transform.

What exactly did Alexei know of the woman he planned to marry? So far it seemed he expected her to be obedient, possibly unintelligent and good at spending money. It was a distorted picture of Mina's friend, and didn't recommend her as a wife.

Which begged the question, why marry her?

More and more, the idea of an arranged marriage between him and Carissa seemed odd.

'Carissa?'

'Sorry?' She blinked. She'd missed what he said.

'If you need hygiene products, talk to Marie. She also has a supply of suncream and spare hats for visitors.'

Mina's smile was perfunctory. She refused to feel embarrassed by his assumption. 'Thanks, but that's not what I had in mind.'

'Later in the week, when your father's here, we'll go to one of the larger islands and you can visit the boutiques.'

Didn't that sound like fun? Steadfastly Mina yanked her mind from the inevitable scene when her masquerade was uncovered. She hoped Carissa and Pierre were safely married by then.

'Surely I could take the boat before that? This afternoon perhaps?'

'You're that desperate?' Alexei angled his head as if to survey her better. His expression didn't alter, but the flare of his nostrils hinted at impatience. 'I'm afraid not. The boat's being repaired.' Mina opened her mouth, but before she could ask he added, 'It will be available again in a day or two. I'm sure you'll enjoy an outing to the boutiques after that. I'm assured they stock an excellent range.'

'I can't wait.' Mina manufactured a smile and sank back in her seat. She didn't need a high-end boutique that catered for the rich at play. But there was no point explaining that. For now she'd simply wash her underwear every night.

Inevitably her thoughts jagged back to her unmasking when Carissa's father arrived. Her stomach squeezed uncomfortably.

She could almost hear her own father's pained voice, telling her she'd been reckless and headstrong. That she shouldn't have dared to disrupt a father's plans for his daughter.

But how could she regret helping her friend? She couldn't sit and watch her forced into marriage.

Mina wasn't afraid of Alexei's reaction when he discovered the truth, or Mr Carter's. After all, what could they do to her? And it served them right for putting Carissa in such an invidious position. Yet now the first rush of indignation on her friend's behalf was fading, Mina wasn't looking forward to the moment of revelation. It would be uncomfortable at best, especially as she relied on Alexei's goodwill to get off the island. He was bound to be furious.

What would an angry Alexei Katsaros be like? Loud and belligerent, or icily condemning?

Mina could withstand anything he threw at her. That went without saying. Yet she found herself wishing she were back in Paris, busy working instead of playing this cat-and-mouse game.

Suddenly the lack of underwear seemed the least of her concerns.

CHAPTER FIVE

ALEXEI TRIED AND failed to read Carissa's expression. She seemed distracted, almost uninterested, as if her need to shop wasn't urgent after all. He couldn't get a handle on her. Every time she confirmed his estimation of her as shallow and opportunistic, she confounded him.

Marie served drinks and a substantial platter of food but Carissa barely touched the lavish spread.

'You'll be glad to see your father again.'

Her soft eyes widened as if in surprise, and Alexei felt his own narrow.

What was going on? Had father and daughter fallen out? Surely not. If it appeared Carissa was on the verge of securing a marriage with Alexei, her father would be eager to give the match his blessing.

'Of course.'

'It's been a while since you saw each other?'

'A while.' She shifted in her seat, crossing her legs. Despite his determination to ferret out her motivations, Alexei was distracted by the toned golden skin on display. The ploy of a woman bent on seduction? Why else would she wear a micro miniskirt and a tight top that so lovingly moulded her breasts?

Unwanted heat flared as he considered the generous bounty barely concealed by Carissa's new clothes. How had he thought her lacking in curves? She was slender yet definitely feminine. And those legs went on forever.

Yet when he dragged his gaze to her face, she was staring, not at him but towards the horizon, her brow knitted in thought.

Alexei experienced an odd sensation, a clamping in his

gut. It took a moment to realise it was pique. He wasn't used to being ignored by anyone, especially women.

Especially a woman who thought she was here to marry him.

Was Carissa so sure of herself that she didn't feel the need to pander to his ego?

She turned her head, her gaze meshing with his, and his blood pumped powerfully. How would it feel if she reached out and touched him? The notion quickened his pulse to a hard, heavy throb.

'Something's on your mind.' His voice was rough. 'What is it?'

She blinked, as if surprised at his words. For a second he almost believed he'd unsettled her, though that was unlikely. When she'd arrived she'd been very vocal. There'd been nothing reticent or uncertain about Carissa. He'd enjoyed their sparring. It was rare Alexei had someone confront him, much less take him to task for his actions.

Carissa seemed to gather herself. She sat higher, those slim shoulders forming a straight, uncompromising line that even after such a short acquaintance was familiar. Her jaw angled up and Alexei felt anticipation thrum.

'Why do you want an arranged marriage? Why not marry someone you know?'

Again she surprised him. He hadn't suspected Carter's daughter would look a gift horse in the mouth. But clearly Carissa was intelligent. Even if she craved his wealth, she wanted to understand his expectations.

'I haven't found anyone I want to marry.' That, at least, was true.

'But why arrange a marriage this way?'

'Are you trying to back out?' He sat forward, fascinated.

'No.' She paused. 'I just want to know more about you.'

'It seemed an efficient way of proceeding.'

'Efficient?' She tilted her head and recrossed her legs.

He heard the faint sibilant whisper of fabric on skin and fought to keep his eyes on her face. If she thought he'd be distracted by the obvious tactic she was mistaken, but that didn't prevent arousal clamping his groin.

'You make it sound as easy as ordering from a catalogue.' She gestured dismissively. 'Wanted, one female of reasonable appearance and education. Must have all her own teeth and be of child-bearing age.' She snapped the words out, and again Alexei heard that edge of disapproval. Yet instead of annoying him, it stirred a desire to provoke more of the same. Heat simmered in his blood at the idea of Carissa aroused to heightened emotion.

If he had to wait for her father to come out of hiding, he might as well enjoy himself.

'Why not? Look what it's brought me.' He let his gaze drop, trailing down her long, proud neck to her collarbone, the high curve of her breasts and lower.

Her fingers dug into the arms of her chair, the tendons in the backs of her hands tensing.

'And since you mention child-bearing…' He lifted his eyes to hers. They blazed back at him with a banked fury that might have made him pause in other circumstances. He didn't want Carissa calm and dismissive or, worse, distracted. He preferred her hot under the collar, concentrating on *him*. 'How do you feel about starting a family straight away?'

'That's why you want to marry? To have children?' Surprising how stunned she sounded. Surely the thought of kids must have occurred to her?

Alexei shrugged. 'Why else? When I have children I want them to have my name, to be part of a family unit. There's nothing else I can get from marriage that I can't have already.'

Alexei *did* want a family. Kids of his own. He'd spent years driven by the need to drag himself out of poverty and hadn't looked beyond securing success and financial security. Determination had kept him climbing to the top. But one day, yes, a family of his own…

He had a few precious memories of happy family life before his father died but he knew how lucky he was to have those. The miserable years after his mother remarried made him appreciate what he'd had so briefly. He'd like to recreate that with his own children.

When this debacle with Carter was over he'd think of finding a woman suitable to share his life. Someone who'd make a wonderful mother.

'There's nothing else you can get from marriage?' Carissa's mouth twisted superciliously. 'How about emotional intimacy? Trust? Love?'

'Love?' He frowned. 'You believe in love?'

Yet she was happy to sell herself into a marriage of convenience. The woman was a mass of contradictions.

Carissa hesitated. Her hands plucked at the arm of her chair. 'I believe it exists,' she said eventually.

'But you've never been in love.' It was a guess, but Alexei always backed his hunches. The idea intrigued, that a pretty woman in her mid-twenties had never fancied herself in love.

'Have *you*?' She raised one eyebrow.

'No.' People talked of love but it was rare.

His parents had married for love and he admitted the idea held allure. But look where it had left his mother. When Alexei's father died she'd been heartbroken. Even as a young child he'd understood that. She'd forced herself to go through the motions of life but she'd never been the same. Her sense of loss had been behind her disastrous second marriage. She'd admitted it to Alexei before she died and he'd had to bite back a howl of protest that she hadn't been alone. She'd had *him*. But clearly that hadn't been enough. *He* hadn't been enough.

Almost as bad, it turned out her other reason for remarrying was to provide Alexei with a father. Because of that she'd condemned them to life with that miserable excuse for a man.

Futile anger boiled in his belly. Alexei wouldn't let anyone make him weak the way his mother had been.

He'd triumphed over adversity and made himself a man his father would have been proud of. He had no intention of falling into some sentimental trap.

'So you don't expect to love the woman you marry.'

Carissa's cool tone cleaved his thoughts. She surveyed him with faint disapproval.

'If you're waiting for a declaration from me, Princess, you'll be disappointed.'

Predictably she didn't bat an eye. This woman had grit.

'What if you fall in love with someone else after you marry?'

'I can't imagine it happening.' Alexei saw her open her mouth to object and raised a hand. 'But if, after some time, we divorce, you needn't be concerned. The legal agreement will ensure you're recompensed.'

Her jaw inched even higher. 'And if your wife fell for someone else?'

Alexei met her challenging stare and felt a tiny beat of surprise. At the idea of the woman he married preferring another man. And at Carissa's determination to speak in the abstract. As if discussing some faceless woman instead of herself.

Why did she pretend lack of interest when she was here for marriage? Even now, staring along the length of that straight nose like a monarch surveying a vulgar yokel, she couldn't hide her awareness of him. Alexei read her shortened breathing, the pebbled nipples pressing invitingly against taut fabric. He understood, with the experience of a man who'd attracted women since his teens, that Carissa was anything but uninterested.

The knowledge sent a frisson down his spine, to circle his body and lodge in his groin.

Carissa Carter might be a necessary encumbrance for now but increasingly Alexei recognised a woman he'd enjoy knowing better.

Perhaps when his business with her father was resolved they might come to a mutually enjoyable arrangement.

'You want to bring children into a family where there's no love, just a…commercial agreement?' Carissa's tone jabbed through his pleasant imaginings. 'Don't you think that's selfish?'

Alexei frowned. 'Children need stability.' His own childhood was a case in point. 'They'd have the love of their parents, and a caring, settled environment. That's more than many kids ever have.'

He took in the flat line of her mouth and the opaque look in her eyes, and wondered what Carissa was thinking. Had his words struck a chord?

Yet she'd been one of the lucky ones. The Carters had been a tight-knit family. There'd been no mistaking Ralph Carter's devastation over his wife's death, or his concern for his daughter.

Alexei recalled the late-night conversation he'd had with Carter after his wife's death. Alexei had been leaving his office and been surprised to see the older man still in the building, though his glazed eyes had told their own story. Alexei had taken a seat, unable to walk past the man, reading the small, telltale signs of fiercely suppressed emotion.

In that moment Ralph Carter had reminded him of his father, who, while devoted to his family, closely guarded deep emotions. Alexei had known he was loved, not by words but by his father's actions.

That night Alexei had felt a bond to Carter, enough to unbend and admit he'd count himself lucky to have a marriage such as Carter had enjoyed. It had been a moment of unfamiliar, unguarded sentimentality that surprised him.

No wonder Carter's subsequent betrayal stuck in his craw. For the first time in his life Alexei had opened up about his most private desires, while trying to help the other man. He'd felt a brief moment of shared understanding. Then a couple of months later the guy had ripped him off, proving Alexei's trust had been totally misplaced.

Not only that. Carter remembered Alexei's admission that since he'd never have a love match, he'd settle for marriage based on respect and common goals. Carter had tried to exploit that. Last week, before his embezzlement was uncovered, he'd suggested Alexei consider marrying his daughter. He'd described her as beautiful, gentle and generous, if impractical at building a career.

Alexei gritted his teeth. Clearly she wasn't impractical enough to resist the lure of marriage to a billionaire.

'So, Carissa,' he drawled. 'You're not in favour of marriage without love, but here you are on my private island. Why?'

She curled her fingers into the arms of her chair, discomfited. Then she shrugged, the movement making those lush breasts jiggle. 'I didn't say I'm not in favour of it. But I like to know where I stand, hence my questions.'

Alexei sat forward. 'Where *do* you stand, Carissa? Do you want to marry me and have my babies?'

Strange how saying it jolted heat through his belly. At the thought of Carissa in his bed. He had no trouble imagining that lissom body beneath his or astride it or against the wall of the shower as he took her with the water streaming over them. As for her pregnant with his baby—Alexei was stunned by the heavy whump of desire that slammed into him.

Carissa Carter was lovely to look at but far from the most beautiful woman he'd met. She was mouthy and opinionated, avaricious enough to marry a stranger for money. Yet, after knowing her mere hours, Alexei wanted her in his bed.

Had his wits taken a hike?

She sat back in her seat, taking time to recross her legs. Was the seat uncomfortable, or was she nervous?

More likely she was employing the not-so-subtle means of drawing his attention to her stunning legs.

Did she think he'd be so mesmerised she could manipulate him when they negotiated a prenuptial agreement?

'The jury's still out, Alexei. Surely you don't expect me to make up my mind within a couple of hours of meeting you.'

He applauded her aplomb. Her answer was designed to buy her time, and improve her bargaining position, making him more eager to seal the deal. It worked. Though there was no marriage contract to seal, Alexei felt his interest quicken. He'd always found it hard to resist a challenge.

'What if I don't want to wait?'

Her dark eyebrows arched. 'Then perhaps I'm not the woman you need. I'm happy to return to Paris…' She let the words hang but shuffled forward in her seat as if ready to get up and go right then and there.

As if he'd let her go! She was his bargaining chip. The reason Ralph Carter would believe it safe to come out of hiding.

If Carter baulked at showing himself, there were other possibilities. The man doted on Carissa. All Alexei had to do was suggest he'd make the daughter pay for her father's sins, in his bed, since she didn't have money, and Carter would come running to her rescue.

'No. You'll stay here, where we can get to know each other better.'

Did he imagine she tensed? Then she shrugged and the illusion vanished. 'That sounds ideal. I'm sure neither of us want to make a mistake on such a significant…'

'Merger?'

Fascinated, Alexei watched the faintest tinge of pink colour her cheeks. Was she thinking, as he was, of their bodies merging in the most intimate of ways?

'Decision.' Carissa's voice was crisp. She reached out and took a bread stick from the platter, broke it in half and crunched.

Alexei suppressed a laugh and reached for a piece of Marie's fried chicken. The delicious aroma made him inhale appreciatively.

'I look forward to getting to know you better, Carissa. And as for the question of starting a family immediately—' her eyes locked on his '—we can negotiate.'

She inclined her head slightly, the picture of cool condescension.

Which made Alexei want to ruffle her composure all the more. The urge to reach out to her made his fingers tingle but he refused to follow through. No matter how enjoyable that would be, he needed to keep his eye on the main game.

It was almost a shame that this was all a front. He'd enjoy negotiating with Carissa over sex. Perhaps he *would* see if she was interested in an affair when this was over.

Except by then her father would be ruined and in prison. It was unlikely she'd want anything to do with Alexei after that.

Reluctantly Alexei decided the best thing for now was to keep things low-key. He'd treat her as a guest rather than a prospective bride. He didn't need the complications that would follow if he acted on this attraction.

'When you've finished eating, I'll show you around.'

Mina enjoyed Alexei's voice, she realised. Its deep, suede quality was compelling. Worse, it weakened her, as if he brushed her flesh with plush fur that invited her to arch against it. There was his accent too. His English was crisp enough to prove it wasn't his first language; he had rich, round vowels, and the occasional soft consonant gave his voice a seductive quality.

Or perhaps he did that deliberately. He'd been toying with her, occasionally flirting as they spoke.

To see how she responded? Or because that was the nature of the man?

All she knew for sure was that Carissa had had a lucky escape. She'd have been miserable with Alexei, a man who viewed finding a wife as a matter of efficiency, and no doubt the woman herself as a possession!

It would do him good to discover she wasn't a chattel to be acquired so easily.

'That sounds marvellous. But please, don't let me keep you from your work. I can find my own way.'

Mina selected a skewer of tropical fruit and settled further into her seat, taking her time. She wasn't going to jump to his bidding.

'And neglect you?' He shook his head and a lock of dark hair tumbled over his brow, making him look more like a beachcomber than a business tycoon.

Mina's gaze strayed towards his unbuttoned shirt and the display of taut, packed muscle. She tried not to stare but it became tougher by the second. Why didn't he do up his shirt? Did he think himself so sexy he had to flaunt himself? That she wouldn't be able to resist him?

The idea was laughable. Yet Mina admitted the sight of his powerful frame set tremors running deep inside her.

She'd seen plenty of men wearing less than he did. She'd drawn nudes, even sculpted them, yet this was different. *She* felt different as she slanted a look at all that unvarnished masculinity. Not like an artist with an eye for angle and perspective. But like a woman.

There was a curious buzz in her bloodstream and her breath seemed far too shallow. The feeling was somehow both enervating and exhilarating.

Mina met his remarkable eyes. Malachite or tourmaline? The green was as deep as a fathomless ocean and just as unreadable. Beautiful yet dangerous. Like ocean depths where an unwary diver might be lured to disaster.

Setting her jaw, she put down her food and stood up. She reminded herself she was pragmatic, not fanciful, despite her creative nature.

'I'd love a tour, if you have time.' Anything was better than sitting, trying not to ogle a man she didn't even like.

The tour proved fascinating. More so than she'd anticipated. Alexei showed her the main rooms in his sprawling villa. Big, airy spaces that invited you to relax. And despite the presence of some stunning pieces of art that made Mina desperate to return for a longer study, the place didn't feel ostentatious, like a rich man's showpiece. It was luxurious but, above all, comfortable. Mina could imagine living here.

Nor did Alexei insist on a detailed tour of every designer detail. A wave of the arm indicated the cinema. Another incorporated his private wing. Then guest suites, gym and so on. As they passed outside, Alexei swept up two broad-brimmed hats and passed her one.

'It's easy to get sunburned.'

Mina didn't argue. She had a healthy respect for the power of the sun. In her country everyone covered up to shelter from its rays. Casting him a glance, she realised he looked more like a beachcomber than ever. An incredibly fit, sexy beachcomber who clearly didn't spend all his time lolling in a hammock with a cold beer.

They passed through a lush garden, with more sculptures she promised herself she'd come back to. Then they were out on a white sand beach, where small waves shushed ashore with the regularity of a heartbeat. There were no footprints on the sand. No other houses, only water and the birds in the trees and the warmth of the sun on her body.

It was paradise.

Mina dragged in a deep breath, rich with the tang of the sea, and sighed. How long had it been since she'd spent time away from crowds and cars? Not since her last visit to Jeirut. There she'd been rejuvenated by the rough majesty of the arid mountains, the sparkling clean air with its unique fragrance and the quality of the light that was unlike anything else.

'This is glorious.'

'I think so. There aren't many places like it.'

'With no neighbours?' She scanned the opposite end of the beach, seeing only the rise of a headland covered in a tangle of green forest.

'Partly that. But the island itself is pretty unique. It was never cleared for farming so a lot of the natural forest is left. Its conservation value is tremendous, especially for several species of endangered birds.'

Mina swung around to discover Alexei surveying her rather than their surroundings. She wasn't used to being the centre of attention, not since she'd given up her royal duties in Jeirut and disappeared into her life in Paris. Yet it wasn't just the fact Alexei watched her, it was the intensity of his regard. As if *he* were the artist and she a model.

'What are your plans for the island?'

'Plans?'

Mina turned back to the stretch of white sand, imagining it lined with buildings and an oversized marina. 'Eco-tourism or some other sort of development?'

'You assume I'm going to develop it?' Something in his voice snagged her attention and she looked up at him. His gaze was shadowed by the brim of his hat and unreadable.

'You're a businessman. Anyone with commercial sense would see it has enormous money-making potential.'

'Is that what you see?' His voice dipped to a gravelly note that made her skin shiver.

Mina shook her head and tried to repress regret at the

thought of it transformed into a busy holiday resort. 'I can see it, yes.'

'But you don't approve.' Had he read her so easily?

She shrugged. 'Not all progress is an improvement.' Her gaze took in the forest and a flash of bright colour as some small bird curvetted into the blue sky before disappearing again into the green.

'I agree.'

Mina started and swung back. 'You do?'

'Why so surprised? Even businessmen can appreciate beauty when they see it.'

Not all businessmen. Mina had met enough, so wrapped up in building more wealth or power, who never considered the impact of their actions on others or the environment.

At fifteen she'd had a stand-up argument with her father about a development proposal for the foothills near the capital. The scheme would bring short-term jobs but most profits would go offshore and the environmental damage would be catastrophic. In the end the plan was modified. It was one of the few times her father had been swayed. A local company had won the contract in a compromise between development and conservation. Now that area attracted tourists, drawn by the natural beauty and nearby facilities.

'Carissa?'

'Sorry.' She blinked and focused, reading the lines around his mouth that spoke of disapproval. 'What did you say?'

'I asked what you have against businessmen.'

'Nothing.' Just selfish rich guys who expected others to dance to their tune. Yet the vibe she got now from Alexei was a million miles away from that.

That intrigued her. Standing with the ocean lapping near their feet and Alexei's dark gaze heavy as a touch, Mina felt something new shiver through her. More than sexual awareness. More than impatience and indignation. Something that spread warmth and niggled at her protective, no, her combative attitude.

'So you're not going to change the place?' It seemed too good to be true.

'Oh, there'll be changes.' He waved his hand in an encompassing gesture.

Disappointment was sour on Mina's tongue. Why had she allowed herself to think otherwise? 'Such as?'

'Some cabins near the landing strip for visiting scientists and a small research facility.' Mina looked up and caught his fleeting smile. 'That's all.'

He'd deliberately led her on, and she'd fallen for it, because she was primed to believe the worst of him. And he'd guessed. Yet instead of taking offence, he was amused.

She hated to admit it but Alexei Katsaros threw her off balance. He was arrogant and annoying but he was perceptive and had a lighter, warmer side. Plus he valued this pristine environment as it was.

'Truly?'

'Truly. I spent my teens in a crowded city. Believe me, I realise how special this place is.' A slow smile curled his mouth and Mina felt the same curl etch a scrawl of heat deep inside. 'Now, how about I show you the spot where the turtles come in to lay their eggs?'

Silently Mina nodded. Then, following his example, took off her sandals, her feet sinking into fine, damp sand.

Because of Carissa, Mina and Alexei Katsaros were on opposing sides. When he discovered her deception he'd be livid. She couldn't afford to let her guard down. Yet spending time learning about him could only be to her advantage and Carissa's, couldn't it?

An inner voice warned Mina she was playing with fire. She should make an excuse and go back to her room.

But Mina had always been fascinated by fire and playing safe had never seemed so unappealing.

CHAPTER SIX

MINA'S HAND MOVED swiftly over the sketchpad, but her thoughts focused on the role she played. She should end this farce now.

She wouldn't betray Carissa and leave her prey to Alexei. Yet, with each hour, Mina grew more desperate. After two days on his island, the atmosphere grew thicker, more intense. He'd kept his distance physically but that only accentuated her catastrophic response to him.

As if it had a mind of its own, her body woke in his presence. The symptoms were depressingly irrefutable. Budding nipples, a surge of heat that threatened to flood her cheeks and flickered like wildfire in her veins. Butterflies the size of circling vultures in her stomach and a heavy, pulsing throb between her legs.

Sexual interest.

She could view it clinically. The trouble was that when they were together Mina felt anything but clinical detachment.

Frowning, she stared at her less-than-impressive sketch, then shoved it over the spiral spine of her drawing book to start afresh.

To make matters worse was Carissa's news, received via text. The elopement was delayed. Pierre was still in the USA, finishing negotiations on the tricky deal that he hoped would cement his professional success. Despite Carissa's pleas he was determined to stick it out, saying their future hinged on it. Mina sympathised. If his family disowned him for making a marriage they didn't approve, one of the pair needed a steady income. Carissa was talented but only starting her commercial design business.

Which meant Mina was stuck here for at least a couple more days, pretending to be someone else. Pretending to be impervious to Alexei. The strain was unbearable.

No other man had got under her skin like this. Just the mellow sound of his rare laugh or the deliberately confrontational twitch of one black eyebrow and her pulse revved out of control. Fortunately he never got close enough to touch. Despite those daydreams where he touched her in the most delicious, disturbing ways.

Mina set her chin and tried to focus on her drawing. She had work to do. An exhibition to prepare for. She couldn't sit in the Caribbean twiddling her thumbs. She needed...

Her hand stilled. There *was* a way out. Why hadn't she seen it?

Probably because her head was too skewed by thoughts of Alexei Katsaros.

Mina had accepted Carissa's assumption that her father's job would suffer if the marriage fell through. But surely it *must* fall through. Once Carissa was married to Pierre there'd be no question of a match with Alexei.

Besides, though Alexei could be daunting and demanding, the last couple of days had revealed another side to him. His manner with Marie and Henri indicated a man far more approachable and likeable than she'd imagined. A man who didn't expect to be treated as a superior being because he paid their wages. A man who could be surprisingly considerate.

He wasn't the complete ogre Carissa had imagined.

If Carissa, or, more accurately, Mina, were to say she couldn't go through with an arranged marriage, he'd have to respect that.

Mina blinked down at the half-formed sketch as she ran through the scenario in her mind. All she needed to do was say she'd considered but decided against the match. She'd be free to return to Paris, her work and her routine.

Funny how the thought didn't fill her with relief or anticipation.

Instead, Mina felt a pang of regret at the idea of leaving the island. And Alexei.

Her pencil dropped to roll unchecked across the paper. Mina blinked as it described a half circle on the page.

Was she serious?

Alexei Katsaros?

She huffed out a fierce breath. But it did no good to tell herself she didn't like big, bold, bossy men whose dark eyes twinkled with amusement just when she was about to explode with indignation.

Because she did. She liked him too much. Though he made her weak in ways she never wanted. For weakness was an invitation for men to trample you. She'd seen it too often.

'You look annoyed. Trouble with your drawing?' The deep voice came from beside her and Mina jumped. It was as if she'd conjured Alexei out of thin air by thinking of him.

She turned, her gaze on a level with snug faded jeans. Mina's heart rapped out a new, frantic tattoo as she fought not to let her eyes linger on the outline of muscled thighs. Instead she tilted her head up and up, till finally she met his quizzical gaze.

A jolt, like the impact of an electrical current, drove down through her body. Her breath stalled and the blood coursed faster in her veins.

This wasn't right. She didn't want to feel this or anything like it for Alexei. Despite his occasional charm he was the sort to stomp all over a woman.

'It's not going well.' She dragged her gaze back to the sketchpad and flipped it closed. The black cover mocked her with its blankness. That was how her brain was when he got near, and her artistic ability. How could she finish her designs when all she could concentrate on was him?

Suddenly it was imperative she put an end to this farce.

Mina was on her feet before she had time to think about it. 'I need to talk with you.'

Alexei stood so close her nostrils quivered at that delicious tang of citrus and cedar with base notes of warm male. Mina wanted to step away but he'd notice. He noticed everything.

'Of course.' He gestured to the chairs grouped on the wide veranda. 'Shall we sit?'

Mina was too agitated to sit. 'Let's walk.' Now she'd decided on her course of action she wanted it done. With luck, in a few hours she'd be on her way to Paris. Fiercely she smothered a pang of disappointment at the idea.

He wasn't good for her. No man who distracted her this way could be.

'Of course.' He turned towards the path that led to the beach. When they reached the fine sand Mina tugged off Carissa's pink sandals and put them to one side. Alexei, she noticed, was already barefoot. She liked the shape of his feet, the strength and composition of bone, vein, heel and arch.

The next time she sculpted a male nude she'd search for a model with feet and hands like Alexei. There was something powerful and appealing about them.

Catching her thoughts, Mina closed her eyes in self-disgust.

'Carissa? What is it? Surely nothing too bad?' For once there was no challenge or humour in Alexei's tone. He sounded concerned. 'Are you okay?'

'Absolutely.' She wiped her face of expression. 'But I need to tell you something.'

'I'm all ears.'

He began walking along the beach, heading for the hard-packed sand near the water. Mina fell into step beside him, wondering how to proceed. In the end she decided a direct approach was best.

'I've been doing a lot of thinking, Alexei, and I can't marry you.'

For a heartbeat he said nothing. Then he turned his head to survey her, his easy stride never faltering.

'Can't? Is there some barrier I don't know about?'

Because, of course, it would never occur to him that she didn't *want* to marry him.

'I'm not ready for marriage. I'm just turning twenty-three.' Yet many of her peers in Jeirut were married with children.

'Whereas I'm past thirty.'

'It's not that.' As soon as she said it, Mina could have bitten her tongue. Predictably Alexei pounced on her comment.

'So what is it?' His tone was even, yet she fancied she caught something sharp behind the smooth cadence.

'It's not the right decision for me.' She should have known he'd probe. She should have taken time to get her excuse straight instead of grabbing the first opportunity to talk.

Alexei stopped and Mina was forced to halt. Reluctantly she turned and looked up at him. Behind his head, out to sea, dark storm clouds built, promising rain and relief from the sultry weather. For Mina, raised in a dry climate, the air felt heavy and close, almost claustrophobic. It made her edgy.

Or perhaps that was Alexei's sharp scrutiny. No trace now of the understanding, almost easygoing man she'd glimpsed lately.

'So it's not the age gap. What, then? The idea of having my children?'

Mina stood, mesmerised by the gleam in those stunning eyes. She felt something burgeon deep inside. Excitement.

A well of tenderness as she imagined a toddler with black hair and green eyes, its expression morphing from serious to mischievous. Alexei's child. And hers.

Her heart dipped and a vast tremor shuddered through her.

It was preposterous. She'd known the man mere days. She had no plans for kids anytime soon.

Yet what she felt at that deep, visceral level couldn't be denied.

'No, you want children, don't you, Mina?' Alexei's voice was a soft thread, drawing through her, making her suddenly, shockingly aware that he was right.

Marriage had never been her goal. She hadn't played brides or pretended her dolls were babies. She'd only had one doll, a gift from a neighbouring monarch that was too precious to play with. She'd assumed she'd missed out on the so-called maternal instinct.

Yet with the right partner, Mina could imagine motherhood being wonderful.

With the right partner.

Suddenly Mina felt completely, devastatingly out of her depth. All these years she'd known herself and what she wanted—the right to choose, the chance to be an artist. She'd worked hard and that work was beginning to pay off. Now, out of nowhere, this man made her feel and want things she'd never wanted before.

He undermined her certainties and her understanding of herself. And he'd done it in mere days!

Her breath clogged in her chest and she looked away. 'It doesn't matter. I've considered this carefully and I can't marry you.'

Silence. So complete even the birds in the trees seemed to stop singing. All Mina heard was the soft shush of waves.

'You'll have to give me more than that.'

'Pardon?' She swung around and met his steady look.

He didn't seem at all put out. Instead Alexei looked merely intrigued and perhaps…amused? No, that couldn't be.

'You'll have to give me a reason. Your father assured me you were interested. *You* led me to believe—'

'I led you to believe nothing!' *He* was the one who'd dragged her here. 'I'm telling you marriage is off the agenda.'

Relief buoyed her. How much easier to stand up to Alexei when he riled her than when he was likeable.

'I'm afraid I can't accept that. Not unless you give me a reason.'

'Can't accept?' Mina couldn't believe the gall of the man. Her hands found her hips and she gave him a laser stare that should have singed a few inches off his height but sadly seemed to have no impact on that oversized ego. 'Then how about this? I'm not attracted to you. If I'm going to play happy families with any man, I'd like there to be some chemistry between us.'

Her chest heaved and her chin tilted high as her gaze collided with his. Then he inclined his head and her breath came more easily. He'd got the message. See? It had been simple after all.

'I'll go and pack. I'm sure you'd rather—' Mina paused in the act of turning when a large hand wrapped around her arm.

'Not so fast, Princess.'

Alexei took in her startled expression, and the quick, convulsive swallow, the darted look at his hand on her arm—her warm, bare, silk-fleshed arm.

For two days he'd been careful not to touch her. Not even to brush against her, for his awareness of Carissa verged on the primal and he preferred to keep a cool head where the Carters were concerned. Especially as her father still proved elusive, despite the efforts of a top investigator to locate him.

Alexei breathed deep, scenting her, that tantalising aroma of exotic spice that made him want more. Far more than a single touch.

More than a provocative game of advance and retreat.

More than this brush-off.

The marriage arrangement was a sham, yet Carissa's dismissal rankled. Did she really believe she could simply turn her back on him?

'You want *chemistry*?' His voice hit a bass note and he felt her shiver. Her eyes widened and he caught a hint of vulnerability in that sherry-brown gaze. But then she lowered those long lashes, veiling her eyes before turning her head to survey his restraining hand. Her pointed stare and haughty expression were a silent demand that he release her.

Why silent? Because she didn't trust her voice? Alexei watched Carissa's pulse thrum at the base of her throat.

How could she say there was no chemistry when the air was charged with animal attraction?

He stepped close and still she didn't look up. Alexei frowned. She wasn't scared, was she? The bizarre thought hit out of nowhere, tangling his thoughts. It was contrary to everything he knew of her.

Carissa was proud, opinionated and brave, considering how most people bowed to his wishes. It wasn't as if she were inexperienced. Carter had mentioned a failed affair with a Frenchman.

No, it wasn't fear holding her still. He read the shallow rise and fall of her breasts, the rushing pulse.

'I can give you chemistry,' Alexei murmured. He put his hand beneath her chin and lifted it till she had no choice but to look at him. Her mouth was a mutinous line but her eyes... Her eyes glowed dark gold. Desire slammed into him.

She lifted a hand to his chest, pushing as she opened her lips, no doubt to protest. So Alexei stopped her with his mouth, muffling her words, drawing in her warm breath.

For a moment there was stillness as shock tore through him. Just this simple touch and he felt poised on the brink.

Then Alexei gave himself up to instinct and delved deep, cradling her head with one hand, shuffling his legs wider as he lashed his arm around her and fitted her in against him.

He'd known this would be good. How right he'd been.

She tasted like every desire made flesh, rich and tantalising. Different from any other woman yet somehow familiar. Alexei pressed harder, simultaneously demanding and coaxing a response till finally her tongue slipped against his, tentatively at first, almost shy.

This was unlike anything he could remember. A judder of pure need ripped through him. His hands tightened as she caressed him again, slowly, learning the taste and shape of his mouth. As if he were some new treat to be savoured.

That slow, cautious exploration was more arousing than anything he'd experienced in years. It was all he could do to stand there, letting her take her time, when every lick threatened to blow the back off his head. He shuddered and his groin tightened as if she'd reached out and taken his burgeoning erection in her hand rather than simply returned his kiss.

Alexei's breath expelled in a huff of satisfaction as her responses grew more voluptuous. Leaning in, he demanded more.

Their kiss became fervent. She trembled but there was nothing tentative about her caresses now. Her lips and tongue were bold and sensual, carnal and eager. Carissa had given up playing games. The honest hunger, the lack of pretence, fuelled Alexei's desire towards the point of no return.

At his chest her fingers dug into his shirt as if to stop him pulling back. He pushed closer, trying to assuage his body's demand for more. Carissa met him with demands of her own. Her slim body arched against him, her small, plump breasts thrusting up, her nipples hard and arousing as they scraped his torso.

A growl built at the back of Alexei's throat. A sound of satisfaction and need. She'd taken him from zero to a hundred in less time than a supercar on a circuit. His blood surged in his ears and his body clamoured for more.

Dropping both hands to her rump, he lifted her higher, inserting his thigh between hers. He was as taut and hot as newly worked metal. When she moved, rotating her hips, tilting her pelvis against him, Alexei wondered if he might shatter. His hands shook as he fought the impulse to strip her naked and take her here, on the sand.

Yet why hold back?

Despite that intriguing initial hesitation, Carissa was no innocent needing protection. Her kisses were the deep, drugging caresses of a woman ready for sex, and her body told its own story, of a highly sensual woman eager to mate.

He breathed deep through his nostrils, inhaling the scent of musk mingled with exotic spice and sea salt. There was no mistaking her arousal.

Alexei shuddered at what her undulating body did to his. He was more than hard. He was in pain. A pain that could only be assuaged by more, much more.

He lifted one hand, grazing it up her ribs to her breast, pulling back from her enough to close his hand over her.

Yes! Her breast filled his hand perfectly. Excitement flooded him as she arched further, thrusting herself into his palm. His erection throbbed against her softness and he heard her hiss of pleasure.

His qualms evaporated. Why wait? Why not?

Suddenly Alexei felt pressure on his chest. Two palms pushing at him. Carissa wriggling as if to get off his leg.

Her mouth broke from his and he heard her raw gasps. Still, he didn't relinquish his hold. He couldn't. His brain was locked onto the elemental need to mate. It wasn't what he'd intended when he kissed her but chemistry like this couldn't be ignored.

'No.'

At first the word didn't register as anything other than a sound. Then she said it again and he focused on her lips, red and slick from their kisses. Heat flooded his gut as he watched her mouth move and imagined her lips caressing his bare body.

He'd wanted Carissa before. From the moment she'd crossed his threshold and pretended to be unimpressed with him and his home. Her disdain had the perverse effect of sharpening his interest, especially when he had no trouble identifying the passion beneath it.

Now his need tested his control to the limit.

'Alexei, let me go!'

He frowned down into her beautiful face, seeing her mouth tighten, her jaw bunch, and her words filtered into his brain.

She couldn't be serious.

But she was. He caught what looked like desperation in the flicker of her eyes and immediately let her go. She stumbled back and he grabbed her by the elbows, holding her steady. She shook as if her legs wouldn't support her.

'Thank you.' Her eyes fixed on a point near his mouth and delicate colour washed her cheeks, highlighting her patrician features. Her hair had come undone, spilling a wash of dark silk across her shoulders. It had felt like gossamer in his hands. With the sun on it, it looked like some glossy, fabled treasure. Alexei wanted to catch it up in his hands.

He wanted to kiss her and feel again the triumphant moment when her yielding became a sensual demand.

Instead he released her and stepped back, disconcerted at the lingering strength of his desire. That was supposed to be a kiss to prove a point. Yet he felt he'd walked into an ambush. His gaze sharpened on Carissa but she looked just as poleaxed.

Yet as he watched, she regrouped. Her hands went to her hips and her chin rose. She drew a deep breath and Alexei's attention dropped to those proud, perfect breasts pouting against her pink T-shirt. His fingers twitched as he recalled the feel of her breasts. He wanted to discover if she tasted as good all over as her mouth did.

Inhaling sharply, Alexei took another step back and felt a rush of warm water around his bare feet as a tiny wave came ashore. He wished it were icy, and deep enough to wash away the erection still jutting against his jeans.

He wasn't in the habit of losing control. His mouth tightened.

'I'll go and pack.'

'Sorry?' He scowled down at her determined features. Carissa made a vague gesture with one arm. 'I'd like to go home now.' Her gaze lifted briefly to his before skittering away again. 'If you can arrange the transport.'

Alexei shook his head, a harsh laugh grinding from his throat. 'You've got to be kidding. You're not still pretending we're not attracted.'

'I...' She chewed her lip.

'Because if you are, maybe I should kiss you again. Then when we're naked on the sand and I'm deep inside you, you can tell me how sexually incompatible we are.' His voice dropped to a husky cadence as he imagined it. 'One more kiss is all it would take, Princess. You know it and I know it.'

Her nostrils flared and her eyes flashed. Alexei loved

her passion. He wanted to reach out and touch it, bask in its heat.

'Nevertheless, I want to leave. I told you I won't marry you.'

Alexei shoved his hands into the pockets of his jeans as he surveyed his confusing guest. A woman who'd tampered with his peace since she arrived. Who'd distracted him more than was advisable when he still had to bring her father to book.

What game was she playing? Some elaborate sexual tease? Except it was clear she suffered as much as he from unfulfilled desire.

Impatience stormed through Alexei. At himself for being diverted. At Carter for not showing himself. At Carissa for making him feel like an out-of-control teenager instead of a mogul with the world at his feet.

'That's a shame, Princess. Because you're not going anywhere.'

CHAPTER SEVEN

MINA STARED UP into Alexei's set face—the haughty winged eyebrows, the set jaw, the calculation in those gem-bright eyes—and knew she'd blundered terribly.

How had she imagined leaving would be easy?

It would have been if you hadn't kissed him back. If you hadn't tried to climb onto him like some sex-starved nymphomaniac.

Her naivety was truly remarkable, she realised belatedly.

Not only was the attraction between them real, but Alexei was a man used to getting his way. Right now he wanted a bride. And since Mina had demonstrated how sexually compatible they were, he also wanted her, physically.

Excitement eddied deep inside at his possessiveness. It should annoy her. It *did*. And yet…

Heat flushed her throat and breasts as she recalled the weight of his erection. The way she'd ground herself against his thigh, trying to ease the desperate ache between her legs. The way one kiss had made her cast aside a lifetime's caution.

Maybe she was sex-starved after all. In twenty-two years she'd never felt anything like this compulsion. No man had come close to breaking her absorption in her art and arousing such fire.

'Don't call me Princess. I don't like it.'

Those expressive eyebrows lifted higher as if he were surprised she'd choose that to complain about. But the way Alexei said it in that deep, roughened voice cut too close to the real Mina.

In her youth she'd chafed at the title 'Princess,' for it encompassed all the restrictions placed on her life by her father and her birth. Yet it was indelibly, undeniably hers, something she could never erase, though she didn't use it.

Hearing it now, from this big bear of a man who smashed through all the layers of civilisation and control she'd built up over a lifetime, evoked an atavistic fear that he *knew* her as no one else did. That he recognised the real Mina. More, that the wild, reckless woman who'd lost her mind and her self-respect when he kissed her, *was* the real Mina.

Her jumbled thoughts were crazy, surely, yet she had to put at least an illusion of distance between them. Hearing him use her title, even if he didn't know how apt it was, made her feel he saw past her attempts to be indomitable.

Besides, the cynical way he said it made her shiver thinking of his retribution once he learned the truth.

'Then of course I won't call you that. Carissa.'

The name was a deliberate caress, the soft sibilant curling around her vital organs like a silken cord.

The terrible knowledge hit that Mina wanted to hear him say her real name like that. Not that it was nearly as musical. It was plain and ordinary, but the longing to hear it on his tongue was almost overpowering.

She folded her arms across her chest and stumbled back a step. He'd see that as proof of weakness but that wasn't as important as retaining her sanity.

What had he done to her?

How had a kiss tumbled her defences and addled her brain?

But it had been more than a kiss.

It had been momentous. Life-changing. Mina felt as if she'd woken from a dream to a new world where everything took on a sharp clarity. Where every sense was heightened and alert. Where light and shadow were more defined, colour brighter, feelings more vivid.

She hefted a deep breath, saw his eyes flicker on the movement and angled her chin.

Weakened she might be, but she was no pushover.

'I'm sorry if my response just now misled you, Alexei.' She faced his stare head-on, telling herself this was nothing compared to challenges she'd faced as a royal. Except then she'd been confident in her own abilities. Now, suddenly, she realised she wasn't as strong as she'd believed. This man made her feel unexpectedly weak. 'But I'm serious. I don't want marriage.'

He folded his arms over his chest, the movement mirroring her posture. Yet on him the gesture was challenging rather than self-protective. She watched his biceps bulge and tried not to remember the iron-hard strength of his embrace. His virile power had been part of the magic she'd felt in his arms.

'So what do you want? An affair?'

'No!' Mina heard the shock in her voice and gave up any hope of pretending to be insouciant. 'My response was…a mistake.'

'A mistake?'

'You're a very persuasive kisser.' She refused to look away, despite the heat warming her face. 'But I've decided I'm not ready to settle down and marry.'

Mina paused, waiting for him to respond but Alexei said nothing. 'I'm sorry to disappoint you. But it's better to know now than later.' She drew a slow breath, annoyance rising at his continued silence. 'In the circumstances I'd like to return to Paris.'

'That's not possible.'

'Not possible? Is there a problem with the plane?'

Alexei shook his head. 'I need you here until your father arrives.'

'Sorry?' Still dealing with shock at her physical response to Alexei, Mina found it hard to grasp his meaning.

'Have you heard from him recently?'

Mina frowned. 'Heard from him?'

'A phone call? Text or email?'

She shook her head.

That shadowy green gaze bored into her but now he didn't bother to hide his expression. It was sharp with disbelief. With distrust.

'It's true!' Mina had been thankful Carissa's father hadn't arrived, because it delayed the moment of her unmasking, giving her friend time to get away with Pierre. Now Mina's stomach sank and her skin tightened. She had a bad feeling that this situation was more complex and fraught than she'd suspected. What had she walked into?

'Then lend me your phone. I'll check the number I have for him. Clearly the one I've got is wrong. It's vital I contact him.'

Mina bit her lip. This conversation got odder and odder. But she could hardly refuse. 'I'll write it down for you.' She'd have to get it from Carissa.

'Hand over the phone, Carissa. That will do.'

There was something about the way he spoke, the air of ruthless command that sent warning cresting through her. Something was very wrong.

Drawing on years of royal training, she masked her tension. 'Of course. I'll go and get it now.'

She felt his suspicion like tiny pinpricks on her skin but eventually he inclined his head and relief juddered through her. For a moment she'd thought he'd insist on walking her back to her room.

Mina turned away, forcing herself not to run. But all the way to the house she felt shaky. From the sudden sense of foreboding when Carissa's father had been mentioned? Or from that kiss?

In her room she turned the latch to lock her door and sagged against it, knees wobbly with reaction. But she had no time to waste.

Seconds later she had the phone in her hand, punching

out Carissa's number. But her relief when her friend picked up was short-lived. Mina recognised the panic in Carissa's voice as she admitted she hadn't heard from her father. It wasn't like him to be out of contact so long. Worse, Pierre had rung again to confirm he wouldn't be back in Paris for two days. Could Mina hold out till then?

Mina pressed a hand to her forehead, her thoughts frantic. Two more days here wouldn't affect her work schedule too much. But did she really want to stay with Alexei Katsaros? Especially now the stakes seemed infinitely higher. What had started as a defiant plan to save her friend grew tangled and risky.

Then Carissa sniffed and said Mina should tell Alexei the truth. She'd done more than enough and it was time Carissa fought her own battles.

Mina was tempted to agree.

Except Carissa would be bulldozed by Alexei. She'd be cowed and if not browbeaten then emotionally blackmailed into doing what her father and Alexei wanted. Could Mina stand by and see that happen to her dear friend?

There was even a part of her that protested at the idea of Alexei with Carissa, not for Carissa's sake but Mina's.

Where had that come from?

Mina drew a steadying breath and thrust aside the wayward thought. She warned Carissa to move out of her apartment as a precaution, in case the masquerade came unstuck and Alexei came looking for her.

Then she ended the call and stared at the phone in her hand. If she was to play this role any longer she couldn't let Alexei see her call history or contacts. It would be obvious she wasn't Carissa.

Which meant refusing to hand over her phone.

Adrenalin rushed her bloodstream at the thought of Alexei discovering the truth. But there was no other option.

All she had to do was hold out for a couple more days.

A rap on her door made her stiffen.

'Carissa?'

Mina's heart thumped and she knew a craven desire to admit defeat. To open the door and tell him everything.

Except Carissa relied on her. Carissa, who'd been there when Mina was desperately homesick and convinced she'd never make it as an artist. Carissa, whose warm, gentle nature made her the best friend Mina had ever had. The only real friend, since all the people she'd mixed with in Jeirut had been hand-picked by her father.

Carissa didn't care about her royal status. She liked Mina for herself. She was genuine and caring and Mina refused to see her throw her happiness away for some moody tycoon.

Mina breathed deep and tiptoed to the glass door that led outside.

Behind her the door rattled. 'Carissa?'

The sound sent her catapulting into the garden, eyes on the path to the beach, her phone gripped in one clammy hand.

He wouldn't be happy. In fact, Alexei would be furious. The thought lent her speed, though of course there was no real escape. The best she could do was ensure he didn't discover she wasn't Carissa. It still amazed her that he hadn't bothered to check her photo. No one but the immigration official had bothered to view her passport.

Her stride slowed as she approached the beach. Did she really mean to—

A rhythmic thudding reached her ears. Louder than her pumping heart. Mina looked over her shoulder and saw Alexei covering the ground between them in long strides. For a second, a primitive thrill of fear engulfed her, freezing her limbs. But Mina was no cornered prey. Her hand tightened on the phone. Then she turned, hauling her arm back and letting go.

Alexei grabbed her arm a moment too late. She heard his rough breathing, felt the clamp of his fingers on her wrist and the heat of his massive frame behind her as the phone arced over the water and disappeared into the endless azure sea.

The die was cast.

With a sense of disbelief, Alexei watched the phone plummet into the sea.

He'd almost convinced himself that despite her contrariness Carissa was an innocent pawn in her father's scheme.

Because her kiss blew you away.

A kiss meant nothing. Logically he knew that, yet Alexei had been close to believing in her.

Because he'd wanted her since she stepped across his threshold. Her feisty attitude and subtle sexiness were a unique turn-on, especially combined with that indefinable sense of connection, as if behind the charades they played he knew her and she him. As if at a level so deep it defied logic, they understood each other.

When they'd kissed it was combustible. *He'd* been combustible.

She'd been far more than he expected. Responsive. Blatantly hungry for him, wildly passionate and yet, when he'd first tasted her he'd sensed a hesitance that felt almost like innocence.

Innocence! She was in cahoots with her thieving father. She was messing with his mind.

'You're so desperate that I don't contact your father?' He slid his free arm around her waist, holding her back against him in a travesty of the passionate embrace they'd shared on this very beach.

Now the passions he felt were fury and jarring disappointment. He'd actually wanted to believe in Carissa.

Because you want her in your bed. You'd begun to trust

her. Even now, knowing she's part of his scam, you can't turn off your hunger.

It was true. His arm around her middle wasn't lover-like and his grip on her wrist was unbreakable, yet his body reacted to the soft pressure of her rump against him, the underside of her breasts brushing his arm and the scent of her hair teasing his nostrils.

If anything, ire hiked his arousal higher. His sharpened senses picked up her ragged breathing and her quick, thrumming pulse and the tension of her muscles, as if she waited for him to slacken his hold so she could run.

There was nowhere she could go that he wouldn't find her.

Suddenly, their situation took on a whole new, delectable piquancy.

'I didn't want you prying into my private messages.' Her voice was choppy, and Alexei felt as well as heard her harsh breathing.

'Why's that, Carissa? Have you been sexting with your French boyfriend?'

Her hissed breath confirmed it. Alexei's constraining arm tightened. At the idea of her sharing erotic messages and images with another man?

Impossible.

Yet he felt a deep satisfaction that while she was on his island she'd have to devote all her attention to him. There'd be no other men in her life.

'You know about him?' Her voice was wary.

'Was he supposed to be a secret?' Of course he was. She'd even faked a show of tremulous innocence when her lips met his. Not that it had lasted.

'My messages are my affair. You have no right to pry. You're a bully.'

She yanked her arm, trying to free it. The movement was so violent it slammed her into even more intimate contact with Alexei's hardening body. Flame shot through him as she rubbed against his groin.

Carissa froze, her breath a shocked hiss. He felt the pulse at her wrist sprint out of control as if she only now realised how intimately close they stood.

'You think I care about seeing your nude photos? All I want is to bring your father out of hiding.'

'Hiding? What are you talking about?'

Alexei applauded her acting skills. She sounded confused rather than guilty. 'Spare me the dramatics. Only a woman desperate to hide the truth would pitch her phone. You're in this with your father.' He hadn't quite believed she'd do it, even as she drew her arm back in that perfect curve. 'You've just proved it.'

She was silent for so long he wondered if she were about to admit defeat till she said in a completely different tone, 'In what?'

Furious and sick of her lies, he spun her round, his hands on her narrow waist.

Yet, reading her expression, Alexei felt a splinter of doubt.

'What has he done?' Instead of avoiding his stare, she peered up at him, a tiny wrinkle between her eyebrows, her look searching.

Probably hoping to pretend that she didn't know.

'Embezzled a fortune. And that's just the funds he's stolen in the last couple of months. Who knows what the total is in the years he's worked for me?' Alexei spoke through clamped teeth, watching her eyes grow wide.

He'd thought his financial systems the best. The rigorous accounting and auditing processes were held up as the gold standard. But when the man who designed them was the one with his fingers in the till...

'You're sure?' Carissa looked the picture of shock. He felt a tremor pass through her and held her more firmly, telling himself he didn't want her pretending to faint. It wasn't dramatics he wanted but retribution.

'Absolutely. There's a complete audit underway. You can be sure it will uncover every cent he's stolen. Including the money that's supported your party lifestyle while you pretend to be an artist.'

The fact some of the stolen money had funded this woman's taste for idle self-gratification twisted the knife. Alexei had laboured hard for everything he possessed. It had been tough, especially scraping together capital to invest in his first innovative software package when he'd had no track record and only a mediocre education. He hadn't even had a permanent roof over his head.

Nothing had been handed to him. And he knew all about leeches who fattened themselves by living off the hard work of others.

Yet he'd allowed himself to be conned by Carter.

He stared down into soft brown eyes and knew they lied. His voice held bitter amusement. 'After this you'll have to work for a living like the rest of us. That will be a novel experience for you.'

Now Mina understood the rage flaring in that deep green gaze, the snap of his words and the harsh jut of his chin. It was like staring into the boiling heart of a volcano.

The raw quality of his emotion should unnerve her. Yet at the same time, that elemental ferocity drew her.

Was she mad?

Her father had always said she was reckless, yet there was something so vital about Alexei in this moment. Even as she warned herself to be careful, her artist's eye was busy cataloguing the changes in him, the way potent masculine anger imbued every sharp angle and bunched muscle.

Already his hold on her waist loosened. Was she ridiculously naive? Yet the vibe she picked up from Alexei was the same as she got from her brother-in-law, Huseyn. When he'd first appeared, Huseyn had been the enemy, storming in to snatch the kingdom and her sister in marriage. Big, abrupt and deliberately provoking, he'd nevertheless proved appearances wrong. He'd turned out to be a devoted family man and an unobtrusively kind brother-in-law, whose bark was worse than his bite, at least with those he cared for.

Was Alexei like him? Or did her instinct lie because she was attracted? And because she battled a compulsion to commit that sparking, urgent energy to paper? Mina wanted to capture his aura of power.

Almost as much as she wanted that energy focused on kissing her again.

She blinked. She couldn't take her safety for granted.

'Do you plan to hurt me because of him?' Mina had no idea if confronting Alexei directly was the right approach but she had to know.

His head reared back, a scowl settling on his forehead. 'I suppose you'll find it tough to work for a living instead of living off your father's ill-gotten gains. But I'd hardly call that hurting.'

'I mean, are you so angry you'll *hurt* me.'

She saw the moment her meaning registered. Alexei's instinctive recoil and the horror in his eyes.

His hands dropped to his sides. 'No! Of course not.'

'There's no *of course.* Some men do.'

Slowly he inclined his head, his breath expelling in a rush of warm air that feathered her hair. 'Not me. Not ever.'

Mina surveyed him steadily, wondering whether to believe him, and her instinct.

'I think you're wrong about the theft. I think it's a mistake. Maybe someone else stole the money and made it look like he did it.' What she knew of Carissa's father pointed to an honest man, though his idea of engineering an arranged marriage was bizarre. Maybe his recent bereavement had affected him more than Carissa feared.

Alexei shook his head. 'There's no doubt. It was definitely him.' He raised his eyebrows as if challenging her to prove otherwise.

'Well, if so, he didn't fritter it away funding parties in Paris.' Carissa's father had paid his daughter's art school tuition and now helped with part of her rent, but Carissa was talented and hardworking, supplementing her income from her art by waitressing and modelling. Even her shopping addiction for second-hand clothes was a source of income since she sold items she'd refurbished.

Alexei merely crossed his arms over his chest. He looked as unmoved and unmovable as the rocky outcrop at the far end of the beach.

Mina suppressed a sigh. What was the point of protesting Carissa's blamelessness? He'd never believe her. And, if he'd been ripped off so badly, who could blame him?

She slicked her tongue around her parched lips, feeling the rush of her pulse and the jitter of nerves still unsteady after that sprint to the beach, with Alexei at her heels. And Alexei holding her against him as if he'd never release her.

In fury, Mina reminded herself. Not desire. She was the one plagued by that. To Alexei she was a conniving thief, or as good as.

She shivered and looked away, out over the water where the dark clouds grew more threatening by the moment. The humid air felt heavy, sultry with ominous foreboding.

It was hard not to see it as a sign, a warning that Alexei had some revenge planned.

Of course! Abruptly she swung towards him. His gaze was already on her, sending sensation wrinkling down her backbone. Mina's mouth tightened. She had to stop *reacting* to him!

'Why am I here, Alexei? What do you really want?'

'Don't look so worried. Nothing's going to happen to you that you don't want.'

Mina took a second to digest that. It should have reassured except the dark speculation in his eyes and her answering tremor of awareness undermined certainty. As if their bodies spoke a different language. As if he expected her to *want* far more than was good for her.

Mina refused to go there. Bad enough to find her first stirrings of real desire were for a man who didn't trust or like her. Who was, to all intents and purposes, her enemy.

She crossed her arms, mirroring his posture. 'Why am I here, Alexei? And don't give me that line about wanting to marry. That's clearly a lie.'

One dark eyebrow slanted. 'You take offence at a lie?'

Mina was about to tell him she abhorred dishonesty as much as she did selfish men who manipulated women for their own ends. Then she remembered she was here under false pretences. For the best of reasons, but still...

'Spit it out, Alexei.'

His eyes held hers. 'You're bait, to draw your father out. Since he had the front to suggest I marry you, I figure when he learns you're here, he'll assume his theft hasn't been discovered or that I'm willing to come to some agreement with my soon-to-be father-in-law.' His disdainful tone and chilly stare told her how likely that was.

'And until he gets here?' She swallowed. Her throat was tight and she had a hard time projecting calm.

'Till then you're my trump card.' His lips curved in a smile she could only describe as dangerous. 'I'll keep you close.'

CHAPTER EIGHT

THE SOUND OF the wind finally distracted Mina. She looked up from the intricate design taking shape on her sketchpad and realised the noise she'd been vaguely aware of was the howl of a strong wind from the sea. The dark clouds had moved closer in the hours since her confrontation with Alexei and the light was lurid green.

The hairs on Mina's nape and arms lifted. She didn't know tropical weather, but that eerie light reminded her of the explosive storms that occasionally devastated the mountains of her homeland.

A crash made her jump. Mina put her drawing down and crossed to her bedroom window.

A sun umbrella had fallen, knocking over a wrought-iron chair. As she watched, a cushion tumbled past and came to rest against a gardenia hedge.

Mina opened the door and went out, feeling the whip of the wind. Another cushion floated in the pool. She concentrated on saving the rest, gathering them and dropping them inside her room.

As she turned around, a chair slid, screeching across the flagstones. Mina chewed her lip, looking beyond the garden to the taller trees, bending in the wind. If the storm worsened, unsecured furniture could be dangerous, especially in a house with so many big windows. As for that umbrella…

She was grappling with it, trying to close it against the force of the wind when she heard a voice behind her.

'Leave that to me.' Large hands took over, Alexei's shoulder nudging her out of the way. She watched the strain of bunching muscles and tendons in his arms as he fought to close it, then heard a grunt of satisfaction as he finally succeeded. 'You get inside. This will get worse before it gets better.' He was already lifting the long umbrella pole and marching away.

Mina frowned, staring as he disappeared around the corner of the house. What had she expected? Thanks for trying to help? She should have known better.

But as another chair careered across flagstones, she set her mouth, grabbed it and followed him.

Nearby, yet screened from the house, was a large garage. Inside, in addition to the four-wheel drive, she discovered a couple of jet skis, a windsurfer, canoes and Alexei, stacking the furled umbrella against a pile of outdoor furniture. He must have been working for some time, securing it all. Mina had been so busy working she hadn't noticed.

'Where's Henri?'

Alexei's head jerked up. He hadn't heard her approach over the noise of the wind. 'Gone with Marie to the larger island for supplies. But the storm's changed course, coming in faster than expected. They'll have to stay there till it blows over.'

Even in the gloom Mina could see the gleam of Alexei's steady stare. Did he expect her to panic at the idea of a powerful storm?

'What can I do?'

'Sorry?'

Behind her the door banged shut, leaving them in almost darkness. But not completely. Mina could make out his towering form, close now. The wide spread of his shoulders, the jut of his jaw as if he were still furious.

Mina didn't step back. To retreat would be to admit fear. She might be stuck here, an unwilling guest of an angry host who saw her as an avaricious plotter, but she refused to show anxiety. Even if there *was* something about Alexei Katsaros that made her breathing ragged and her pulse skip.

But it's not fear, is it?

It's desire.

Mina inhaled a breath redolent with the tang of citrus and Alexei, and strove to ignore the flurry in her belly.

'You said the storm's coming more quickly than expected and Henri's not here to help. What can I do to prepare?'

Alexei peered down at the slim figure before him, wishing it were light enough to read her expression.

It wasn't the first time she'd surprised him. When he'd rounded the house to find her struggling with the oversized umbrella his heart had almost stopped. Did she have any idea how dangerous that would have been, if the wind had ripped it out of her hold? How much damage it could do as a projectile?

'Get into the house and stay there.' He had enough to do without worrying for her safety. The wind was still rising.

For answer, she spun on her foot, headed for the door and yanked it open. Alexei saw her silhouetted against the light, long legs, short white shorts and a tight top that outlined a deliciously willowy body. He remembered the feel of her against him; the combination of taut flesh and enticing, feminine softness had been irresistible.

Then she strode towards the house.

Good riddance. Alexei had more to do and time was running out. Yet, as he carted more furniture to the garage, he found Mina marching towards him, carrying another chair. The wind had strengthened and her long dark hair whipped around her face.

'What are you doing? Get inside. Now!'

For answer she kept walking, would have passed him if he hadn't caught her arm.

Her haughty stare could have stripped bark from a tree. 'There isn't time to argue. Accept my help and do what you have to. What about shutters? I can't see any. How do we protect the windows?'

Alexei paused, surprised to discover she was serious. She planned to help him batten down for the storm. 'They're electric. They'll come down at the punch of a button.'

'Then shouldn't you go and punch that button before we lose power?'

She was right. Plus he wanted to double-check the backup generator.

Alexei considered picking her up bodily and carrying her inside. She'd be safe. But no doubt she'd race back out here as soon as his back was turned.

'Very well.' He cast a look at the trees bending in the wind and, behind them, the inky, threatening sky. 'But only five minutes more. The main entrance will be open. Come in that way.' He lowered his head to her level, watching her pupils dilate. 'No longer than five minutes. Got it?'

Silently she nodded.

But when the time was up, Carissa was nowhere to be seen. The wind was stronger now, the sound like a freight train approaching from a distance. They had to take shelter. They didn't have much time left. Fat drops of rain fell and a second later he faced a grey sheet of solid water.

His mouth tightened as he scanned the exterior of the house. All the furniture was shut away. The house was secure, storm shutters in place. But Carissa was nowhere to be found.

Alexei called her name but the wind tore the sound away. Anxiety nipping at him, he sped through the garden, drenched by the needling deluge.

He couldn't see her. Not near the pool or house. He ventured further into the garden, blinking to clear his vision. With each passing second tension coiled tighter, his pulse racing faster.

Alexei rounded a curve in a path to see something staggering towards him. The sight was so unexpected, the shape lurching drunkenly, that it took precious seconds to process what he saw. When he did, he stifled an oath and raced forward, anger vying with stupefaction.

A sculpture! She'd stayed out in *this* to save a sculpture.

Arms out, he grabbed the ungainly wooden shape as Carissa staggered against him, blown by the force of the gale.

'Leave it! It's not worth it.' He felt her flinch. Saw her eyes widen as he tugged it from her.

She clung on like a limpet, mouthing something he couldn't hear. 'Save…together.'

Alexei shook his head. 'Inside. Now!'

Whether she heard him over the wind's rising scream, Alexei didn't know. But her mouth set in a mulish line as she held on tight. They didn't have time to argue. The wind was still picking up speed. Soon the flying debris would be larger, more dangerous.

Hefting the sculpture more securely, Alexei grabbed her hand and started back down the path.

The way back took forever. The sodden ground was treacherous and the wind buffeted mercilessly. More than once he saved Carissa from falling when her foot skidded. Then, as they approached the house, the wind caught Alexei and the wildly rotating sculpture full force and almost plunged them into the pool. He would have dropped it there and then, except this time Carissa was dragging at his arm, holding him steady.

Cursing, Alexei regained his balance and lurched forward. His muscles strained at the effort of carrying the cumbersome sculpture that wanted to fly from his arms into the screeching wind.

Darkness. The slam of the door. Stillness after that riot of rushing air and hammering rain.

Alexei struggled to the control panel on the wall, jamming his elbow against the switch that brought down the final storm shutter. Another jab and light filled the foyer.

His breath came in rough gasps that tore his throat. Water sluiced down his face and he almost lost balance in the spreading pool of water as he bent to lower his ungainly burden.

Finally he straightened to stare at the convoluted collection of carved sails that still spun and shivered with the dying momentum of the wind. No wonder it had felt as if it might take off from his arms. It was designed to move in a breeze. Breeze, not a cyclone!

Alexei had bought it as a brilliant, evocative piece that paid homage to the centuries of seafarers who'd passed this way. Now, looking past the still-turning sails to the woman beyond, he wished he'd never seen it.

She could have been hurt. More than hurt.

The savage clench of his ribs around his organs wrapped fiery pain around Alexei's torso.

Mina was bent forward, hands on knees, dragging in desperate, gasping breaths. Her hair was a slick, dark curve that arrowed over her shoulder. Her nipples stood proud against the dark cherry pink of the top that plastered her breasts. Her slim legs glistened with water and there was a long red scratch on her shin.

'What. The. Hell. Were. You. Thinking?' He ground the words out.

Her eyes lifted. A second later Carissa straightened, abandoning her recuperative pose for that now-familiar haughty stance. Chin forward, slender neck stretched high, eyebrows slightly raised. She did obstinate condescension to perfection.

'Saving a wonderful work of art.' She reached into a back pocket of her shorts and produced a large screwdriver. That explained how she'd dislodged the sculpture from its plinth. She must have grabbed it from the garage.

'What on earth possessed you?'

Still not quite believing what she'd done, he watched as she turned away and put the screwdriver down on a side table. It landed with a clatter. There was a jagged tear at the hem of her T-shirt and another scratch down the back of one toned thigh.

Alexei felt something surge high inside. Something rough and sharp, scrabbling and clawing at his control. He clenched his jaw so tight he wondered if he'd ever unlock it.

A spasm shook him as he remembered the waving boughs, the lashing storm and thought of the lucky escape she'd had.

Carissa turned, eyes dark and wide in her too-pale face. 'We couldn't leave it there. It's a masterpiece.'

Alexei stared. He couldn't believe what he heard.

'You know it is.' Her voice was clipped. 'Otherwise you wouldn't have bought it.'

He knew all right. He wouldn't have paid the exorbitant amount he had for it otherwise. But that didn't matter.

'That was the single most stupid, irresponsible thing I've witnessed in years.' His voice lashed as he relived the sight of her, refusing to budge without her precious sculpture. 'I don't care about the money.'

She flinched, her face paling even more. 'Of course you don't! Obviously I was mistaken. You probably bought it because it had a big price tag to match your big ego.' She drew a breath that emphasised how shaky she was, despite her show of defiance. She looked proud and glorious and frighteningly vulnerable. And Alexei couldn't understand why the vein of fury ran so deep and strong within him.

It was a good thing they were on opposite sides of the room. Dimly he realised fear fed his anger. That terrible moment when he'd discovered her missing. Guilt that she could have died out there because he hadn't forced her inside earlier.

'It's not worth your life. Do you have any idea how dangerous it was out there?' Alexei heard his voice rise from a hoarse whisper to something close to a roar. 'Are you really that thoughtless? That unbelievably stupid?'

His loss of control stunned him. When had he ever been this angry? When he'd discovered her father's theft he'd been livid, determined to get justice. He'd felt personally betrayed, made a fool of by the one person he'd trusted in years. But he hadn't experienced this visceral level of dismay. This gut-scouring scrape of horror.

Carissa didn't flinch. She faced him with cool—almost *too* cool—composure.

Finally the echo of his words died. Outside the wind wailed, but in here there was nothing but the sound of heavy, uneven breaths and the tumble of rushing blood in his ears.

'If you'll excuse me, I have a cut I need to attend to, before I stain your floor.'

Carissa spun around and walked away down the dark corridor towards her suite. Belatedly he realised she was cradling one hand. And that she walked with the careful precision of someone marshalling their strength to stay upright.

The red mist edging Alexei's vision began to clear. The cyclonic rage eased. His brain kicked into gear, enough to suspect her superior bearing hid something other than disgust at his fury.

His gaze dropped to the floor. A spatter of dark droplets led down the corridor. The sight was a kick to the belly.

Her hand was bleeding and he hadn't noticed. He'd been too busy berating her.

Alexei slumped against the wall, palming his wet face, trying to scrub away the last vestiges of blinding fury.

He still reeled from the fact Carissa had pitched in to help secure the house, making herself useful as if she wasn't the spoiled, self-absorbed woman he'd pegged her as. Alexei had expected her to demand he spirit her off the island. Or that she'd cower in the house, frightened by the ferocity of the weather. He wouldn't have blamed her.

Carissa never did what he expected. *She* wasn't what he expected.

Now she made him feel as if *he* were in the wrong.

Residual anger made his heart pound his ribcage. Yet that didn't explain the unfamiliar, queasy feeling in his belly. It wasn't fear, not now she was safe.

Surely it wasn't guilt? She *had* risked her neck out there. The woman was trouble.

Alexei straightened from the wall, circled around the sculpture that had caused this drama, and headed towards the light streaming from her suite. He needed to see how badly she was hurt.

Mina bit her lip and tried to stop shaking enough to tear open the box of sticking plasters she'd found in the bathroom. It dropped to the floor and she sagged against the wall, eyes closing.

She'd pick it up in a minute, when the shaking stopped.

She was so angry. But soon she'd be calm.

Except it wasn't simply anger that made her tremble from head to foot. Mina wiped her uninjured hand across her cheeks, scrubbing away the fresh trails of wetness that had nothing to do with the sodden hair dripping down her face.

There was a blockage in her throat, hot and sour, making it hard to swallow. A ball of emotion that refused to go away.

Stupid. Thoughtless.

The words circled again and again. She didn't know how to silence them.

Mina told herself she was in shock. The storm had been

terrifying. When she'd started out to save the sculpture, the wind hadn't been so bad and she'd been sure she'd have time. Then all hell had broken loose and she'd been stunned to realise danger was upon her, upon *them*. It was her fault Alexei had been out there too.

What if he'd been hurt trying to save her?

Her mouth crumpled and a sob seared her clogged throat.

Mina shook her head. She didn't cry. She never cried. Not even when her father died.

Stupid. Thoughtless.

She swallowed again and this time tasted tears.

The last time she'd seen her father they'd argued. She'd wanted to go to art school and he'd already enrolled her in university to major in economics. It was one of the rare times he'd lost his temper. Usually he was cool and distant. He expected his daughters to obey, to do whatever he expected, including acquiring appropriate qualifications to prove women in Jeirut could play a part in the country's modernisation.

There was no room for an artist in the royal family. Mina's value, like her sister Ghizlan's, lay in being *useful*.

Their father's focus was the country, not them. He'd never cuddled them or laughed with them. Never been close, let alone shown love. They were tools in his grand plans. Her mother had died when she was an infant so there was no one to argue on her behalf.

But at seventeen, Mina had believed she had a right to choose her career. Her father had put paid to that. He'd been brutally frank about her purpose in life. As a princess she'd be a model for Jeiruti women and have a key role in royal events. In time, she'd make a dynastic marriage to a man her father chose.

Mina was stupid, thoughtless and selfish to question his plans.

Two days later he'd dropped dead from a brain aneurism.

She'd never had a chance to mend the breach between them. She told herself it didn't matter because her father hadn't loved her, or she him. Yet regret lingered. Hearing those words again, whiplash sharp—

'Carissa? Are you all right?'

Mina's eyes popped open, horror enveloping her. She caught sight of herself in the mirror and groaned. Her eyes were pink and she couldn't stop her mouth quivering.

'Yes.'

The door rattled. 'Why have you locked the door?'

Mina sank her teeth into her bottom lip. She didn't need this. She didn't have the energy to face Alexei. She needed time to marshal her defences.

'Carissa?'

'I want privacy. Is that too much to ask?' Her shaking grew worse, not better. She wrapped her arms around herself, trying to hold in the ache. And the cold. She felt so cold.

'Open the door, Carissa. I need to make sure you're okay.'

Great. Another man who refused to take a woman's word or believe she could look after herself.

But Alexei thought her stupid, didn't he?

To her horror, fresh tears prickled her eyes and she blinked frantically. She felt…raw, unprotected, unable to summon the assurance she projected to keep people at a distance.

It was ridiculous. Words couldn't hurt her. Yet Alexei's expression as he'd spoken… The knowledge he'd been right—

'Open the door *now*, Carissa, or I'll break it down.'

'I said—'

'Now!' He didn't shout like before. But the low resonance of his voice convinced her more than any ranting threat.

Mina stumbled to the door and flicked the latch. It swung open and Alexei surged in, making her back up.

She refused to meet his eyes, turning instead to the packet she'd dropped on the floor. 'Since you're here—' she tugged in a swift breath and tried to sound nonchalant '—would you mind picking that up? My hands are a bit unsteady.' There was no way of hiding that so she might as well admit it.

Without waiting for a response Mina turned to the basin and ran water over the jagged cut in the fleshy part of her hand, cleaning away the dripping blood. Her grasp of the screwdriver had slipped on the last screw and dug into her flesh. Strange, she couldn't feel any pain.

'Here, let me.' A large hand took her elbow and Alexei pushed her down onto a chair beside the vast bath. His touch was surprisingly gentle. Mina opened her mouth to protest but found she didn't have the inclination. Her shoulders slumped as her energy ebbed.

Alexei wrapped a fluffy white hand towel around her hand. Mina frowned, thinking of blood on the pristine cloth, but said nothing. It was his towel.

He took her other hand and pressed it to the cloth to keep the pressure steady. Then he collected the packet she'd dropped plus a bottle from the cupboard and hunkered before her.

She was aware of his heat above all, like a furnace sending out warmth to tease her frozen body. But she refused to meet his eyes. Instead she concentrated on those hard, beautiful hands. They worked deftly.

'This will sting.' He unwrapped the towel and dabbed the wound. Mina felt the burn of antiseptic but didn't flinch.

'It doesn't look too deep.'

'No. Fortunately it drove along my hand instead of in.' If it had surely she wouldn't feel so calm. A major injury to her hand would be catastrophe.

Alexei's grip tightened for a second, then eased. Mina frowned, watching him work. A moment later it was all over.

'How does that feel?'

'Fine.' She flexed her hand, discovering she'd stopped shaking as he held her. 'Thank you.'

He didn't move. Beyond the thick shutters, Mina heard the rush of the wind driving against the building. It reminded her of the danger she'd put them both in.

Her heart thudded against her ribs as if trying to fly away on the storm. She drew in another breath, this time through her mouth, trying not to inhale Alexei's spicy scent. The storm seemed to have heightened it rather than washed it away.

'Carissa, I'm sorry. I—'

Mina surged up, stepping sideways, away from him. It felt wrong, hearing him apologise, when she'd been at fault.

It felt even more wrong, hearing him call her by someone else's name. She wanted *her* name on his lips. How crazy was that?

'No. Don't.' She swallowed. He rose and she fixed her eyes on his collarbone. 'I apologise. I was wrong to put you in danger by making you look for me.' She sucked in a shallow breath. 'You're right. A sculpture isn't as important as a person.' If he'd died because of her...

Reluctantly she lifted her eyes and met his deep green gaze. A thrill of recognition and awareness shot down her spine. Strangely, he didn't look angry any more.

'It *was* stupid of me. I thought I had more time. Obviously I underestimated the force and speed of the storm.'

'I applaud your desire to save the sculpture. Just not your timing.' His mouth flattened. 'I shouldn't have spoken the way I did. That was fear talking. But it was no excuse.'

'You were frightened?' Alexei had seemed so in control, so competent, it hadn't entered her mind he was frightened.

'I was frantic. You could have been badly hurt.'

His eyes locked on hers and Mina felt as if she were being pulled under by a jade-green sea, sucked into an undertow where, no matter how she struggled, she couldn't break free.

Or had she forgotten to struggle? She tried to rouse herself from this strange torpor but couldn't.

'I'm tougher than I look.'

Alexei inclined his head. 'So I'm learning. It took guts to do what you did.' His words astounded her.

'And stupidity.' She couldn't let it go.

Something shifted in his expression. 'You thought it important. That made it courageous.'

His words sowed a kernel of heat deep inside. Heat that glowed and spread as he stared down at her.

'Does that mean you don't despise me quite as much as before?' Better to remind them both that they were on opposing sides than be lulled into surrendering her guard any further.

'I don't despise you.' Alexei's voice was gruff as he lifted his hand to wipe the tear tracks from her cheeks. His touch ignited a terrible yearning. Mina had to fight to not lean closer.

'I find that hard to believe.' Mina moved back, breaking contact, injecting hauteur into her expression.

Alexei followed, hemming her in and planting a palm on the wall beside her head. 'You infuriate me. Intrigue me.' His voice dropped to a low note that resonated through her. 'Attract me.'

Mina's pulse thundered as she read the stark determination in his eyes. She struggled to hang on to anger but it slipped like precious water from her hands.

'That's impossible.' It had to be. Because she feared she didn't have the strength to remember they were enemies.

'Then perhaps you'll believe this.' Alexei leaned in and every emotion, every sensation Mina had tried not to feel, exploded into life.

CHAPTER NINE

THE TOUCH OF his lips on hers was gentle yet not tentative. As if he gave her time to adjust to the inevitable.

And it *did* feel inevitable.

As if she'd waited half her life for this. As if the kiss they'd shared on the sand hours ago had evoked a longing that, once roused, couldn't be assuaged or argued away by common sense.

Common sense?

Where was that as Mina curled her fingers around those hard, wet shoulders?

Where was it as his kiss deepened and Mina not only opened for him but slicked her tongue against his, curling, inviting, *demanding* more?

She'd learned a lot from their earlier kiss. It had blasted away the little she'd thought she knew about kissing. Her limited experience hadn't prepared her for Alexei's wholesale takeover of her senses.

He didn't even touch her, except for his lips and tongue, but that was enough to create a sensual storm. Mina was swept away, clinging to his shoulders for support and to prevent him pulling back.

She'd been the one to withdraw last time. His hand on her breast had broken the moment, terrifying her. Not because he'd overstepped the bounds. But because Mina had been overwhelmed by how much she'd wanted more. How reckless he made her.

Stupid. Thoughtless.

The words lost their sting as Alexei's heat swamped her and she felt his body all down hers. He angled his head for better access to her mouth and growled his appreciation as she sucked his tongue hard.

Had she ever heard such a sexy sound? It made her nipples pebble and heat blossom at the apex of her thighs where she felt an achy emptiness.

Mina might have an impulsive streak but in some things she was innately cautious. She'd never given herself to a man. Never been attracted enough to trust someone so intimately. Never been so swept away that it wasn't a matter of *if* but *when* she surrendered.

Alexei made her feel more than she'd thought possible. *That* scared her. He didn't.

Fingers still curled into his shoulder muscles, she turned her head, breaking the kiss. The sound of their ragged breathing filled the air.

'You don't really want me here.' Mina struggled to find an argument that would end this.

'But I need you here.' His words were hot on her sensitised skin, his mouth moving against her cheek in a caress that made her tremble.

'Only as bait to lure him.' She gasped the words, trying to catch her breath. Trying to find the strength to push Alexei away. If she had any self-respect, she'd stop this.

His fingers gripped her chin, inexorably turning her head. Alexei was so close she fell into that malachite gaze.

'He can go to hell. All I can think about is you.' Alexei frowned, his look almost savage, his breathing as uneven as Mina's. 'If you'd been seriously hurt out there…' He shook his head. 'You have no idea how I felt, thinking about that.'

Mina read the echo of her own stark emotions in Alexei's flared nostrils, tight jaw, grim line of mouth and shadowed eyes.

'Believe me, I know.' Mina couldn't hold back the words. 'When I thought about how I'd put you at risk I felt sick.' Alexei's hand softened against her face, palming her cheek, inviting her to turn her head into his touch. She did, luxuriating in the comfort of it, even as it sent a buzz of adrenalin ricocheting through her body. 'It's crazy. I don't even know you—'

'And you don't like me,' he added with a wry tilt of his mouth.

'I don't think this is about liking.' What she felt came from a deep, vital part of herself and it demanded honesty. She was beyond prevarication.

The hint of humour in his expression died. 'Carissa, I—'

'No!' She pressed her fingers to his mouth, desperate to stop his words. Mina couldn't bear for him to call her by her friend's name. Not when she trembled on the brink of something so huge. 'Don't say anything. No more words, please.'

There were lies enough between them. But what she felt, however unexpected, was real. More real than anything she'd felt for any other man.

It had to be just sex. It couldn't be anything more. Yet this felt as unstoppable as sunrise. As wondrous as a child's smile.

She could no more turn her back on this than she could stop the storm outside.

Even if she could, she didn't want to.

It was time.

Instead of smiling, Alexei's expression grew more serious. There was no triumph in his eyes, or greedy anticipation, just a steady regard that told her he felt the same.

Or was she impossibly naive, painting her own wash on circumstances?

Before she could decide, Alexei bent, slid an arm around her back and another behind her legs, and lifted her off the floor. Mina slipped her hands around his neck, torn between dismay at being hoisted high against his hard chest and quivering delight at how strong and sure he felt. How utterly feminine he made her feel.

She'd never ceded control to any man. Had resisted it, she now realised, after seeing so many acquaintances pushed into unwanted, arranged marriages. Her sister included. Now she discovered the delight of being with a man whose physical strength far surpassed hers. Surprisingly she didn't feel vulnerable but treasured.

He carried her out of the bathroom and Mina's pulse quickened as they approached her bed. But Alexei kept going, through the door and down the corridor that formed the spine of the house. Towards the master suite.

The hall was gloomy and the wind sounded like the malevolent howl of the desert djinns her nurse had told her about when she was little. Mina shivered.

'We're safe here.' Alexei must have sensed her thoughts. 'The main house is built to withstand worse than this.' He stopped walking and fixed her with that steady gaze. 'But if you prefer, we could sit this out in the basement storm shelter.'

He was giving her the opportunity to change her mind. One last chance at sanity.

For answer Mina slid her fingers into his wet hair and tugged his head down, pressing her lips to his. She slicked her tongue along his mouth till he opened. Alexei shuddered, then gathered her closer still, his hold so tight he crushed her breathless.

When, finally, he lifted his head, she couldn't hear the wind over the thunder of her blood and Alexei had lost that veneer of calm. She read naked hunger in his dark eyes.

Mina squirmed as arousal coursed through her, coalescing in a sensation like wax melting and softening between her legs.

Then Alexei was striding down the dim hall, eating up the distance to his room.

Fleetingly Mina wondered about mentioning her inexperience, but she shied from anything that might delay or even stop what lay ahead. Besides, instinct had worked fine so far.

Alexei lowered her feet to the floor and switched on a bedside lamp. Mina had an impression of space, of furnishings the colour of parchment with azure accents, then Alexei put his hands on her waist and she had eyes for nothing but him.

His black hair glistened, wet against his skull. Lamplight highlighted the severe, beautiful angle of his cheekbones and threw into relief the stern set of his nose.

Mina's gaze dropped to his mouth, so sensual and generous. Her heart dipped and she felt again the liquid rush of desire.

She swayed closer, grabbing his shirt. Of their own volition her fingers began undoing his buttons. Gone was the deft quickness of a woman who worked with her hands. She fumbled first one, then another, but Alexei didn't help, just stood, still as a breathing statue.

A breathing, hot statue of majestic proportions. Mina finally slid the final button free and pushed her hands between the open edges of his shirt. Damp heat, heavily moulded muscle, the crispness of chest hair, the quick throb of his powerful heartbeat.

A quiver ran through him as she slid her palms over his pectorals to his collarbone, pushing the shirt wide across his shoulders and down his arms. Alexei shrugged and it fell, leaving Mina in possession of a view that stole her breath.

She wanted to sculpt him. She wanted to run her hands over every contour and angle, from the heavy weight of muscle to the masculine symmetry of ribs and hips. She wanted to taste him, to see if he responded to her lips on his body.

'My turn.' Alexei caught her as she leaned closer. She was still processing his words when he tugged her T-shirt up. Obediently Mina lifted her arms and tossed it free.

His gaze dipped to her breasts. Mina felt her nipples harden and, realising her bra was probably transparent when wet, felt heat rise in her throat. Not from embarrassment, but from a cocktail of pride and daring at Alexei's expression. There was glazed heat in his eyes, while his tight mouth and flared nostrils spoke of immense control.

'Not pink?' His voice was hoarse, as if his throat had dried.

To her surprise Mina found herself pushing her shoulders back, inviting him to stare. Was this the same woman who never flaunted herself? Who found male attention more often a nuisance than anything else?

But this was different. With Alexei nothing was as it had been.

'No, not pink.' Her bra and matching knickers were of silk and cobweb lace in dark anthracite grey. The combination of bold colour and soft, exquisitely worked fabric was pure Mina, who'd never chosen a pastel in her life.

'I like it.' His mouth barely moved on the words. 'Take it off.' His voice was as harsh as the sanding block she used to finish a stone sculpture.

Suddenly his eyes were on hers, the cool green no longer cool. Mina felt a judder pass through her, something shared between them. Understanding. Desire. Desperation.

Not allowing time for second thoughts, Mina reached back and unclipped her bra. Her breasts swung free as she tugged it off. A flash of exaltation filled her as she watched Alexei's expression, his sudden swallow, the tension in his jaw.

Alexei might be more experienced, he might be bigger and stronger, but Mina had her own power.

Then a hard palm centred over her nipple, closing gently on her breast, squeezing with just the right amount of pressure, and Mina's self-satisfaction disintegrated.

Something zipped like lightning from her breast to her

womb, leaving a scorched trail. Her knees rocked and for a second she wondered if they'd hold her, till Alexei curled his arm around her waist and pulled her close. Her hips pressed the damp denim of his jeans.

Her breath was a choked moan and his mouth rucked up in a smile that looked as if it bordered on pain.

Still, he worked her breast and Mina felt something vital inside her give and break free. She leaned closer, desperate for more, overwhelmed at the escalating pace of desire.

Alexei pressed his mouth to the side of her neck, near the curve that opened to her shoulder. But instead of kissing, he grazed with his teeth, then nipped gently. Mina jumped as another electric charge passed through her, exacerbating the neediness low in her body. She wriggled against him, desperate for relief.

Her hands went to his jeans, flicking the button undone as if she'd done this so many times before. Then his zip, harder to open because of the erection straining the fabric. Finally she succeeded, inserting her hands between his hips and the fabric, drawing slowly down.

A shudder passed through him, his hold tightening, then the hot length of him sprang free to rest against her.

Mina moulded him with her hands, her touch inquisitive, wondering, testing the fascinating weight and surprising silk-over-steel sensation.

But not for long. Alexei captured her wrists, pulling them away. He muttered something under his breath and stepped back. But before she could protest he shucked his shoes and shoved his jeans down.

Mina had thought his upper body beautiful, his erection arresting. But those thighs, even the carved shape of his knees and, when he turned away from her, the bunch of muscled buttocks... She breathed deep and felt herself quiver and quicken. An artist's response to beauty melded with a woman's need. It was an irresistible combination.

When he turned back from the bedside table, he was rolling on a condom. It was the most erotic thing Mina had ever seen.

She wanted, how she wanted.

But suddenly she couldn't bring herself to move or touch. Her feet were welded to the floor and a curious weakness stole through her. Nerves? Now?

Alexei didn't smile as he flicked open the snap at the top of her shorts. His expression was serious as he tugged the zip down. Mina shifted but not from embarrassment or doubt. She found herself tilting her pelvis towards him, till he cupped her with that big hand and she felt pressure just where she needed it.

So good. She closed her eyes as they rolled back, which meant she didn't see him push the last of her clothes down her legs. When she opened them again he was crouched before her, undoing the tiny buckles on those flimsy pink sandals.

Mina's legs were so wobbly she put her hands on Alexei's shoulders as he slipped off her shoes, then freed her shorts and underwear.

She stood naked before him, primed and ready. Mina felt the moisture between her legs, knew it would help when they came together, yet still Alexei didn't rise. Instead he surprised her by leaning in, dipping his head to the soft curls above her thighs.

Obeying the silent pressure of his hands, Mina moved one leg wider. She heard a grunt of approval, then nothing but a roaring in her ears as he touched his tongue to her. More than touched. Dipped and swirled and probed.

Mina's fingers turned to talons, raking his shoulders. Her knees shook so much she'd have fallen if not for his grip. And then, suddenly, coaxed with a delicacy and precision that spoke of generous expertise, Mina exploded into rapture. Lights blurred behind closed lids, piercing pleasure filled her, so sweet it made her ache and throb, so shocking she felt as if the world collapsed in on itself.

Or maybe that was her. She was no longer standing, but lying on the bed and the soaring, intense orgasm kept going as Alexei pressed his hand where his mouth had been and kissed his way up her stomach and ribs to her breast.

Mina sucked in a desperate gasp. She'd died and gone to paradise. But surely she couldn't take any more delight.

Which proved how innocent she truly was. For Alexei proceeded to illustrate with ease exactly how much more she could enjoy.

Her senses blurred. The only constant was the heat of Alexei naked against her, the tender touch of those hard hands, his scent, sharp and addictive, and the taste of salty skin as she kissed his shoulder, chest, throat, wherever she could reach.

Finally, when she thought she'd go mad with desperation, he gave in to the urging of her hands and restless body and settled between her legs. Mina lifted her knees, wrapping her calves around his waist and linking her ankles. She was so ready, she wouldn't allow any more delay.

Alexei's hot eyes held hers as he tested her then, with one hard thrust, embedded himself deep within.

Mina's breath snared in her throat and for a shocking moment she couldn't get enough oxygen. She read Alexei's puzzlement in that furrowed brow and questioning eyes. But her attention was on her tight lungs and even tighter body. She felt pinned to the bed, fuller than she'd imagined possible. She couldn't move, couldn't possibly—

'Breathe. Slowly, sweetheart.' Alexei's voice infiltrated her stunned brain. His fingers trailed her cheek in a touch that was as delicate as a butterfly wing, so different from the invasive weight of his possession.

Belatedly Mina sucked in air. Relieved, she breathed in and out with him, watching his mouth, watching the flare of his nostrils and matching her efforts to his. Gradually her frantic pulse eased a fraction, the fog in her brain clearing.

Panic subsided and she felt her taut muscles soften. There was no pain. Simply surprise, a sensation that was neither good nor bad.

Alexei moved, beginning to pull back, and despite her reaction a moment before, Mina couldn't bear the thought of him leaving her. This might feel strange but she craved more. She tightened her legs around him, digging her fingers into his shoulders.

'Don't go.'

He shook his head, his wavy black hair flopping endearingly over his brow, making him appear younger, despite the lines of tension etching his features. 'Don't worry, sweetheart. I'm not going far.' Holding her gaze, he withdrew, then, at the last moment thrust forward.

'Oh.' Mina blinked, stunned at the fizz of appreciation his movement stirred.

His smile looked close to a grimace. 'Exactly.' He repeated the movement, this time with a little more force, and the fizz became of zap of arousal.

With each tilt of his hips, each surge towards her, Alexei kept his attention on her, reading her reaction in her expression. As she'd guessed, her body knew what to do, even if she didn't. Already she'd learned to tilt her pelvis to accommodate him. Yet Mina wanted to do more. She wanted to be as generous as he'd been. She wanted to see him lost to the world, floating in rapture.

'What can I do to make it better for you?'

His laugh was a harsh, grating sound. 'Nothing. It's already too good.'

Mina frowned, fighting the urge to acquiesce and simply enjoy the wonderful new sensations. Her knowledge was all theoretical but it gave her a few ideas.

The next time Alexei thrust, she didn't just grip him

with her thighs, but clenched her inner muscles too. She was rewarded with a hoarse gasp that bordered on a groan. Beads of sweat broke out on his brow and he shuddered.

Delighted, Mina tugged at his right hand, lifting it from the bed and clamping it over her breast. It stayed there, moulding and plucking and adding to her pleasure.

Another thrust, another squeeze and this time Mina had to swallow a gasp of delight. Her tactic worked, she could see it in Alexei's febrile, almost vacant stare and the way his fluid movements grew suddenly jerky.

Then he seemed to gather himself. His eyes focused on hers and his mouth opened. 'Car—'

No! Not another woman's name now.

In a flash she reached up and drew his head down, kissing him with all the desperate yearning he'd awakened. Mina sucked his tongue deep into her mouth, palming the back of his head, drawing him closer with her whole body.

Suddenly Alexei's control broke. Hard fingers dug into her buttock as he angled her body higher. He took over the kiss, driving into her mouth as he drove into her body, with a shocking, wonderful synchronicity that pushed her straight over the edge into spasms of ecstasy.

His body was steely hard, his movements convulsive, and the moan of release she swallowed sounded as if it had been drawn from the depths of his soul. Through it all they stayed locked together as one. Each explosion of sensation in one echoed in the other.

Finally, when the last shudders subsided to tiny tremors, Alexei broke their kiss and rolled onto his side, pulling her with him.

Struggling, Mina opened weighted eyelids. That sea of green engulfed her again and this time she didn't mind. She felt weightless and languorous and so very, very good.

No, it was more than that. It felt as if they were one. It

was remarkable, far more fantastic than she'd believed possible. Surely there was some magic involved that made this more than a mere physical act. It felt…momentous.

Slowly she smiled, though even that took too much energy. 'You were right. There's definitely chemistry.'

CHAPTER TEN

ALEXEI STARED INTO those beautiful, sleepy, sherry-brown eyes and didn't know whether to laugh or run for the hills.

Except running wasn't an option. Problems had to be confronted. And no matter how delightful she was in his bed, Carissa Carter was a problem with a capital *P*.

He should be annoyed she hadn't warned him she was a virgin. He should be worried that in her inexperience she could misread great sex for something more. He should be checking the storm shutters and weather warnings. And he definitely should be disposing of the condom.

Alexei stayed exactly where he was, surrounded by firm, silky heat. Her legs around his waist were a perfect fit. His eyes flickered shut as he replayed the moment when she'd gripped him hard, everywhere, and he'd been ready to explode like an untested kid.

Speaking of untested… He opened his eyes and focused on the dreamy smile still lingering on Carissa's lush, red-dened mouth. He recalled the taste of her, the hungry, avid kiss that had sent him hurtling over the edge. It made him throb within her and he saw her eyes pop wide.

It surprised him too, the fact that there was a spark of life when he'd spilled himself so completely.

'Are you okay? Are you sore?'
Move. You need to leave her alone.

Yet he couldn't bring himself to do it yet. Not when she was so inviting, clinging as if she never wanted to let him go.

Alexei had never liked post-coital pillow talk. He kept a definite line between sex and friendship, not giving lovers the idea they might be in his life long-term. And still he couldn't bring himself to move.

She shook her head, her dark hair, still damp, sliding around her shoulders and onto the pillow. She wore not a trace of make-up and her only adornment was the pair of tiny, intricate gold earrings she'd worn since she arrived.

Yet she was one of the most alluring women he'd seen. Not a perfect beauty, but then the supposedly perfect beauties he'd known weren't either. The more time Alexei spent with Carissa, the more fascinated he was by the line of her cheekbones, her lush mouth and speaking eyes.

'No, I'm not sore.' She clenched her muscles, gripping him tight, and Alexei felt himself quicken. That should be impossible.

But he was learning to expect the unexpected with Carissa.

'Still, you should have told me I was your first.' The words filled him with a mix of feelings. Privilege. Triumph. And, he was stunned to discover, possessiveness. As if he wanted to lay claim to her.

Carissa shrugged, the movement dragging her breasts teasingly across his torso. Another shimmer of tension arrowed to his groin.

'Maybe. But I was afraid you might stop.'

Did she have any idea what her words did to him? How they encouraged the half-formed lascivious, proprietorial thoughts in his befuddled brain?

'It would have taken much more than that to stop me.' He tried to imagine pulling back and couldn't. As well he hadn't been put to the test. Alexei prided himself on mastery over his animal instincts. But with Carissa that untamed side came to the fore. He was tempted to see how far this gathering arousal could take him, take them.

Witnessing Carissa lose herself so totally, spread before

him like a delectable feast, had been better than anything he remembered for a long time.

Too long. He told himself it had been all work and no play recently. That was why the sex had seemed so preternaturally spectacular.

'But you enjoyed it.' It was couched as a statement but Alexei read the question in her eyes. It was a timely reminder that this was new to her. She had no reference point, no way of knowing that they'd shared something out of the ordinary.

How had that happened? Why had such a sensual woman remained celibate? Alexei had no doubt her responses were genuine, not feigned. She enjoyed sex as much as he did. Her patent enthusiasm had added spice to his pleasure.

Why end her virginity now, with him? Because, like him, she'd been unable to resist the elemental attraction that had sparked since she stepped over his threshold?

No, even before that. Alexei had felt it as she stood, arms akimbo, surveying his house. When she'd stared up at him with such arrogant confidence. He'd never experienced anything like it—so instantaneous and compulsive.

But the question remained, why end her virginity today?

Because it could be a useful negotiating tool?

The thought eddied like a circling shark.

Did she think to convince him to go easy on her father, despite his crime? His mouth tightened. Distrust was hard to shake when it was so ingrained.

'Oh, yes. I definitely enjoyed the sex, Carissa.'

Something passed across her features. Something he couldn't define, but it made heat score her cheeks. Instantly he wished he'd chosen his words more carefully. No matter what her ultimate motivation, she'd been generous with him and deserved the same. He prided himself on being a considerate lover. But even to him, the words had sounded harsh, almost dismissive.

With a stab of self-loathing he stroked her hair back from her face. 'Thank you, Carissa. It was wonderful. *You* were wonderful.'

It was true. What they'd shared was beyond anything he recalled. Was he so jaded it had taken sex with a virgin to turn him on?

No, the truth lay elsewhere. It was something about Carissa and the way she made him feel. She was different. Enticing and provoking and more besides. Alexei breathed deep, drawing in her evocative spice-and-cinnamon scent. He could easily become addicted to it. To her.

Lightly he grazed the base of her neck with his teeth. Carissa shivered and clutched at him.

Alexei closed his eyes, savouring her responsiveness and the prospect of more voluptuous pleasure. It would be a simple thing to coax her into more. As he thought it, he recognised the tightening in his groin. He could stay here and sate himself. She was willing. He felt it in the way she arched into him, and in her quickened heartbeat that throbbed against his chest.

Yet he couldn't do it.

He was the experienced one. He was the one who'd initiated this. It was up to him to act responsibly. To be considerate.

Dispose of the condom. Let her rest. All sensible, but it was difficult to make his body obey his brain.

With one last open-mouthed kiss on her satiny flesh, Alexei sighed and pulled back. He gritted his teeth, for in his semi-aroused state the friction was a powerful inducement to stay where he was. As were Carissa's limbs around his body.

'Must you go?'

He opened his eyes to find her watching him with an expression of such disappointment he knew he'd been right. Staying here, luxuriating in her sensuality would be a mistake. It would probably leave her aching. Plus it might convince her this was more than an act of simple physical intimacy. That she should expect more than he was willing to give.

Alexei grabbed her wrists from behind his neck and drew them down between their bodies. Her soft breasts and plum-coloured nipples brushed his hands, diverting him as erotic energy zapped through him.

He was crazy, denying himself. It was clear from her hitched breath and dilated eyes that Carissa wanted more.

But his conscience wouldn't let him stay. She'd change her mind if he made her chafed and sore.

'Be honest with me. Did I hurt you?'

She shook her head. 'No. It felt…odd but not painful.'

'Odd?' His brows drew together and she laughed, a rich chuckle that reminded him of melted chocolate and sunshine.

'Unusual. But good. Very, very good.' Her smile was two parts sultry seductress and one part carefree woman.

Alexei was intrigued by the latter. It struck him that he wanted to learn about that woman, discover what made her tick. He couldn't meld her in his mind with a conniving accomplice to theft he'd imagined.

'Good. That gives us something to aim for next time.'

Her smile lit her face. 'There'll be a next time?'

'Oh, yes.' Alexei wasn't strong enough to abstain permanently.

He lifted one of her hands and kissed it, starting on the back of her hand and working his way around her wrist, where her pulse fluttered wildly, to her palm. He licked it slowly, savouring, and watched her shiver.

'I want it to be soon,' she whispered. Her eyes were sultry and enticing. Alexei had to force himself to move away.

'As soon as you've rested.'

'I'm not tired!'

Was that a pout? Heaven help him—that mouth tempted him to forget good intentions.

'Perhaps *I* am.' It was a fabrication but better than telling her he acted for her own good. She hated any hint he had power over her. Except when he'd had her beneath him.

Her gaze shifted down his body and his erection stirred. 'You don't *look* tired.'

Alexei muffled a bark of laughter. She was right. He felt energised.

He should simply get up and leave her to rest, but that was beyond his powers. What he needed was a distraction. 'How's your hand?' He angled it to inspect the bandage.

'I can't feel any pain.'

Alexei darted a glance at her. It would probably hurt later when the endorphins faded. It was a nasty gash. But then, he'd realised as he treated her, she'd had a few accidents in the past.

He slid his thumb over the fine skin at the back of her hand, seeing two tiny scars, faded now. And on the palm some rougher patches, as if it had seen work instead of simply lotions and manicures.

Alexei turned her hand over again, considering the supple strength in those slim fingers, the lack of jewellery, the short nails.

Why hadn't he noticed? This wasn't the hand of a pampered socialite.

'What sort of art do you do?'

It was only because he held her that he noticed her flinch. It was momentary, so brief he almost thought he was mistaken. But now her hand was stiff, not relaxed. His curiosity deepened.

'All sorts of things. Drawing, oils, sculpting, even some pottery.'

His sixth sense stirred. She was being evasive. Why?

'Surely you specialise in one? Don't successful artists focus their energies?'

Mina read the acuteness in Alexei's gaze and wondered at his instinct for pinpointing vulnerability. It was as if he knew exactly what to ask to uncover the truth. Carissa was a successful graphic artist but Mina's expertise and passion lay in sculpture.

No wonder he was such a successful businessman with that uncannily accurate instinct. Or was it a fluke? Was she overreacting?

In the distance she heard the furious rush of the storm. It echoed the abrupt warning clamour surging within her.

Mina told herself it was just as well she was no longer crammed up so close against him he might feel her response to his words. Even so she was still desperate for his caresses, for more of the glory they'd shared. That had challenged her preconceptions about him and made her wonder if Alexei was someone more than simply a demanding tycoon, used to getting his way.

Or was that her bias? The virgin fixating on the man who'd introduced her to sex? Because what she'd experienced with Alexei had felt almost transcendental, as if they'd achieved a union that was unique and precious.

Her thoughts were in turmoil, her emotions all over the place. She was in danger of letting feelings cloud her judgement. But, oh, how she wanted to bask in what Alexei made her feel!

'Carissa?'

'Sorry. Yes, artists do tend to specialise.'

What harm was there, telling him about her work? Remarkably, this was the man who hadn't bothered to look at Carissa's photo before bringing her here. If he wasn't interested enough to do that, he wouldn't have checked out her work.

It was a startling reminder that, despite the intimacy of the moment, they were still opponents in a dangerous game. That left a sour tang on Mina's tongue and an ache in her middle.

It grew harder and harder to reconcile that imperious tycoon with the man lying naked beside her.

'And your specialty?'

Mina hesitated, then took the plunge. She was finding some success but it wasn't as if her work was well known. Soon, hopefully. 'I sculpt.'

'*Now* it makes sense.' His rueful smile made her heart hammer and warmth unfurl inside. It was as if they shared a private joke. Mina realised she wanted more of this. More of Alexei's warmth and understanding.

'Saving the sail sculpture? It's a masterpiece. I couldn't leave it.'

He nodded. 'Of course not. I see that now.' His tone held no rancour, just understanding. Why not? It was obvious the man loved sculpture too. The pieces scattered through his home were superb.

'I was working in Paris on ideas for something similar, but with stylised birds' wings that will move, propelled by the wind. It's far more difficult than you'd imagine.' If she could bring it off it would be perfect for Jeirut's first royal art exhibition. Mina had promised Ghizlan she'd contribute something special and she could imagine the piece at the Palace of the Winds.

'I'd like to see that.'

'I've got drawings...' Mina closed her mouth over her eager response as doubt welled. What else was in her current sketchbook? Anything that would give away her true identity?

'I'd be fascinated to see them.'

Slowly Mina nodded. She'd like to show him and hear his thoughts. She suspected his response would be informed but honest.

'I'll check to see if I have them with me,' she said finally. Mina looked away, hating the dishonesty of her situation. She had the strongest desire to strip away the lies. To know him properly and have him know her.

She wanted…more.

Except Carissa relied on her.

Mina swallowed, bitterness filling her mouth.

'Are you sure you're okay, Carissa?'

She suppressed a shiver. Even being called by her friend's name felt wrong.

'Of course.' Mina darted a glance towards him, but didn't quite meet his eyes. 'Maybe you're right. I think I need a rest after all.'

It was another lie. For Mina felt sparking with life and eager for more of Alexei's loving. What did that say about her? She'd known the man mere days!

She knew so little about him. Except that he felt deeply. That he abhorred cheats, was impatient yet surprisingly kind, determined, outrageous and used to getting his own way. That when he made love to her she felt as if she could fly and that everything in the world was bright and fresh. When she was with Alexei everything was more intense.

With him she had the strangest feeling she could be more herself than she could with anyone else. And that wasn't just about sex. The realisation was disquieting.

'I'll leave you to rest.' He rose and Mina had to clench her hands rather than reach out and draw him back.

She missed the warmth of Alexei's powerful body and the feeling of oneness. She wanted to see that smile in his eyes and bask in that wonderment again.

'Okay?' His hand brushed her cheek and delight coursed

through her. Such a simple gesture, yet it affected her profoundly.

When had she let anyone close? Mina had spent so long hoarding her emotions to herself, first as self-protection, then because she'd focused on achieving her dream. Only Carissa had suspected Mina's air of assurance and practicality masked innate loneliness.

Mina looked up into Alexei's alert green gaze and her chest pinched tight.

'Yes, I'm okay.' And she was. Despite the circumstances, despite the lies between them that she so wanted to obliterate. In this, she reminded herself, she had no choice...yet. But soon she'd be free to explain. 'Just tired.' And suddenly that too was true. Mina stifled a cracking yawn.

'Sleep then, lover. I'll be back later.'

Mina settled her head on the pillow and watched him go, hearing that *lover* as an echo that refused to die.

Tall, shoulders back, he sauntered towards the bathroom with the grace of an athlete utterly at home in his skin. What exercise did he do to keep so fit?

Her gaze traced the curving sweep of his spine, the tight bunch of his backside, the powerful, well-formed legs.

Mina wanted to sculpt him. Almost as much as she wanted to run her hands over all that warm, muscled flesh.

Her last thought before sleep took her was that she enjoyed being with Alexei Katsaros. Too much.

Alexei checked the house, the generator and the radio. The storm had hit quickly but was even now easing. The forecast predicted it would pass over soon.

Yet all the time he busied himself with what had to be done, his thoughts tracked back to Carissa. How she'd felt in his arms, in his bed, her body yielding and soft yet strong. Her slick heat driving him out of his mind. And those little growls of pleasure she gave. The memory sent a judder of longing through him.

Which was why he spent as much time as he could away from the bedroom. He knew next to nothing about virgins. There hadn't been many in the rough streets where he'd grown up. But common sense dictated he should let her sleep.

Yet an hour later he was back in his room, staring down at the woman who'd turned his life upside down in a mere couple of days. Unbelievable that it was such a short time. It felt as if she'd been in his world much longer.

He drew a steadying breath and shoved his hands in his pockets as he surveyed her, sprawled across his bed. In the lamplight her glossy, dark hair splayed around her shoulders and her lithe, gold-toned body was a masterpiece, more alluring than any work of art.

Alexei was surprised at the depth of his desire to possess her. Not just possess her body, as he fully intended to when she woke, but to claim this woman as... What? His mistress? Carter's daughter shouldn't be for him.

Yet, when he was with her, it wasn't her father's wrongdoing that came to mind. It was the tug of something else that drew him inexorably. Desire. Attraction. Curiosity. Appreciation that she gave as good as she got. And for her humour, her unpretentious attitude, the way she'd developed a bond of friendship with Marie and Henri so quickly.

So much about her intrigued.

She mumbled and rolled over. Alexei's thoughts frayed as he watched those tip-tilted breasts jiggle. The curve from breasts to narrow waist, then out to her hip was so sweet it stole his breath. One slim leg slid over the other, almost hiding that V of dark hair. The memory of their coupling, of her virginal tightness and shocked ecstasy, created a jolt of triumph so strong it flattened his good intentions. She'd been delectable, so charmingly enthusiastic.

Alexei's resolve disintegrated as a wave of need slammed into him. He'd done his best, he told himself as he reefed his shirt up. He really had, he assured himself as he reached for the box of condoms in the bedside table.

But he was a man, not a saint.

Minutes later he gathered her to him, his chest against her back, his legs curved into hers from behind, the burning heat of his groin hard against the sweet curve of her rump.

'Alexei?' She turned her head, her hair falling back against his chest, a sliding silk curtain that tickled and aroused.

'Yes?' He slid his hand around to cup her breast. Immediately her nipple puckered, hard against his palm. The tension in his lower body screwed another notch tighter.

'I'm glad you're here.' She sounded breathless.

'So am I.' He bumped his groin against her and felt her chuckle resonate through him. Her hand covered his, pressing down as she arched into his touch.

'Are we going to have sex again now?'

Her words sent a flurry of need rushing through him. 'If you're not sore.' If she was he'd have to be inventive. He was definitely up to that challenge.

'I'm not.' She turned, trying to roll towards him but Alexei held her where she was. 'Don't you want to be on top?'

The question reminded him how inexperienced she was. That he was the first man she'd been with. This time the surge of erotic excitement was so profound it threatened to blow the back off his skull. Or make him come before he was ready. Her soft, warm flesh against him was almost too good.

'There are other ways,' he murmured and bit her neck. She sighed and angled her head to give him better access. Alexei released her breast and arrowed his hand down past her ribs, her belly, to her hidden core. He found her slick and hot, unmistakeably ready. His erection throbbed needily and Carissa pushed back against him.

'Show me,' she demanded, fingers stroking along his arm, then back up, sending shivers across his flesh to coalesce at his nape and groin. He liked her bold acceptance of pleasure.

Alexei inserted one knee between hers, opening her legs a little. He nudged between her thighs, positioning himself.

'You don't have to do anything but, if you like, in a minute you can push back when I…'

His words died as he thrust forward, slowly at first. But then she wriggled, taking him deeper with a sexy little shimmy of her hips and Alexei found himself bucking hard and strong, as deep as he could go.

Behind his closed lids stars burst. So good. It felt so unbelievably good that it took a second to realise Carissa had gone rigid in his arms.

Was he too much? Had he hurt her? Heart pounding, Alexei began to withdraw, silently cursing. He should have taken more time, pleasured her more.

Her hand clamped the back of his upper thigh like a talon.

'Don't!'

'Carissa?' He frowned, disorientated by the contradiction of her sharp voice and the clench of her inner muscles that threatened to destroy the last vestiges of thought.

For answer she drove back against him, impaling herself. 'That feels…'

'What?' For the life of him he couldn't move away. His hand circled her hip, then crept up to her breast. Her breath caught. 'How does it feel?'

'Wonderful,' she whispered. 'So wonderful.'

And that, to Alexei's amazement, was all it took for him to feel the fierce rush of power as a climax tore through him. He barely had time to ease back and surge again, right to the heart of her, and hear her laugh of shocked pleasure. Then the madness was upon him, fire in his blood, a roaring shout of ecstasy and the hard pump of him spilling into her beautiful body.

It took a long time to come down from the high. Aftershocks rocked him, setting off Carissa's orgasm, which in turned drove him on a desperate, slowly diminishing cycle of delight.

Finally, what seemed a lifetime later, he slumped against her, head in the curve of her neck, arms encircling her as if to prevent her leaving. Dazed, Alexei realised he didn't have enough energy even to pull away and lie on his back. His body was locked with hers and there it would stay.

'I think…' Her words were so faint they were a shadow of sound.

'Yes?' Alexei struggled to focus.

'I think I could get addicted to this.'

His mouth curved against the satiny skin of her neck. He knew the feeling. Sex with Carissa Carter was either the best idea he'd ever had or the worst mistake of his life.

CHAPTER ELEVEN

MINA STRETCHED, BLINKING, and surfaced from one of the deepest sleeps of her life. She felt wonderful, apart from a little tenderness. When she recalled why she was tender, she smiled. So this was what all the fuss was about!

Being with Alexei was unlike anything she'd imagined. Better. Wonderful. She felt…different.

She rolled over to find the storm shutters open. Beyond the windows was the vivid blaze of green foliage, scarlet flowers and turquoise water. A songbird trilled and the hush of waves on sand proved yesterday's maelstrom was over.

How long had she slept? Long enough for Alexei to be up and about.

Cravenly she wished he hadn't gone. If she'd woken wrapped around him, she wouldn't have a chance to think. She'd be too busy exploring *him*. Carnal excitement filled her.

In his absence thoughts crammed her head, vying for supremacy over her feeling of contentment.

With a sigh she stuffed pillows behind her and sat up. The fine linen sheets felt heavy over her sensitised skin, grazing her nipples as she tucked the fabric under her arms. Making her remember last night in delicious detail.

If Alexei walked in now, she'd fling the sheet aside and indulge in her new favourite pastime. Sex.

Except, what they'd shared seemed much more than a mere physical coupling. It had felt…

Mina shook her head, her hair sliding around her shoulders. Whatever it had felt like, it had to stop.

She caught her lip between her teeth. It would be easy to tell herself she wasn't thinking straight after such mind-boggling pleasure but she couldn't escape her conscience. Responsibility, doing right, had been drummed into her from childhood.

Despite what her eager body urged, it wasn't right to sleep with Alexei while he believed her to be someone else!

A selfish part of her wanted to thrust that aside. After all, he'd given Carissa no choice. He deserved whatever he got for his high-handed actions. And yet... Even in so short a time, she knew he was far more complex than the bogeyman they'd made him into. For one thing, Carissa's father had stolen from him, on a large scale. Who wouldn't be irate in the circumstances? Alexei was a victim of crime and deserved sympathy, not more treachery.

Besides, this wasn't a question of Alexei's culpability but hers. This masquerade didn't sit well with Mina's conscience. True, she did it for the best reasons, but it was still a lie. It was one thing to be swept off her feet in heightened passion and not reveal the truth. It was another to share Alexei's bed while duping him. She'd feel cheap and tainted, prolonging that lie while they were physically intimate.

Mina hugged herself as a chill enveloped her. She wanted to be selfish and have more of what she'd had last night.

But she couldn't, not without telling Alexei who she was.

Her conscience urged her to find Alexei and reveal the truth. Surely he'd understand. He wouldn't insist on dragging Carissa into this.

Then she remembered his fury when he'd spoken of Carissa's father. That adamantine set of Alexei's jaw as he'd spoken of retribution. A chill spread through her like mountain frost. Mina hoped he'd change his mind but she couldn't guarantee it. There was a chance he'd go through with his plans for Carissa.

Nausea swirled in her stomach and bile rose in her throat at the idea of Alexei with Carissa. *Marrying* her.

She wanted to scream that it wasn't possible. He wouldn't do that, not now, he'd more or less admitted that had been a ploy to get her here. But there were no guarantees. Alexei was a powerful man used to getting what he wanted.

She couldn't risk it. Carissa had pleaded for another couple of days. If Mina revealed the truth now Alexei might still use her friend as a pawn. Mina hated to think it but she had to face facts.

Which left her lusting for a man she couldn't fully trust. Lying to a man she liked more than she'd expected. Yearning for—

Mina thrust aside the sheet and scrambled out of bed. Two things were clear. She couldn't tell Alexei who she was until she knew Carissa was safe with Pierre. And in the meantime, honour demanded Mina didn't sleep with Alexei again.

'Alexei?'

He looked up from the tray he was filling and saw her framed in the kitchen doorway. His heart did a crazy somersault.

She wore a miniskirt the colour of ripe watermelon and a sleeveless white shirt that tied at the waist, emphasising her slenderness. There was plenty of honey-toned skin on display but it was her hair, a dark cloud around her shoulders, and her glowing eyes, that captivated.

Heat scudded through him. Desire. Satisfaction.

He'd had her all night but that hadn't sated his need.

She was delectable. A mix of hesitant, innocent and wanton sensualist.

'You should have stayed in bed. I was bringing brunch.' Then Alexei registered the stiff way she held herself. 'Are you okay?' He was across the room in an instant, taking her hands. 'Tell me.' Uncharacteristically, Alexei felt anxious. He told himself women lost their virginities all the time.

She swallowed and his eyes tracked the movement, senses alert. Especially when he realised she hadn't yet looked directly at him.

As he thought it, she raised her eyes, her expression serious. His gut tightened.

'I realised I never told you I'm sorry about the theft. About…my father's actions.' She grimaced. 'I didn't really think about the impact on your business. Is it a complete disaster? Will the company recover?'

Days ago Alexei would have been astounded to feel relief at her words. Yet that was what flooded him. Carissa was okay; she wasn't hurt. Or having second thoughts.

He brushed his thumbs over her wrists. 'Thank you.' Strange how something as simple as her concern, and her apology, acted as a salve on the raw wound to his pride. Because he hadn't seen the betrayal coming. Because despite excellent systems, his enterprise had still been vulnerable. 'It's…manageable.'

The theft caused major problems but not enough to destabilise the company, if handled carefully.

'Manageable?' She tilted her head, trying to read him. 'Is that code? He hasn't bankrupted you, has he?' No missing her sharp note of worry.

Alexei felt her tremble, saw her features pale. For once Carissa's thoughts were easy to read. Horror and distress.

'No, nothing like that.' He squeezed her hands. 'The company wasn't that vulnerable.'

'Good.' She nodded. 'I'm glad.'

The words were simple but he knew her well enough to realise her sentiments were genuine. Had he really believed she'd connived with her father? Watching her now, it was hard to credit. Her concern and sincerity, clear in her eyes and taut body as well as her words, made a mockery of his doubts. She might not want to betray her father but she was innocent of his crimes.

Belatedly it hit him how difficult this had been for her.

'I've put you in a tough situation.' The words emerged without thinking. It was too late to regret his actions, especially since he couldn't regret having her here with him. But given his time over, Alexei would have taken a different approach.

Those brown eyes widened in shock. Then she lifted one shoulder. 'I've survived worse.'

She made light of it but suddenly Alexei couldn't. He felt wrong-footed. 'I acted rashly. For that I'm sorry. I assumed you knew about the theft.' When her eyes widened, he shook his head. 'My default position is not to trust anyone. I learned long ago it was safer than being disappointed.'

Even Alexei was surprised by the admission. He never explained himself. But in this case, he knew he owed her an apology.

Carissa's hands grasped his. 'Could we, maybe, put all that aside for a little?'

She looked so earnest he had to smile. Especially since, after giving an apology, Alexei wasn't quite sure where to go next. This was unfamiliar territory.

'With pleasure.' He brushed the fall of long hair off her shoulder and wrapped his other arm around her waist, tugging her close. 'I'm sure we can find something else to concentrate on.' He was leaning in to kiss her when a palm on his chest stopped him.

Carissa was staring at his collarbone, not his face. High colour flagged her cheeks.

'About that,' she said to his shirt. 'We need to take a raincheck.'

Alexei frowned. He couldn't believe it, especially as she arched sinuously against him. He could tell when a woman wanted him and Carissa did, without doubt. 'Sorry? You don't want to have sex with me?'

Her crack of laughter unlocked something tight that had

formed in his chest. She shook her head. 'You're so sure of yourself.'

'With good reason.' His hand wandered lower, to the hem of her miniskirt. She stiffened.

'The fact is, I can't. I…' She lifted her face and met his eyes with an unblinking stare. 'I've got my period.'

Disappointment seared him. It was so savage it felt like pain. Alexei opened his mouth to suggest there were ways they could, but seeing her blush deepen, recalling she'd been a virgin yesterday, he shut it again.

He dragged in a slow breath. 'I won't say I'm not disappointed. But I've survived worse.'

When she registered the echo of her own words, Carissa grinned. Suddenly she looked more like the vibrant, confident woman he knew. A weight he hadn't registered lifted from his chest. Alexei slung his arm around her shoulder and turned towards the tray he'd prepared.

'Things will seem brighter after we've eaten.'

If only food could cure sexual frustration. Because the next few days would surely test him to the limit.

'For someone who's never been on a boat you look right at home.' Alexei's voice stirred Mina from her reverie. She looked across the dinghy's bench seat to find him watching speculatively.

Three days ago his questioning stare would have made her wary, consumed with worry that he'd unmask her, for, unlike Carissa, she'd grown up in a desert kingdom with no experience of the sea. But a lot had changed. By mutual consent they didn't speak about business or revenge or the future. They existed totally in the present.

Their relationship was fragile. It could only last until the outside world intruded. But for the first time in her life it was enough just to *be*.

To be with him.

All her life, she'd strived to live up to others' expectations. First to meet her father's impossible demands. Then, finding a niche in the competitive art world, working harder than her peers to prove she hadn't achieved her initial success because of her connections.

Being with Alexei was like breathing fresh air after stale. Even though they weren't physically intimate since her lie about her period—the only way she could think of to keep him at arm's length—to her amazement he hadn't shown annoyance or frustration.

Alexei made her feel good about herself. Not because of her royal status, but because…

Because he genuinely liked her? The thought was tempting. But she couldn't afford to dwell on it. She adjusted her wide-brimmed hat.

'I'm adaptable,' she murmured, taking in the crystalline ocean and white beach. 'Besides, the view is fantastic.'

'It sure is.' Heat simmered in his dark jade stare and Mina felt the familiar tickle of awareness. It began in the soles of her feet, climbing up her legs to swirl and intensify between her thighs, then rise, via her breasts to her throat where her breath caught.

Every time Alexei watched her she felt that same drag of muscles, the quickening, the eagerness. The sensations grew stronger with each day they spent together.

Henri and Marie hadn't returned, their boat damaged in the storm, which had hit the main island badly. They could have returned by Alexei's helicopter but it was busy on relief work and Alexei and Mina were more than able to look after themselves while the others waited for repairs.

'When you invited me out on your boat I'd pictured a massive cruiser. But this suits you better.' Her gaze drifted over his open shirt, cotton shorts and strongly muscled legs. Her pulse revved pleasantly.

Alexei shrugged, his expression wickedly knowing. 'I

prefer something a little laid-back unless I have to entertain for business.'

'I can relate to that.' Mina extended one bare leg and wriggled her toes in the sunshine. How fabulous to be free of the formal clothes appropriate to the royal court. That was something she hadn't missed in France.

'You don't like dressing up?'

'I prefer comfort.' Carissa's clothes might not be her style, but at least they included shorts and summer skirts rather than evening gowns and high heels.

Alexei reached out and stroked his finger across the arch of her foot, then up to her ankle and calf.

Mina shivered. His touch evoked a memory of his loving. It had been days now and abstinence was tough, tougher than she'd imagined.

'I can imagine you in some glamorous outfit. You'd look spectacular.'

Mina smiled. The deep timbre of his voice told her he meant every word. 'Why, thank you. I'm sure you clean up pretty well too.' He'd look stunning in formal clothes. Her insides clenched just thinking about it.

She hesitated on the brink of suggesting they go out one night in the future, he in a tuxedo, she in something slinky and feminine. Except that would mean a date and that was impossible. Once the truth came out Mina wouldn't see him again.

A sudden tightness in her chest stole her breath.

This interlude was a snatched moment out of their real lives. Neither were interested in long-term relationships. Mina had a career to build. She couldn't afford distractions. And Alexei…

'What are you thinking?'

Mina became aware of Alexei's hand, warm on her knee, of his quizzical stare fixed on her face. Regret pierced her. She wanted what they shared to last longer than a few days.

Underlying regret was surprise that Alexei understood her well enough to read her expression. Mina had spent years keeping her emotions private. She was an expert. Discovering a man who saw beyond her projected calm and sensed her disquiet should make her feel vulnerable. Yet Mina felt a thrill of excitement that Alexei was so attuned to her emotions. As if she mattered.

What did he read in her face?

Surely not her foolish longing for what could never be.

'I'm thinking you should grab that fishing line. I saw it move.'

Alexei muttered something beneath his breath and grabbed the neglected reel.

It had surprised her that he hadn't produced sleek, professional-looking fishing rods. Yet these battered hand reels, like the unpretentious boat, seemed as right for Alexei as his architect-designed home and priceless art.

He was a man who couldn't be labelled and stuck in a box. She wanted to find out more, discover what made him tick. But she resisted the temptation to pry. It could lead to places she couldn't go.

'Have you got a fish?' She leaned forward, fascinated by his sudden alertness.

'Could be.' He held the line in one sinewy hand, his attention on the water.

Mina peered over the side but couldn't see anything.

Alexei felt the tug on the line and began to reel it in.

There'd be fresh fish for dinner. Not that there was any danger of starving. Marie's well-stocked kitchen would keep them till she came back with supplies.

Strangely the thought of having company, even Marie and Henri, who were friends as much as employees, didn't appeal. He wanted more time alone with Carissa.

When she wasn't driving him to distraction with sexual

frustration she was surprisingly restful company. She didn't pry or quiz him about his private life, yet Alexei had found himself talking far more than usual.

They'd discussed music and art and found more areas where their tastes overlapped than where they'd diverged. They'd discovered a shared passion for football, which made Alexei reassess his unconscious sexism. When, in the past, had he discussed sport with a lover? He'd assumed women weren't interested.

A chance comment about doing business across continents led to a discussion about the global economy and international trade. Alexei again realised he'd underestimated Carissa.

He felt ashamed that he'd been so shallow. Carissa was unique and she clearly hadn't been coached by her father. They'd veered into areas he knew were beyond Carter's expertise. Besides, Carissa had been distracted at the time, cooking. She'd got so caught up in their discussion she'd forgotten the food, till Alexei salvaged it.

She'd shrugged and admitted she wasn't much of a cook. Then she'd described her one attempt to bake a soufflé and the disastrous result. Carissa's laughter had wrapped around him like warm silk as her eyes lit at the memory.

Now she looked like an excited kid.

It hit Alexei that if she'd never been in a boat, she'd probably never caught a fish. The thought snagged.

His childhood had been short on fun experiences after his stepfather got his feet under their table. But Alexei had one precious memory of his father teaching him to fish.

He recalled the sun on his face and the breeze off the water, and the scent of baking as his mother laid out a picnic on a blanket. Alexei remembered walking to her, one hand in his dad's big, sure grasp and the other holding up the fish he'd caught. He'd been so proud, so secure, so innocent that he'd taken everything he had for granted.

It was his final happy memory before the dark days.

'Here.' He gave Carissa the line. 'You do it.'

The excitement in her eyes hit him like a shot of liquor.

'I can feel it!' She reeled in, carefully at first, then with more confidence. 'There it is!'

Silver flashed near the water's surface but it was Carissa, animated and happy, that captured his attention. Belatedly he grabbed a scoop net and secured the fish as she brought it in.

'It's on the small side, isn't it?'

He saw her gnaw her bottom lip. Her forehead creased as if she were unhappy. Carissa's frown deepened as the fish struggled. It seemed she had a soft heart.

'Not the biggest I've seen.' He paused, watching her. 'It's almost too small to keep.' It was a reasonable size, but Carissa was already nodding.

'Can we let it go? Give it a chance to grow? I read fish stocks are dropping because the population doesn't get a chance to reproduce.'

'*That's* why you want to let it go?'

'Well…' She shrugged. 'I liked the thrill of catching it but we're not desperate for food. I could make a salad and there's plenty of other stuff to cook.'

Alexei nodded and unhooked the fish, then put it over the side. A second later it wriggled out of his hand and away. Carissa's beaming grin as she watched was worth it.

'Thank you, Alexei.'

'No problem. Especially since you've offered to cook.' He paused and tilted his head to one side. 'I know. How about you make us a nice cheese soufflé?'

He ducked and grabbed her wrist as she swept off her sunhat and batted him with it. Then, catching her off balance, he dragged her onto his lap. The boat rocked wildly.

'That was a low blow. Just because I'm not a good cook.' She pouted but her eyes sparkled.

'But look what it got me. Who wants a fish when they can have a mermaid?'

Alexei slipped his hand behind her head and pulled out the pin securing her dark hair. He'd become adept at that. Carissa began the day by brushing her hair and securing it back from her face but Alexei preferred it loose.

His breath huffed out in satisfaction as he threaded the satiny locks through his fingers. Then he stroked lower, down her side to the couple of inches of warm, golden flesh showing between her pink shorts and cropped, polka-dotted shirt.

Carissa shivered and he saw the hard points of her nipples rise against the thin fabric. She stilled, looking up at him with a sultry, heavy-lidded look before she caught herself and tried to pull away. 'You know we can't—'

'I know. Kisses only.' Knowing she wanted him as much as he wanted her was strangely satisfying. Even though holding her and knowing he couldn't have her was an exercise in sexual frustration.

Alexei pulled her closer. He heard a splash but focused instead on that wide, delectable mouth.

'Alexei?' Carissa struggled to sit up. 'I think that was the net going over the side. Alexei?'

'Leave it.' He hauled her closer, hand splaying low on her hip. 'I've got more important things on my mind.'

Their gazes collided. A shower of sparks rained down, peppering his body with pinpricks of fire. Her expression changed and in one swift move she grabbed his shirt and tugged his face down to hers.

Alexei covered her lips with his and felt her open up. Despite the turmoil of thwarted lust, he had no desire to pull back. He couldn't recall ever feeling so…light, so unencumbered by life's burdens.

Since childhood he'd been focused on the need to survive, to succeed, to secure his place in the world. With previous lovers there'd always been a part of him that wasn't engaged. That focused on business or fending off unwanted expectations.

With Carissa, he simply enjoyed the moment. He felt just plain happy. It was a revelation.

CHAPTER TWELVE

'WHEN DID YOU know you wanted to be an artist?' Alexei watched as Carissa's sketch took shape. A couple of swift strokes and there was the outline of his hands. Another and the hint of a wrist appeared.

Watching her work, as he had these last days, left Alexei in no doubt Carissa really *was* an artist, not a spoiled daddy's girl playing at being something she wasn't.

She didn't look up. 'I never consciously decided. It's just me. I was always interested in art.'

'So your father organised for you to attend classes?'

Strange how the mention of Ralph Carter didn't make him feel that heavy twist in the gut it had before. The anger remained, and indignation, but not the seething sense of urgency. The investigator had a lead on Carter in Switzerland, but for once Alexei wasn't impatient to confront the man. That would come.

Alexei had other things to occupy him.

Carissa's brow knotted as she rubbed out a couple of lines and replaced them with others more to her liking.

'Sorry?'

'You had art lessons as a child?'

She snorted. 'I wish. I was self-taught till I went to art school. I'd have loved to have learned sooner. I couldn't even take art at high school. My father didn't approve.'

'He didn't?'

Carissa shook her head and a tendril of hair escaped her severely pulled-back hairstyle. It flirted over her collarbone as if inviting his attention to the tight white top clinging to her breasts.

Her clothes reminded him that she wasn't as Alexei

had first assumed. Instead of glamorous designer outfits from expensive shopping sprees, she favoured shorts and skirts, skimpy and incredibly sexy. And that black outfit, the leggings and loose T-shirt that didn't fit with the rest yet seemed right for a woman so obviously comfortable with her body and uninterested in primping.

Carissa didn't need fancy clothes to hold his attention. She was sexy, vehement, impulsive and had a mischievous sense of humour. She was full of energy and surprising depths.

And he wanted her more than he'd wanted anyone or anything in a long, long time. Perhaps ever.

Acknowledging it made something inside him still. As if the treadmill of his world, driving him on and on, paused, allowing him to take stock.

It was a strange sensation. As if he were an onlooker to his own life, his wants and needs.

And the result of that self-examination? The realisation that, after a lifetime of self-reliance, he wanted more. The laughter and sharing, the warmth of having someone special.

The revelation stopped Alexei's breath, crushed his lungs and made his heart thunder.

Share his life?

It shouldn't be a surprise. He had the example of his parents' loving partnership. Days ago he'd begun toying with the idea of finding someone to start a family with. But now the idea wasn't abstract. It wasn't a theoretical, faceless woman who came to mind.

It was one specific woman. One spirited, restful, infuriating, generous woman. A woman about whom he knew so little, yet felt he knew everything important.

Not that this was *love*.

Alexei wouldn't fall victim to sentimentality. But Carissa and he shared more than sex. They'd exercised abstinence for days and he grew more, rather than less, interested. This warmth, respect and liking could form the foundation of a solid relationship.

Instead of rejecting the idea, he felt a quiver of anticipation. It was like the moment he'd realised his first software innovation really worked. That it had the makings of a runaway commercial success. He was a loner but deep down he'd always wanted more than solitude.

Alexei waited for common sense to kick in and object that he'd known Carissa just a week.

It stayed silent.

And all the while the effervescence in his blood signalled he was onto a winning idea.

He always trusted his instincts.

He stared at Carissa, absorbed in her drawing. She never tried to charm or flatter. It was refreshing not to be fussed over, to be treated as an equal, or, Alexei realised with a silent huff of laughter, as an inanimate object to be sketched. But he knew one touch, one word, even a *look*, would have her burning for him. She was her own woman, but she was his too.

For the moment.

Did he really want more?

If so, what about her father? Alexei couldn't let Carter off the hook.

She'd want nothing to do with Alexei once he brought her father to justice. Yet she knew that was Alexei's goal and it hadn't deterred her.

'Why didn't your father encourage you to study art?' Maybe father and daughter weren't as close as he'd imagined.

'He wanted me to do something useful. Like *economics*.' Mina's tone echoed horror. 'It would have been a disaster!'

That didn't sound like the man who'd spoken indulgently about his artistic daughter. But Carter had said she wasn't suited to business. Perhaps he'd originally wanted her to follow in his shoes. As for Carissa not coping with economics, Alexei recalled their conversations and knew she had a better-than-average understanding.

'So you persuaded your parents to let you try art.'

Her hand stopped on the page, her knuckles tightening. Had he hit a nerve?

'I didn't ask. I just applied.' Slowly her hand moved again, though her strokes weren't as bold as before. She stopped and raised her head. Alexei's curiosity rose as he saw her flushed cheeks.

'How about you?' Her bright eyes snared his and awareness throbbed. How easily they struck sparks. 'How did you start in IT? Did you spend all your free time as a kid on the computer?'

'Hardly. We didn't have one.'

He read the question in her expression yet she didn't ask. She kept to their unspoken agreement not to pry.

Alexei was the one pushing the boundaries. His curiosity was insatiable. He had to decide if he wanted more than the time they had left till the showdown with her father.

He needed to know more about this woman who engaged his mind as well as his body. To do that he'd have to share things he never shared with anyone. He paused, considering.

'There wasn't money when I was growing up, and what little we had my stepfather spent on himself.'

'He sounds unlikeable.'

'You could say that.' Alexei's vital organs knotted. 'He targeted my mother for the insurance money she inherited when my father died. It wasn't a fortune but it would have paid for a roof over our heads and a decent education for me.'

Instead the money had gone on his stepfather's whims. A sports car that he crashed while drunk. A 'get rich quick' scheme that failed. Expensive clothes, 'business' expenses for unspecified enterprises that involved late-night entertaining.

'You didn't have a home or decent education?' He heard sympathy in Carissa's voice as she bent her head, concentrating on a new sketch. Of his hands clenched in fists rather than relaxed as before. There was something soothing, almost hypnotic about watching the lines appear on the page, seeing form appear out of what had seemed random scratchings.

Though she worked, he knew she focused on his words. There was a tension about her that hadn't been there earlier. But she didn't push. She gave him space, and a measure of privacy, avoiding his gaze.

'We had a roof for the first couple of years. Mum remortgaged the place to finance his spending but he ran through that soon enough. He lived off her for years but when the money went, so did he.'

Alexei raked a hand through his shaggy hair, then realised what he'd done.

'Sorry.' He dropped his hand, fisting it on his thigh like its mate.

'Don't worry.' Her upward look, with that fleeting smile, eased the old tension brewing inside. 'I'll sketch your hands however you hold them. I love them. I'm thinking of using them in a piece I want to do.'

Alexei scowled down at his tight hands. For reasons he couldn't define her words unsettled him. Love. She'd used the word casually, yet he'd experienced a pang of...could it be *yearning*?

It was easier, suddenly, to think about the past than the knotty issue of how she made him feel.

'He sounds despicable,' Carissa said, her quiet voice vibrating with rage. 'To target a woman. To *use* her. There are too many selfish people in the world.'

Alexei's stare sharpened. 'You sound like you've met some.' He'd imagined she'd led a cosseted life.

'A few.' Her mouth flattened and she flipped the page. 'Actually, can I move your hands?' Her eyes held his. Something passed between them that inexplicably loosened the tension in his shoulders.

'Sure.' He watched as she turned his hands so they lay, palms up and fingers cupped. Her own hands were narrow and warm. Alexei liked the brush of her fingers.

'You must have been relieved when your stepfather left.'

'Definitely. He was a difficult man at the best of times and, believe me, there weren't many of those.' Alexei remembered the sound of his mother's sharp cry, waking him in the night. The hard crack of a beefy hand against his jaw and the lash of a belt around his backside. 'But the trouble didn't end when he went.'

'It didn't?' She lifted her head.

Alexei shrugged. 'He'd somehow run up debts in my mother's name, and loan sharks have no sympathy for defaulters.' Even if the defaulter was a defeated, desperate woman struggling to make ends meet. 'My mother worked three jobs to keep us safe from the enforcers.' Was it any wonder she'd worked herself into an early grave?

Warm fingers clasped his. Carissa didn't say anything but the gentle pressure was wonderfully soothing. Not that he needed sympathy. He'd conquered his past long ago. Yet he didn't move, just let her fingers curl around his, enjoying the sense of connection.

'That doesn't explain your education.'

'Sorry?'

'You indicated your education was patchy. Surely school was free.'

Alexei added tenaciousness to Carissa's qualities.

'I missed school to earn money to help out.'

'How old were you?' Her brow scrunched.

'Eleven. Early teens.'

Carissa shook her head and covered his cheek with her palm. The gesture felt like balm. How long had it been since anyone had tried to soothe his hurts? No one had since his mother. 'Your mother must have been so worried about you.'

Surprise jabbed him. But of course Carissa understood his mother's concern. After they'd stopped sniping at each other, he'd quickly recognised empathy as one of her core traits.

'She was, but I had to do my bit for the family.' There it was again. Family. Until this week he hadn't let himself think about how it had felt to be part of something bigger than himself. To care and be cared for.

'Having a mother to love you. That's special.'

'At least you and I were lucky enough to know our mothers.'

He frowned, registering Carissa's brittle smile and wistful eyes. Did she miss her mother? It wasn't long ago she'd died. 'I'm sorry, Carissa. Sorry for your loss.'

'Thank you.' She blinked, her eyes bright. Then she pulled her arm away and sat back.

Mina had no memories of her mother. She'd told herself that didn't matter. Her older sister, Ghizlan, had been as good as any mother, making up for their father's distance.

Yet Alexei's words reopened a raw wound. One she'd refused for years to recognise. She felt it now, the sharp pain of loneliness, of being rejected by her father, abandoned by the mother who'd died.

Self-pity was pathetic. She had Ghizlan and she couldn't wish for a better sister. And Huseyn, her brother-in-law, was a sweetie beneath that incredibly gruff exterior. She had her little niece and nephew in Jeirut, and there was her friend Carissa.

But no one just for her.

Mina hated the direction of her thoughts. *Look at Alexei.* He'd lost his father young and had all sorts of trouble as a kid but he didn't give in to self-pity.

'So how *did* you start in IT?'

'A community youth centre.' Alexei shook his head. 'One of the staff was particularly persistent. I look back and realise how hard he worked even to get me to talk. But the place was heated and relatively safe so it appealed.'

'You weren't safe?' Silly to feel concern now. But Mina hated the idea of a young kid alone and scared.

Alexei shrugged. As usual, his shirt hung open over his broad chest and she watched the play of his muscles. It made her slightly dizzy. She wanted to plant her palm there, where his heart beat.

'It wasn't a good neighbourhood. There were gangs.' His tone was dismissive. 'And it didn't matter where we moved, the heavies collecting the money we owed always found us.'

We owed. Not his mother, or even his stepfather.

We.

Alexei had assumed responsibility for something that shouldn't have been his concern. He should have been running around a school playground without a care.

A lump rose in Mina's throat and she swallowed hard. Why was she so sentimental? Millions of children lived in harsh conditions they didn't deserve, some in her own country. She and Ghizlan were particularly active in supporting disadvantaged children. But why did Alexei's past hurts specifically unsettle her?

Because you care for him.

You care too much.

'They had an old computer. One of the guys taught me and I discovered an aptitude for it.'

'You make it sound easy. You don't go from being a kid

with a second-hand computer to launching a megasuccessful software and communications company.'

'True. But I won't bore you with a blow-by-blow description.'

Mina opened her mouth to protest. She was fascinated. She wanted to hear more about Alexei. Anything about him. But she sensed he'd had enough of the subject.

'How did they meet, your parents?'

His winged eyebrows lifted, giving him the look of a particularly rakish fallen angel, especially with that tousled hair threatening to flop over his forehead.

Fire ripped through her.

'Don't move a muscle.' She flipped a page and started drawing, trying to get the haughty angles, the stark beauty of spectacular cheekbones and determined jaw, the sensuality of his mouth.

As she worked, darting looks at him and then back to the paper, something changed. His expression grew less arrogant and more focused, the gleam in his eyes brighter. Mina became more than ever aware of Alexei's scent—cedar, citrus and male, with an undertone of musk. She inhaled deeply, her hand moving furiously across the paper. If Ghizlan could bottle that scent at her perfumery, the enterprise would make a fortune.

'Finished?' Those malachite eyes glinted more brightly than any faceted gem.

'Almost.' Mina read his impatience, sensed his arousal and strove for something to distract him. 'You didn't tell me how your parents met.'

'At the Olympics. He was an athlete and she was a physio travelling with the Russian team. They fell in love and eloped the day before the closing ceremony.'

'Wow! That's fast. They must have been head over heels.'

'They were. Completely and utterly in love. When my father died, my mother was devastated. It was almost too

ANNIE WEST

hard for her to go on.' His mouth twisted and Mina felt a
thud of pain in her middle. 'That's why she remarried. She
couldn't face the loneliness.'

Mina watched emotions play across Alexei's face. He
looked angry, as if he blamed his mother. She'd made his
life miserable with her rotten choice of second husband.

Yet things were rarely black and white. 'Maybe she
wanted someone to take your father's place, for your sake.
So you'd have a dad.'

The spasm of pain across his face lasted only a moment
but it told her so much.

He felt guilty about his mother's choice?

And maybe for blaming her?

'How about you?' he asked. 'How did your parents
meet?'

Mina felt a flutter in her chest. A battle between innate
honesty and her need to cover for Carissa. Mina was increasingly uncomfortable with these lies. Surely Carissa
was safe. The elopement was supposed to happen this weekend. She wanted so badly to blurt the truth but couldn't
risk it.

*Because you don't want this to end, do you? You want
to stay here with Alexei and dream of impossible things.*

She closed her sketchbook. She wouldn't give Carissa
away, nor would she pretend to have lived Carissa's life.

'They didn't know each other before the engagement.'

'It was an arranged marriage?' He looked stunned.

'It's a tradition in my family.' Mina suppressed a pained
smile. As far as she knew, her sister was the only woman in
a long line of ancestors to find love in marriage. It wasn't
something either of them had believed possible, having
been bred as dynastic bargaining chips.

Now finding happiness with the man you loved, and
who loved you, seemed incredibly alluring.

Mina put her sketchbook down, ignoring the drag of unhappiness. Her time with Alexei was limited. She refused to mar it. Instead she stood and stretched, forcing her attention away from *if onlys*.

'I've sat too long. I need exercise. How about another archery contest?' She'd been delighted to find it was a sport Alexei enjoyed, and one of the few she was proficient in, since it was Jeirut's national sport. 'Or a swim?' Her gaze turned towards the pristine beach. She'd had no qualms about using the brand-new swimsuit Carissa had packed. An errant thread of heat circled her womb at the thought of dispensing with the swimsuit and swimming naked with Alexei. If he knew the truth about her maybe they could...

Suddenly he was beside her. The fine hairs on her arms and neck prickled and her insides melted.

'If it's exercise you want—' his voice was an earthy growl that tumbled down her backbone and drew her belly tight '—I know just the thing.' His green eyes darkened and she swayed towards him.

Then, abruptly, he stepped back and groaned, shaking his head. 'You'll be the death of me yet.' But his lips curved in a smile as he reached for her hand. 'Come on, we need to work off some of this surplus energy.' He tugged her hand and she followed.

That was the problem. She was long past resisting Alexei. She wanted to be with him, all the time.

She was headed for disaster and couldn't pull back.

CHAPTER THIRTEEN

PHONE TO HIS EAR, Alexei sat back in his desk chair, grinning. Ralph Carter had been found in a casino in southern Switzerland. Either through cunning or sheer luck, he'd led the investigators a merry dance, but now there was no escape. Carter would face the consequences of his theft.

Satisfaction warmed Alexei.

Until Carissa's face swam in his mind. He recalled her sparkling eyes, the throaty husk of her voice as she cried his name in ecstasy, her decadently addictive mouth.

How would she react when he made her father pay for his crimes?

Doubt stirred Alexei's gut. He'd learned this week that she was anything but a selfish social butterfly. He admired her honest, generous spirit, even her obstinacy. This would hurt her.

He stiffened his resolve. She couldn't expect him to forget her father's crime. She knew it was coming. She hadn't asked for mercy on Carter's behalf. Though now Alexei considered that odd, surely.

Carissa was passionate and unafraid of ruffling his feathers, yet she'd never tried to intercede for her father.

As he listened to his PA, Alexei reached idly for Carissa's sketchbook and flipped it open. She'd left it by the pool and he'd brought it inside when he took this call. Clearly she'd forgotten it, focused instead on the fact it was her turn to cook.

Tomorrow Henri and Marie returned and the food would be restaurant quality again. But Alexei would far rather have another week alone with Carissa, sharing responsibility for chores, than any amount of exquisite dishes.

His insides twisted. Alexei told himself it was from eagerness to face Carter. Not concern as he anticipated Carissa's reaction.

'Excellent. See to those arrangements and we'll wrap this up.'

'There's one more thing.' His PA sounded unexpectedly tentative. 'A woman has been ringing, insisting she speak with you.'

Alexei frowned. He paid his PA an excellent salary. In return he didn't expect to be bothered by importunate strangers. Obviously this woman was out of the ordinary. 'And?'

'She gave her name as Carissa Carter.'

Arrested, Alexei sat straighter. 'Say that again.'

'She claims to be Carissa Carter, daughter of Ralph Carter.'

Alexei looked at the sketch before him. It was one he hadn't seen before and there was something incredibly intimate about it. Not just the fact that he was asleep on a sun lounger. He felt tenderness in the way Carissa had drawn the rumpled hair shadowing his forehead, and the lines of his mouth.

Was that really how she saw him?

A curious buzz started up in his ears.

'Obviously the woman is lying.'

'That's what I thought. But she gave enough detail to be very convincing.'

The fact his PA pressed the point was significant. She was not only loyal but intelligent. She must have good reason for pursuing this. 'Very well. Give me her number.'

Minutes later Alexei made the call.

'Hello? Carissa speaking.' Her voice was high and breathy and slightly familiar.

Alexei leaned forward, hand splayed on the desk, pulse quickening.

'Carissa Carter?'

'Yes, I… Who is this?' Her voice wobbled and Alexei felt the blood drain from his face. He recognised the voice now. It was the woman he'd spoken to a week ago. The woman he'd arranged to have collected in Paris. He'd assumed the line had distorted her voice because she sounded different in person.

He pinched the bridge of his nose with his thumb and forefinger. 'It's Alexei Katsaros.'

He heard a gasp, then a noise as if she'd dropped the phone. Adrenalin shot through him and his stomach lurched.

'Are…are you there?'

'I'm here. What do you want?' The person responsible for this elaborate hoax would pay. Alexei was in no mood for games.

'I rang to tell you I got married. I know my father led you to believe I was…available but he was wrong. A match between us isn't possible.' Her words were rushed, her breathing so uneven the words slurred together. 'I should have told you my plans sooner. I'm sorry. But I was too… That is, I wasn't thinking clearly when you rang. Pierre said I should have told you straight, and so did Mina, but I was too…' She hiccupped as if holding back a sob. 'I've tried and tried to call Mina but I can't reach her. Is she all right?'

Alexei's head spun. His pulse throbbed so hard it felt like a hammer against his temple.

He wanted to tell this stranger to quit wasting his time. But something stopped him. The suspicion this was no joke. That the impossible was about to become possible.

Twenty minutes later Alexei stared unseeingly across his desk, the phone silenced.

He'd got to the bottom of the situation all right. He'd taken some convincing, and more checking, but he was absolutely sure the woman on the phone was Carissa Carter.

He reeled at learning the truth. All this time he'd thought

his guest was his employee's daughter when she was Princess Mina of Jeirut, sister of the country's Queen. A rich royal who'd played the part of Carissa, duping him.

Making a fool of him.

Alexei imagined the field day the press would have with this. What impact would that have on his business? He screwed his eyes shut and tried to focus his scrambled brain on damage limitation.

But focus was impossible. It was all he could do to accept the preposterous truth. The two women had conned him. And he, so wrapped up in the pursuit of vengeance and the need to act decisively, had made it easy, not bothering to check details.

This wasn't business. It was far more personal. Briefly he acknowledged he'd made it so when he'd brought Carter's daughter to his private retreat. But his actions didn't sink to these depths of deception.

Alexei's gaze drifted to the abandoned sketchbook on his desk. He turned it over, opening it at the very beginning, to the images he hadn't viewed before. Why? Was he so desperate to believe, even now, that the woman in his kitchen was genuine? That the woman he'd come to care for was real, not some pretend persona adopted to dupe him?

Alexei stopped on the second page, on a series of intricate designs for a flask. They were exquisite. But it wasn't the design's beauty that caught his eye, it was the stylised calligraphy around the base. Calligraphy in Arabic. A talented artist could have copied the flowing script. Except there were also what looked like scribbled notes on the edge of the page in the same language.

Alexei turned the page. There was another bottle, again with scrawled notes in Arabic.

His mouth tightened. If he'd only taken the time to look, instead of being so caught up in that blaze of attraction for Carissa. For *Mina*, he corrected himself.

Despite Carissa Carter's breathless, half-defiant, half-apologetic explanations, Alexei knew they'd made a fool of him.

He looked down to see he'd again reached the page where she, *Mina*, had drawn him sleeping. With new eyes Alexei realised it wasn't tenderness revealed in the portrait. That wasn't vulnerability in his sleeping features but weakness. She'd been laughing at him.

She'd sashayed in, daring him to make a pass at her, teasing him till he didn't know which way was up. Pretending to be someone else, pretending to be honest and open and vulnerable. Had her virginity also been a lie?

Alexei shoved the book so hard it toppled off the desk as he surged to his feet and stalked to the window. It wasn't the view he saw. It was himself, laughing with... Mina. Telling Mina about his past, his stepfather, because he'd actually considered extending their relationship into something else.

Relationship!

He snorted. They had no relationship beyond sex and lies. The sex he could cope with, but not the lies.

He'd been conned as a kid and that had brought disaster.

He'd trusted Carter, had actually liked him, believing he and the older man shared an understanding. Till Carter knifed him in the back and stole his money.

Now Alexei found himself tricked again. By a slip of a woman with big brown eyes and a devious mind. A woman who'd burrowed her way into his—

Alexei yanked his thoughts to safer ground. To the blaze of anger searing his gut.

She'd made him reconsider his single status. She'd made him think about babies and belonging and all the while...

He swore, a mix of Greek and Russian that was far more potent for cursing than English.

Only when he had himself under control did he turn towards the door.

* * *

Mina hummed as she took the casserole from the oven. The aromas were mouth-watering. This was the one meal she could cook well, a traditional spicy vegetable dish from her homeland. It had been worth the extra time and effort.

For once Mina would be able to present Alexei with something delicious. There was a spring in her step and a smile on her face as she crossed to put it on the counter.

Alexei never complained about her culinary efforts. Nor did she aim to become a domestic goddess. Yet there was something deeply satisfying about cooking something nice for your man.

Mina blinked, staring down at the fragrant meal in astonishment.

Your man. Where had that come from?

This was temporary. Alexei Katsaros wasn't her man and never would be. Yet some tremulous, defiant voice inside disagreed.

He *felt* like her man.

She *wanted* him to be hers.

Mina stumbled back against the big island bench and slumped there, her mind racing at the enormity of the revelation.

She crossed her arms over her chest as if she could contain the swelling sensation inside. The rising demand that she face the truth.

What she felt with Alexei was more profound than sexual attraction. She'd spent her time on the island studiously ignoring that, pretending this was animal magnetism and no more. Because the truth of what she felt was too enormous, too life-changing. Too preposterous.

She'd imagined herself immune to romance, to dreams of being with one special man. No one had come close to distracting her from her drive to make art. But Alexei did that, even though they hadn't had sex in days. No one had ever made her *feel*, made her want to be part of a couple.

Mina put her hand to her breastbone. Her heart pounded high and hard.

A noise on the other side of the room made her look up. Instantly the tightness in her chest eased, and something inside her soared.

Alexei stood in the doorway, one shoulder propped against the doorjamb, arms crossed over his chest in a way that accentuated the curves of well-developed biceps and pectorals.

Desire throbbed through her. And more, far more. When he was with her she no longer worried that she was out of her depth. With Alexei she felt utterly right. It should be crazy to feel this way after a mere week, but there was no avoiding her feelings.

Mina smiled, not bothering to hide her delight. 'Smells good, doesn't it?' She leaned over the dish, inhaling the aroma that reminded her of Jeirut. What would Alexei make of her homeland? She'd love to take him there. 'And I promise it's not charred or undercooked. I'll get the plates.'

'Surely you shouldn't be waiting on me, *Princess*.'

Mina's head jerked up as if yanked on a string. It wasn't just Alexei's words but his tone that shook her. She looked into that searing green gaze, registered the flaring nostrils and savagely flattened mouth. Her stomach plummeted.

He knew.

And he was livid.

Alexei watched the laughter and the blood drain from her face, leaving her features pale and proud.

In that moment his last hope that this was a mistake died. And with it the foolish desires he'd entertained.

He waited for her to show embarrassment or guilt. There would have been some satisfaction in that. He might even have listened to an explanation if she'd shown regret and shame.

Instead, she drew herself up, shoulders straight and pushed back. Her neck lengthened as her chin came up. The welcome in her eyes died, replaced with a hauteur Alexei recognised from her arrival on the island.

It was like watching an actress don another persona. Except instead of seeing a make-believe character, the woman confronting him with that cool stare and regal bearing *was* the real woman. A conniving, lying woman.

The enthusiastic, caring person he'd known was a chimera. She'd been created to hold his attention long enough to distract him from the fact he was being fooled. How much of her had been real? Any of it?

He slammed the lid on such thoughts. He refused to search for pitiful fragments of a woman who didn't exist beyond his imagination.

The anger that had been brewing since the phone calls bubbled over. 'You must be used to having servants scurrying to do everything.'

Her face changed even more, shutters coming down behind her eyes, making her unapproachable. No wonder he'd likened her to that Russian ballerina. Both could project regal hauteur fit for a queen.

But no blue-blooded princess would play a part for public entertainment like a dancer. How much had her roleplaying been for personal entertainment? Had she laughed at how easily she'd fooled him?

A knife twisted in his chest.

'You're wrong, Alexei. I have no servants.'

Maybe it was the way she said his name, her voice husky and low, reminding him of her throaty purrs as she climaxed, that fuelled his ire to spilling point. More probably it was the unblinking gaze that revealed the barriers she erected between herself and the hoi polloi.

After all, despite his wealth, Alexei had spent most of his early years living in slums. Whereas she was descended from generations of royalty.

This was the woman he'd wanted in his bed, his home, his life. She'd laugh if she knew exactly how much of a fool she'd made him.

'Quit lying, Princess. The pretence is over.'

He spoke like a stranger. A looming, ice-cold stranger. Shock made Mina shuffle back a step.

If there was ever a time to call on those early lessons in self-control, this was it. This furious stranger wasn't her lover. She knew without question this man wouldn't respond to appeals for mercy or reason. He had no softer side.

Mina had known there'd be trouble when the truth emerged. But lately she'd convinced herself it wouldn't be so bad. Maybe she and Alexei might even laugh it off.

Only sheer willpower stifled the hysterical laughter bubbling inside. Again she'd been naive.

Desperately she wrapped herself tighter in that cloak of composure she'd learned to wear since childhood. The cloak she'd worn when facing her father's beetling regard, or the curious stares of the public. Both had been more concerned with the appearance of royalty than the real girl behind the façade.

'You're right.' She breathed deep. 'It's time for the truth.' With every hour she'd sunk deeper into that hazy world of self-deception, where Alexei cared for her as much as she did him.

'Past time.' He spoke through gritted teeth. 'You *are* Princess Mina of Jeirut, aren't you?' He said it as if it were a mark of shame rather than honour.

Wearily Mina nodded. 'I am.' She searched for what to say next, then surprised herself by blurting out, 'But it's true. I don't have servants. I look after myself.'

Why she insisted on telling him, she didn't know. His expression showed he wasn't interested. Yet it seemed important he understand she was an ordinary person despite her lineage.

'Is that a ploy for sympathy?' His eyebrows rose mockingly. 'Did you do this scam for money? Because you've spent your inheritance?' His words bit so deep it was a wonder they didn't leave marks. 'Are you looking for someone to fund your lifestyle?'

The insult wasn't camouflaged. Even someone as inexperienced as she could read the curl of his lip and the dismissive gaze flicking her from face to feet.

Something inside Mina shrivelled, like a delicate bloom blasted by the desert sun. The ache inside became a tearing pain but she wouldn't let it show. 'Don't be ridiculous. I—'

'Ridiculous?' He straightened from the doorjamb and prowled towards her, arms still crossed. He didn't stop till he was right in front of her, toe to toe.

Mina blinked and widened her stance, grounding herself rather than stepping back. He intimidated her. If she weren't shell-shocked by his reaction she'd probably be scared. But pride refused to let her reveal that.

'Of course it's ridiculous. I'm not after financial support.' How could he believe that? Did he think everyone was out for what they could get from him?

'Then what was this past week? Some social experiment for a cosseted princess to see how the other half lives? Was royal life so tame you wanted to spice it up with someone who grew up on the other side of the tracks?'

Horror stole her voice for precious seconds. 'You can't believe that!' It was a scratchy whisper.

'Why not?' He leaned close and Mina read nothing but contempt in his eyes.

'I'd hardly call a man with your power and finances anyone's idea of a bit of rough.' How dared he attack *her*? Yes, she was culpable. She'd lied and she hadn't been comfort-able with it but she'd had good reason. 'Secondly, you need to take responsibility for what happened.'

'Me?' He had the nerve to look outraged.

'Who else?' Through the pain anger erupted. 'You put Carissa through hell. And I—'

'You what? You can't tell me this last week has been your idea of hell.' He leaned in and Mina inhaled the cedar-and-citrus scent that always made her senses tingle. To her horror she felt a softening between her thighs, as if, even facing Alexei's scorn, she wanted him.

She drew herself up, slowly reciting in her head the names of her five favourite sculptors, then another five, till she trusted her voice.

'I did what I did for my friend. You threatened to kid-nap her.'

'I did no such thing. Her father offered her to me and I simply invited her here to—'

'Rubbish!' Mina's control frayed and she prodded her fingers into the solid muscle of his shoulder. '*You* started this when you decided to use Carissa for your own ends. Have you any idea how scared she was when she got your call?'

'Because she was in cahoots with her father.' If possible he looked even grimmer than before.

Mina shook her head. 'If you knew Carissa you'd know that was impossible. She can't tell a lie to save herself. She couldn't even think of an excuse to fob you off when you sent your goons to collect her.'

'But it wasn't Carissa who came, was it? It was you, lying through your teeth.'

'You expect me to apologise for that?' The nerve of the man stupefied her. 'I've known some manipulative men. Men who'd use a woman as a convenience as if she weren't a real person. But I thought they were dying out. Until I met you.'

Mina refused to think about the man she'd fallen for this past week. He'd either been a mirage invented by her yearning soul or a cruel joke.

'You brought this on yourself. Poor Carissa was beside herself, thinking her father would lose his job unless she agreed to come.'

Mina stepped back, not in retreat but so she could turn and march across the kitchen. She couldn't stay still, couldn't pretend to be calm. Not when everything had gone up in flames.

'Don't you walk away from me!' The growl came from just behind her and the hairs at her nape stood to attention.

'Or what?' She spun round and fixed her tormentor with a furious stare, barely able to believe how this confrontation had exploded. 'You'll lock me up? Hold me to ransom?'

'You're so sure your royal status exempts you from the consequences of your actions.'

'This has nothing to do with being royal.'

Alexei's eyes blazed. 'You deliberately connived to keep me from finding Carter. The man's a thief.'

'All I did—' she jammed her hands on her hips '—was buy time so my friend wouldn't be railroaded into marrying an arrogant jerk who treats people like disposable toys.' Mina drew a deep breath. 'Did you ever, once, stop to consider the collateral damage to other people from your actions?'

'Like you, I presume? You're claiming to be an injured party?' His contemptuous stare incinerated her last, frail hope. 'I'm no expert on Jeirut but I know it's very traditional. A royal princess who has casual flings would be frowned on. What's your plan? To claim I forced you into my bed when it comes out we've been alone for days?' His voice was a snarl, ripping through her stupid fantasies.

'How can you think such a thing?' Tears of indignation and pain needled the backs of her eyes.

His eyebrows lifted, the only sign of animation in a face turned mask-like.

'Then what? A kiss-and-tell story for the media? You'd get a small fortune for that, and revenge for your friend. But you'd wreck your reputation at home if it came out you had an affair.' He paused, his mouth tightening. 'Or am I to expect a demand from the King of Jeirut that I pay for the privilege of having despoiled your supposed virginal status?'

Mina flinched at his brutal accusations. How could he *think* such things? A yawning pit of hurt opened up inside.

'I see.' Abruptly Alexei's fury vanished, replaced by a look of weariness and bitter disillusionment. His voice turned flat. 'So that's it. You have your bit of fun and expect someone else to pay the price.'

Mina opened her mouth and shut it again. She was without words. How had she given her heart to a man who thought so little of her? For it was her heart she'd lost to Alexei, not just her innocence.

She pressed her hand to her middle, trying to hold in the lacerating anguish that felt as if her insides had crystallised to glass and shattered. She'd gone from heady delight to the depths of humiliation and pain so fast her head spun.

She needed to find words to make him understand. But what was the point? This wasn't her Alexei. This was a man who could believe the absolute worst of her. Her Alexei was nothing but a phantom.

'I'd like to leave the island now.' Her voice was stilted but she was beyond caring. 'I assume you can arrange that?'

'Nothing would give me greater pleasure.'

Mina turned to the door, unable to face his disdain any longer. 'Excellent. At least that's one thing we agree on.'

CHAPTER FOURTEEN

PARIS WASN'T FAR enough away.

Mina stared at the blinking light of her message bank and knew if she hit Play, Alexei's deep voice would fill the room. Worse, it would inveigle its way inside her, reinforcing the hollow ache she carried.

She knew because that was what had happened earlier. She'd come out of the shower and hadn't thought twice about checking her messages. Only to find herself fighting a rush of pain at the sound of that familiar voice. She'd slammed the phone down and deleted his message, unable to listen.

It didn't matter if he'd rung to berate her some more, or even to apologise for his sniping accusations. The fact was she *had* lied to him. But worse, she'd made the mistake of falling for the man.

Even if he called to say he was sorry he overreacted, which was about as likely as snowfall in the desert, it wouldn't be enough. Even if by some miracle he'd forgiven her and decided the sex between them was so good he wanted an affair, Mina knew she needed more.

She needed all or nothing.

Nothing was the only logical option.

Mina turned and paced. She needed space to think. Somewhere with no reminders of him.

A tattoo on the front door made her heart leap. It couldn't be. She didn't want it to be. Yet her hands shook as she opened it. Savage disappointment sliced through her at the sight of her best friend.

Mina really was desperate. And delusional. As if Alexei would turn up at her door!

'Carissa!'

Her friend enveloped her in a hug and a cloud of rose perfume. 'Are you okay? You look like hell.'

Mina managed a chuckle, despite the scratchy throat that made it hard to swallow. 'Lack of sleep. I'll be fine. But you look fabulous. Marriage agrees with you.'

Carissa grinned. She'd never looked prettier. Something tugged at Mina's heart but she refused to feel jealous that her friend had found happiness with the man she adored.

'It *is* wonderful. Pierre's the best. And I have you to thank. Without you stepping in—'

'I was glad to help.' Mina shut the door and led her towards the lounge room. But Carissa stopped her.

'I'm sorry, sweetie. I don't have time. Pierre and I are heading off to see his family. He's going to introduce me, so wish us luck.'

'They'll love you once they get to know you.' Mina pressed her hands. 'Give them a little time.'

Carissa nodded. 'That's what Pierre said. But I'm not sure and—' Her eyes rounded. 'How could I forget? Are you in trouble? That's what I came to ask.'

'Trouble?'

Carissa nodded. 'You must have got home very late last night. I didn't even know you were back. Then just now I was coming up the street when I saw those men. The ones who took you to Alexei Katsaros. They were coming out of our building and drove away in a big black car.'

'You're sure it was them?' Had she missed a knock on the door as she dried her hair?

Emotions stormed through Mina. Excitement vied with hope that she knew she had to crush. She and Alexei had no future.

'As if I'd forget.' Carissa shivered. 'I got a good look through the peephole the day they took you away. What do they want? Why are they here?'

'Probably checking I got home safely.' Maybe Alexei's conscience was troubling him and he wanted to make sure. Last night she'd refused an escort from the airport, insisting on finding her own way home.

'You're such a bad liar, Mina. I'll tell Pierre we can't go yet—'

'No. You have to go.' Her words were sharp, yet her mouth quivered. Reaction, she told herself. She'd barely slept. She needed time alone.

'Then what can I do to help?' Carissa put her arm around her and Mina had to fight the urge to weep on her shoulder.

Mina never ran from trouble but she felt too raw, too destroyed by the enormity of her feelings to cope. She needed to lick her wounds and recoup. 'Help me pack a bag. I'm going to Jeirut.'

The royal palace of Jeirut was imposing and warlike. Only the banners snapping in the wind alleviated its grimness. Perched on a high plateau, it commanded views of the city spread around it and the desert below.

Alexei followed a courtier through an oversized portal into a series of antechambers, each more magnificent than the last. But Alexei wasn't in the mood to be impressed. His mind was on the upcoming interview.

His one chance. The knowledge tightened his gut.

Finally he was led into an audience chamber with a forest of pillars around the perimeter. His gaze went to the golden throne and on it a tall, powerfully built man in white robes. His face was rugged, his nose uneven and eyes piercing. This man—Alexei knew, his pulse quickening in anticipation—made even the best negotiators nervous.

Introductions were made, complete with a scraping bow from Alexei's companion. Sheikh Huseyn, colloquially known as the Iron Hand, remained stony-faced. It was only when the doors closed behind the courtier and Alexei was alone with Mina's brother-in-law that the Sheikh raised one eyebrow in interrogation.

'You have a request?'

Alexei met that assessing stare with one of his own. 'I want to speak with your sister-in-law.' As if Sheikh Huseyn didn't already know that. As if Alexei hadn't been through this multiple times with officials.

'If you have something important to say, I can pass on a message. At present she's busy.'

Alexei wasn't deterred. He'd missed her in Paris but he *would* see her here. Mina might be furious and hurt but she wouldn't hide from him. She was too proud.

At least he hoped so. Unless he'd given her such a disgust of him that even her pride wasn't enough. He shoved the idea aside, refusing to countenance the idea of defeat.

'Thank you. But I prefer to speak with Mina.'

Sheikh Huseyn's eyes narrowed as if questioning his use of Mina's name.

'Why should I let you see her?' His even tone held an undercurrent of menace.

Instead of being abashed, Alexei stepped closer. Royalty or not, he refused to let the Sheikh stand in his way. 'Surely that's Mina's decision.'

The Sheikh didn't reply and as the silence lengthened, ice-cold sweat trickled down Alexei's spine.

'Are you saying Mina refuses to see me?' Nausea rolled through him. He tasted acid and recognised it as fear. Would Mina send him away without a chance?

'Why should she? What's your relationship?'

'That's between me and Mina.' Alexei's gaze followed the perimeter of the room. Did one of those doors lead to her? Frustration rose. The palace was enormous. If he made a break for it he had no hope of finding her before the royal guard stopped him.

'And if I make it my business?' The Sheikh rose and

stepped onto the floor. He moved with the ease of an athlete and, sizing him up, Alexei guessed they'd be well matched in a tussle.

'I can only repeat that my business is solely with Mina.'

'I am her King and head of her family.' Huseyn moved to stand toe to toe with Alexei. The air was redolent with latent danger. 'It's my role to protect her.'

Alexei met his eyes. 'I respect your desire to protect her, but Mina can manage her own concerns. I doubt she'd be impressed by anyone, even family, speaking on her behalf.'

A ripple of expression crossed the Sheikh's features, then, to Alexei's surprise, his face creased in a smile.

'You know Mina well.' He paused. 'What brings you to Jeirut? Surely not simply seeing my sister-in-law. Are you opening an office here? Or perhaps one of your youth centres. Such a laudable programme.'

Huseyn had done his homework. Alexei respected that. It was what he would have done. Due diligence was second nature.

Except that one vital time when he hadn't checked out Carissa Carter because he'd been determined to snaffle her quickly as bait. Technically that had been a grave error, but Alexei couldn't think of it in those terms since it had brought him Mina.

Elusive Mina. He stifled impatience with difficulty.

'I congratulate you, Highness. Not many know of my link to that initiative.' Alexei made sure of it. His community training and support scheme for disadvantaged teenagers wasn't done for kudos but to make a difference. Those kids didn't need their problems aired for public sympathy when Alexei could quietly provide the start-up money for programmes that eventually became self-funding.

'I make it my business to know about men who take an interest in my sister-in-law.'

Huseyn was toying with him. Mina had been a sexual

innocent until she'd come to him. Despite what he'd thought in the white-hot sear of anger.

'So, would you be interested in working in Jeirut?'

'It depends on the result of my discussion with Mina.' Alexei set his jaw. 'Is that the price for letting me see her?'

For a moment longer the Sheikh watched him through narrowed eyes. Then he nodded abruptly as if coming to a decision. 'You're not what I expected, Mr Katsaros.' He paused. 'Come, I'll take you to her.'

So he'd passed a test. Alexei should have felt relieved. Instead, as he followed Huseyn he felt more nervous than he could ever remember.

Perhaps that was why, when the Sheikh ushered him into a lavish chamber, it took Alexei a moment to recognise Mina. There were two women, both focused on a velvet-lined jewellery case open on a table. One he knew from his research as the beautiful Sheikha of Jeirut. The other... His breath stopped as she looked up and eyes of rich brown snared his.

Mina. One look and the ground shuddered beneath his feet. Yearning filled him.

Instead of the casual clothes he was accustomed to, she wore an evening dress of crimson with a square-cut neckline that emphasised the purity of her slender throat and graceful posture. Her hair was up and a tiara of brilliant diamonds sparkled in that dark mass.

How had he ever imagined her to be Carissa Carter? She was every inch a princess.

She was the most stunning woman he'd ever beheld.

Alexei's heart battered his ribs as he fought not to cross the room and pull her close.

As he watched her mouth flattened into a straight line and her beautiful eyes clouded. The hurt he saw there tore his conscience and his hopes.

All his resolve, all his certainty he could set things right, were shaken to the core.

* * *

He looked the same. No, not the same. Bigger, sexier, more charismatic than she'd let herself remember.

Heat swamped Mina. Her quiver of awareness was proof that, if anything, memory had done Alexei Katsaros a disservice. The only change in him, apart from the suave suit, was that he looked hollow around the eyes. Tired from travel. She wouldn't allow herself to imagine their parting had interfered with his sleep.

She was the one cursed with wakeful nights.

She drew a deep breath, hands clenching. That was when she remembered the diamond necklace in her palm. She moved to put it in its box but her hand shook ridiculously. Fortunately Ghizlan reached out and scooped it from her.

Mina had been on tenterhooks all day, unable to settle, after Huseyn told her Alexei was coming. Ghizlan's insistence that she decide on some finery for an upcoming royal reception had been a welcome diversion that stopped her checking the time every two minutes.

Now she'd been caught all glammed up. Full-length silk rustled as she shifted. Diamond drops swung from her earlobes and she was conscious of the pins securing the heirloom tiara.

Her chin tilted as she took in Alexei's stare. So what if he had a problem with her royal status? She wasn't ashamed. She was what she was, as much at home in a formal gown as old jeans.

'Mina.' Alexei's voice was the same, a deep cadence that did crazy things to her self-control.

She drew a sustaining breath. 'Alexei.' Then she turned to her sister. 'Ghizlan, this is Mr Katsaros.'

'Mr Katsaros.' Contrary to her usual friendly manner, Ghizlan gave the tiniest nod, her expression a degree short of glacial.

Alexei didn't look fazed by the lack of welcome. 'Your Highness.' His eyes tracked back to Mina.

She'd arrived here unexpectedly, desperate for the comfort of her sister's presence. Like when she'd been a child. Ghizlan and Huseyn had, in their different ways, provided that comfort. Huseyn's expression now made it clear he'd intervene if Alexei upset Mina, and Ghizlan bristled with protectiveness. She'd guessed Alexei had caused the unhappiness Mina couldn't hide. Bless her, and Huseyn too, for closing ranks.

But this was Mina's battle.

'I'd like to speak to Alexei alone.' It was a lie. Facing him was torment. But this had to be done. One final conversation and their abortive relationship would be over. Pain crested to a point behind her ribs and Mina rubbed the spot, till Alexei tracked the movement. She dropped her hand.

Huseyn folded his arms. 'Anything he wishes to say can be said before your family.'

'But surely,' Alexei said, without taking his eyes from her, 'Mina has the right to privacy.'

Mina stifled the urge to roll her eyes. The air was thick with testosterone, the two very alpha males each determined to stand their ground.

'This won't take long.' Mina ignored the pang of regret she felt at that, and sent a pleading glance to Ghizlan. 'Then I'll come and join you.'

After a searching glance Ghizlan nodded. 'We'll finish this later.' Not just the choice of jewels, but, she made clear, a conversation about Alexei Katsaros.

Wearily Mina nodded. She owed Ghizlan an explanation even if it was a truncated version of the truth. For no matter how she'd tried, since arriving in Jeirut she hadn't been able to hide the fact that something was terribly wrong.

Her sister took Huseyn's arm. For a moment he stood, unmoving. Then he nodded. 'Very well. We'll be in my study.' His tone held a warning as if daring Alexei to step out of line.

'Your family is very protective,' he said when the door closed.

'They are.' Sometimes overprotective. But there was comfort in having family who cared.

'I'm glad. You deserve to have people who care.'

Surprised, she shot Alexei a wary glance and was snared by those green eyes she'd tried to avoid.

It was impossible to look away, no matter how she ordered herself to do so. It was as if he drew her to him, compelled her against her will.

No, not against her will. That was the problem. Despite everything, Mina couldn't eradicate her weakness for Alexei. All she could do was pretend it didn't exist. It *shouldn't* exist. They'd only been together for a week. Far too short a time to fall in love. What she felt was infatuation.

A lump rose in her throat as she fought to stifle her feelings. She felt so wretched, not like herself at all. Once she'd have lost herself in work no matter what was going on around her. Now work took second place to the pain she carried like a layer beneath her skin.

Mina propped her hands on the table, grateful for something to lean on. She hadn't thought he'd come. Whenever she thought of that last day his words burned her soul. She'd told herself he'd spoken in the heat of the moment. That he didn't really believe what he'd said. But maybe he had.

After days of thinking herself at her lowest possible ebb, Mina knew she'd finally hit rock bottom. Shame, outrage and, yes, sheer hurt, scraped every inch of her flesh, making it smart. She tore her gaze away, pretending to tidy the gems that blurred before her eyes.

'I know because you're standing there, unscathed, you didn't suggest to Huseyn that you owed him a fee for taking my virginity.' She spat the words out, hating their acid taste. 'So let me reiterate, once and for all, I don't need your wealth. Nor does my family. There's no fine to pay.'

In the old days it would have been called a bride price and the suitor would have been ushered into a hasty marriage. But Alexei was no suitor. He despised her.

Mina clasped her hands, projecting as much calm as she could when her heart pounded like the hoofs of a runaway stallion. 'So there's no reason for you to stay. I can arrange for you to be on the next flight out.'

'I didn't come for that, Mina.'

His voice didn't sound right. She was used to lazy cadences, the mellifluous sound of a man confident and at ease. Her senses quickened at that too-tight timbre, as if something squeezed his voice box. Till his meaning sank in.

There was only one other reason for Alexei to come.

Another scrape of pain, this time so deep Mina was surprised she didn't see blood.

She lifted her head and met his eyes. The shock of what she saw reverberated through her. He looked gaunt and strained where minutes ago he'd looked solid and strong. His olive complexion was a sickly grey that made his eyes look sunken.

The alteration was so profound she actually moved towards him, then stopped mid-step.

'If you've come to check if I'm pregnant, you can relax.' Her voice was harsh. 'Those condoms did the trick. No inconvenient accidents to worry about.'

To her surprise Alexei recoiled as if from the lash of a whip.

'Are you sure?' His voice held a husky quality that reminded her too much of his words of praise and encouragement when they'd made lo—when they'd had sex. 'I assumed your supposed period was a sham.'

Mina's fingers pressed tight together. 'Absolutely sure.'

She'd been amazed to find herself fighting tears when

she arrived in Paris and discovered her period really had started. She should have been relieved, she *was* relieved there was no pregnancy to complicate things. Yet it had been final confirmation that the fantasy was over.

'I'm sorry, Mina.'

She blinked and realised he'd closed the space between them. Instantly she stiffened. 'Sorry there's no baby? I can't believe that.'

'Sorry for *everything*.' He lifted both hands in a gesture that was at once open and weary, as if he carried an impossibly heavy weight. 'If I could eradicate everything I said that day I would. I'm *ashamed* of the accusations I threw at you. That's why I came, to apologise.'

Mina stared, grappling to connect this desperate man with the one she recognised. They were both Alexei, both real, but this one, with the anguished eyes, was new.

'You were right, Mina. I need to take responsibility for my actions. Instead I got wrapped up in my disappointment.'

'Disappointment?' At last she found her voice. 'It was more than that. It was rage.'

He inclined his head, but paused as if gathering himself. His mouth lifted in a bitter curve.

'You probably won't believe this, but I'm renowned for never losing my cool, even when things go badly wrong, even in highly pressured situations. I don't waste energy on anger because I prefer to focus on fixing things and moving on.'

Mina opened her mouth to argue when Alexei put up his hand. 'Please, hear me out.' Reluctantly she nodded and watched as he drew a breath that expanded his chest mightily. He looked intimidatingly big and bold and heart-breakingly desirable, yet his expression indicated a pain that might even match her own. She didn't understand what he wanted but she had to hear him out.

His hands dropped. 'As a kid I had a lot of anger, directed at my stepfather. Then at the people who harried my mother into an early grave. But I learned to control my feelings and focus on the future. It worked. Once I had that goal I had somewhere to channel my energies.'

Alexei waved an impatient hand. 'Sorry. Too much information.'

Mina was fascinated. But she was desperate to discover why he'd come. 'Get to the point, Alexei.'

A brief smile curled his lips but it wasn't reflected in his eyes. 'The point is I never lose control. Only twice. First when I discovered Ralph Carter had swindled the company and betrayed me.' His voice dropped to a sombre note. 'I'd trusted him, you see. The first person I'd actually trusted in...' He waved a dismissive hand again. 'Not that it matters.'

It mattered. It didn't take an expert to understand Alexei had major trust issues.

'Then, when I realised you weren't who you said, I lost it. Totally.' He shook his head and the lock of dark hair that had been combed back ruthlessly from his forehead tumbled over his brow, reminding her of the rumpled, gorgeous beachcomber she'd known in the Caribbean.

Brilliant green eyes focused on Mina. 'I told myself I was furious because you'd fooled me, that you and Carissa were laughing at me. I know now you weren't. But at the time all I could feel was hurt that I'd believed in you, *trusted* you and you'd betrayed that trust.'

There was that word again.

Alexei stood straighter. 'I lashed out because I cared for you, Mina. I wanted more from you than I'd ever wanted with anyone else. That's why I was furious. Because I hoped...' He stopped and she leaned forward, eager for more. 'As I said, it doesn't excuse my behaviour. You didn't deserve that and I apologise.'

Mina stared, trying to read his thoughts. She saw regret and shame. But what else?

'What did you hope, Alexei?' Her nerves were shredded, her heart racing.

Those stunning, familiar eyes locked on hers. 'I'd hoped we might have a future together.' His voice dropped. 'I'd even wondered how you felt about children.'

Mina gaped at him. 'But we'd only known each other a week.'

He shrugged, the usually fluid movement jerky. 'I trust my instinct. A week was long enough for me to feel things I've never felt before.'

'Things?' Her breath was a shallow draught of oxygen scented with warm male. Her brain froze.

Large hands took hers, their touch gentle yet compelling. 'Emotions. Not just desire but affection. Trust. Pride. Caring.' His eyes clouded. 'Not that you'd think so, the way I went for you when the truth came out.' His hands tightened on hers. 'The way I overreacted has nagged at me ever since.'

Mina watched him swallow. 'It made me realise the way I've stifled my emotions all these years isn't healthy. I'm determined to learn a better way to deal with my feelings. I need to make changes.'

Mina stared into Alexei's determined features, her emotions splintering in a dozen directions.

Wonder that he was here, baring his soul.

Sadness that his childhood experiences had affected him so profoundly.

Pride that he should confront his problems head-on and take action. Most men would run a mile from the idea of examining emotions and their own behaviour.

Regret that Alexei took all the blame when there'd been fault on both sides.

But above all excitement that he was here because he

cared for her. He'd wondered about the future…with her! Did he still wonder? Or was he here simply to explain? Surely he couldn't be so cruel.

'I'm sorry too, Alexei. I lied to you and I wasn't comfortable about it—'

'You were protecting your friend.' His hands squeezed hers. 'Loyalty like that is a wonderful thing.'

'Even if I acted impulsively?' Her eyebrows rose.

'If you hadn't, we wouldn't have met.'

The look he gave her, grave yet intense, turned her heart over. No man had looked at her that way. As if he spoke to *her*. Not the artist or the princess but the woman who sometimes struggled to find her way, who loved her life, yet made mistakes and sometimes doubted herself, like everyone else.

'You're not saying anything.' His hands tightened.

'We both overreacted.' Mina drew a shuddery breath as if she'd inhaled a field full of butterflies. 'I was so attracted to you but scared of what I felt.' Even though it was glorious it was far beyond her experience.

Was that why she'd given up so easily, scurrying away rather than forcing him to accept the truth? Because she was frightened of where such a relationship might lead? Because she was used to being alone, not trusting anyone to know her fully?

'Was? In the past?' His voice was harsh, cracking on the last word.

Mina stared into that proud, handsome face, drinking in the familiar features that could seem intimidating or playful and right now looked drawn with tension.

She tilted her face high, defying the cowardly impulse to lie. 'Am. Right now.' It felt like the bravest thing she'd ever done, admitting that.

Mina swallowed as he stroked the line of her jaw from ear to chin.

'Me, as well. I'm attracted and scared too.'

Her lips curved in an unsteady smile. 'Who are you and what have you done with Alexei Katsaros? He's not scared of anything.'

He shook his head. 'I'm scared of losing you. Scared I blew my chance.' His words made everything within her still.

'Your chance for an affair?' She had to ask, though she knew, deep inside, what he meant. She needed the words.

Alexei cupped her face in both hands, leaning in so his words feathered her mouth. 'My chance to build a future with you. I know it's too early. I know we barely know each other, but there's something about you, Mina, that I can't do without. I want you in my life and I'll do whatever I must to convince you to give me that chance.' He drew a deep breath and she felt his hands shake. 'I think I'm in love with you.'

His words resonated like the echo of a bell, the sound filling her with not just joy, but recognition.

'It's unsettling, isn't it?'

For a moment Alexei looked dumbfounded, as if he couldn't believe his ears. Then his face creased into a smile so broad it blinded. He released her hands and instead wrapped his arms around her, yanking her close so she was pressed against his hot, hard frame. It was heaven. Mina melted into him, her hands clutching, wearing a grin of her own.

Was this really happening?

'Unsettling in the best possible way.' He paused, his eyes locked on hers so Mina felt as if she were falling into a deep, bright sea. 'You mean that? You feel—'

'I've been falling in love with you since the day I reached your island and you made me furious and turned on at the same time.' Mina shook her head. 'I thought love was supposed to be all hearts and roses but you make me feel—' she struggled for words to convey at least some of her feelings '—*everything.*'

He nodded, his smile fading, eyes serious. 'Exactly. I want you even when we're arguing. Even when we don't agree. I want to make love to you all the time, but I also simply want to be with you, to share with you. To grow together.'

'Even though I live in Paris and you live—'

'I'm flexible. I can move.'

Mina's eyebrows shot up. He was a CEO with a business to run. She was the artist who could work almost anywhere. 'Even though I'm a princess?'

'You're not getting away from me that easily.' He lifted a hand to her hair and began to tug out the pins that secured it up. 'Besides, you look hot in a tiara.'

Mina saw a devilish glint in his eyes and sweet heat pierced her middle.

'Even though my best friend is Ralph Carter's daughter?'

Alexei shook his head. 'Stop trying to distract me. It won't work.'

'Distract you?'

Alexei's face lowered till his lips almost touched hers. 'I'm going to kiss you, Mina, till you stop throwing up objections. I'm going to kiss you till you agree to let me into your life so I can prove how good we'll be together.' All tension was gone from his face, replaced with a smug determination that made Mina want to laugh. For the first time today he looked like the man she'd fallen in love with.

For the first time since she left the Caribbean she felt happy.

'And if I don't agree?'

'Then, my sweet, sexy, Princess, I'll have to keep kissing you till you do.' There he was again, the confident tycoon with lurking humour in those slumberous eyes. But the tension humming through him, and the racing flick of the pulse at his temple, revealed Alexei took nothing for granted. He was still tense, waiting.

That, most of all, showed the change in him.

His lips brushed hers and Mina's knees went weak. Her arms tightened around his neck.

'If I agree, we need to take things slowly, get to know each other properly. We barely know each other.'

'I believe we know each other in the ways that count.' Alexei nuzzled the base of her throat and delight shuddered through her. 'But I won't rush you.'

'I should warn you, I'm no pushover.' Yet she arched against him.

Alexei lifted his head, his smile wickedly knowing. 'I'm counting on it. I'm here for the long haul.' Then he took her mouth with his and Mina entered a world of bliss.

Ages later she heard a man clear his throat. Huseyn. It had to be. But Alexei didn't react and Mina was too lost in a haze of delight to pull back.

Her brother-in-law wasn't used to being ignored. Would he march over and pull them apart? Then she heard Ghizlan murmur something and the door clicked shut.

Alexei pulled back enough to look down at her. The gleam in his eyes made her heart tumble. 'So, your family is tactful as well as protective? I like them better all the time.'

Mina dragged air into starved lungs. 'Don't think they'll make it easy for you. They'll give you the third degree about your life, goals and intentions.'

His smiling eyes held hers. 'I can't think of anything else I'd rather discuss.' He stepped back the tiniest fraction, unhooking one of her hands from his neck and bringing it to his lips. 'My intention is to be the man who'll make you happy. Always.'

EPILOGUE

A YEAR LATER, to the day, Alexei entered their Parisian home. Not the cramped place Mina had rented, but a spacious, high-ceilinged house with space for a studio. He smiled. That was where she'd be, working, even though there was barely time for him to shower and change before they headed to tonight's exhibition.

He ripped off the tie he'd worn for a press conference and tossed it over the back of a settee. His pulse quickened as he headed for the studio. Thinking of Mina filled him with a heady excitement he didn't think would ever fade.

But for once his sweetheart wasn't up to her elbows in clay or working with metal. The place was empty, save for the usual clutter. A half-finished piece stood near the window. Sketches were pinned to one wall near a scuffed workbench.

Alexei's eyes went to a small, familiar piece in bronze on a nearby table. A man's hands, *his* hands, cupped and holding the slim fingers of a woman. *Mina's*. Though he appeared to support her hands, their fingers were intertwined as if sharing strength. Sharing a bond.

Whenever he saw the piece, Alexei felt a thump in the region of his heart. An awareness of how lucky he was to have Mina. This year had been everything he could have hoped and it made him more determined to keep what he had.

Smiling, he put his hand to his pocket and turned towards the door, only to pull up short.

The woman he adored stood there, wearing a curiously unreadable expression and a stunning dress of flame red. Alexei's lungs expanded on an appreciative breath as he took in the tiny shoulder straps and flirty skirt that were an invitation to explore.

'Mina! You look stunning.' He imagined his hands skimming her taut thighs beneath the fabric. Heat circled his chest and drove straight to his groin.

'You don't look so bad yourself.' She crossed the room and kissed him. Alexei gathered her up, relishing the fire that ignited between them and the sweet sensation of coming home. Coming to Mina.

When he ended the kiss, he kept his arms around her. Her exotic spice and cinnamon scent was warm in his nostrils and he savoured how right this was.

'I heard from Carissa today.'

'Hmm?' He looked down into velvety eyes. She was smiling.

'She and Pierre are visiting Ralph in Jeirut. He's thriving and even picking up some of the language.'

Belatedly Alexei caught the thread of the conversation. Ralph Carter. In Jeirut.

Mina walked her fingers up Alexei's chest, making him wish she'd found him naked in the shower.

'It was a stroke of genius, getting him involved in your programme there.'

Alexei shook his head. 'It was as much your idea as mine. You suggested Jeirut.' Because the opportunities for gambling there were limited, so Ralph would have less temptation.

Alexei had revised his view of Ralph when he learned of his gambling addiction, a coping mechanism to deal with overwhelming grief at his wife's death.

After hearing of the older man's shame and desperate plan to pay back the money by gambling more, and his near suicidal despair when that failed, Alexei hadn't pressed charges. Prison wouldn't get his money back. Instead he'd co-opted Ralph into the initiative he and Sheikh Huseyn had begun to give unemployed youth the skills and confidence to start up innovative businesses.

After a rocky start, Ralph, with his financial expertise, pernickety attention to detail and genuine interest in his budding entrepreneurs, was a surprise hit. It helped them and gave him back a sense of purpose and self-respect.

'But you were the one who suggested including him.' Mina's fingers reached his chin and traced his jaw, teasing. 'You gave him a second chance. Not many people would do that.' The way she looked at him stirred Alexei's soul. His chest swelled.

'Everyone deserves a second chance, sweetheart.'

She smiled and Alexei felt the radiance of it all the way to the centre of his being. 'Which shows how right I was about you, Alexei Katsaros. You might be savvy and über-successful, but there's more to you than business.'

'Oh, much more.' He slid his hands down Mina's back, over that pertly rounded rump, and pulled her against him. That was better. Much better.

Mina wriggled and Alexei was tempted to forget their plans to attend a new exhibition. Except he had other plans too. A romantic dinner for two in one of the city's best restaurants as a prelude to something much more significant.

But looking into Mina's smiling face, Alexei knew it wasn't a picture-perfect setting that mattered. It was her. And how she felt. Suddenly he couldn't wait.

'Mina.' He swallowed, trying to eradicate the betraying husky edge to his voice. 'I have something for you.'

She blinked. 'That's a coincidence. I have something for you too. Over there—'

'Sweetheart.' Alexei turned her head back towards him and reached into his pocket. 'I've waited a whole year to give you time to be sure of me and what you feel. I'm in love with you, Mina. I want to spend my life with you.'

He'd spent hours thinking of how to say this, searching for something unique and memorable. But when he looked into

Mina's warm gaze, each carefully crafted word disintegrated and he was left with the bare truth. 'Will you marry me?'

He lifted his hand and showed her the ring he'd had made for her. A unique, modern piece of white gold and a square-cut ruby. Sparks shot off the facets as it trembled in the light.

Mina's hand closed around his and he realised they were both shaking. He heard a muffled gasp and saw her eyes were overbright.

'Mina? Sweetheart?'

She shook her head and smiled, her mouth a crumpled curve. 'That sounds like a wonderful plan. I love you too, darling. And yes, I want to be with you, always.'

Elation surged so high he felt ten feet tall. Alexei bent to kiss her but her fingertips on his lips stopped him. 'You don't want to see my gift?'

'Sorry?'

'My gift.' Mina reached over to a nearby table and picked up a small box. She flipped the lid and there were two matching wedding rings. 'I thought a year was time enough. I want you with all my heart, Alexei.' She laughed, the sound like liquid crystal, shining with promise. 'It seems we both had the same idea.'

'Because we're perfectly matched.' He spared an appreciative glance for the finely crafted wedding bands, then lifted her hand and slid the engagement ring onto her finger. Emotion threatened to overwhelm him.

'We definitely are.' She moved her fingers, admiring the ring. 'Thank you, Alexei. I never thought I could be so happy.'

'Nor did I.' He raised her hand to his lips and kissed it. 'And this is just the beginning.' Then he scooped her up and swung her round till the room rang with her delicious laughter. It was a sound he looked forward to hearing for the rest of his life.

* * * * *

COMING SOON!

We really hope you enjoyed reading this book. If you're looking for more romance, be sure to head to the shops when new books are available on

Thursday 7th February

To see which titles are coming soon, please visit
millsandboon.co.uk/nextmonth

MILLS & BOON

Coming next month

A VIRGIN TO REDEEM THE BILLIONAIRE
Dani Collins

'I went to the auction for an earring. I kissed a man who interested me. I've since realized what a mistake that was.'

'It was,' Kaine agreed. 'A big one.' He picked up his drink again, adding in a smooth, lethal tone, 'I have half a mind to accept Rohan's latest offer just to punish you.'

'Don't,' Gisella said through gritted teeth, telling herself she shouldn't be shocked at how vindictive and ruthless he was. She'd already seen him in action.

He smirked. 'It's amazing how quickly that little sparkler brings you to heel. I'm starting to think it has a cold war spy transmitter in it that's still active.'

'I'm starting to think this sounds like extortion. Why are you being so heavy-handed?'

'So that you understand all that's at stake as we discuss terms.'

She shifted, uncomfortable, and folded her arms. 'What exactly are you asking me to do, then?'

'You're adorable. I'm not asking. I'm telling you that, starting now, you're going to portray yourself as my latest and most smitten lover.' He savored that pronouncement with a sip of wine that he seemed to roll around on his tongue.

'Oh, so you blackmail women into your bed.'

For a moment, he didn't move. Neither did she, fearing she'd gone too far. But did he hear himself? As the silence prolonged, she began to feel hemmed in and trapped. Far too close to him. Suffocated.

'The fact you didn't hear the word portray says more about your desires than mine,' he mocked softly. He was full out laughing in silence at her. So overbearing.

'I won't be blackmailed into playing pretend, either,' she stated. 'Why would you even want me to?'

He sobered. 'If I'm being accused of trying to cheat investors, I want it known that I wasn't acting alone. I'm firmly in bed with the Barsi family.'

'No. We can't let people believe we had anything to do with someone accused of fraud.' It had taken three generations of honest business to build Barsi on Fifth into its current, iconic status. Rumors of imitations and deceit could tear it down overnight.

'I can't let my reputation deteriorate while I wait for your cousin to reappear and explain himself,' Kaine said in an uncompromising tone. 'Especially if that explanation still leaves me looking like the one who orchestrated the fraud. I need to start rebuilding my name. And I want an inside track on your family while I do it, keeping an eye on every move you and your family make, especially as it pertains to my interests. If you really believe your cousin is innocent, you'll want to limit the damage he's caused me. Because I make a terrible enemy.'

'I've noticed,' she bit out.

'Then we have an agreement.'

Continue reading
A VIRGIN TO REDEEM THE BILLIONAIRE
Dani Collins

www.millsandboon.co.uk